THE
BEE-GINNING

THE BEE-GINNING

Icalos

Podium

THE
BEE-GINNING

THE BOY AND THE BEE

A young boy, just a bit over a decade old, stumbled into the house. He had scruffy brown hair, lighter skin with a healthy tan, and freckles across his face.

As well as a black eye.

"Ah, you're home? Welcome back, Belissar."

He winced as he heard the elderly woman's voice. He . . . didn't particularly want Mrs. Imkomos to see him at the moment, but she shuffled out regardless, supporting her shaking legs with a cane. Her eyes widened when she caught sight of him, then she heaved a sigh.

"Are you okay?"

Belissar silently nodded. She sighed again.

"Here, help me get the salve, would you? We'll get you fixed up."

Belissar nodded again and then silently did as she said.

A bit later, he stumbled into his room, holding a small piece of honeycomb Mrs. Imkomos had given him. He was about to collapse in his bed when something caught his eye. In the corner near his window was a spiderweb, and he could see something squirming on it. As he got closer, he found it was a little worker bee, missing half of one antenna. He frowned.

Mrs. Imkomos had told him to respect spiders. They were a crucial part of the cycle of the world, a creation of the gods intended to keep the pests under control. But she had also trained him to take care of her bees, and they were anything but a pest.

And Belissar knew all too well what it felt like to be helpless and at someone's mercy.

He didn't see the spider on the web, so he wouldn't have to hurt it, in any case. So, he grabbed the heavy gloves he wore while beekeeping and knelt by the corner.

"Don't hurt the bees."

He reached out to the web and gently broke through the sides of it, reaching his finger for the little insect.

"Please don't sting me, okay?"

He brought his finger under her legs and began lifting her up, using his other hand to detach the web stuck to her. The bee scrambled about and attempted to sting his finger, but her stinger failed to pierce into the thick glove. She then stopped and tried to beat her wings, but they were still entangled.

Belissar grabbed the small piece of honeycomb and brought it up to his finger.

"See? I'm not going to hurt you. Here, have something to eat."

The bee paused for a bit before slowly crawling onto the honey. She slowly lowered her proboscis down until she tasted the sweet liquid. After that, she stopped trying to sting him or fly away, settling down onto the honeycomb.

Belissar gave a small smile. He may have been powerless in his own life, but at least he could save a trapped little bee. Mrs. Imkomos had taught him to take care of them, and that's what he would do.

He managed to get some rest, just a bit less upset than before. And the little bee watched him for a few hours until the web dissolved and she was able to fly away.

Belissar never noticed the faint glow of light around her . . .

CHAPTER ONE

THE BEE-GINNING

About a decade later, Belissar stood in a dark cellar, holding a small candle for light. He was now a young man past his second decade, dressed in the well-worn tunic and pants of any other frontier peasant. He was surrounded by barrels. Opening the top of one, he scooped out some of the liquid contents into a jar, then closed the barrel and walked toward the rickety stairs leading out of the cellar. He extinguished the candle and climbed back up.

He made his way across the apiary he now managed on his own, where wooden boxes stood in rows and bees buzzed all around, climbing in and out of holes in said boxes. Belissar smiled and watched them work for a second before making his way to his house. Once inside, he poured a bit of the golden liquid from the jar and took a drink. He held it in his mouth, tilting his head before he swallowed and smacked his lips.

"Hm, a bit too many juniper berries, I think. I'll have to tone it down for the next batch."

He heaved a sigh as he put away the jar. That was the last one of the batch, and it would take some time before the next attempt. Apparently, the local tower lord's son was coming to visit their little village, and every household was required to donate tribute for the welcome banquet. Losing entire barrels of mead for free would not help him survive the winter, so he'd have to stick to tried-and-true recipes he knew he could sell for the foreseeable future.

The date for the visit had come and gone a week ago, and of course, the tower lord's son was nowhere to be seen. And yet, the village chief hadn't returned any of the tribute, just in case the noble scion decided to show up at his own convenience.

Some of the villagers had raised eyebrows at that, but Belissar had just kept his head down. It wouldn't help for him to complain. It never had. So, he just sighed and shook his head.

He stretched and walked over to the window, where he had a few flowers growing in pots. A bee was hovering around and flew to him when he walked over. He held out a finger, the bee obliging and landing on it. Belissar smiled as he noted the bee had half her antenna missing.

"Working hard, huh? Great job today." The bee buzzed and spun around. Belissar had saved a bee with a missing antenna once, freeing her from a spider's web. He knew it was silly, especially since it had been years since then, but he liked to imagine it was the same bee that visited him, and that they were friends, even. Well, he knew the bees landed on him because he had coaxed them by dipping his finger in honey, but it didn't hurt anyone to pretend.

Just then, Belissar heard shouting and screams.

He frowned and grabbed his spear by the door. Their village was at the very edge of the local tower's influence. Attacks by the Hunger were rare but not unheard of, and there were plenty of other wild animals that could cause trouble besides.

Belissar peeked his head out the window in the direction of the screaming . . .

. . . and gasped as his eyes went as wide as they would go.

The village was on fire. Armored soldiers marched through the town, right over the bodies of the village chief and those who had gathered with him. Hooded mages were setting fire to the buildings one by one while the soldiers cut down the villagers trying to flee. They each bore the image of a lizard curled around a stone tower—the crest of the local tower lord—on their armor, and a young man in plate armor and a cape rode atop a horse at the center of the formation.

Belissar turned and ran out the back door. He had no idea why the local tower lord would do such a thing, but he was of no mind to ponder it. He ran past his beehives toward the tree line at the edge of his home.

Running off into the wilderness bordering the Hunger was not exactly a great idea, but Belissar was barely thinking at all at this point. All he wanted was to get as far away as possible.

Feeling a sharp pain in his back, he stumbled to the ground, falling into some overgrown fields leading to the forest. An arrow had lodged itself in his back.

Tears ran down his face as he gritted his teeth, trying not to scream from the pain. Maybe, if he was lucky, they'd think he was dead. That is . . . if the wound wasn't bad enough to actually kill him.

But, as he lay there . . . slowly, he began to relax. As he thought, he wondered why he was trying so hard. Bad break after bad break, and for what? There was no one at home waiting for him; no one would even realize he was gone. The entire village was gone too, and no one beyond even knew he existed.

Nothing would change if he lived, and nothing would change if he died, so how was one better than the other? What was the point of fighting his fate? If the gods had decreed this was his lot in life, then what could he do but accept it?

He felt his heart calm even as he began to feel cold. He went ahead and closed his eyes. Perhaps this was for the best. Maybe if he let himself go, he'd get to see Mrs. Imkomos . . . and his parents.

Only a slight murmur in his heart caused him to hesitate, to wonder if this was truly the end. But that, too, passed as all around him grew dim.

It was at that moment that a little bee landed on his back. A bee with half an antenna missing . . . and a slight glow around her body, too faint to be noticed in the afternoon sun. She buzzed and danced around Belissar's back, but the young man stirred no longer. The bee buzzed again, and again the man lay still.

The bee began dancing faster and faster, buzzing her wings more and more frantically. As she did, the glow around her began to pulse, growing brighter each time. Eventually, a small bit of the light moved from her into Belissar's back . . .

The face of the man on the horse scrunched up as the smell of smoke and blood filled his nose. Ruckanos was not fond of such dirty and laborious affairs. Normally, he resented his lord father for forcing them upon him, but well . . . today was different.

The augurs had spoken. It was time for a new tower to rise, and it was time for a new tower lord to rise with it. The gaze of the gods had turned toward his father's lands, and so the day Ruckanos had long awaited had arrived. He would become the master of the new tower, the chosen of the gods.

Riches, power, and long life would be his, as well as grand armies loyal only to him, and he would finally be free from the authority of his father. He was not doomed to languish as generations of his siblings had before him. He was the one who would ascend to greatness.

So great was his joy that he had thrown a grand banquet that lasted for a week straight before his lord father intervened. His father . . . had been displeased with the delay. So displeased, in fact, that he had ordered Ruckanos to come straight to the site himself.

Normally, the tower guard would have cleared the way, ensuring the area was free from all riffraff and obstructions. No one save the augurs, the tower-lord-to-be, and the tower guard were permitted to witness such a sacred event. But Ruckanos now lacked the time to wait, and so he was here during the cleanup, waiting for his men to finish their dirty work so that the ritual could commence.

But it was good that he was present. The incompetent fools had been bumbling about, waiting for the peasants to gather and pack their paltry possessions. Ruckanos knew that time was of the essence and could not be wasted on such irrelevant riffraff, so he'd ordered his men to clear the way immediately, by any and all means necessary.

He knew his lord father would be upset, though why a tower lord saw any value in such impoverished peasantry, he would never know. But it didn't matter. Once he had ascended and become a tower lord of his own, his lord father's will would no longer be his law.

Just then, an old man to his side began to frown. This was one of the augurs, dressed in fine robes and carrying all sorts of tomes and crystals on his person.

"My lord, the mana stirs, and the gods are on the move. We must hurry if we are to prepare the bindings."

Ruckanos scowled and turned to one of the soldiers. "Captain, what is taking so long? Do not tell me that my own guard cannot handle some dirty peasants?"

His captain bowed his head. "My apologies, my lord. We should be finished up shortly. My men will be sweeping the perimeter, but I believe you should be able to proceed soon."

Ruckanos sighed. "You had better. This is the moment of my ascension, Captain. Nothing shall be permitted to go wrong—"

Just then, the augur gasped. Before Ruckanos could react to the interruption, a bright column of light shot into the sky from behind one of the houses.

"We are too late! It has already begun!"

Ruckanos dug his heels into his horse. "Move, you fools! Whatever's happening there, stop it!"

He and his guard rushed toward the house in question, his horse galloping around to the back. Ruckanos arrived just in time to see a dirty peasant lying on the ground, an arrow in his back and surrounded by the column of light, before there was a crack of thunder and a bright flash of light that blinded the tower-lord-to-be.

When it faded and his eyes could see again, the peasant was gone, and the column of light with him. The augur turned pale.

"We . . . were too late, my lord. The tower has been born . . . and the bindings were not prepared."

Ruckanos narrowed his eyes. "What are you saying?"

The augur gulped. "If the bindings are not in place for the tower's birth . . . then we cannot adjust its course. We . . . have failed, for the first time in my career. For the first time since my grandfather's grandfather . . ."

Ruckanos's eyes widened as he processed those statements. "I-It was only moments ago; surely there is something you can do!"

The augur slowly shook his head. "The tower has been born and moved beyond my sight. I know not where it has gone . . . and I can no longer bind it to you."

Ruckanos turned pale. The tower was gone? It . . . was not bound to him, and they didn't know where it went?

But that meant . . . that he would not ascend today. And his lord father would be most displeased . . .

CHAPTER TWO

WELL, I'LL BEE

Belissar awoke with a start, sitting upright. He blinked for a moment, then gasped and reached for his back. He didn't feel anything there: no arrow shaft, no wounds, no pain, not even blood. He blinked again.

Had it all been a dream?

Just then, vivid memories passed through his mind. He could smell the smoke of flames just outside his window . . . and the scent of blood. He could hear the screams of the villagers, the roar of burning houses, and the angry shouts of soldiers. He could see sunlight reflecting off metal blades before they plunged into his neighbors. He could remember the sharp pain stabbing into his back.

He turned pale and began to sweat. No, he didn't think all that was a dream, after all. Not to mention the fact that he hadn't awoken in his bed . . . or on the ground where he had fallen.

He finally thought to look at his surroundings. He was . . . Well, he didn't know where. All around him was empty white space with only a single feature: a glowing sphere hovering in the air a bit in front of him.

"Am I . . . dead?"

He couldn't think of any other explanation for his current surroundings and the sudden lack of mortal wounds on his back. But at the same time . . . this did not match anything he had been told. Where was the Hall of Judgement? Where was the God of Death?

Just then, he heard a buzzing noise. He began glancing around until he saw it—a single bee buzzing around the glowing sphere. She flew up to him, and he held up his hand by reflex. Belissar's eyes widened as she landed right on his finger. She was missing half an antenna, just like the one from the spiderweb and the one from this morning.

"Don't tell me you died too?!"

That seemed impossible. Even if this was somehow the same bee, only humans went to the Hall of Judgement when they died . . . or so Belissar had been told.

On the other hand, this place didn't match any description of the Hall of Judgement Belissar had heard. Not that any human had actually seen it and lived to talk about it. They couldn't, by definition. There was also the lack of a god passing judgement on the events of his life.

He looked at the bee on his finger. Unless . . . the God of Death was a bee?! Or had he somehow ended up in the Hall of Judgement for bees?! Did bees *have* a Hall of Judgement?!

Said potential god buzzed her wings and danced around, brushing his finger with her uninjured antenna before taking off. She hovered in front of his eyes and flew in a figure eight before turning and flying toward the sphere. Belissar blinked. The bee flew back in front of him and repeated her actions, heading back toward the orb.

"Um, do you want me to do something with this?"

The bee buzzed her wings and began dancing on top of the sphere.

"Um, what exactly?"

The bee just repeated her actions. Belissar gulped before stepping forward. He had no idea what was going on, but if a potential bee god of death wanted him to act, then he'd have to try his best.

He looked at the ball. Even though his surroundings were nothing but white light, he could somehow tell the sphere was glowing faintly. It was perfectly smooth, with no protrusions or marks anywhere—which meant no hints whatsoever as to what he was actually supposed to do with it. But the bee kept dancing and buzzing around on top of the orb.

"Um, like this?"

He reached out to touch it, for lack of any better idea. Once he did, Belissar grunted and shielded his face as the sphere began to glow brightly, to the point it hurt his eyes. He tried to pull his hand back . . . but it was apparently stuck to the orb. He felt it heat up, hotter than anything he'd ever felt. Yet, he didn't feel any pain nor smell any smoke, so it didn't seem like it was burning him.

The heat passed from the sphere into his hand and traveled along his arm. It circulated through his whole body, leaving his entire being feeling hot, burning without pain. And then . . . something appeared before his eyes.

Beginning dungeon binding . . .

Strange words began to appear before his eyes. He was blessed that Mrs. Imkomos had taught him how to read, but knowing the words didn't help him make any sense of them. Dungeon . . . binding? Was he . . . Was he in some sort of prison? Was this the Hall of Judgement, after all? And had he just been judged as wicked?!

"Wait! This is some sort of mistake! I didn't break any of the commandments!"

Well, there was that one about not lying, and that time he'd snuck some cookies. And he didn't actually know all the doctrine; Mrs. Imkomos had made it clear she didn't possess all of the holy texts, so he couldn't rule out that he had broken a rule he hadn't known about. But beyond that, he was pretty sure he had followed the rest! Don't murder, don't steal, pay taxes, obey any and all commands from the tower lords without question, etc.

Please select a starting defender:
- Slime (Rarity: Common. Random default option.)
- Goblin (Rarity: Common. Random default option.)
- Zombie (Rarity: Common. Random default option.)
- Monster Bee Queen (Rarity: Rare. Unlocked by Dungeon Conduit's records.)
- Clockwork Puppet (Rarity: Epic. Random option.)

Belissar blinked again. "Um, what?"

Select a defender? From . . . a list of monsters? What did that mean? Was this some kind of test? Was he choosing his own punishment?! Would whatever he pick arrive to eat him alive?!

He glanced at the bee who was still on top of the sphere, but she didn't react.

Well . . . the choice should be obvious, right? Or rather, Belissar had only heard stories about the others—if he had heard of them at all—but he knew bees, had worked with them for most of his life. He even pretended they were his friends and talked to them when no one else was around. Or so he'd thought; he hadn't become known as the "weird bee guy" for nothing.

He hung his head at that thought.

In any case, if he had to be killed or tormented or whatever this was, he would prefer it be done by his long-time companions.

Monster Bee Queen selected.

Please select a starting room:
- Flower Meadow (Rarity: Common. Unlocked by starting defender.)
- Forest (Rarity: Common. Unlocked by local environment.)
- Stone Labyrinth (Rarity: Common. Random default option.)
- Enchanter's Laboratory (Rarity: Uncommon. Random option.)

Belissar tilted his head. Okay, now he was getting *really* confused. *Pick a room?* Was the God of Death letting him choose where he would be punished? Why would he be allowed to choose that? Was it a consolation prize for good behavior?

Well, if that was the case, the choice was pretty obvious here, too. Of all the places he could be punished, a flower meadow sounded the least bad.

Flower Meadow selected.

Completing binding . . .

The heat from the sphere grew even hotter and began to change. Before, his entire body had been filled with the same amount of heat all over. Now . . . it felt like it was concentrating on his hand.

Suddenly, it vanished all at once, leaving only a dull warmth in his body. Belissar stumbled back as his hand was freed, and then, turning his palm back toward him, he blinked.

There was now a glowing pattern on his hand in the shape of a stone tower.

More words passed before his mind.

Constructing dungeon . . .

Belissar stumbled as the ground began to tremble, feeling as though he was rising into the air. The sphere began to change as well. Colors began to swirl inside of it, and the warmth now inside his body grew hot once more.

Eventually, the rumbling stopped. Belissar glanced around . . . but he was still in the pure-white space. And he was not, in fact, being eaten or tormented by monster bees. Indeed, nothing had changed at all, save for the orb.

He stepped forward to peer inside of it . . . and blinked.

Within, he could see a large meadow full of flowers, a field of color broken up only by the occasional tree. The sphere was blinking toward the top, which drew Belissar's attention. As he focused, additional words appeared before his mind.

Please place Monster Bee Queen Spawner(s).
Upkeep: 20 mana per active spawner.
Available Mana: 95/100

Belissar blinked again. "Um . . . just what is going on here?"

As he spoke the words, the view in the orb shifted, displaying a small circular building. It was a single story tall and made of some kind of white stone with perfectly smooth walls. At its top was a ring of stone holding some sort of glowing sphere. All around it was a sea of an amorphous black substance with faint rainbow undertones, constantly shifting and twisting like a stormy sea.

Words again appeared before his eyes.

Dungeon Status

Floors:	1 (Rooms: 1*/1) (*Pending completion)
Available Mana:	95/100
Available Monster Types:	Monster Bee Queen
Available Room Types:	Flower Meadow
Core Corruption:	0%
Dungeon Master:	Belissar
Dungeon Conduit:	Unnamed Bee
	Complete at least one room.
Current Missions:	Complete initial purification.
	Earn the favor of a patron.

The words did not help him understand the situation, but Belissar was hardly paying any attention to them, for his eyes were fixed upon the image inside the orb. It was a sight he recognized. It was a sight that every person alive could recognize.

"It's a . . . Tower of the Gods?"

Though he recognized the sight, Belissar found himself even more confused.

CHAPTER THREE

DOTH QUOTH THE BEE

Well, calling a single-story building a tower was a bit of an exaggeration, but Belissar couldn't mistake the material, the perfectly smooth round exterior, or the glowing sphere held by a ring of stone at the top.

Descriptions of the towers were taught to frontier children; illustrations filled every book on the subject, and stylized designs adorned the crests and banners of every tower lord. The old beekeeper who had taught him her craft had also made sure to instruct him on the doctrines, so Belissar was quite certain he wasn't wrong.

Moreover, the moment he saw it in the sphere and the "Dungeon Status" appeared before his eyes, he knew. He could feel it . . . quite literally, in fact.

The warmth inside him resonated and confirmed his thoughts. He was now aware that the tower he viewed was the place he was standing in. He could *feel* its boundaries like the edges of his skin. He could even feel the empty spot the flower meadow was waiting to fill. It felt like he was on the verge of sneezing or had something stuck in his teeth, as the room was somehow there but not. Every inch of it had the same warmth flowing through it as the sphere and his body.

He, an unworthy peasant, was standing inside a Tower of the Gods . . . and yet, he had not been smote.

No, that wasn't all . . .

He looked at his hand, searching for the symbol, which responded and began to glow. His eyes widened as he saw the same mark as in the dungeon status—as he saw *his* name listed in the place of the dungeon master. If this place was the dungeon . . . then that was what the strange words called a tower. And if he was the master, then he was a . . .

"No, no, no! That's blasphemy, Belissar!"

He grabbed his head and turned away from the sphere. It didn't make any sense. The Towers of the Gods were special gifts granted to humanity to keep the Hunger at bay. And as gifts from the gods, only those specifically chosen by them were even allowed inside. And to become a tower lord? Only those truly favored were worthy of such an honor.

So Belissar, a random peasant from the frontier, certainly could not have become a tower lord. Such an event would go against everything he had ever been taught about towers, the world, the gods, everything!

And yet . . . here he was. Everything he could see and feel told him this was a tower. And everything he could see and feel also told him that this tower was now connected to him.

Belissar trembled and fell to the ground. This had to be a mistake. How could this even have happened? He'd been minding his own business and dying in the dirt, and now he had somehow not merely defiled a tower with his presence but had gone and taken a tower lord's place somehow? What would happen to him when everyone found out? What would the tower lords do to him? What would the *gods* do to him?

. . . Probably accuse him of stealing it, even though he didn't know the first thing about what had happened, much less intended it.

Of all the unlucky things to happen to him in this life, this must have been the worst yet. How was he going to explain himself to the *gods*? Would anyone believe that *stealing a tower* was some sort of completely unintentional accident? Would they care even if they did?

If he hadn't been doomed at the Hall of Judgement before, he definitely was now.

Just then, the bee buzzed and flew in front of his face, flying around in different circular patterns.

Belissar froze.

"What wrong? Queen still hurt?"

He heard . . . No, that was wrong. He didn't hear anything but buzzing. And yet, somehow, he could tell what the bee was saying, as if her dancing was somehow converting into words.

Well, that or his mind had broken under the strain.

"You can talk?!"

The bee paused and then began quickly zooming around.

"Queen can dance now?!"

Belissar's jaw dropped. "Wait . . . *now*?! You've always been talking?!"

"Yes?"

Belissar's mouth opened and closed a couple of times before he managed to make any noise. Eventually, though, he shook his head. The bee talking now—or, rather, him now being able to interpret the bee's dancing and flying as words— was . . . well, deeply concerning, but it paled in comparison to the rest of the issues at hand. Since the bee had seemed to want him to touch the sphere that had led to all this, perhaps she knew what had happened.

Belissar froze again, then quickly scrambled to his feet as he rushed to bow toward the bee. Because if this was a Tower of the Gods, and this bee had been here from the start, seeming to know how it worked, then wouldn't that mean she was a . . .

"A-Are you a god?"

The bee buzzed and wobbled about on her flight.

"No? Am worker! Your worker now, Queen!"

Belissar blinked and exhaled his breath, standing back up.

"Well, um, if not . . . do you know what happened, then? How we ended up in a Tower of the Gods?"

The bee began to dutifully weave her story through the air. "Queen was hurt! Wanted to help, like Queen helped worker! Then moved here and became core! Core want choose queen, so made Queen the queen!"

Belissar blinked again. "Wait, you became a . . . core? What's that?"

The bee flew over to the sphere and landed on it. "This!"

Belissar blinked as the gears turned in his mind. "Wait, so . . . you became a Tower of the Gods?"

The bee flew about a bit unsteadily. "Tower . . . is dungeon? Then, yes?"

Belissar's jaw dropped. "How?"

"Don't know."

He grunted and held his head at that, taking a deep breath. "Um, look, Miss Bee, I'm grateful that you helped me and saved my life, from the looks of it. But, um, this is a Tower of the Gods, and I'm definitely not one of the chosen. It'll probably be a *big* problem once everyone finds out. So, um, could you . . . unconnect me, or something? Undo whatever happened?"

The bee flew slowly. "Sorry, can't."

Belissar's heart sank into his stomach. "*Can't?*"

The bee flew a little quicker. "Can't. Core says once queen, always queen. And Queen is worker's queen! Can't make not queen! No other queen!"

Belissar held his head and sank to the ground again. He sat there as his heart pounded before eventually taking a deep breath and trying to organize his thoughts and what he knew.

Okay, first of all, he had almost been killed.

Next, the bee, which apparently had been intelligent *before* this, had tried to save him . . . and somehow succeeded.

Well, he should be grateful to her for that. In fact, didn't that confirm she actually *was* the same bee all along? That they were actually friends?

Belissar shook his head. He was getting distracted.

After that, they had somehow ended up here. The bee said she'd become the . . . core? Of a Tower of the Gods? How did that work? He had no idea; none of the doctrine actually detailed the process by which the gods created their towers. Such things were beyond mortal minds, so who's to say they *weren't* formed from intelligent bees? In any case, as far as he knew, that was what had happened.

And then she'd gotten him to touch said core, and now, the tower was somehow connected to him and listed him as its master. *Him.* An unworthy peasant who *definitely* hadn't been chosen by the gods to be here. Unless the bee was somehow connected to them? The tower listed her as a "conduit" or something, if that meant anything. And if true, it would explain the talking-bee thing . . . and the lack of smiting for his very presence defiling the gods' gift.

Finally, the bee had said whatever had happened could not be undone. The "stealing the tower" thing was permanent, no matter how much he wanted to give it back.

Belissar nodded to himself. *Yep.* He still had absolutely *no* idea what was going on here.

"What do I do now?"

Well, he was mostly speaking to himself, but there *was* someone in the room who could respond. And she did.

"Queen says, not worker!"

He tilted his head. "Hm?"

The bee was flying in front of him in excited loops. "Queen is queen now! Queen of core! Queen leads, builds hive, lays brood! Worker listens!"

Belissar heaved a sigh. Being in charge was *exactly* the issue here. And being told he was supposed to lead did not help him figure out what to do, not to mention the whole "build hive, lay brood" thing. He was pretty sure the bee was under a fundamental misconception of his capabilities.

Well, she was also calling him *queen.* He should probably correct her on that. Later, though, as he had to figure out how to avoid the wrath of the gods first. And also, something was drawing his attention and distracting him from solving his impending doom.

The flower meadow room felt like it was poking at his side as a light kept blinking within the sphere . . . core . . . thing. Even if he turned away, it remained present on his mind and in his perception. He felt bloated, or maybe constipated?

He sighed and stood up, walking over to the orb. Looking over the status that lingered before his eyes, he noticed something he had seen before.

	Complete at least one room.
Current Missions:	*Complete initial purification.*
	Earn the favor of a patron.

Okay, so apparently, tower lords had missions? That made sense; they had the duty of watching over the gifts of the gods, which meant . . . these missions might be assigned by the gods to the tower lord.

He crossed his arms and frowned.

The question was, would the gods be angrier if he messed around with one of their towers even more than he had . . . or if he neglected these missions and left them unfulfilled after taking the place of the chosen who was supposed to handle them?

The bee flew over to the core and landed on top of it as he pondered which decision was less likely to lead to divine judgement. She looked up at him, faintly buzzing her little wings. Belissar looked at her for a moment and then sighed.

If the bee responsible for his presence here—who may or may not be connected to the gods themselves—wanted him to do something with this tower, then his best bet was probably to follow through.

Reaching for the core, he really hoped he wouldn't regret this.

CHAPTER FOUR

THE BEE KING

Belissar touched the orb and frowned.

"Okay, then . . . we'll finish the, um, room or whatever. Now, how do I actually do that?"

As he thought, his vision went white. A moment later, he found himself *floating above* a field of flowers. He gasped, but he wasn't falling. He was . . . flying? How was that possible?

Trying to look down at himself for any hints, he gasped again. He couldn't see his body—at all. But as he focused on it, he realized he could still feel it. As far as he was aware, he was still standing in the white room with his hand on the core.

Weird.

But that was nothing new for this situation. This was a Tower of the Gods, after all! Who was he to say what was weird and what was normal? Maybe tower lords thought it weird that peasants had to walk around on their feet . . . and stay inside their bodies?

In any case, he was getting distracted again, and the room was still poking him. So, he set out to work.

Once he had that thought, something changed.

Please place Monster Bee Queen Spawner(s).
Upkeep: 20 mana per active spawner.
Available Mana: 95/100

A tree with a larger beehive than Belissar had ever seen appeared on the ground below. It was transparent, as if made of light.

"Place, huh? Does that mean it can move?"

Belissar waved his hands around . . . or did the ghostly equivalent, he supposed. The tree moved as he did.

"Huh."

Moving it around a bit more, he spun it around, tried to lift it into the sky—which didn't work—and then tried to sink it into the ground, but it turned red. It also turned red if he moved it on top of an existing tree.

Eventually, however, he got tired of moving it around, and with no better ideas, he just put it back where it'd first appeared.

"Okay, um, the tower seems to respond to my thoughts or something? In that case, place it here?"

The tree rooted into the ground and slowly grew solid from the top down.

Monster Bee Queen Spawner placed.
Available Mana: 75/100

Flower Meadow can now be completed. Confirm?

Belissar blinked . . . or tried to as well as he could with his body elsewhere. "Um, confirm?"

Suddenly, he felt as if he were being pulled up into the sky . . .

Flower Meadow placed.

Mission "Complete at least one room" completed!
Reward: One room feature selection.

Preparing for initial purification attempt.
Initial purification attempt in 2 days, 23 hours, and 59 minutes.

Belissar found himself back in the room with the core, feeling as the tower shifted. A doorway appeared in the room he was in. Blinking at it, he looked at the bee, then back at the door.

"Um . . . should we check it out?"

The bee flew up off the core and landed on his shoulder. "Okay!"

"Right . . ."

Belissar slowly began to step forward. Opening the door, he found the scene of a meadow before him, slightly shifting and distorting as if under a pool of water. He tried to stick his head through and peek outside, but his head passed right through the doorway and back inside the white room.

Taking a step back, Belissar frowned.

A moment later, he shook his head. The situation wasn't going to change if he just sat there pondering things he didn't understand, so he might as well try something.

He stepped through the door.

Immediately, Belissar stopped and blinked at the sight before him. He was standing in a meadow full of flowers surrounded by a wall of trees. The sun was shining down on him, and yellow dandelions covered the ground. A gentle breeze blew across the field, causing the flowers to sway. The occasional tree provided a bit of shade.

Behind him, the wall of trees stretched out to either side, the trees growing so closely together he couldn't move or see past them. A glowing doorway made of white light appeared among them, and far in front of him, a large wooden gate stood in a second wall of trees. Belissar glanced around in a daze.

It was exactly the field he had seen in the sphere.

"I . . . made this?"

He bent down and picked up one of the dandelions. It looked real. It felt real. It smelled real. He stopped himself just before putting it in his mouth, as he recalled he did not particularly enjoy the taste of raw dandelion.

". . . A Tower of the Gods, indeed."

After all, what else could he call something that could make an entire field like this out of nothing, and in moments?

He gulped as his heart sank. This truly was the work of the gods . . . and that meant he had truly, if accidentally, stolen said work from one of the chosen. To see their power at work made him dread to see their wrath.

He slowly walked through the field until he came to the center, where the tree with the beehive stood. As he approached it, he felt the warmth inside of both him and the tower begin to concentrate within the hive. Soon, the entrance began to glow, and then a bee emerged. She was larger than any he had ever seen, about the length of his finger. As he looked her over, words appeared before him once again.

Monster Bee Queen

Vitality:	*Minimal*	*Defense:*	*Minimal*
Strength:	*Minimal*	*Resistance:*	*Minimal*
Speed:	*Average*	*Special:*	*Above Average*
Magic:	*Minimal*		*Poison Sting*
		Notable Skills:	*Brood Mother*
			Command Offspring

A honeybee queen that has accumulated enough mana to become something more.

Mostly similar to her mundane cousins, but more aggressive and with a slightly magical venom.

This one is a queen, and capable of building a hive of monster bees.

As Belissar was trying to process the words, the monster bee queen shook herself and then flew toward him. Belissar tensed for a moment, but she stopped in the air before him, watching his every move. He could . . . feel her intentions, somehow. She wanted . . . orders?

"Um, well . . . you're the bee. Go and do bee things, I guess."

The monster flew in a pattern Belissar now perceived as a salute and then headed off into the field. She began gathering pollen from the flowers before flying off to one of the trees. There, she started building a small wax honeycomb and laying eggs.

Belissar just watched in silence while the first bee flew off his shoulder and danced around in the air before him.

"Queen built hive, laid brood!"

Belissar rubbed his chin before nodding. Now was as good a time as ever. "Um, you know I'm a guy, right?"

The bee paused. "Guy?"

Belissar nodded. "A boy, a man, a male?"

The bee's flight grew unsteady. "Queen is . . . drone? But Queen made hive, laid brood? Drone can't."

Belissar opened his mouth to object, but then glanced around at the field of flowers he had apparently made . . . and the monster queen bee he had apparently chosen . . . and the spawner he had apparently placed.

"That's . . . um . . . Well, I guess that's true? But, like, I *am* still a guy, you know?"

The bee shook in flight. "But . . . how can Queen be a drone? Drone is not queen."

Belissar blinked. "Uh . . . then how about a king?"

The bee flew unsteadily. "King? What king?"

Belissar nodded to himself. "It's, um, like a queen, but male. Rules countries, raises armies? It's, ah, a human thing."

The bee flew slowly. "King like queen, but also drone? Do both job? Humans have drone queens?"

Belissar furrowed his brow. "Erm, kind of?"

The bee continued her slow flight. "Queen want call King?"

Belissar slowly nodded. "Yes, please, if you don't mind."

The bee paused for a moment, then flew in a quick salute.

"Okay! Will call Queen King now!"

Belissar gave her a small grin. "Thanks."

Well, he had a feeling he hadn't exactly resolved the fundamental misunderstanding, but close enough. As long as she didn't expect him to lay eggs directly . . .

With that situation . . . *resolved* somewhat, Belissar made his way to the other unique feature in his field: the large gate on the other side—two large wooden doors standing alone in the middle of the field. Belissar walked around the gate and found nothing behind or around it. It truly appeared as just a door randomly standing in the middle of nowhere.

He frowned and then shrugged.

"Might as well . . ."

Begin initial purification attempt?
Initial purification attempt in 2 days, 23 hours, and 37 minutes.

Belissar immediately shut the door and braced his body against it once he saw a writhing, amorphous black mass outside.

The Hunger. Outside the door was a *sea* of the Hunger.

The doom that haunted the world. The punishment from the gods upon the wicked. It consumed everything it touched, be it human, beast, plant, or even metal and stone, and turned them into twisted shadows of their former selves. Those shades would then assault the living and continue to spread the Hunger.

Belissar would die in seconds if exposed to it. Even now, his heart pounded as he slowly backed away from the gate. He was completely surrounded . . . which meant, soon, this place would be corrupted too. There would be no escape.

Suddenly, he paused. He remembered that he was standing inside a Tower of the Gods, the gift they had granted to combat that very Hunger. To protect the chosen from doom.

He watched the gate for a few more minutes, but it seemed the Hunger somehow couldn't make it past the supposedly wooden gates. He exhaled his breath. It seemed he was safe . . . for now.

In fact . . . weren't the Towers of the Gods supposed to purify the Hunger from their surroundings or something like that? Or had this one failed to do so because it was being defiled by him?

Belissar gulped and once again prayed that the gods might forgive him. And given what he'd seen outside that gate, hopefully sooner rather than later . . .

CHAPTER FIVE

BEE THE BUILDER

Belissar walked back over to where the monster bee queen was still making her first little hive. His heartbeat slowed and his mind calmed as he watched the bee buzz around, little comb cells taking shape.

So, he was trapped here, waiting either for the gods to judge him or for the tower to purify the Hunger surrounding it. Oh, and the local tower lord's son had burned his village to the ground, cutting down everyone in it, including himself, so even if he escaped this place and somehow gave back the tower, he couldn't exactly go back to his old home.

Belissar frowned. He wasn't particularly close to anyone in the village, not since the old beekeeper who took him in had died. And even before that, the rest of the village had had little interest in him after he lost his parents. But still, the idea that everyone he knew, good or bad, was gone . . .

He shook his head. His had been an unlucky life, and now, it seemed that misfortune had spread. Perhaps that was why he was now out here, besieged by the Hunger. But what could he do? The situation wouldn't change if he just sat here moping about it. The gods hadn't smitten him yet for defiling their gift, so he may as well do . . . something.

Walking around the field, passing by the trees and scouring the field around them, he picked up whatever fallen branches he could find. He wasn't sure *why* there were fallen branches when the trees had just grown today, but he wasn't about to complain, especially not about the inner workings of a Tower of the Gods. He also began to pick some of the dandelions as he made his way back over to the monster bee's tree.

Once there, he got to work.

Picking the flowers off of the dandelions, he gathered their stems and tied them together, then found a low-hanging branch to hang them from. Now, he just had to wait for the sun and the breeze to dry the stems out.

While he was waiting, he thought about what else he could do, but frowned as he realized his priorities were wrong. If he was going to be trapped here for who knows how long, he would need food, water, and shelter. So once again, he walked through the field.

When he was done, Belissar grimaced. There was nothing there but dandelions and a handful of trees. Hypothetically, the bees would produce honey eventually, but that would take a while, and the bees would need it for themselves. He also didn't have any of the heavy robes needed to approach the hive safely. Although, since he could apparently talk to bees now, maybe he could just ask them for some?

In any case, that was something for the future. Right now, all he had were dandelions for both food and drink, and he did not relish the idea of subsisting on them alone, though what choice did he have?

He sighed once again and started to gather more dandelions. He would eat them once he got hungry or thirsty, but until then, he'd at least start gathering some material. Maybe he could make a cushion or something if he gathered enough . . .

Initial purification attempt in 2 days, 22 hours, and 41 minutes.

After gathering and hanging as many dandelion stems as he could, enough time had passed that the first stems had dried out. Or close enough. Belissar was getting tired of doing the same thing over and over and wanted to move on, so he gathered the driest stems and began to make basic cordage out of them. He then took some sticks and started to tie them together into a basic square.

It was something he had discovered back when he was young. The old beekeeper had shown him that hanging branches from the top of a basket would help the bees shape their hive and give a way to pull out the honeycomb without destroying the entire colony.

Belissar had experimented with different shapes and sizes in order to find what the bees liked best, and he'd eventually found that if he put straight square boxes in rows, the bees would build their comb within them. He especially liked that he could just pull the boxes out when he wanted the honeycomb, and so didn't have to destroy the hive.

Looking at the rickety square made of twigs and dandelion rope, he sighed. This . . . wasn't exactly what he had in mind, but he didn't exactly have his wood-cutting axe with him, and the knife he kept on his person wasn't going to chop through a tree branch. He wasn't going to be making nice beehouses anytime soon, it seemed.

He could see the bee watching him, so he held up the square. "What do you think?"

The bee buzzed and flew around rapidly. "King making hive! Worker help!"

Belissar chuckled. "Well, at least you like it."

He went ahead and made some more dandelion rope, then hung the square from a branch near the monster bee queen. She looked at it curiously, and then started to build her new comb within the frame. Meanwhile, his other bee companion flew around to the corners, adding some beeswax to hold the sticks together.

Belissar blinked. That . . . definitely wasn't normal bee behavior. But then again, these also weren't normal bees . . .

Still, he felt a smile grow on his face as he watched the two work, going over to see if any of the other dandelion stems had dried yet.

Belissar ended up working until the sun began to set, making as many frames as he could and hanging them together. He didn't notice that he wasn't hungry, even after hours of work . . .

Belissar frowned as the sun went down. How was there night when he was inside a tower? In fact, why was there a sun and sky inside?

But he shook his head. Such things were the purview of gods and tower lords, not of peasants like himself. So, he stretched, gathered what dandelion cords he had . . . and promptly realized that he had spent all day building improvised bee-house frames and not actually preparing a shelter for himself. It was growing too dark to work on anything as well.

With a sigh, he made his way over to the other side of the field, where the door to the core room was. Stepping inside, he found it just as he had left it: a room of pure white where he had trouble distinguishing where the floors and walls even were . . . assuming there actually *were* floors and walls. Maybe he'd try exploring the edges of the room later.

For now, he used the light of the room and the core to gather up some dandelion cords into something of a pillow, then lay down and placed his head upon it. The ground felt like . . . Well, it felt solid, but it didn't really feel like anything, which was kind of weird to Belissar . . . and grew weirder the more he thought about it. So, he tried his best not to, and to close his eyes.

He lasted about half an hour before deciding that the weird floor that was there but not really and the white room that seemed the same color and brightness everywhere at all times were not conducive to his rest and stepped back out into the flower meadow. He ended up just lying down wherever and staring up at the night sky.

Well, the meadow wasn't very cold, and the field of flowers was soft enough; he had slept on worse before. He sighed and tried to get as comfortable as he could, putting aside the thoughts of gods, Hunger, and burning villages.

Initial purification attempt in 2 days, 10 hours, and 23 minutes.

Belissar had a fitful sleep and awoke as soon as the sun peeked over the horizon. Strangely, though, he didn't feel tired. Or hungry . . . or thirsty . . . or even the need to relieve himself. He narrowed his eyes.

At this point, Belissar was getting weirded out, but maybe he shouldn't? The tower lords were supposed to be something beyond the ranks of mortal men. They lived ageless lives and wielded powers the common folk couldn't comprehend. Belissar had always thought that was why they were chosen to rule the towers . . . but maybe some of it came from the towers themselves?

He shook his head to clear his thoughts and rose to his feet. In the end, Belissar was no thinker or theologian, so he'd do what he did best: Keep his head down and take care of his bees.

He walked over to the monster bee queen's tree . . . and gasped. Dozens of worker bees now buzzed around the frames, some filling the rows with comb, others forming wax into an outer wall around the edges, while still others were off harvesting from the flowers. The queen herself was now busy laying eggs into the cells as the workers formed them.

Belissar blinked. Bees grew quickly, but he thought it took a few days for an egg to grow into an adult worker at least. Well, they *were* supposed to be monster bees, so he supposed they might grow faster than a normal hive or something?

Crossing his arms, he hummed. They honestly had enough frames . . . and he wasn't even sure they needed them, seeing as how they could form their hives with those basic outlines on their own.

In which case, what should he do today?

At that moment, his bee companion buzzed in front of him. "King! New queen coming!"

"Oh, another one?"

He walked over to the center tree just in time to see another monster bee queen climb out of the spawner hive. She shook herself then flew over to him like the first had. He gave a small smile.

"Let's build you a hive."

The monster bee queen danced her salute before gathering pollen as Belissar went to collect his frame materials. Another day saw another hive taking shape . . . and yet another day where Belissar forgot to build any accommodations for himself.

Initial purification attempt in 1 day, 10 hours, and 15 minutes.

Belissar again tossed and turned that night, but still didn't feel that tired in the morning, so he got to work as soon as it was light enough for him to see. Again, another day came and went, another hive was built, and he again forgot to prepare anything for himself.

But he didn't mind. He apparently didn't really need much, and he preferred working on the hives, in any case. In fact, as the sun set, a few of the bees from the first one came and danced in front of him.

"You want to show me something?"

Belissar followed them back to the first hive. It was very nearly complete, a box shape very reminiscent of the beehouses he had back home, only made of wax and hanging from a tree branch.

The queen bee came out and danced in front of Belissar.

"You want . . . to give me some honey?"

The queen bee continued her dance. "Tribute for King."

A few workers guided him to one of the frames, and he climbed up the tree, pulling out the frame in question, filled to the brim with golden honey. He broke off a piece and took a bite, his eyes widening. "Delicious."

A delectable sweetness graced his tongue. And more than that, he could feel warmth spreading through his body of a similar sort as the core had filled him with at first. The entire hive began buzzing and dancing at his word, the queen bee most of all.

Belissar felt a smile grow on his face, and he held out the frame. "Please, have some too."

The queen bee began to refuse, but Belissar shook his head. "A diligent worker deserves her reward."

The queen bee hesitated before slowly flying over to the comb and sipping from one of the cells. Belissar's smile grew.

As the night grew dark, Belissar gathered his materials into the core room and continued working on more frames with the light of the core. All other thoughts left his mind save for the task before him.

Initial purification attempt in 8 hours and 51 minutes.

Initial purification attempt in 2 hours and 13 minutes.

Initial purification attempt in 35 minutes.

Initial purification attempt in 4 minutes.

Initial purification attempt in 30 seconds.

Initial purification attempt in 5 . . . 4 . . . 3 . . . 2 . . . 1 . . .

CHAPTER SIX

INITIAL PURIFICATION ATTEMPT

Initial purification attempt in 5 . . . 4 . . . 3 . . . 2 . . . 1 . . .

Belissar was hanging another frame on a tree when, suddenly, his body went hot. His eyes widened as he realized it wasn't just him. The entire tower had gone hot; he could feel streams of heat flowing through the ground and the air.

Initial purification attempt commencing.

The gates to the Hunger swung open, and Belissar gasped as the black oil-like substance began to whip and reach into the flower meadow, only for the edges of the gate to begin glowing with bright light which made the Hunger screech and its tendrils retreat back through the gate.

So instead, the black substance began to condense and warp. Belissar fell on his behind as he heard snarling and growling, then a black paw with rainbow highlights broke out of the writhing mass and stepped inside the gate, black mist emanating from it like tongues of fire as huge claws crushed the dandelions underfoot.

A second paw stepped through, and then a snarling snout began to emerge above, dripping with bits of the Hunger that melted into the ground and caused the flowers below to wilt. Glowing red lights appeared where the creature may have had eyes—only there were *six* of them in pairs climbing up its head.

Belissar began scooting back through the dirt as the creature fully exited the Hunger and stepped into the field. The black mist emanating from it made its full body shape hard to distinguish, but it was vaguely in the shape of a canine, though larger than any dog or wolf Belissar had ever seen. What he could make out were the sharp claws on its feet, the fangs lining a snout that was a bit too long, and the sharp spike at the end of a snakelike tail.

Belissar turned pale. "A-A . . . shade?"

The shade threw its head up into the sky and let out a roar. Belissar let out a whimper and then spun around, pulling on the dirt with his hands as he tried to stand up and start running at the same time.

"H-Help!"

Initial purification attempt has begun.
Remaining hostiles: 1

The shade snarled and took off running, chasing after Belissar. The flowers wilted beneath its feet every time it stepped, leaving a trail of death in its wake.

Belissar wasn't a stranger to violence; he had warded off wild animals and such, as all rural villagers must. But this . . . *this* was a shade of the Hunger, the disaster that brought ruin to the wicked kings of old and laid low the civilizations of the subhumans. This was a threat that even the tower guard could not defeat without sacrifice.

It was far beyond a single farmer with a spear—and Belissar didn't even have his.

Belissar could hear the snarling and growling behind him, could feel bits of dirt collide with the back of his legs as the shade chased after him. He began to feel cold as bits of dark mist flickered around him, whimpering as he felt the fell creature's breath upon his back and smelled the stench of death.

It was then that his companion buzzed on his shoulder.

"King retreat. Worker save."

Belissar turned to glance at his shoulder. "What?!"

But the little bee didn't answer. Instead, a faint light began to glow around her, and Belissar could feel a spot of heat growing on his shoulder. Before he could say anything else, she flew off his shoulder . . . and straight toward the shade's forehead.

A moment later, there was a small flicker of light, and the creature roared. It skidded to a stop, letting Belissar gain some distance. He could see the small spark of light fly off the shade's head and into the side of its torso, making it roar again.

The spark flew away once more, but this time, the shade was ready. It whirled around . . . and its jaws snapped around the spark.

"No!"

Conduit Unnamed Bee has fallen.

Belissar gritted his teeth and shut his eyes, but he kept running. There was nothing he could do now . . . and the shade had turned to face him once again, starting to run toward him once more.

Belissar could hear more buzzing, and his eyes shot open. Bees were turning away from the flowers and flying toward the shade. First one, then two, and then a dozen. The creature growled and snapped around at the air, swatting with its paws and tail.

Belissar saw a small cloud of bees approach from the nearest tree, where his first hive stood. He could feel his first monster bee queen as she rallied her forces and sallied out from the hive, urging him to move faster.

The creature snarled and took a deep breath, letting out a cloud of black mist from its mouth that surged forward. The bees dropped from the sky as the mist passed over them, the queen bee falling with them. Belissar could feel as his bond with her faded.

Monster Bee Queen has fallen.

The shade then ran and pounced through the air toward the tree, crushing the entire hive in a single bite. Belissar gritted his teeth even harder as he pushed off the ground with all his strength. His legs were burning, his heart was pounding in his chest, and his eyes were growing blurry, but he kept running.

On Belissar ran, and on the shade chased.

He passed by the tree in the center even as another monster bee queen was just emerging, only for the shade to coat the hive in a breath of deadly mist once more.

Monster Bee Queen has fallen.
Monster Bee Queen Spawner disabled.
Monster Bee Queen has fallen.

The second hive flew into battle, only to again be brought down by the mist. The shade was sprinting as fast as it could, and quickly gaining on Belissar. He saw the light of the second door just ahead of him . . . but his legs were slowing down. He ran as fast as he could, but he had no further strength to give. He could not move any faster than he already was.

And the shade was about to reach him. It would catch him before he could reach the core room . . .

But the third and final monster bee queen arrived. Her hive was not yet complete, and her brood was the smallest of the bunch, but she had watched the first and second queens fall, and so she did not have her workers swarm the foe as her instincts demanded.

Instead, small groups of bees rushed in one by one, stinging and then fleeing. The shade snarled and bit at them, but they had already passed, and another group stung its unprepared back. It whirled around, but they too had already fled.

In the meantime, Belissar reached the door and leapt through with one last push of his legs. He tumbled into the room and willed the door shut, but it remained open. Belissar's eyes trembled as the core's interior shifted, showing the fight in the meadow.

The shade let out a breath, but the bee groups scattered from one another, and only a few were caught. It snarled and snapped at the air, but the bees kept up their assault.

With only a few of them falling at a time, Belissar began to hope.

"Come on, you can do it . . ."

The queen bee paused at Belissar's words, and then the bees sprung into action, intensifying their assault. The groups were flying in at maximum speed, stinging the shade over and over, which growled and roared, then took a deep breath.

Suddenly, a cloud of mist burst out of the shade, surging in every direction. The bee groups fell one by one, and the queen barely had time to react before the cloud passed over her too.

Monster Bee Queen has fallen.

Belissar's heart sank. The shade still stood in the end.

Stalking forward slowly, it growled softly as it stepped toward the door of light in front of it. It did not seem to have forgotten him nor lost his trail.

Belissar thought of grabbing his knife, but what was the point? How could he dodge its breath of death when flying bees couldn't? How would his little knife fare against this shade's fangs and claws?

He shut his eyes and whimpered, waiting for his death.

The shade dug its claws into the ground and lowered its body before snarling and leaping toward the door of light.

And the moment it touched the door . . . it exploded.

The whole tower rumbled and shook, startling Belissar and causing him to open his eyes. He gasped as he saw the black tendrils of the Hunger spreading across the featureless white room, feeling as the heat running through the tower turned cold. He could see in his core as the Hunger spread across the flower meadow. He could see the Hunger pouring in through the gateway as the light around its edges faded.

And then Belissar collapsed to the ground.

Initial purification attempt failed.

CHAPTER SEVEN

BEE-COME THE MASTER

The gateway slammed shut, locking the Hunger out once again. The black tendrils that had spread through both the core room and the meadow began to slow down until they eventually stopped. The entire tower fell silent.

Beginning cleansing.

Belissar slowly rose to his feet as the rumbling stopped, glancing at the black tendrils within the core room, but they didn't move any further. He glanced in the core, but there was no sign of the monster, so he crept to the door and gingerly stepped outside.

He gasped.

The flower field was black and wilted. Everywhere he looked, tendrils of the Hunger reached across the ground, leaving dead flowers in their wake. The breeze carried dried leaves through the air, and the trees in the fields were black and crumbling.

And everywhere he looked on the ground, he saw dead bees.

He walked through the field in a daze. It was silent, not a flower left to rustle in the wind, not a single bee left to buzz about.

Not even the one who had saved him.

Falling to his knees as he came to one of the trees, Belissar reached out to a pile of debris under the branches. There lay the remains of one of his hives. Reaching in, he picked up two sticks. The wax and dandelion cords holding them together crumbled as he held a dead bee within his hand.

He clutched his head. Something cracked inside of him, and memories he rarely thought about now surged into his mind . . .

*

A young boy, scarcely more than half a decade, stood at the side of the bed. Two adults lay across it, their faces pale and drenched with sweat. Their bodies were taut, their breaths ragged, and they kept coughing. The young boy gripped his pants tight with both hands as he looked down.

And then he felt a trembling hand slowly touch his own. His eyes shot up.

His mother had turned her head to him. She tried to smile, but broke out coughing. Her eyes began to moisten.

"I'm . . . sorry, Belissar. Please . . . live . . ."

The young boy broke into tears.

A young teenage boy of around fifteen years, just old enough to be considered an adult, once again stood in an adult's bedroom. A frail old woman lay upon the bed. The boy, or perhaps young man now, kept his eyes glued upon the ground.

"Now, what's with that look? I know these old bones aren't the prettiest, but I can't be that bad to look at, can I?"

The young man slowly raised his head, glancing at the old woman out of the corner of his eye.

". . . No, Mrs. Imkomos."

She began a chuckle that turned into a hacking cough.

"Come closer, would you?"

The young man slowly obliged as Mrs. Imkomos gave a wry smile.

"Now, don't you worry about me, Belissar. I'm going to the gods, to the Hall of Judgement, where the God of Death shall evaluate my life. I can't say I've been perfect, but I can say now I'm happy with the life I've lived. Most of all because of this."

Belissar felt a wrinkled, trembling hand grasp his. Feeling his eyes start to moisten against his will, he slowly turned to glance at the woman again. She gave him a sad smile as she rubbed the back of his hand with her thumb.

". . . I know, boy. This is going to be hard for you, I won't lie, but this isn't the end. Just remember what I taught you and do the best you can, alright? Follow the doctrines, honor the gods and their chosen, and live a good life regardless of what anyone else says. Then, when your time comes, we'll meet again. You, me . . . and your mom and dad. You'll have to introduce me, okay?"

Belissar slowly nodded. He began to sob mid-motion, and a tear dripped down Mrs. Imkomos's cheek as well.

"And take care of our bees, you hear?"

With that, she let go of his hand and lay back against the bed to rest as Belissar's vision filled with tears.

Back in the present, Belissar let out a long scream as he fell to the ground, curling up in the ashes, tears streaming from his eyes as sobs wracked his body.

Why? Why him? Why *always* him?

He had lost his parents, he had nearly starved, he'd lost the old beekeeper who'd taken him in, he'd lost his entire village . . .

And now, he had lost his bees, including perhaps the one real friend he had ever had. All because he, someone unworthy, had dared to take a Tower of the Gods from those who had been chosen. This dead and barren field was the result.

His heart constricted at the thought of the little bee he had helped out of that spiderweb. Who had brought him to a Tower of the Gods just to save him. Who hadn't hesitated before jumping into the jaws of a monster just to buy him a little time.

And with those thoughts came the thoughts of others. The beekeeper, the old woman who had taken him in when he was lying in the dirt. All the days she'd spent showing him her bees and how to care for them. All she had taught him: how to read and write, how to take care of himself, and how to honor the gods. And even further back to a time when he rarely wept at all, comforted in the arms of his mother and father.

His sobs grew louder. He had done his best. He had worked his hardest. He had never made a fuss. He had kept his head down. He had followed every law. He had given honor to the gods and the tower lords. He had been agreeable to everyone. He had never complained no matter what they did: Not when they had stolen his food. Not when they had trampled his fields. Not when they had taken his mead and his honey. Not when they had left him to starve.

And yet . . . time and time again, more bad things happened. He would brush it off, hold his tears, say that it was just plain old bad luck.

But it only ever got worse. And now, even when the gods were coming for him, the world was not content to let him have *anything*. Everything he had, everyone he cared about, had to be stripped from him.

"Mom . . . Dad . . . Mrs. Imkomos . . . my friend . . ."

He finally broke.

Belissar didn't know how long he lay there. He wept and he wept until he could weep no more, and then he lay there, staring blankly at the dirt. But then . . . something changed. His body began to grow warm; in fact, the whole tower began to grow warm once more. The ground, the sky, the air, it all began to glow and shine.

Belissar slowly sat back up and rubbed his eyes, which then widened at what he saw.

The black tendrils of the Hunger began to recede, shrinking and streaming toward the core room. Shoots of grass and dandelions broke through the dirt and began to bloom. Color returned to the tree branches, and green leaves began to cover them once more.

Cleansing complete.
All spawners and features reenabled.
Core corruption at 37%
Core cannot be cleansed until dungeon is fully established.
Next initial purification attempt in 3 days.

Conduit respawning.

Belissar watched as the room returned to normal, the flowers sprouting as if nothing had ever happened. And as he read the last message before his eyes, his heart began to pound, and his eyes began to tremble. He glanced every which way until he looked back at the door to the core room once more. His eyes went as wide as they could go.

A single bee was flying toward him. He held his breath as she approached. "King! You alive!"

He held up trembling hands as she danced in the air, and she landed on his palms before dancing happily. Tears filled Belissar's eyes once more.

There she was: the bee with half her left antenna missing. His friend.

Gently cupping his hands, he brought them to his chest, hunching over to curl around them as best he could.

"Thank goodness . . ."

Tears streamed down his face again, and he began to sob once more, only this time for a different reason.

When Belissar had finally calmed down, he stood back up and looked over the flower meadow. As the breeze began to blow in his face, he closed his eyes and took a deep breath, smelling the flowers, then opened his eyes again.

His friend had survived . . . or had been brought back, more accurately. The flowers had regrown, the meadow had healed, and the tower still stood.

But all was not as it was. The frames he had built were gone. The monster bee queens, the hives they had built, and all the workers they had borne were gone, too.

Belissar watched as a new one crawled out of the monster spawner, and he instantly knew: she was different; not one of the four who had perished. Only his friend had been brought back.

Initial purification attempt in 2 days, 23 hours, and 47 minutes.

He knew now what those words meant. He knew now the process by which the towers purified the Hunger. He knew now why the tower lords wielded such great powers, and why only those chosen by the gods could take care of them.

And he knew now the consequences of someone unworthy taking that job. Like him.

The shade would be back. It would once again seek his life, once again bring death and ruin to these fields. And as the dungeon master, it now fell upon him to fight it, to take up the mantle he had found himself wearing and fulfill the duty issued by the gods to the chosen tower lords. A duty that he was entirely unprepared for and that would have deadly consequences for every living thing who dwelled here if he failed.

He looked at the monster bee queen as she shook herself and then flew in the air before him, waiting for him to speak. His friend buzzed and flew off his shoulder, joining the queen in watching him. A fire grew in his chest, and he began to scowl. Grinding his teeth as he remembered the sight of the dead bees littering the ground, he clenched his fists until his knuckles turned white.

Belissar decided no more. He no longer cared if he died, no longer cared if the world wanted to crush him. He no longer cared if he had accidentally stolen from the tower lords or if he was one of the chosen. He no longer cared if he was prepared or if the gods would smite him for what he had done.

The shade—the Hunger—would pay. And they would never again do what they had done today. Belissar wouldn't let them. He would stop them, or he would die trying. And if he had truly defiled the tower with his deeds, he would let the gods judge him—but until they did, he would use everything at his disposal without worrying about what laws he broke in the process.

He would do the best with what he had. Which at present, was a *Tower of the Gods*. And he would use it as best he could.

He looked at the two bees buzzing in the air and nodded.

"Let's get moving. We have a lot of work to do."

The two danced a salute then rushed off to begin building a new hive. Belissar nodded to himself as he watched them go. They rushed to obey his command without complaint or hesitation; he, who had gotten them and their sisters killed.

Belissar swore in his heart that day. The world had taken his mother, had taken his father. It had taken the old beekeeper, then taken his village, his home. It had tried to take his very life. But from now on, whether they were man, beast, god, or Hunger . . .

They would *not* take his bees.

CHAPTER EIGHT

SO, WHAT'LL IT BEE?

Belissar stood as he rubbed his chin. He may have made a bold statement, but implementing it was another matter entirely. At the end of the day, he was still a peasant whose grandest deeds were warding off hungry wild animals. Tower lords using the gifts of the gods to battle the Hunger were a bit outside of his expertise.

Eventually, he walked back to the core room, deciding to start where this all began: at the core.

He placed his hand on the sphere once again.

Dungeon Status

Floors:	_1 (Rooms: 1/1)_
Available Mana:	_75/100_
Available Monster Types:	_Monster Bee Queen_
Available Room Types:	_Flower Meadow_
Core Corruption:	_37%_
Dungeon Master:	_Belissar_
Dungeon Conduit:	_Unnamed Bee_
Current Missions:	_Complete initial purification._
	Earn the favor of a patron.

*One room feature selection available.

Belissar hummed as he looked over his tower and the words that had appeared before his eyes once again. He noticed a new addition from the last time he'd checked and focused on it. As he did, the words shifted, spinning in such a way that he could no longer read them, before they stopped, having rearranged themselves.

Please select a room feature:
- Basic Resource Plants (Rarity: Common. Type: Nature, Resource.)
- Pit Trap (Rarity: Common. Type: Ground, Trap.)
- Thorned Roses (Rarity: Common. Type: Nature, Trap.)

Belissar rubbed his chin. Room selection had let him build a flower meadow within the tower. Defender selection had resulted in the monster bee queens appearing in that room via the spawner he'd placed. So, he figured this choice would let him place whatever he chose within the room as well.

And all of this was to enable him to fight the Hunger and the shades it would send to kill him. To purify the world, as a tower lord was mandated by the gods to do. So the question was: which of these would enable him and a few beehives to kill that monster? His life, the life of his bees—including his friend—and the very existence of this Tower of the Gods hung on the answer.

Belissar turned his attention back to the original status and the flower meadow. He wanted to see what else he could do with this tower before he made his choice.

Frowning, he looked at the spawner in the center of the room. It had been disabled when that shade had reached it.

Well, it only spawned one monster bee queen a day, so it hadn't mattered much when the shade had torn through the tower. But still, it'd been a mistake, if a small one, to have placed it right in between the gate to the Hunger and the door to the core room, right in the center of the path the shade had taken. Another sign of how unprepared and unworthy Belissar was for this job.

"If only I could move it . . ."

The moment he thought that, the core shifted its view to center on the tree.

Move Monster Bee Queen Spawner?

Belissar blinked. "Oh."

Apparently, he *could* move it.

Agreeing to the question, a faint outline of light surrounded the tree, and a transparent image rose from it. He blinked and shook his head. The tree followed his vision.

Quickly willing it to move, the image flew all the way across the meadow . . . and promptly halted. Try as he might, Belissar couldn't move it any further beyond the door to the core room. The trees there seemed to form a solid wall.

Belissar frowned and sighed. He couldn't help but feel that a real tower lord would have known all of this already. But he didn't, so he had no choice but to try things and see what worked.

He tried again in all directions, but the wall of trees remained solid. He finally decided to place the spawner by the door to the core room. If the shade reached there, then he had lost anyway.

But even if the spawner wasn't as far away as he had hoped, it had demonstrated something to Belissar: He apparently could make some adjustments to the room; at least to the spawner. So, what else could he do?

He began to focus on different parts of the room, starting with the flowers.

Manage flower types?
Available types:
*- **Dandelion** (Mana Upkeep: 0) (Selected)*

Well, that was helpful. He tried the trees next.

Move tree?

. . . Slightly more helpful. Maybe. At the very least, he could move some of the trees toward the back of the room, by the spawner and the core room door, and the queens could then build their hives further away from where the Hunger would attack. Still, that wouldn't help them actually slay the shade . . .

Belissar found he could add a few more trees, though there seemed to be a maximum number allowed. Guess they didn't want him turning a flower meadow into a forest. Not that more trees would particularly help. He could also remove them, but that would help even less than adding them.

He sighed. With nothing better to do, he focused on the dirt.

Adjust terrain height?

Belissar pursed his lips. Surprisingly, the dirt was the right choice, as that might actually be helpful. Getting higher up always helped against land-based predators . . . though he wasn't sure if that helped against shades of the Hunger.

Still, if he could make a wall, then maybe he wouldn't have to fight it directly—

Maximum height reached.

Belissar sighed. Of course. *Of course* he couldn't raise it steeper than a gentle hill; this was a flower meadow, not a castle. For a gift from the gods that could create land and life out of thin air, there sure were a lot of limits. Maybe he should've picked one of the other options. That, or there was something he was missing that a real tower lord would have known.

Initial purification attempt in 2 days, 23 hours, and 23 minutes.

But there was no time to wonder what a tower lord could do that he couldn't. Time was ticking, and it was up to him to use it well.

He sighed and let go of the core. He should at least tell his bee queen to set up her hive on one of the farther trees now . . .

He paused. He hadn't even spoken, but he'd *felt* her salute somehow. He shook his head. He wasn't even in the same room as her; he had to have been imagining things.

But just in case he wasn't . . .

He peeked back at the core. The view shifted before showing the queen bee dancing a salute and then flying toward one of the newly arranged trees. He blinked again.

Okay, so apparently, he could also talk to the bees with his mind now? And somehow know their responses?

He shook his head. He had no time to get surprised at every little thing a Tower of the Gods could do; he would just have to figure things out as he went. And since he apparently didn't need to actually walk to the queen to talk to her, he had no reason to leave the core room anymore.

With a sigh, he turned back to the orb and zipped through the flower meadow once again, checking for anything else he could use while trying to figure out how he would actually fight that shade and which of the room features would help most with it.

Catching a glimpse of one of the ruined hives from before, with twigs sticking haphazardly out of the mess, he sighed, as he was once again reminded how out of his depth he was.

A real tower lord would certainly have used the first three days to prepare their defenses. Meanwhile, Belissar had been trying to build beehouses out of twigs—beehouses he didn't even need to build, since he could apparently just ask them to build their hives in the appropriate shape. His original little twig frames wouldn't even have worked had the bees not tried to follow his instructions on their own . . .

Belissar paused and stared at the ruins of the hive as many thoughts in his mind began to twist and swirl. He thought of how he, a weak and unworthy peasant, could fight a monstrous creature. He thought of the bees trying to build their hives according to his shaky frames, clearly attempting to follow the commands he hadn't realized he could give them.

He thought of his life before, and the various things he had made in his life as a beekeeper. He thought of what he had available in the flower meadow, and the list of room features he could now choose from.

The different thoughts in his head began to intersect.

"I think . . . I have an idea."

Belissar was no tower lord, and he hadn't the first clue of how to fight like one, but he was a beekeeper and a farmer. And maybe, just maybe, with the help of the bees . . . he might be able to fight as what he actually was.

In any case, time was ticking, and if he wanted to attempt what he was thinking, he would need all the time he could get. So, he brought up the list of room features once more and made his choice.

He could only pray it would work.

CHAPTER NINE

BEE PREPARED

Belissar placed the feature he had chosen, adjusting it to his liking. He then tried to place more monster bee queen spawners, and finding it worked, he placed another three, for four total, before he ran out of mana.

Mana: 14/100

He then rearranged some of the trees and made a few hills before letting go of the core. There was nothing left he knew how to do with it that could help, so it was time to get to work with his hands.

Initial purification attempt in 2 days, 22 hours, and 38 minutes.

He walked outside just as three new monster bee queens crawled out of their spawners. They flew in front of Belissar as he walked into the field, with the first queen and the conduit bee joining them.

"King, have command?"

He felt a sharp pain in his chest. He had gotten his friend killed while trying to save him, and yet, she still asked him that without even a hint of doubt.

He took a deep breath and nodded his head.

"Yes, I have an idea. I . . . know I'm not worthy of this tower, and you paid the price for it. You might still pay the price for it. But I'm going to try my best to protect you now. However, I will need your help, all of you, to pull it off. I'm sorry, but . . . will you help me?"

The conduit bee flew around rapidly.

"Of course! King lead; worker help!"

The queen bees danced their agreement. Belissar took a deep breath.

"Okay. Let's get to work, then."

"Okay!"

And so they did. The queen bees flew off to start their hives, and the conduit bee went to help them. Meanwhile, Belissar hunched over and moved through the field, picking as many dandelions as he could while making his way over to the nearest tree. Once there, he began picking up sticks as well. He would need as many as he could find.

Initial purification attempt in 2 days, 5 hours, and 17 minutes.

Belissar continued working till night fell. He thought he would be exhausted, but the warmth from the core and the tower filled him whenever he thought he was getting tired, so he was able to continue working with neither food nor sleep. Still, with the sun setting, it would be hard to do much. If only he could see in the dark . . .

The moment he thought that, his vision seemed to light up. The field was still as dark as ever, but Belissar could somehow see it. Or rather . . . it felt like his vision was still dark, but he somehow knew what was happening in the room anyway. As that thought crossed his mind, his vision seemed to float away from his body. He blinked.

Apparently, he could see *anything* happening in the room, even when he wasn't touching the core.

"Well, that's convenient. Yet another thing I wish I had known before . . ."

He shook his head and went back to work tying some dandelion stems into a cord. It seemed he would be able to work through the night, after all.

Initial purification attempt in 1 day, 23 hours, and 45 minutes.

Belissar watched as the first round of worker bees hatched and got to work. A third of them flew to and from their hives gathering nectar, a third flew to greet the new queens from the spawners and help them get set up, and a third flew toward the gate to the Hunger, carrying the dried-out dandelion stems Belissar had picked yesterday. Belissar focused on one of them.

Monster Bee Worker

Vitality:	*Minimal*	***Defense:***	*Minimal*
Strength:	*Minimal*	***Resistance:***	*Minimal*
Speed:	*Average*	***Special:***	*Minimal*
Magic:	*Minimal*		*Poison Sting*
		Notable Skills:	*Sacrificial Strike*
			Brood Offspring

Largely similar to a mundane honeybee, though the mana flowing through it improves the toxicity of its venom. Can be dangerous in numbers to the unprepared, but generally not meant for combat.
Will be spawned by Monster Bee Queens if available.

Belissar nodded. The monster bee workers were about what he expected from what he'd seen earlier, and barely different from normal bees. He wondered what made them "monsters," then, and if he had made the wrong choice. Should he have chosen something else?

But he shook his head. A tower lord might have, but Belissar was a humble beekeeper. Maybe bees weren't the right choice, but at the very least, they were something he knew. He didn't think he would have come up with his idea if he'd had slimes or clockwork puppets or whatever else.

That is, assuming his idea worked . . .

He bent down as he thought, picking more stems. Bees came to grab them from him and lay them out in the sun to dry. They could carry the stems to and fro, but they had trouble cutting them, so it was up to Belissar to pick as many as he could. They had their jobs, and he had his.

Initial purification attempt in 1 day, 0 hours, and 22 minutes.

"Hunger take you!"

Yet another cord snapped as Belissar tried to pull his fire bow back and forth. He had gathered enough material, and the bees were still hard at work, so now he was testing things to make sure he could pull it off.

It wasn't going particularly well, and he had only a day left to go. But he didn't have his flint with him, and making a fire bow with twigs and dandelion cords wasn't proving to be easy. He had managed to saw through some of the thinner branches of the trees to get something a little more substantial than a twig, but the dandelion cords kept snapping.

A real tower lord would have known some magic, or else had an artifact prepared to do this, but a real tower lord probably wouldn't need to start a fire like this either. Belissar sighed and shook his head.

"Guess I have no choice."

Grabbing the hem of his tunic, he stretched it out then took his knife and cut off a strip from the bottom. Hopefully, it would hold up better to the task than tied dandelion stems did.

His entire plan depended on it, and time was ticking.

Initial purification attempt in 15 minutes.

The conduit bee buzzed and zipped around Belissar's head.

"King, sure?"

Belissar nodded. "For the hundredth time, yes."

The bee picked up speed. "But! Worker job to fight! King, queen stay in hive! Stay safe!"

Belissar shook his head as he walked toward the gate, holding a branch with strips from his tunic wrapped around the top. A fire burned on his makeshift torch, going down the branch faster than he'd like. He could only hope he'd timed it right . . .

"Not this time. I watched all of you die once because I'm unworthy. I'm not going to let that happen again."

The buzzing intensified. "Worker job to fight! Worker job to die for hive! King must live!"

Additional bees flew around him, buzzing and dancing their agreement. But Belissar continued walking forward toward the gate to the Hunger. Two hills rose to either side of it with a small flat path between them lined sporadically with trees. Belissar had wanted two rows lining the path, but the maximum limit on the trees meant it was far sparser than he had hoped. Which was why he would be standing before the gate himself.

"If everything goes well, no one will die at all except that monster. You've done your part; this is mine."

The conduit bee flew unsteadily before him. "But . . . But . . ."

Belissar smiled at her. "You've saved my life twice now. It's my turn to save yours."

The bee picked up a bit of speed. "But . . . worker came back?"

Belissar paused for a second then shook his head. That . . . was true, at least for the conduit bee, but it didn't change his mind.

". . . I'm not going to let it take anything else. Now, fall back. Please."

The bee buzzed a bit more before slowly flying back. The bees weren't happy about this. Large clouds of them buzzed behind him, hovering at the exact distance he'd told them to stay at.

Belissar sighed. He knew he was probably being foolish. The bees could most likely do this job, or at least part of it, and it was true that this was their normal role. Worker bees not only risked their lives—they *killed themselves* to protect the hive. They ripped their bodies apart just to deal a small sting to any would-be invaders. As long as the queens remained, they could replace the losses, and the conduit bee herself apparently could come back from the dead.

But the image of the bees dropping from the sky as a black cloud passed over them flashed before Belissar's eyes. It may have been foolish, but he didn't want to see them die like that again. So here he was, a mere peasant, preparing to face the Hunger.

Initial purification attempt in 5 minutes.

Belissar took a deep breath as he arrived at his position in front of the gate, trying to slow his beating heart. He talked up a big game, but now that he was here, waiting for that monster to approach . . . he couldn't help but have second thoughts. The mere idea of facing the shade again sent a shiver down his spine. Sweat already drenched his body, and he couldn't help but gulp.

But he calmed himself. He had already died once, or at least come very close to it. Everyone in his life who knew him was already gone, save for the bee flying behind him. His life had very little meaning. He was the weird guy nobody cared about, with nothing he wanted to achieve but to take care of his bees and improve his mead recipes.

The bees were different. They lived selflessly and with purpose. They would give their lives for each other—and now for him as well—without hesitation. They deserved to live and to carry on their work. They did not deserve to be slaughtered.

Belissar wanted to protect them. He *needed* to protect them. He needed to prove that he had *some* value, that his life had been worth them saving, even if just a little. To prove he could live a good life and take care of his bees.

So, he calmed his beating heart and his trembling hand as he fixed his eye on the gate.

Initial purification attempt in 1 minute.

CHAPTER TEN

SECOND INITIAL PURIFICATION ATTEMPT

Belissar furrowed his brow as the timer counted down.

Initial purification attempt in 5 . . . 4 . . . 3 . . . 2 . . . 1 . . .

Initial purification attempt commencing.

Once again, Belissar and the tower began to grow hot as every part of the tower began to shine; the sky, the trees, even the flowers glowed faintly.

And the gates to the Hunger swung open once more.

Belissar gulped as the black mass surged into the flower meadow. The nightmare every mother frightened their children with; the horror that no man or woman dared to face; the very wrath of the gods made manifest; the doom of the wicked kings of old. But once again, the edges of the gateway began to glow.

Belissar heard a screeching noise as the tendrils of the Hunger fell back into the writhing mass once more. It condensed down like before, then once again, a black paw with massive claws stepped out and dug into the dirt.

Sweat dripped down Belissar's neck as the shade's long snout emerged, growling as it stepped into the dungeon. Belissar tightened his grip on his torch and pulled out his knife with his other hand. The shade lifted its head into the sky and roared.

Initial purification attempt has begun.
Remaining hostiles: 1

Belissar lifted his torch with a shaky hand.

"C-Come and get me . . ."

He winced as his voice cracked. The shade brought its head down to stare at him, then burst out running toward him with a snarl.

Belissar turned and ran, his heart pounding. He was very much having second thoughts as to this plan. What was he—a peasant who had never experienced an actual battle in his life—doing trying to confront a shade of the Hunger?! Those jaws could snap him in half! The claws on its paws were as large as his hand! The barb on its tail would pierce right through him!

This was a monstrosity who trained soldiers would break and run from, who even the most hardened of the tower guard would tremble at the thought of, who had taken the very intervention of the gods for humanity to confront at all.

And Belissar thought he could face it down?!

He regretted every choice he had made as he ran. He felt a rumble in the ground as the shade's feet pounded behind him, hearing the snarling coming from behind. He thought he could feel the creature's breath on his back . . .

But then he realized that was his imagination, for the creature's snarls weren't coming from behind him at all. Glancing over, his eyes widened. The monster had leapt through the trees and was running along the hill to Belissar's right, trying to run around him and head him off.

"N-No!"

If the monster didn't follow him as he wanted, then his entire plan would fail. He had failed. He should have known a couple of trees and a gentle slope wouldn't bother a monster like that. He should have known no plan thought up by a peasant could match the might of a tower lord. He had no choice but to run now and abandon this foolish recklessness.

Until he heard the buzzing.

"King!"

The conduit bee glowed once again as she flew toward the monster, a swarm of bees following behind her. Belissar's eyes widened as the monster came to a halt, snapping and snarling as the bees buzzed around and stung its black, twisting fur. The creature took a deep breath, and images of dying bees raining from the sky filled Belissar's mind.

"Fall back!"

Heat from the tower filled Belissar's chest and imbued his shout. The bees immediately began flying away even as black mist surged out from the monster. But because of Belissar's shout, most of the bees escaped, only a small handful of stragglers being caught by the edge of the mist.

Belissar gritted his teeth and forced himself to breathe. No, this wasn't how he was going to let it end. Even if his plan was going to fail, he wasn't going to just break and run. The bees wouldn't let him; they would sacrifice themselves if he did, and he wouldn't let that happen. Not after all he had seen; not after all he had sworn.

He took a deep breath then waved the torch in the air. "Come and get me, monster!"

His voice held this time. The shade turned to him and snarled, then leapt at him with a roar. Belissar jumped back and turned to run, but since he had stopped to get the shade's attention, it would take him some time to build up speed, while the shade needed only a single leap to do the same. It would catch him before he made it . . .

Again, the conduit bee and the swarm swooped down from above. Belissar furrowed his brow. He had hoped he could keep the bees back . . . but at this point, it was clear he could not succeed alone.

"Don't go all at once! Keep it moving in my direction!"

The bees buzzed and began splitting up into smaller groups that swooped down one by one. The monster snapped at them, but they would fly off immediately to be replaced by the next group. And when the monster took a deep breath, they all flew back.

Eventually, the creature began to bark, taking a deep breath and waving its head around, sending out clouds of black mist billowing in a wave above. It didn't manage to catch the latest group accosting it, but the next one was forced back, unable to approach through the wall of mist ahead of them. The monster then turned its eyes to Belissar. With a roar, it pounced toward him.

Belissar . . . stopped running. He stood still as the creature rushed toward him, heart pounding in his chest. He felt his legs trying to lift off the ground and the sweat dripping down his face, stinging his eyes. He felt faint as his vision swirled.

But he forced himself to stand still, resisting the urge to shut his eyes even as he stared death in the face. He held the torch in front of him, the flame wavering as his arms trembled and the branch shook. The flame had burned down through enough of the branch that he could feel the heat on his hands.

The monster had nearly reached him. With jaws wide open, it lifted its paws and extended its claws—then promptly vanished with a yelp as the ground vanished beneath its feet. Belissar heard a crash, followed by a second yelp.

His heart leapt in his chest, and his legs turned to jelly, but he resisted the urge to fall to the ground. The hardest part was over, but this battle wasn't finished yet. Belissar cautiously crept to the edge of the hole while the bees began to buzz overhead. He peered over the side.

The monster was tangled at the bottom, twisting, about to get back on its feet. It was surrounded by yellow walls, as honeycomb lined the pit. The black fur covered in mist glistened slightly as honey, twigs, and dandelion stems stuck to it before turning black and wilting. More honey, stems, and twigs covered the bottom in a large mat.

The monster shook its head at it rose to its feet. Looking at Belissar, it snarled and stepped forward to the edge, trying to dig its claws into the wall.

Belissar narrowed his eyes and held out his hand.

"This is for my bees."

He dropped the torch.

The bottom of the pit burst into flames as kindling and honey caught fire. The flames spread to the monster's fur, and the creature roared and fell back, trying to roll across the ground . . . only to set more of the honey and stems alight, spreading the fire.

Belissar knew the one weapon a farmer had that every predator feared was fire. And as a beekeeper, he knew that beeswax made an excellent candle. Even honey itself was flammable if not mixed with anything.

The fire continued to grow as the twigs and honey caught and burned, the wax all around beginning to melt and vaporize, further fueling the flame. The monster roared and raced along the edges, but the fire had spread to the entire pit and even the air itself, on account of the vaporized wax.

The creature crouched down and tried to leap out of the pit, but Belissar had made it as deep as he could, and the creature failed to reach the edge. It tried to dig its claws into the walls, but they couldn't hold its weight, and it fell back once again. Trying to unleash the black mist once again had no effect on the flames, and there was nothing living for it to kill.

Eventually, its movement slowed down, and its roars grew soft. Soon, the creature fell to the ground and moved no more. Black mist began to rise from the flames and mix with the smoke as the monster's body disintegrated.

All hostiles defeated.
Initial purification successful.

Belissar fell back onto his bottom as the message passed before his sight. His eyes began to grow wide.

The monster . . . was dead? The plan had worked?

"We . . . won?"

Belissar blinked and then started to giggle. Soon, he began to laugh.

And all around him, the tower began to glow.

CHAPTER ELEVEN

BLESSED VICTOR-BEE

Belissar took a deep breath and exhaled slowly. It worked. It had actually worked!

He'd figured he could start a fire with flowers, twigs, and honeycomb, which had been even easier since he could directly ask the bees to line the walls and floors with wax. But none of that burned particularly quickly, and it would take a bit for the fire to get going, so he'd needed a way to keep the monster in the flames.

The pit trap had seemed to offer the solution, but Belissar had encountered a problem when he went to make it. It turned out he couldn't place it directly in front of the gate. In fact, he couldn't place the trees or the spawners there either. He didn't know why, but for one reason or another, the gate had to remain clear. It wasn't his place to question the gods, so he could only accept the limitation.

And that meant there had been the issue of how to actually get the monster onto the trap. Since he couldn't make enough trees to form a path, either the bees would have had to fight once again . . . or he would have to. And so, he'd resolved himself to face the shade personally, hoping against hope that he could lure it without getting mauled in the process.

But, against all odds, it had worked. He, a simple peasant beekeeper with no magic or might to his name, had slain a shade of the Hunger. He had fulfilled the role of a mighty tower lord.

And that wasn't all . . .

As Belissar laughed and rested on the ground, the tower's shine intensified. Belissar felt the heat within the tower grow red hot, then suddenly, a wave of light surged out from the core room and across the flower meadow. When it reached the pit trap, it burned away the last wisps of black mist before shrinking down as it approached the gateway, forming a tiny glowing ball before passing through the tower's entrance.

Belissar gasped, feeling as a wave of power surged out of the tower itself in every direction. When he glanced outside the gateway, the Hunger was gone. He could see green shoots breaking through the ground in the wake of the purifying light. Twisted, blackened trees began to right themselves and grow green leaves once again as bushes grew underneath.

The wave carried onward, slowing down over time. Eventually, it stopped. Belissar could still feel the Hunger at the edges, reaching its tendrils into the cleared area, but they burned away like they had in the tower's gateway. An area of about one mile in diameter around the tower was now completely free of the Hunger, and growing life once again.

Initial purification completed!
Dungeon B3353402X is now established. Core corruption may now be purified.

The following gods have noticed your victory and offer to become your patron:
- The God of Fire
- The God of Mischief
- The God of Bees
Please accept or deny the offering patrons before receiving additional rewards.

Belissar froze. He blinked. And then he began to tremble.

The gods . . . had noticed him? And instead of smiting him, they were offering . . . to become his patron?

"W-What should I do? W-What's going on? What—?"

At that moment, the conduit bee buzzed in front of his face. His eyes were drawn to her as she danced in the air.

"King? Need help?"

His beating heart began to calm, and he nodded to himself. Holding out his finger, his bee friend landed on it, staring up at him with her little eyes.

No, he knew exactly what to do. There was only one thing he *could* do.

The God of Bees is now your patron.
Applying Blessing of Bees.

He had never even heard of the God of Bees before, but he knew this was the right choice.

It was his bee friend who had saved his life and brought him here, who had gotten him to take control of this tower in the first place. It was the bees who had saved his life at the cost of their own when the first shade appeared and he was entirely unprepared, and their efforts that had prepared the pit that had slain the shade now. And it was their aid and sacrifice that had enabled him to lure the monster to the pit when he had nearly run in panic.

He would not be here if it weren't for them.

A surge of heat passed through him and the dungeon, and a statue rose by the gateway depicting a bee as large as a person standing on her hind legs, with smaller bees all around and on top of her. She held a small sphere, which began to glow with soft light. A pile of honeycombs surrounded her feet. Two banners rose to either side showing a group of bees on top of a yellow field. A large chest made of wax appeared at the foot of the statue.

A second such statue and chest appeared at the other end of the flower meadow, just outside the core room. His hand began to glow, and the image of the tower engraved on it now had a flower growing at its base and small bees flying all around.

All his bees began to buzz, and the dandelions began to sway. He could feel the heat making its way to his core room, so he turned his attention there. His eyes widened.

The room was no longer an empty white space with neither floors nor walls. Yellow honeycomb now crisscrossed along the edges of the space, and golden honey dripped from the walls. A wax pillar rose in the center with the same giant bee carved into it, lifting her hands up and around the floating core.

Outside, the tower also shifted. It maintained the same overall shape and color, but now, yellow banners unfurled along its sides, depicting the same bees upon a yellow field as the statue banners.

Blessing of Bees applied.
Effects:
- Bee-related options appear significantly more frequently.
- Bee-related option rarity increased.
- Special bee-related options are unlocked and may now appear.
- Bee monster upgrades and evolutions are now cheaper and easier to unlock.
- Bee-related option mana upkeep reduced.
- All bee monsters receive a medium boost to all stats.
- Non-bee options appear significantly less frequently.
- Non-bee option rarity decreased.
- Some non-bee options have been restricted and will no longer appear.
- Non-bee monster mana upkeep increased.

Belissar had but a moment to process it all before the messages continued.

Mission "Complete initial purification" completed!
Reward: Room limit increased to 2. Max mana increased to 200. Receive one room selection, one monster selection, and one room feature selection.

Mission "Earn the favor of a patron" completed!
Reward: One dungeon perk selection.

Belissar stood up and walked over to the statue. He stared at it for a moment.

"It's . . . a god. And you gave me . . . a blessing?"

He looked at the banners next to the statue, then down at his hand. The symbol engraved there appeared again, which now matched the image on the banners. His eyes widened before he fell to his knees, bowing his head.

"T-Thank you for choosing me."

One of the gods had chosen him. He who was unworthy, who was unprepared. He who had not descended from the lines of the tower lords. He who was but a mere peasant with no family or friends. He who had no value.

And now, he had been chosen as a tower lord, the blessed of the gods meant for great deeds and glorious purpose. He felt his eyes grow moist.

"I-I will do my best."

The sphere held by the statue began to glow softly, bathing Belissar in warm light. His bees gathered around him, buzzing and hovering in the air, then they split off and returned to the flowers, continuing their work. Belissar watched them for a moment before he nodded and returned to his feet.

That was right. If this was the God of Bees . . . then the best way to repay the trust imbued in him would be to work as diligently as a bee would. Probably. Maybe. Belissar still didn't actually know anything about the God of Bees or the inner workings of towers, but that didn't seem to bother the gods as far as he could tell, so he'd try not to let it bother him.

Whether he liked it or not, whether he was prepared or not, he was a tower lord now. It was his job to manage this tower, to purify the Hunger, and to protect the land. He could not sit back and keep his head down any longer. He would have to figure things out and find a way when challenges arose.

Turning to watch his bees as they spread across the field, gathering nectar for their hives once again, he furrowed his brow. He would have to lead and protect his bees. They were counting on him, more so than the bees at home ever had. They would follow his lead, and they would live—or die—by his decisions. They would pay for every mistake he made.

He truly was the king of the hive now, with all that such a title entailed.

Belissar gripped his hands into fists and nodded. He swore that they would not die in vain. That he would repay their trust. That he would protect them as best he could. And that he would make his life one worth saving.

CHAPTER TWELVE

DON'T BEE CONFUSED!

First things first, Belissar apparently had some decisions to make.

Please select a room:
- Forest (Rarity: Common. Type: Nature, Field.)
- Apiary (Rarity: Uncommon. Type: Bee, Resource, Settlement.)
- Dirt Tunnels (Rarity: Common. Type: Ground, Labyrinth.)

Part of him wanted to make a choice immediately, but he held himself back. He had made his first choices haphazardly, and while it had worked out, who knew what might have happened if he had known what he was doing? Maybe zombies or clockwork puppets could have killed that monster with ease. Maybe an enchanter's lab would have had features he could have used to defend himself without days of prep work.

Belissar had long lived a life of shutting up and getting to work, but now, his job was to think and make decisions. So, think he did.

Forests were good habitats for bees—their natural environment, even. And greater access to wood might increase his options if Belissar had to build another fire. He could also build other structures as well; maybe some walls or fences might help? Well, that was assuming he could get his hands on some actual tools.

An apiary was where he'd grown up, and obviously having a place for his bees to call home should help, especially now that he'd been blessed by the God of Bees and was going to be relying on bee monsters.

And then dirt tunnels . . . Yeah, Belissar didn't really know what to make of that. He did know there were wild bees who dug in the dirt. If he got monster bees who did something similar, maybe they'd like a place like that?

So, the question was which of these options would be the most helpful for his bees . . . and which would help him fight off the Hunger?

Belissar looked up and found the conduit bee hovering around him.

"What do you think? A forest, an apiary, or some dirt tunnels? What sounds good to you?"

The bee answered without hesitation. "What King chooses!"

Belissar resisted a sigh. He should have expected that.

So, saddled with the burden of leadership, Belissar thought . . . and thought . . . and thought until his head hurt. And he decided . . . that maybe he should check the other options first.

He definitely wasn't just putting it off because he had no idea what to pick yet.

Please select a monster:
- Monster Bee Soldier (Rarity: Common. Type: Bee.)
- Monster Carpenter Bee (Rarity: Common. Type: Bee, Nature.)
- Monster Digger Bee (Rarity: Common. Type: Bee, Ground.)

Belissar rubbed his chin as he looked over the options. Soldier bees . . . definitely were something that could fight, if the name was anything to go by. Carpenter bees sounded like something that would like a forest, while digger bees were exactly the ones he'd been thinking about for the tunnels.

But . . . what would the monster versions of those actually be? Would they be like the monster bee queens, practically normal bees save for their ability to understand his words and intentions? Or would they be something else entirely?

Belissar sighed. If only he had some way to check them beforehand . . .

As he thought that, the words shifted, and the image of a bee a bit larger than a fully stretched-out hand appeared.

Monster Bee Soldier

Vitality:	*Minimal*	**Defense:**	*Minor*
Strength:	*Minor*	**Resistance:**	*Minimal*
Speed:	*Average*	**Special:**	*Minor*
Magic:	*Minimal*		*Poison Sting*
		Notable Skills:	*Death Blow*
			Brood Offspring

Spawner Upkeep: *10 (5 with Blessing of Bees)*

A monster bee specialized for combat. Significantly larger than a regular bee, with a stinger large enough to deal physical damage and with more dangerous venom as well. Still weak alone but dangerous in numbers.

Note: Monster Bee Queens with developed hives may spawn Monster Bee Soldiers once unlocked.

Belissar blinked and then smacked his forehead with his palm. Once again, his ignorance of all things tower-related came back to haunt him. He apparently *could* gain more information on these choices if he bothered to ask.

Well, it was better to learn later than never, and fortunately, he hadn't made any choices yet. He went ahead and checked the next option, seeing a black bee just a bit larger than his current bee workers, with sharper mandibles.

Monster Carpenter Bee

Vitality:	Minimal+	**Defense:**	Minimal
Strength:	Minimal+	**Resistance:**	Minimal
Speed:	Average	**Special:**	Minimal
Magic:	Minimal	**Notable Skills:**	Poison Sting Wood Cut

Spawner Upkeep: 1

A carpenter bee that has accumulated enough Nature mana to become something more.
Sharp mandibles meant for boring into wood allow for painful, if small, bites.

Next came the diggers. They were, like the carpenter bees, a bit bigger than the workers, but still largely bee sized. They were brown and gray and very fuzzy, with short little wings and thicker mandibles.

Monster Digger Bee

Vitality:	Minimal+	**Defense:**	Minimal+
Strength:	Minimal	**Resistance:**	Minimal
Speed:	Below Average	**Special:**	Minimal
Magic:	Minimal	**Notable Skills:**	Poison Sting Dig

Spawner Upkeep: 1

A digger bee that has accumulated enough Ground mana to become something more.
Likes to burrow and tunnel. May ambush enemies from the ground.

That . . . actually helped quite a bit. It seemed monster bee soldiers were related to the monster bee queens and workers, while the carpenter and digger bees were different sorts altogether, each specialized to certain environments. Which meant Belissar could now choose between strengthening his current hives with combat-specialized members, or gaining new and more versatile bee types that were about the same as his current bee workers in terms of fighting.

Well, the monster bee soldiers had the obvious advantage of being something that could fight more directly. They were the first bee Belissar had seen that justified the name "monster bee." Yet, the choice wasn't so clear when Belissar thought about it.

The descriptions of their stats didn't seem that powerful, and they were still quite small compared to a human . . . or a shade of the Hunger. So, would they have been enough to take down a beast like that? Their stingers looked like they would definitely hurt, but would they be enough to kill?

On the other hand, carpenter bees could apparently cut through wood. If Belissar had those and they could listen to him like the other bees, he could gain a lot of options. They could cut through dandelion stems and twigs on their own so that Belissar wouldn't need to pick each one personally.

Depending on how good they were at cutting, maybe they could even cut through branches, or process wood further. If so, that would make it much easier for Belissar to build a fire next time. Or maybe even more. Maybe he could build fences and walls—or a wooden spear.

He . . . wasn't sure any of that would stop a shade like he had faced, but it was something to consider.

He wasn't so sure about digger bees. Sure, they could definitely dig—it was in the name, after all—but would they be able to dig something like a pit trap? It seemed like that would take quite a while for little bees to accomplish. But still, Belissar's plan wouldn't have been even remotely possible if it weren't for the pit trap, so there was proven merit to digging holes.

Not feeling ready to make a choice there yet, he went back to the room choices, trying to see if he could bring up more information on each.

Forest

Type:	*Nature, Field*
Innate Features:	*Wild plant growth boost*
Mana Upkeep:	*10*

An open area filled with trees that restrict visibility and provide cover.
Excellent for Nature-type monsters and features. Excellent for resource production.

Apiary

Type:	*Bee, Resource, Settlement*
Innate Features:	*Beehives*
Mana Upkeep:	*10 (5 with Blessing of Bees)*

A farm dedicated to beekeeping. Comes with beehive nodes that produce honeycomb.
If Bee-type monsters are available, they may settle in beehives for a slight boost in brood growth and beehive productivity.

Dirt Tunnels

Type: Ground, Labyrinth
Innate Features: None
Mana Upkeep: 5

A network of tunnels dug directly into the ground. Soft walls mean new tunnels may be dug by defenders and invaders alike, and that plants and fungi may take root with ease.

Excellent environment for Ground-type monsters and features.

The room descriptions didn't give as *much* detail as the monster ones, but it was something. Unfortunately, it didn't answer Belissar's current conundrums. Apiaries, like he thought, were specialized for bee monsters, but not in the way he'd thought. They appeared to be more focused on the production of honey than on the growth of the bees themselves. Which would be excellent if he were still a beekeeper, but didn't seem that useful against the Hunger.

Unless, again, he was missing something about being a tower lord? Why would the gods include such an option? Could he somehow sate a shade's hunger with honey?

He thought back to what he knew of the Towers of the Gods and their lords. The tower lords certainly were said to have great wealth, but every story he'd been told of the towers depicted them as defending against the Hunger and protecting the land. Were options like this just a reward for the tower lords themselves? Or would the production of honey play some role in the defense he couldn't see?

Belissar shook his head. He didn't know what he didn't know. And he still didn't know what to choose. It sounded like a forest might be more useful for defense, if only to have access to more firewood, but maybe the slight boost in brood growth of an apiary might be more useful? He still wasn't sure.

And, well, he still had some more choices to review.

Please select a room feature:
- Basic Resource Plants (Rarity: Common. Type: Nature, Resource.)
- Sticky Honey Trap (Rarity: Common. Type: Bee, Trap.)
- Rest Zone (Rarity: Common. Type: Recovery, Zone.)

Belissar blinked repeatedly, as this latest set of choices came with yet another set of questions. First of all, some kind of honey trap? Was that the answer as to why an apiary was a room choice? Could he use his own bees' honey in the honey trap?

And then, what was a rest zone?

Rest Zone

Type:	_Recovery, Zone_
Mana Upkeep:	_5_

A safe zone where challengers can rest. Remnants won't pass into the zones, and zones provide slight healing, as well as slightly boosted stamina and mana recovery.

Belissar held his head. Challengers? Remnants? What did any of that mean? Were they supposed to be something important? Were challengers his monsters . . . or the shades from the Hunger? That couldn't be right. Why in any of the gods' names would he ever want to let a shade rest and recover?!

It felt like the more information he learned, the more questions he had. He was no closer to making a decision than he was when he'd first started. If anything, he was more confused and far less certain in his ability to make the right call.

And he still had one more choice he hadn't even checked. Belissar groaned.

CHAPTER THIRTEEN

JUST BEE YOURSELF!

Belissar took a deep breath. He could do this. He had slain a monster of the Hunger! He had been chosen by a god, even! He was a tower lord now, one of the pinnacles of humanity who guided the course of civilization!

So, he definitely couldn't be afraid of looking at the next choice. Maybe it would even help him make all his other choices! At least, such was Belissar's hope and prayer.

Please select a perk:
- Bee Specialist (Rarity: Common.)
- Bee Breeder (Rarity: Uncommon.)
- Enhanced Toxins (Rarity: Common.)

Having no idea what any of that meant from first glance, Belissar looked over each option in turn.

Bee Specialist

Bee-type options offered more frequently.
Bee-type monsters gain slight boost to all stats if more common than all other types.

That seemed useful. He'd been blessed by the God of Bees, so he would be using more of them than anything else. Probably. As far as Belissar knew . . . which wasn't much.

Bee Breeder

Small increase to the rate Monster Bee Queens bear offspring.

Well, more bees wouldn't hurt.

Enhanced Toxins

Small damage and duration increase for all toxins.

So, that would make his bees' stings hurt more. He could choose between slightly stronger bees, some more bees, or bees that stung harder.

Belissar rubbed his chin. He then grunted, crossed his arms, and nodded.

"Yep. I have no idea what to do."

He held his head and groaned.

Belissar thought, and he thought, until the sun went down, but still, he had no idea what to pick. He just didn't know enough about towers to know what he was even supposed to aim for.

The conduit bee flew by once again after a hard day helping the other bees, no doubt. He lifted his finger, and she landed on it.

"King, need help?"

Belissar sighed. "I just . . . I don't know what I'm doing or what I should even do. I'm sorry. I just . . . I don't know how to be a good tower lord."

The bee danced around unsteadily. "Tower lord?"

Belissar shrugged. "Or a good king, if that makes more sense. Or queen for you? I don't know."

The bee began dancing excitedly. "King good king! Best king!"

Belissar chuckled at the sight, then shook his head. "I'm really not. I just . . . I wish there were another tower lord here. Someone who could teach me what to do . . ."

The bee kept dancing rapidly. "King not need other king! King knows! King makes best choice! King builds best hives!"

Belissar shook his head again. "You and the queens built the hives, not me."

The bee began to buzz loudly. "King built all hives! Built hives without core!"

Belissar blinked before tilting his head. "Are you talking about the old beehouses?"

"Yes, those! Warm, safe, good for hive! Old queen said were best!"

Belissar blinked, and then chuckled. He guessed a little bee might indeed be impressed by something like that. But making a wooden box and running a Tower of the Gods were two entirely different things. Still . . . it didn't feel bad to have someone who believed in him. He only hoped he could live up to that trust.

Rubbing his chin, he hummed. Well, he still didn't know much about being a tower lord, and he didn't know what the right choices here were; he was but a humble beekeeper. But that was apparently why his friend wanted him in charge . . . not to mention his patron *was* the God of Bees. Maybe he should just focus on what he knew?

After all, he'd figured out how to fight the Hunger when thinking as a farmer and a beekeeper. Maybe he should forget about being a good tower lord and just go with his gut?

Well, in any case, making *some* choice was better than none. Hopefully. Maybe. There wasn't another countdown for a purification at the moment, but Belissar couldn't be certain if or when another would appear. And the one thing he knew was that he'd certainly like to have more bees to fight it with than a field of dandelions.

Belissar sighed and stood up, then looked at the conduit bee again. He gave her a small smile.

"I think I'm ready to choose. Thanks for your help."

"Worker always help King!"

Belissar paused at that. It seemed there was something important he had forgotten in all this chaos.

"You know, I never got your name."

The bee paused, then danced slowly. "What name?"

Belissar frowned. He guessed that maybe bees didn't have names for themselves?

"No name, huh? In that case, why don't I give you one?"

The bee just stared at Belissar as he thought.

"How about . . . Niobee?"

"Okay!"

Conduit Unnamed Bee is now named Niobee.

Belissar smiled as he watched Niobee dance about before returning to his task. Taking a deep breath, he opened the windows, making his choices as they came to him.

Monster Bee Soldier Spawner now available.
Monster Bee Queens may now spawn Monster Bee Soldiers.

Belissar would love to keep his bees from harm, never letting them fight again . . . but that simply wasn't reasonable. He was no fighter and had no confidence he could continue to protect the bees with his own hands.

Equally as important, it was in the bees' own nature to protect their hives, and Belissar couldn't stop them from doing so forever; he had chosen them as the defenders of the tower, after all. The next best thing he could do was make sure they could fight effectively so that the next time he would not need to watch the hives be destroyed and the colonies fall from the sky en masse.

As such, he went with the monster bee soldiers. Dedicated warrior bees might be capable of taking on an enemy on their own . . . and at the very least should do better than the workers, who were practically normal bees. The soldiers would fight, and the workers would gather, as was their intended roles. And with that in mind . . .

Apiary is now available.

The monster bee soldier description stated that queens could spawn them once their hives were more developed, so Belissar hoped an apiary would help them reach that stage more quickly. And, if it didn't, he had an idea as to how to benefit from the honey it produced.

Sticky Honey Trap is now available.

Sticky Honey Trap

Type:	*Bee, Trap*
Mana Upkeep:	*5 (2 with Blessing of Bees. 1 if honey is provided)*

Spreads sticky honey onto a target or area, hindering target's mobility. Upkeep reduced if dungeon has a source of honey. Effects may vary with type of honey.

With this, he would have a way to weaponize the honey more directly. That would allow his worker bees to contribute to the defense by doing what they did best, while the apiary's honeycomb production would help as well. Perhaps if he could combine this trap with the pit one, he could repeat his firepit strategy without needing three days of setup.

The note about effects varying with the type of honey was also interesting. Could his bees make more than just regular honey? Would different types of bees make different types of honey, then?

The old beekeeper had told him stories as a child about fire bees who could make spicy honey, or ice bees who could survive in the winter and made honey as cool as snow. Up till now, he had thought they were just stories . . . but with a Tower of the Gods, who knew what was possible?

Belissar even smiled. He was starting to look forward to the next monster choice.

And finally, to round it all off:

Bee Breeder selected.

This had been the hardest of the choices. All of them were helpful to his bees, and he still didn't know enough to know which was more important, but at the end of the day, the strength of the bees came from their numbers. Bees worked together, living in colonies of thousands, acting as one single being. They could drive away animals thousands of times their size by swarming as a group. So, Belissar figured the more bees, the better.

Stronger bees from Bee Specialist might have been helpful . . . but he didn't know how much stronger it would actually make them. Even the monster bee soldier wasn't listed as "strong," after all, so how much would the perk actually boost them?

He didn't feel like something described as a *slight* boost would enable a bee the size of his hand to take on the Hunger's shades alone, at the very least. And as for getting more bee options . . . Well, the Blessing of Bees was already doing that.

Stronger venom was also useful, but again, Belissar didn't know exactly how useful. The monster from the Hunger had clearly felt pain from the worker bee stings, but it hadn't seemed to slow down much. And, thinking of normal bees, a single sting generally wasn't that dangerous, unless the person was allergic. But a hundred or a thousand bee stings was a different story. So, again, Belissar figured having more stingers would help as much or more than stronger venom.

And, ultimately, Belissar's goal now was to help his hives develop as fast as possible so they could get access to the soldier bees. Therefore, he'd figured Bee Breeder was his best bet.

With that, he took a deep breath and slowly exhaled it. He had made his choices. He didn't know if they were the right ones, but for better or for worse, he had made them.

Now, he just had to go and actually place some of his new options . . .

CHAPTER FOURTEEN

A HOME TO BEE

The first thing Belissar did was check his tower's mana.

Mana: 154/200

It was a lot more than he'd expected. Not only had he gained another hundred mana to work with, but the Blessing of Bees had also reduced the cost of his existing spawners. A quick check of their information revealed their upkeep had gone down from twenty to ten, a reduction by half. And given that he had spent most of the mana he'd previously had on those spawners, that freed up a massive amount for him now.

With plenty to spare, he proceeded to go place the apiary, walking back over to the core room to do so. Stepping inside the newly decorated room, he took a moment to look around. Kneeling down, he felt the wax on the floor and nodded. It was much less unnerving than the sort-of-but-also-kind-of-not floor that had been there before, or the endless white space everywhere he looked . . . as long as he ignored the black tendrils of the Hunger still lingering on some of the walls.

Walking over to the core, he got to work. Or tried to. He furrowed his brow and crossed his arms as he stared at the orb.

"Okay. So . . . how exactly do I add a new room?"

The first one had just sort of . . . added itself, after all. Fortunately, the core reacted to his intention, and the image inside it zoomed out, showing an angled top-down view of the flower meadow, as well as the core room.

Current rooms for Floor 1: 1/2. Add room?

Belissar blinked a few times.

"Um, yes?"

Available rooms:
- Flower Meadow (Type: Nature, Field.)
- Apiary (Type: Bee, Resource, Settlement.)

"Um, apiary, please."

A transparent room now appeared before his eyes. It featured a small farmhouse in a small field surrounded by flowers and a handful of trees, like a miniature version of the flower meadow. In a fenced yard in front of the house were a handful of tree trunks, each with a basket beehive on top. There were three rows of three beehives each.

Belissar found he could adjust various features of the room as with the flower meadow, but he couldn't change the number of beehives at the moment. He went ahead and moved them behind the farmhouse to give them as much protection as he could. Beyond that, he didn't have anything he wanted to change.

Once he thought that, the view zoomed out again. A transparent image of the room now appeared in between the flower meadow and the core room. Belissar found he could move the room around the meadow, putting the apiary in between it and the core room, between it and the gateway, or off to one side. He could also rotate the rooms and move the doors along their walls as he pleased.

Well, it was all very interesting, but Belissar still had no idea what he was doing or why. So, he ended up putting the apiary where it had first appeared, between the flower meadow and the core room. He figured that if his bees were going to set up there, he'd rather have their hives further away from the gateway.

He even considered putting them off to the side and trying to keep them out of harm's way entirely, but during the failed purification attempt, when the monster had attacked the door to the core room, bits of the Hunger had spread across all of the tower.

Even an untrained peasant like Belissar could tell that was a bad thing. So, he figured the core room should probably be as far away from the gateway as possible.

He did, however, move the door to the core room to the far-left side of the apiary, while putting the hives to the right. He still didn't want them in the direct path of the monsters if he could help it.

He heaved a sigh. "Okay, I think that's it . . ."

Once he signaled he was done, he felt the warmth inside the tower stir once more. The doorway to the flower meadow shifted, now showing the apiary.

Once the tower had calmed down, he stepped through.

For a moment, he simply stared at the sight before him. He was standing in another clearing surrounded by walls of trees, with two doors on either end. Another statue of the God of Bees stood next to the door leading to the core room, and the apiary itself filled the clearing ahead of him.

The little house he'd seen in the core's vision was now a full-size dwelling standing before him, a house about the same size as his own had been. He could see the basket hives in the yard to the right. He frowned at that sight. They were the traditional beehouses which generally had to be destroyed entirely to gather the honey.

He did not like that method, and he and the old beekeeper had worked hard developing their own beehouses to avoid such violent waste. He would have to build some once he had the chance. However, these would suffice for now; he wasn't as concerned about gathering the honey when the bees themselves could move it for him.

Besides, it wasn't like he had to pay tribute to the tower lord this year, seeing as his village had been burned to the ground and all, and that the tower lord's son had been the one to do it, nearly killing him in the process.

Belissar also remembered that, technically, he *was* the local tower lord now. Well, for whatever locale this tower was in, that was. He didn't imagine there were many villages in an area that had been covered by the Hunger until very recently.

Shaking his head, he walked into the house. It was furnished with some basic furniture, though it was largely empty otherwise. Belissar nodded as he noted a storage area with a lot of jars for honey. He then found a bedroom with a very simple mattress and sheet.

On a whim, he lay down. It . . . wasn't as comfortable as his bed back home had been, but it was worlds better than trying to lay down in the original core room.

Belissar yawned as he had that thought. He closed his eyes but for a moment . . .

Belissar slowly opened his eyes as the sun filtering through the window fell on his face. He rose and stretched his arms, then stood up and walked over to the window.

He blinked.

Those . . . were not his beehouses, but rather a bunch of basket hives. Belissar had a brief moment of panic before his mind fully woke up and he remembered the events of the past few days.

"Right. I don't live in the village anymore. And . . . I'm a tower lord now, or something. And this is the tower."

He inhaled sharply as his mind processed the words coming out of his very own mouth, then shook his head and walked out of the room.

He had not intended to sleep, as it had seemed that his body remained in good condition regardless. However, it appeared that his mind was not entirely free from exhaustion, and, well, he had *certainly* had a lot to think about recently.

Furrowing his brow, he checked the dungeon status again, but fortunately, he couldn't find any purification attempt timers. It seemed his little unplanned nap wouldn't hurt him for now.

Sighing at his own inability to focus, he tried to recall what he'd been doing when he fell asleep. He nodded as it came to him. "Right, traps."

His vision floated out of his body to view the room as a whole. He found he could also move his sight to the flower meadow if he wanted. He went ahead and placed a couple more pit traps, as well as some of the new sticky honey ones—little holes that would spray a bunch of honey when something passed in front of them. He found he could, in fact, place them inside the pit traps, and did so.

He also found that while he couldn't put pit traps—or any traps—right in front of either the gateway or the core room, he could put them in front of the door between the flower meadow and the apiary, so he did that with a sigh of relief. If he had to face another monster, it now couldn't reach the apiary without stepping on a trap, so he wouldn't have to lure it with either his bees or his body. All he needed to do was make sure there was a fire set up by the apiary entrance, and he would be good to go.

With the traps in place, it was time to address the spawners. He considered his current mana.

Mana: 111/200

The apiary itself had cost him five mana, while the pit traps and sticky honey traps had cost one mana a piece. He had made . . . nineteen of them, if he recalled correctly, which came out to . . .

Belissar soon ran out of fingers. With nothing to write on, he stepped outside of the farmhouse and found some dirt to scratch marks into.

. . . Thirty-eight mana. He didn't really know if that was a lot or not.

With the mana he had left, he could make a lot more spawners. But how many should he make? And also . . . should he make more of the queen ones, or should he add in some of the soldiers? The queens could supposedly spawn soldiers on their own, but maybe it might be better to get some directly and right away?

Belissar had no idea.

A swirl of the tower's heat caught his attention, and he nodded. With the sun now rising in the sky, it was about time for the queen spawners to activate. He guessed he could decide after getting the newcomers acclimated.

He definitely wasn't just pushing off the decision.

CHAPTER FIFTEEN

BEE THE MAGIC?

O ne, two, three . . ."

Belissar counted once. He counted twice. He counted thrice. He counted with his fingers. He counted with his toes. He counted with the dirt. He counted with some stones. He frowned.

No matter how many times or by what method he counted, he came up with the same answer: There were three monster bee queens hovering before him in the flower meadow, despite there being four monster bee queen spawners. Belissar would admit he wasn't the greatest at math, but he figured those numbers should add up, like they had every other day before this.

With no other way to resolve this conundrum, he focused on one of the spawners, the one which hadn't seemed to work today.

Monster Bee Queen Spawner

Monsters:	*Monster Bee Queen*
Cooldown:	*0/24 hours*
Current Monsters Spawned:	*4/4*

Belissar blinked. "Oh."

It seemed this was, again, something he could've learned ahead of time if he had known to check. Apparently, the spawners could only create so many monsters, and this particular one had reached its maximum.

Belissar furrowed his brow as he rubbed his chin. That certainly changed things. He would need to think carefully now about which spawners to make, if the ultimate number of monsters was fixed.

Belissar thought carefully for a couple more minutes before sighing and shrugging. In the end . . . he didn't really know what exactly that change meant for him any more than he knew anything else about running a tower. So, again, he was left with little choice but to go with his gut feeling.

Mana: 71/200

He went ahead and doubled the number of monster bee queen spawners, placing four in the apiary to match the four in the flower meadow. He figured that the queens could eventually spawn monster bee soldiers on their own, so it was probably better to focus on those. Maybe.

At the very least, he wouldn't use up all of his mana right away. If another purification countdown started and his hives didn't have any soldiers yet, he'd still have the option of spawning some directly. He also wanted to save some of his mana in general, in case more options appeared. He didn't know if these choices were permanent, after all.

Remove Monster Bee Queen Spawner?
Note that mana will remain reserved while spawned monsters remain.
Amount reserved is proportional to the ratio of currently spawned monsters to
spawner's maximum.

Belissar paused again. Well, that answered that. Apparently, monster spawners weren't permanent, after all. Belissar let out another sigh. It was good that he was learning more . . . but every bit he learned just made him more aware of how much he *didn't* know.

At the very least, this bit of information didn't change his decisions. It boosted his confidence knowing he could adjust the spawners if he needed to, though. With that in mind, he walked back to the apiary and up to the beehives, frowning again as he saw their basket shapes.

He focused on one as he got closer.

Apiary Beehive

Occupant:	*None*
Current Product:	*Honeycomb*
Base Production Rate:	*1 honeycomb every 24 hours*

The beehive had a large hole on the bottom, and a large hexagonal honeycomb had gotten pushed out to rest on the tree trunk.

Blinking, Belissar picked it up. He observed it from every angle, and even sniffed it. As far as he could tell, it was pure honeycomb, free from any eggs or larva. Belissar tilted his head, then glanced inside the beehive hole. He heard buzzing, yet he couldn't actually see any bees inside.

"Okay, this is kind of weird. So these beehives just . . . make honeycomb? Without any bees?"

Belissar shook his head. It just didn't seem right. But then again, he was standing in the daylight despite being indoors. He supposed a Tower of the Gods didn't have to play by any rules save its own.

He glanced over as a wave of monster bee queens from the new apiary spawners flew over to him. They hovered around the beehives, observing them. Belissar shrugged.

"What do you think? I'm sorry they aren't the nicest but . . . do you want to use them?"

The nearest monster bee queen paused for a second at his question before dancing a salute and flying into the hive. Belissar watched as the beehive's information changed.

Apiary Beehive

Occupant:	*Monster Bee Queen*
Current Product:	*Mana Honeycomb*
Base Production Rate:	*1 honeycomb every 24 hours*

Slight boost to monster bee growth rate.

Belissar tilted his head. He was a little disappointed the base production rate hadn't improved, but he supposed the queen didn't have any workers yet, so maybe that would change. The slight boost to the bees' growth rate was something he knew from the apiary's description, so not a surprise.

What was a surprise was the current product.

"Mana honeycomb?"

Mana. Magical power. The fuel that granted the tower guard powers beyond mortal men. Belissar had heard stories of it, but had never encountered it before. No one in his village had. After all, it was a power reserved only for the tower guard, granted to them by their lords for the defense of humanity.

It was also stated to be highly dangerous in the wrong hands. It was said a peasant who tried to dabble in such a power could blow apart their entire village or set themselves on fire, turn themselves into a frog, or other such horrors. And those who mastered it without the blessing of the tower lords . . . Well, those were the wicked witches and warlocks who preyed upon the innocent. Or they were cursed by the gods and twisted into demihumans: a tormented existence that was half man and half beast.

Either way, no good ever came of dabbling in such things. That was why any occurrence of mana was to be reported to the local tower lord immediately.

So, of course, Belissar had never heard of bees using it, much less somehow putting it into honey? What would that even look like? Some kind of magical honey? Would it make him explode? Would it turn him into a bee?

Suddenly, Belissar's eyes widened as he had a thought.

If the monster bee queen entering the beehive made it produce mana honeycomb . . . then, didn't that mean it was the monster bees who made mana honey? Didn't their description say something about them gathering mana?

Monster Bee Queen

A honeybee queen that has accumulated enough mana to become something more.

Mostly similar to her mundane cousins, but more aggressive and with a slightly magical venom.

This one is a queen, and capable of building a hive of monster bees.

Oh. It did. Belissar frowned, his eyes trembling. Didn't that mean . . . the honey the monster bee queens had offered him was mana honey?!

He quickly felt his stomach, searching for anything wrong. But everything was as it should be, and as far as he could tell, he hadn't turned into anything . . . *unnatural*—ignoring for a moment the part about him being a tower lord who didn't seem to need to eat or drink or even sleep unless he felt like it.

He thought about the moment when he had eaten the honey and furrowed his brow. He couldn't think of anything strange, besides that sense of warmth filling him which was a lot like the warmth he felt from the tower itself . . .

He paused, his eyes going even wider. Wait . . . was that heat he felt . . . mana?!

That would actually make a lot of sense, now that Belissar thought about it. If the tower guards received mana from the tower lords, then it just made sense that the tower itself would have mana in it, right?

And it would also make sense for the tower lord to have mana, too.

Belissar looked at his hands as he felt the warmth that had suffused his body since the tower had been bound to him.

"I . . . have mana now?"

His first instinct was to report it to the local tower guard before remembering that he was, in fact, a tower lord now. So instead, he focused on the mana, narrowing his eyes and furrowing his brow as he concentrated. A few minutes later, he shrugged.

Well, that was all incredible to think about—but he still didn't actually know *how* to use mana, or whatever. Not to mention the potential dangers of doing so haphazardly, even if he did figure it out. Maybe the mana honey would make a shade explode if they ate it or something, but beyond that, this revelation didn't seem to change much; mostly because Belissar didn't know how it could actually change things.

He sighed. "Is there, like, a guide for tower lords or something?"

He listened just in case, but no one responded to his words, and no strange words appeared before his eyes. He sighed again. The one time he wished there was something there . . .

But it seemed he was still on his own as he dabbled in these powers he didn't comprehend. He could only hope it wouldn't explode in his face—possibly literally.

Shocking revelations about his powers and bees aside, Belissar did still have some work to do, so he walked back to the flower meadow and to the hives on the trees by the door.

The monster bee queens came out and flew before him, dancing in a salute pattern. Belissar nodded.

"So, we only have about nine beehives in the apiary. You girls were first, so do you want to move there? You could also just move your hives to the trees there if you don't like the houses."

The monster bee queens remained still for a moment before starting a slow refusal pattern.

Belissar frowned.

"Are you sure? I know your hives are set up already, but . . . don't you want to move further back? It could be dangerous to keep your hives here."

The queens picked up speed, and Belissar frowned again. They seemed quite resolute in their decision to remain here, indicating that they wished to defend the gateway.

Belissar didn't want them to . . . but it wouldn't actually help to have more rooms if he moved all of the bees to the end of the tower. At the end of the day, they were supposed to be the tower's defenders.

Belissar would just have to do his best to ensure they survived the effort . . .

CHAPTER SIXTEEN

A MISSION BEE-QUEATHED

Belissar sat back against one of the trees in the flower meadow, taking a deep breath as a breeze spread the scent of flowers through the air. He watched as bees moved from blossom to blossom, carrying nectar back to their hives. He watched as they flew in and out of the pit traps, coating the floors and walls in wax in case Belissar needed to light them on fire again.

"Well . . . now what?"

He had spent as much of his mana as he was willing to for now. He couldn't make any more rooms at present, and had a bunch of traps already. He had eight monster bee queen spawners, and the queens were hard at work setting up their colonies. The apiary had made some honeycomb, but Belissar didn't really know what else to do with it.

Well, as a beekeeper, he knew plenty of things he could do with them. The honey had a lot of culinary and even medicinal uses, while beeswax could be used to make sealants, salves, candles, and other products. He'd even heard some of the tower lords' wives could use it for beauty products.

But most of those weren't useful for defense, save for the candles. Maybe he could use the honey as bait for a trap if the shades found it appetizing, but the Hunger itself would consume everything, trap included, so he wasn't sure if its shades cared about food specifically.

Without anything better to do, he went ahead and checked the dungeon status. Maybe there was something else there he had missed.

Dungeon Status

Patron:	*God of Bees*
Floors:	*1 (Rooms: 2/2)*
Available Mana:	*71/200*

DP:	*1*
Available Monster Types:	*Monster Bee Queen*
	Monster Bee Soldier
Available Room Types:	*Flower Meadow*
	Apiary
Core Corruption:	*36%*
Dungeon Master:	*Belissar*
Dungeon Conduit:	*Niobee*
Current Missions:	*None*

Belissar blinked. There were, in fact, some changes from the last time he had checked. The core corruption had gone down by one percent, which was a relief, as core corruption didn't sound like anything good. But more importantly, there was a new value that hadn't been there before.

"*DP*? What's that?"

Dungeon Points

Used for various upgrades or to acquire more choices. Awarded for ongoing purification, remnant defeat, challenger activity, or at the discretion of the dungeon's patron god.

Belissar tilted his head. He, again, had more questions. Upgrades? Choices? And then remnants and challengers were being mentioned once again. Not to mention . . . the patron god.

Belissar frowned. He hadn't really thought about it with everything going on, but the God of Bees had chosen him and had become this tower's patron. He wondered if he should do something for her . . . or him? He didn't know anything about the God of Bees, but *her* seemed more likely, given what he knew of the little insects. Should he be worshiping somehow? Offering sacrifices? Praying?

His little village had had their rituals and whatnot, but they'd been too small for a priest or anything. The worship of the gods was centralized around the towers, so a village on the far frontier like his own was the last thing on the minds of the faithful.

Besides, it was not the place of the unwashed masses to come before the gods. That was the role of the chosen tower lords and the devoted priests: to act as the bridge between the gods above and the common folk below. So, the only thing Belissar's village had ever been told about the gods was that the tower lords required extra tribute from them so they could make the appropriate offerings.

Mrs. Imkomos had gathered what sacred texts she could find and taught him to honor the gods as best she could, but her collection had been far from complete.

Unfortunately, Belissar was now one of those tower lords, and he had no idea what to do. He wished he did. Beyond just the general avoidance of smiting, the God of Bees had chosen him. She believed in him enough to forgive his defilement of the tower, and had granted him her blessing. Belissar thought he should thank her somehow, at the very least.

Just then, he heard a sound directly in his head. A chime, like the sound of a bell.

New mission received: Pray at a Shrine of Bees.

Belissar blinked at the words in front of his eyes . . . and began to tremble. That . . . That mission had to be from the God of Bees, right? Had she heard him? Was she listening to his thoughts? Was she listening to him *right now*?!

That would make sense for a god, if he thought about it. A direct response was unheard of—for a peasant, but since he was a tower lord now, that might not apply anymore. In any case, she had given him a task, apparently; one that seemed to answer his question.

So, he stood up and made his way to one of the statues that had appeared when he'd received the Blessing of Bees. He figured that had to be what "shrine of bees" referred to.

Pausing, he made his way to the apiary instead, where he gathered up a bunch of the honeycomb produced by the beehives. He didn't really know how to pray to a god or anything, but he figured he at least shouldn't show up empty-handed, since tower lords often mentioned offering tribute and all. He didn't know if the honeycomb produced by the apiary would be to her liking, but it was the best thing he had at present.

Walking now to the shrine of bees in the apiary, he placed the honeycomb in the chest before the statue, then knelt down and bowed his head.

"Um, I'm sorry. I don't really know how this is supposed to go, but, um, God of Bees, if you can hear me? Uh, thank you for your blessing, and for not smiting me for defiling one of your towers. I'm, uh, not really sure what I'm doing here, but I'll try my best?"

Belissar winced with each word he spoke. Even he could tell that was no prayer anyone would approve of. But the sphere held by the statue started to glow softly, bathing Belissar in warm light. The chest then began to shine brightly for a moment, flashed once, and then fell dark. Belissar slowly reached for it, opening the lid.

He blinked. The honeycomb had all disappeared, and lying in its place was . . . an axe and a saw?

Mission "Pray at a Shrine of Bees" completed!
Reward: One woodcutting axe and one woodcutting saw.

New mission received: Build a beehouse.

Belissar lifted the axe out of the chest with both hands. He looked at the words before his eyes, then down at the axe, then up at the shrine of bees. He glanced back and forth several more times.

"You want me . . . to build a beehouse? You mean, like the ones I used to?"

The shrine glowed a bit brighter. Belissar blinked a few more times.

That was not the mission he'd expected to receive. His first purification had failed because he had spent his time trying to make beehouses instead of doing tower lord things. Shouldn't he continue doing tower lord things now? Worshiping the gods, purifying the lands, defeating the Hunger, mustering the troops?

But the shrine continued glowing, the axe remained in his hand, and the mission stayed unchanged in the dungeon status. Belissar looked up at the statue above him and nodded.

"Um, okay. I'll, uh, do my best?"

The shrine grew bright once more in a flash of light before falling dim. Belissar took a deep breath and then rose to his feet, picking up the tools.

Well, at least this was something he knew how to do, if not why he was doing it. Besides, if this was what the God of Bees said she wanted, who was he to question her?

With that, he grabbed his tools and got to work, finding a tree none of the bees were using and beginning to chop away at it.

While Belissar began working to acquire some wood, the bees spread across the flower meadow. With over a dozen colonies at this point, the field was getting rather crowded, and so the workers spread out further and further.

Eventually, they began to reach the edges of the field in all directions, coming upon the doors to either side. Those who reached the apiary door went no further, for such was the territory of the next generation, and so not a good direction to expand their efforts.

But the ones who reached the gateway leading outside the tower had no such qualms. A group of scouts gathered in the air before the gates, which began to open on their own, leading to the outside world. The scouts flew outside . . . and found a world of plenty.

Green grass now covered the ground, shoots of various plants continued to grow, and even some flowers had started to bloom—flowers of colors and shapes the bees had never seen before, far different from the dandelion field that was all they had ever known.

The workers began to fly around excitedly and land on each of the blooms in turn, sampling the nectar and its suitability for honey making. Some flew back to report their findings, while others spread out even farther, exploring the land the tower had reclaimed from the Hunger . . .

CHAPTER SEVENTEEN

A BEE-NEFICIAL FIND

Belissar grunted as he hauled branches and logs back toward the farmhouse. Fortunately, this was something he had done before. Everyone in his village was capable of some basic logging and woodwork, as no one had such abundance that they could hire a specialist at any given time.

This went doubly so for Belissar and the old beekeeper, neither of whom had extensive family assets or extensive families who could come and help.

Unfortunately, Belissar found that whatever tower magic kept him free of need for food and drink did not extend to muscle fatigue from extensive exertion. He could very much feel the burn all across his body as he plopped another large piece of wood onto the pile he had gathered. The pile that still needed to be dried and processed into usable shapes before he could even begin to work on one of his old beehouses.

This may have been a task he was used to . . . but that didn't mean it was easy.

The gates of the tower opened up into the world beyond once again, and a swarm of bees flew out in a buzzing cloud. The scouts had reported back on their findings, and the queens were now sending out a full wave of harvesters to gather from the flowers outside.

The scouts themselves continued onward, searching for even more locations to gather from as the harvesters availed themselves of the first finds. The scouts flew beyond the immediate area around the tower into a more heavily forested area. The flowers were more difficult to find here with the trees and brush barring the way, but still, they found much to report. Some of the trees and bushes had flowers of their own as well.

But a few of the scouts did not settle for these finds, pushing far into the forest instead. They had detected something, their antennas twitching as they caught faint wisps of a scent on the wind, as small lights seemed to flicker just beyond the sight of their eyes and something resonated with the mana flowing within them. It was almost as if something was calling to them.

Eventually, a handful of the scouts came across something. Something beyond the simple plants and trees that had regrown in the light of the tower. Something far older; something that had existed in ages past, before the Hunger had ever swallowed this place.

Ancient stone ruins rose above the brush, covered in moss and vines. Stone arches and pillars had crumbled, the walls and roofs they'd supported long gone. Ancient markings faded on the stone, wind and rain leveling out the grooves carved into the surfaces. Small flickers of light were all that remained of ancient enchantments, the barest hints of mana that had once powered wonders.

And yet . . . something lingered in this place. The air held still. The leaves fell around the structure. The rot and decay seemed to hesitate. It was as if this place were pushing against time, as if something remained that wanted to preserve what memories still endured.

And the bees ignored it entirely and flew instead to the flowers growing on the outskirts of the ruins. They began to buzz and dance about as they sampled the nectar then flew back toward the tower at maximum speed.

Belissar ended up taking a rest in the farmhouse once again after laying out some sawed planks to dry. He chewed some honeycomb from the apiary beehouses before turning in for the night, sleeping better than he had ever since his village had burned down.

He stretched his arms as he awoke, smiling as he moved about and found no pain in any part of his body. The magic of the tower may not have prevented exhaustion, but it sure did an excellent job of repairing it.

Stretching one more time, he then prepared to resume his work for the day when Niobee came buzzing through the door, flying about at maximum speed. "King, come quick!"

Belissar's eyes widened. "Niobee? What's the matter? Did something happen?!"

Niobee just kept telling him to come and then zoomed out the door. Belissar grabbed the axe and hurried after her, running through the apiary and into the flower meadow. Niobee led him onward until they arrived at the gate of the tower itself. Belissar's eyes widened when he saw the gate was open, and yet, he didn't see any of the Hunger trying to force its way inside.

"Come quick!"

Belissar gasped as Niobee zoomed out the gate, then noticed dozens of other bees flying in and out as well. His eyes widened further for a second, but he gulped and followed after them.

He blinked at the sun shining down on his face. The *real* sun. Before him was a small clearing in the middle of a forest; it was covered in grass, with flowers adding occasional specks of color. Bees flew everywhere in the field, landing on each of the flowers in turn. Belissar stood still for a moment, taking in the scene.

"What is this?"

He rubbed his eyes and looked again. Previously, he had seen nothing but the Hunger behind the gate. He knew the tower had pushed it back, but . . . the scene before him was more than that. He had expected barren rock, maybe some dirt and lichen at most.

Instead, the land was filled with life and color, with his bees happily buzzing and gathering the bounty of nature. It was like the Hunger had never been there.

Belissar slowly turned around. Walking to the edge of the gateway, he placed a hand on the walls of the tower. *His* tower.

"Tower of the Gods indeed . . ."

For what else could this be but a miracle? The Tower of the Gods had not only pushed back the Hunger, but it had also reclaimed the world from it. It had restored what had been lost and healed what had been twisted. And it had been his work—his victory over the shade—which had made this possible.

So long did Belissar stand staring at the scene that Niobee flew back and buzzed in front of his face. "King, come quick!"

Belissar shook himself out of his daze and followed after Niobee once more. He narrowed his eyes as he followed. "Can you tell me what's going on now?"

"Scouts find something! Something important!"

Belissar nodded and followed after her—before promptly tripping over a lifted root and falling into a bush. "Ouch . . ."

"King! King okay?!"

Belissar slowed down a bit, carefully making his way through the forest after that. He had to hack his way through some particularly thick bushes when he couldn't find a path forward, but eventually, he rounded a final tree and found what the bees wanted him to see.

His eyes widened as he saw the ruins, the ancient stones still standing tall even as the majority had already crumbled. There was a faint buzzing and heat from the mana remaining in long gone enchantments; he could still make out the nearly faded markings—messages of an ancient script he couldn't decipher. He saw a once towering statue now but a crumbling torso, as its head and arms had long since broken apart.

He stepped forward. "What is this place?"

And then Niobee buzzed before him. "King! This way!"

Belissar blinked and turned his head as Niobee flew . . . off to the side. He glanced at her, then back at the ruins, shaking his head back and forth between them.

"Are you sure? Not these?"

"This way!"

She seemed very insistent, so Belissar shrugged and turned to follow her.

"Here! Look!"

Belissar followed until he arrived at a small bunch of flowers; several of his bees were hovering around them. At first, he tilted his head. They were pretty pale-blue flowers, but they seemed little different from any of the others in the field around him. He was about to question the bees about it when he saw it.

A faint shimmer of light passed through the petals. Belissar nearly thought it was simply the sunlight passing through the canopy above . . . except he felt a slight warmth and heard a very faint hum at the same time.

Crouching down, he reached for one of the flowers, gently holding one of its petals in his fingers. His eyes widened. The warmth he'd felt was emanating from the flowers; a warmth he now recognized. And he knew immediately why the bees were drawn to it.

These flowers contained mana. He already knew that a bee colony's honey could vary slightly based on what flowers they gathered nectar from. Likewise, his bees were monster bees who produced a kind of mana-infused honey. So, what would happen if they gathered nectar from a flower already filled with mana?

. . . Well, Belissar had no idea. But his intuition told him it was something he wanted to find out. Plus, the bees seemed very excited about this.

"Good flowers! Queens think we should bring home but workers can't lift. King can?"

Belissar nodded. In fact, they were so excited that they had come to find him and ask for his help.

"Good idea."

He crouched down and began to dig into the dirt with his hands, careful not to tear up any of the roots he encountered. Soon, he lifted a handful of dirt held together by the roots of the flower, carrying the whole plant with it. He gave one last glance at the ruins before he set off back toward his tower.

Whatever was there could wait; his bees had made a request of him, and he would deliver. Besides, he was a bit excited to see what the result would be.

CHAPTER EIGHTEEN

CURIOSI-BEE

Belissar brought the flower back to the tower. He was planning to carry it to the far corner of the flower meadow, but a message popped before his eyes the moment he stepped inside.

Absorb Mana Flower?
Current samples: 0/5

Belissar stared at the message for a bit. He had a feeling this was yet another important tower lord thing he didn't know about. He had no idea what would happen if he absorbed the flower . . . but he felt the tower wouldn't have prompted him if it wasn't something important.

He thought for a minute, then put the flower to the side. Stepping outside the gate again, he crouched down and picked some of the other flowers in the area until he had five of the same one. Once he brought them back inside, the message appeared before him again.

Absorb Lily?
Current samples: 0/3

It turned out the sample number wasn't consistent. Belissar shrugged and confirmed. Three of the lilies in his hands were covered in glowing light before vanishing.

Lily absorbed. Sufficient samples gathered.
Lily now available.
Current applications: Flower Meadow, Apiary.

Crouching down, Belissar focused on the dandelions in the flower meadow once more. He had a hunch as to what had just occurred . . .

Manage flower types?
Available types:
*- **Dandelion** (Mana Upkeep: 0) (Selected)*
- Lily (Mana Upkeep: 0)

He smiled slightly. It seemed his hunch was correct. He went ahead and selected lilies.

Flower types:
*- **Dandelion** (Mana Upkeep: 0) (Selected)*
*- **Lily** (Mana Upkeep: 0) (Selected)*

Belissar watched as new shoots began to pop out of his flower field. White lilies grew among the dandelions, adding a new shade of color that spread across the meadow. The bees gathering nectar all paused, then many of their numbers began to fly to the new flowers.

Belissar nodded in satisfaction. It was nice to have correctly guessed what the tower was trying to do. Focusing on the apiary next, he saw there weren't as many flowers there, but there was a small field he was able to manage, along with flowers growing around the beehouses, so he went ahead and added lilies there too.

"I think I'm getting the hang of this."

"King is best king!"

He couldn't help but chuckle as Niobee danced before him.

Stepping outside the tower once more, he walked back toward the forest. Now that he had confirmed what was going on, he *definitely* wanted these mana flowers.

A short while later, Belissar returned, several more plants in his arms.

Mana Flower absorbed. Sufficient samples gathered.
Mana Flower now available.
Current applications: Flower Meadow, Apiary.

He again focused on the flower field.

Manage flower types?
Available types:

*- **Dandelion** (Mana Upkeep: 0) (Selected)*
*- **Lily** (Mana Upkeep: 0) (Selected)*
- Mana Flower (Mana Upkeep: 3)

He paused and frowned. The mana flowers were apparently a bit different from the normal ones and were going to cost him. Three was a lot when the entire flower meadow had only cost him five.

He crossed his arms and hummed.

He . . . honestly didn't have enough information to make a decision. Mana-filled plants were legends and stories to a former peasant like him, so he had no idea what this flower was or how valuable it would be. But . . .

He glanced at his bees. They were extremely excited about this flower; enough to report it to him immediately. And to Belissar . . . that was reason enough. He didn't want to be wasteful, but the bees were the ones who were going to work and fight and die for this tower. They deserved whatever consideration he could give them.

And if it turned out mana flowers had other uses, then all the better.

He went ahead and selected it for the flower meadow.

This time, the changes were more subtle. The field itself didn't change in color, and Belissar frowned at first, but the words confirmed he had selected the flowers. But then, he felt it. A light current of what he now knew was mana flowing through the field unlike before.

He followed the current until he eventually found a spot of blue in a field of yellow, green, and white. A subtle thing, easy to miss. A lone mana flower growing amid the dandelions and lilies.

Walking around the field, he found a few more. He did wonder if such a small and sparse number of flowers was worth the mana upkeep, but all the bees nearby had stopped what they were doing and were congregating around the flowers wherever they grew. One of the queens herself had flown over and frozen midair at the sight. She turned to him and simply hovered in the air, watching him.

Belissar motioned to the flower. "Go ahead. I made them for you girls, after all."

The queen dipped in her flight and began a dance of gratitude . . . and respect? Or, perhaps, something more? Then the worker bees swarmed the flower, quickly forming a long line to gather as much nectar from it as possible.

Belissar nodded, and his face relaxed. If his bees liked them that much, then he considered it a worthwhile expense.

With that, he moved on to his next task.

Belissar made his way through the forest once again, coming before the ruins. He couldn't help himself; he was curious about them.

"King, what doing?"

Niobee buzzed around him, along with several of the other bees who had followed him when he left the tower. Belissar shook his head.

"I'm . . . not sure. But I wanted to check this place out. It looks like people lived here; other humans like me."

"Okay! We help!"

Belissar smiled as the bees spread out and began to fly around the ruins. Even when neither he nor they knew what he was doing, they never hesitated to help. They really were the best.

But Belissar wasn't about to let them do all the work, so he got to exploring as well. Stepping closer to the stone, he traced his hand upon some engraved words, but he still couldn't make heads or tails of them, so he moved on.

The ruins were arranged in a small circle that rose into the air. The stones that remained reached about two stories, but Belissar thought they might have gone higher. He couldn't say for sure, as everything above that point was long gone, but it seemed like some sort of tower; maybe a watchtower for a guard outpost?

As he walked, he could feel small spots of warmth. Small bits of mana still imbued the stone, and occasionally, he could feel it move about slowly. He rubbed his chin.

"How did this stuff survive the Hunger? I thought it consumed everything . . ."

He'd thought the tower had simply grown everything back from scratch . . . but then, why would there be ruins? Why wouldn't the tower just create a brand-new structure if that was the case? Or did the gods want to restore things exactly as they were when the Hunger arrived? Had these ruins already been like this before the Hunger got there?

Well, Belissar didn't have even the beginnings of the knowledge required to answer those questions, so he shook his head and kept exploring. The ruins were mostly empty. Little remained besides the stone itself, either time, nature, or the Hunger having claimed everything else.

There was a stone path leading out from the far side of the structure, but the structure was close to the edge of the safe zone around the tower, so right now, it just led to the Hunger. Instead, Belissar found himself wandering back toward the entrance, where the broken statue was.

He noticed something lying behind it: a rectangular stone, a bit on the flat side. He thought it was just another piece of debris at first, but on closer inspection, its shape was too neat, too regular. And most of all—there was a faint hint of mana inside.

He dusted it off before flipping it over.

It turned out it was some sort of thick stone tablet engraved with the same letters as the ruins themselves. There was also a carving showing some sort of soldier, and a crest he didn't recognize.

Belissar glanced at it for a couple of minutes before he shrugged. It didn't mean anything more to him than any of the other carvings had. And even though he felt hints of mana inside, they didn't seem to do anything. He may have been able to feel mana now, but he didn't know how to actually do anything with it . . . and wasn't willing to risk spontaneous combustion attempting some experiment.

He picked up the tablet. He figured if nothing else, maybe the tower would try to absorb it if it was anything useful.

He nodded at Niobee as she flew over to rejoin him. "Find anything?"

"Sorry . . . couldn't . . ."

Belissar smiled and held his hand out for her to land on.

"Don't be. I was just curious about this place. Besides, you girls were the ones who found it, and the mana flowers, too."

She didn't respond, but her wings buzzed a bit. The rest of the bees began to rejoin them, and Belissar nodded at them all.

"Let's go home."

Belissar took the tablet back to the tower, but nothing happened when he passed through the gateway.

He shrugged and carried it over to the apiary, placing it inside the farmhouse. It was an easier walk than trekking back through the forest would be, so he figured he might as well keep it.

After that, he stepped outside and gathered a bunch of the flowers surrounding the tower, absorbing them and applying them to the flower meadow and the apiary.

He smiled as he looked over the now colorful field filled with bees. He felt that, honestly, this sight was much better than some dusty old ruins would ever be.

THE FIRSTBORN

Back in one of the hives in the flower meadow, a monster bee queen watched as her workers processed the new honey. She was the First Queen of the First Spawner's Second Dynasty, the first of her line, and the Firstborn of all the queens. The first guardian of the gate to the beyond.

She watched as her children finished their work, leaving a cell full of glistening honey. Honey that occasionally shimmered with a subtle glow, a golden light lost in the yellow colors of the wax and the bees all around it. The queen felt the warmth of mana stir within the cell, resonating with the mana inside of her. She felt a heat grow within her torso.

It was time.

She and her spawner siblings were the only ones to bear the title of the Second Dynasty. But every bee in the dungeon knew the reason why. Back when she was born, she'd thought she was the first of the King's defenders . . . but she'd been quickly dissuaded of that notion.

She'd felt the bond with her king moments after her birth—a being beyond mere bees, with depths of emotion and existence she couldn't yet fully comprehend—and she had been nearly overwhelmed by the sensations of that moment. But there had been two things she could understand: Loss, and a desire to protect.

The Conduit had later explained to them what had happened. An entire dynasty of queens had lived before them. They'd spread across the King's fields and formed their civilization upon his generosity. They had grown their colonies in grand constructions formed by the King's own hands. They had been the first to offer their tribute to the King.

And then, the invader had come. The armies of the First Dynasty had risen to meet it, led by the Conduit herself.

But they'd failed.

The armies of the First Dynasty had fallen in droves. They'd given their lives in the multitudes, as was their duty, but they'd failed to stop the assault. The invader had torn through them all the same and laid waste to their civilization. The mighty structures the King had forged, the pillars upon which the hives had been built, were crushed in the jaws of the enemy. The queens themselves had fallen, leading the last of their armies in a final, desperate stand.

It had not been enough.

Only the King and the Conduit had survived, and the Conduit only by her bond to the dungeon and the King. And in the aftermath, the King had changed. No longer did he build the hives by his own hand. No longer did he use his wisdom for prosperity and shelter. No longer did he leave the defense to the queens. The bees had proven too weak to do as he required, and so the King himself had been forced to intervene.

At first, the Firstborn of the Second Dynasty had been pleased to serve as her King had commanded. She devoted her workers to the tasks he ordered, though she understood not the meaning behind them. She sent her workers to aid her siblings and those of the other spawners, gifting resources to what would have been rival hives under any other circumstances.

She had her workers carry the stems of the flowers instead of the nectar. She constructed a hive that was not a hive, leaving empty cells deep within the ground.

She had not understood these things, but she'd seen the intensity and the drive of her King as he worked. She'd heard from the Conduit that he had devised a grand plan, and she was honored to be a part of it, even as she drilled her hive with the lessons of the first battle.

And then, the day arrived. The invader had returned, and the Second Dynasty would be put to the test. Or so the Firstborn thought.

Instead, the King's wisdom had been revealed. The invader was lured into a trap, and the empty hive they had built was set ablaze, and the invader joined the ashes. The battle was won without the loss of a single hive, and only token casualties among the assembled armies.

And the Firstborn's heart *burned*.

The King himself had stood before the invader, placing his own life before its jaws. He had not permitted them to fight. Nay, he had *forbidden* them from doing so. The Firstborn had not led her army into battle, only being permitted to contribute a token diversion from her scouts.

As the invader burned within the flames, the Firstborn had realized the truth. The Second Dynasty was no better than the First. They, too, had failed.

The King had not trusted them to fight the invader. He could not. The Conduit had spoken of the sheer casualties the First Dynasty had experienced, all in vain. The Firstborn herself had felt the deep pain of the King at those losses.

He'd resolved to avoid the needless death and destruction that had befallen the First Invasion by turning his hand to war; his wisdom, his plans, and his grand constructions devoted to the delivery of death. He'd taken on the job that should have been their duty, all because they were too weak to defend their King and his realm.

No, they could not even defend themselves. Their King had risked himself to protect *them*. He, who should have been the last to face danger.

The Firstborn would not let it stand.

Her entire hive had redoubled its efforts, all of her children devoting themselves to their work with even greater fervor than before. Her scouts flew into the beyond, past the sight and protection of their King, in search of new lands and resources.

And she thought they had found a shining treasure, a worthy tribute to offer to the King. But once again, he had demonstrated his power and his charity. He had not taken the sweetest of flowers for his own but spread them across his lands. And he'd offered them to her, freely.

His generosity knew no bounds, but she could not help but feel disappointed. Once again, she had failed to be of use to her King, who continued to sacrifice for the sake of those who should serve him.

But now . . . that was about to change.

She dunked her head into the cell before her and drank deeply. The warmth of mana filled her body and set it ablaze. For the first time since her birth, she had more mana than could be spent on the laying of her brood.

Monster bee eggs required mana to lay, and even more mana to grow; the small amounts they received from mundane honey and their own bodies were barely enough to sustain the colony's growth. But now, thanks to the King's generosity, they had more than enough.

Mana began to fill her body and push against her chitin. She buzzed as she began to glow with light.

A few minutes later, the light died down, and a new queen several times the size she was before stepped forward. She drank more of the mana honey to fill her reserves, then strode over to a new section of the hive. One with cells far larger than any her hive had built before.

The King had not rejected them entirely. The Firstborn had felt as his power stirred within them, changing them. She'd seen visions of mighty warriors; giants bred for battle who stood tall and strong among all of beekind.

Soldiers with lances long and sharp, clad in armor so thick even the deadly hornet could not pierce it. Warriors of a kind who could face much larger enemies directly, who could defeat the invader without sacrificing their entire civilization in the process, who would not require the protection of the very King they'd been born to defend.

She'd known then that her King still believed in them; that he had seen beyond their present weakness. She understood now his generosity, for it would take far more mana to birth these children than the Firstborn had ever possessed.

With the mundane flowers, she would have had to cut an entire generation of workers to store up the power for even one of these giants. Even her hive, the most developed and numerous of all, could not endure such an interruption. It would have taken a long time before she was established enough to do so.

But now that her King had granted them access to nectar overflowing with mana, she had power in abundance. She herself had advanced to a new stage and grown beyond the limits of her mundane ancestors. Her body now produced ten times as much mana as before, and she would scarcely require external nutrients to expand the ranks of her children. She could lay dozens of worker eggs at a time and still devote all of the honey they produced to grow and sustain the next generation.

And most importantly, a giant egg packed with mana would be no great burden to her now.

She came to a large cell even as the workers lined the sides with mana honey. And then, she began to lay her army: the first true army amongst any dynasty of any spawner within her King's dungeon. And with them, her hive would prove its might to the King. They would take up their role as the dungeon's defenders. They would defend the King and all that belonged to him.

They would be weak and helpless no longer.

CHAPTER NINETEEN

GOTTA BEE DILIGENT!

After gathering the flowers, Belissar returned to his woodworking. He did think about searching the forest for more specimens, or maybe trying to absorb other plants like bushes and trees, but ultimately decided to prioritize the beehouse construction.

He figured the bees would let him know if they found a flower they really liked, and moving bushes, much less trees, into the tower seemed . . . difficult. Besides, this was a mission tasked to him by the God of Bees herself, so he should probably focus on it if there were no other pressing matters.

He had already cut some planks and set them out to dry. Now, all he had to do was wait six months to a year.

Belissar paused, then sighed. At home, they had stocks of wood to work with, but since he was starting from scratch, there wasn't much he could do but wait if he wanted quality.

Well, in his village, people couldn't always wait for the best of things, so he also knew how to build with freshly cut wood, which meant he didn't *have* to wait for fully dried planks. But this was a mission from a god! How could he accept cutting any corners?!

Well . . . he was already going to cut some corners, since all he had was an axe, a saw, and his knife. He didn't have all the tools a true woodworker might use, after all, so some of the details and finishes might be a bit rough by necessity. And, well, the God of Bees had accepted his mess of a prayer for the shrine mission. In fact, he could argue the God of Bees had accepted cut corners by blessing some peasant beekeeper instead of a chosen tower lord.

Belissar thought for a moment before he stood up and went to grab his axe and saw.

Yeah, he had no idea what quality of a job was acceptable for this mission, but there was no sense sitting around for six months doing nothing. He figured he'd make one now with green wood, and if it wasn't acceptable, then he'd wait for fully dried planks. Worse came to worst, he'd have an extra beehouse which might be a bit rough around the edges but would still be a roof over his bees' heads.

Belissar tilted his head as he wondered if it would rain in his tower. There was a sky with a sun; there was also night and day, so maybe? And what about seasons? Was winter coming?

Flower Meadow upgrades:
- Randomized Weather (Cost: 100 DP)
- Weather Control (Cost: 1000 DP)
- Seasonal Cycle (Cost: 500 DP)

Belissar nodded. Of course there were more upgrades that he didn't know about. At this point, it just made sense.

Well, at least he knew something he could use the DP on now.

DP: 2

He pursed his lips. Yes. He was currently getting DP at a rate of one per day. Well, he could randomize the weather before the planks finished drying, at least? And it'd only take over a year and a half to get seasons! Less than three years if he wanted to control the weather, apparently!

He decided he was fine with things as they were. Who wouldn't want a nice, sunny flower meadow with a pleasant breeze? Why would he want a winter, anyway? His bees would have to go and hibernate . . . maybe, if monster bees still had to do that.

In any case, Belissar decided he would save the DP for something else. After all, who knew what else he might need it for?

DP Shop
- Room Feature Choice (Cost: 1000 DP)
- Monster Choice (Cost: 3000 DP)
- Room Choice (Cost: 3000 DP)
- Perk Choice (Cost: 10000 DP)
- Additional Room Slot (Cost: 5000 DP)
- Boost Maximum Mana (Cost: 5000 DP)

. . . Belissar now knew, apparently. And it seemed like 100 DP was really cheap? He had a feeling the one DP per day may not be what other tower lords relied on.

Well, he'd worry about that when he figured out how to actually get any more. Ongoing purification didn't sound like something he was ready for if it was anything like the initial purification. Remnants and challengers were still terms he didn't know about, and at the discretion of his patron meant that he should keep focusing on the mission assigned to him by the God of Bees.

Remnant

A portion of corruption condensed into corporeal form.
Allows challengers to assist in ongoing purification.

Challenger

A being independent from the dungeon with enough intelligence to acknowledge the patron god.

. . . And now Belissar technically knew what those terms meant. Not that the descriptions made him any less confused. Condensed corruption so that challengers could assist with purification? Um, okay? And beings with enough intelligence to acknowledge the patron god . . . did that mean people? Then why didn't it just say that? Maybe that was supposed to be the tower guard specifically?

After all, peasants weren't supposed to be capable of entering a tower without defiling it, so there should be some sort of distinguishing feature . . . right?

And then there was Belissar, who had not only entered a tower but taken command of it without being smitten by the gods. He wasn't actually sure if his tower was defiled or not, but it seemed to still work fine as far as he could tell. If a god was blessing it, then surely it should be fine?

In any case, the information still didn't really answer Belissar's original question of how to get more DP, so he put it aside as he originally intended and moved on to his task. He left the tower and headed toward the tree line, figuring that he may as well take some wood from outside so his bees could use all his trees for their hives. And who knew, maybe the tower would absorb the tree?

So, he went to work and began chopping.

Absorb Pinecone?
Samples: 0/100

It turned out the tower didn't absorb the wood itself but could absorb the pinecones from the tree he cut. Maybe because he only brought part of the tree instead of the whole thing?

Well, it was nice to know he could just carry pinecones instead. Uprooting an entire tree on his own was beyond Belissar, much less carrying it. It would, however, take a lot of samples to produce any results.

Belissar decided he'd absorb them here and there but wouldn't go out of his way for the moment. The flower meadow and apiary couldn't have that many trees to begin with, so switching up the types wasn't all that impactful. Maybe if the bees found one with flowers they liked he'd work at it a bit more diligently.

Belissar instead busied himself by carrying pieces of wood across the meadow and to the apiary, almost dumping them on the ground as he arrived by the farmhouse. He rubbed his aching arms as he looked at the pile of wood on the ground . . . and thought about the larger pile still out in the forest. He grimaced.

For a brief moment, he wondered what might have been if he had chosen a human-size defending monster, but he quickly banished those thoughts. He was doing this for the bees, and they deserved his best. He certainly wouldn't fault them for being unable to help with his current task.

So he told himself as he dragged his feet back out toward the flower meadow and the exit to the tower. It took a couple more trips to get all the wood inside, after which Belissar stumbled into the farmhouse and collapsed on the bed, trying to ignore his burning muscles.

Belissar woke up the next morning and stretched his arms. He smiled, as once again, he had made a full recovery. Sometimes, this tower business wasn't half bad.

He had a quick breakfast of honeycomb before stepping outside.

And stopped and blinked at the sight waiting for him.

One of the monster bee queens hovered in the air before him—only, she had somehow grown *significantly* larger, now the size of a hand and a half. And hovering in the air behind her were half a dozen monster bee soldiers: hand-size bees with solid-looking chitin and stingers like small daggers.

Once Belissar stepped outside, the queen made a motion, and the soldier bees performed a salute dance, all moving in sync. The queen bee joined them in the movement, and then they all hovered motionless before Belissar.

"King!"

Niobee flew over and greeted him as well.

"Niobee, these are . . . the soldier bees?"

The little bee flew around happily. "Yes! Hive now has soldiers! Will fight for King next time!"

Belissar furrowed his brow at that but looked over the monster bee soldiers. He imagined the shade attacking again, only this time, it wasn't tiny bees flying to their deaths. This time, he imagined the bees before him, their large stingers plunging into the shade's side. He imagined a swarm of bees like that meeting the monster as it arrived.

The shade was still terrifying to Belissar, and he couldn't help but think of the fallen hives when he thought of it. But with the soldiers before him now . . . it didn't seem so unthinkable that they could face such a monster directly.

He smiled. "Well done. I think we'll be much better prepared if we have to fight again."

The queen buzzed and gave another salute, the soldier bees following suit.

CHAPTER TWENTY

BELISSAR'S BEEHOUSE

Belissar sawed away as best he could at the piece of wood before him. He was working on one of the beehouse walls at the moment, trying to cut some grooves he could slot the trays into. He looked at it and sighed.

It was not his finest work; a rough cut that looked more like some creature had taken a bite out of the wood than a detailed woodworker's craftsmanship. But that was the limit of his current tools and material. Since he was working with wet wood, he would have to leave room for it to bend or shrink, or any number of other such things he couldn't necessarily predict. He wasn't going to get it to fit perfectly together; he was just hoping he could get it to fit together, period.

He sighed and put it aside, beginning to work on the next wall. He wanted to make sure all this would actually work before he went and cut a bunch of the grooves.

A while later, he had a basic three-sided box that fit together . . . sort of. There were holes and gaps and whatnot, but at the very least, it stood up without collapsing. Belissar then went and cut out a floor piece, seeing if he could get it to fit in. It did . . . sort of. Again, there were gaps on the edges Belissar would have preferred to do without, so he tried to cut some pieces to line the edges.

Next, he began to cut some thinner long pieces for the frames. Getting the grooves and shapes so the frame parts would fit together was challenging, but eventually Belissar got one assembled. He placed it down into the box . . . and it managed to fit into the grooves he had carved in the wall. He heaved a sigh of relief.

With the proof of concept confirmed, he could begin to assemble the rest of it.

It took most of the day, but eventually, Belissar finished. He took a step back and beheld the work of his hands.

. . . It was a rickety thing, leaning to one side where he'd misjudged the length of one of the legs, and with gaps all over the place. But it was a complete box, with some frames to guide the bees that could be pulled out—with a lot of effort and grunting. Belissar sighed.

And then he heard a chime.

Mission "Build a beehouse" completed!
Reward: 225 DP

He blinked and looked over the beehouse again. The God of Bees . . . approved of this work? Belissar frowned, but then glanced over at the existing beehives, and his face relaxed.

Maybe the point wasn't to get the best that Belissar could produce but just to get something that would work without having to destroy an entire bee colony with each harvest. Compared to that, he could understand why the God of Bees would prefer even the rough construction he had made.

But in the end, it was neither his nor even the God of Bees's opinion that would truly determine if the hive was sufficient.

"Well, okay then. What do you think?"

He glanced over at some of the bees circling around him. He caught sight of Niobee—and the queen from the nearest basket hive. Both of them began buzzing and flying around the house at maximum speed.

"Great! Amazing! King is best king!"

Belissar chuckled at that before nodding. "As long as you girls like it."

He moved to pick up the hive, grunting at the weight of the wood. The rough construction meant he'd made things a bit thicker than normal, and he was paying for that now. But eventually, he moved it over to the closest basket hive, intending to make it as easy as possible for the queen to transfer over.

But it was then that the beehive and the basket hive began to glow.

Compatible design confirmed.
Upgrade Apiary Beehive to Belissar's Beehouse? Cost: 25 DP

"Oh, sure? That would be helpful."

Light covered the two hives, then with a flash, the basket hive vanished. Belissar's beehouse moved in its place, sitting on top of the tree trunk now.

His eyes widened, and he rushed over to it.

Replacing the basket hive was all well and good, but that queen had been working hard in the basket hive. The very last thing Belissar wanted was for her to lose her brood growing inside. So, he quickly removed the lid of the beehouse and began pulling out the frames. He exhaled his breath.

Honeycomb now filled the frames, and Belissar could see little eggs and larva in some of them. The queen herself flew in front of Belissar and began a dance of happiness and gratitude. It seemed the process had transferred over the queen's brood to the new house without issue.

A smile grew on Belissar's face as he put the frame and lid back where they belonged. "Enjoy."

The queen gave her gratitude once last time, saluted to Belissar, and then flew into the beehouse to continue her work. Belissar turned his attention to the words he had ignored in his panic.

Apiary Beehive upgraded to Belissar's Beehouse!
Product Mana Honeycomb changed to Mana Honeycomb Tray.
Maximum products stored increased from 1 to 3.
Bee productivity increased.
Bee happiness increased!

Belissar blinked. The last line was written in glowing yellow letters. Soon, though, he began to grin. That message alone made all this effort worthwhile to him. He went and focused on the next basket hive. Since the tower could upgrade them, he figured he wanted all his bees to have one.

Upgrade Apiary Beehive to Belissar's Beehouse? Cost: 100 DP (25 if beehouse provided)

Belissar frowned and rubbed his chin. It seemed it would be a bit more expensive to upgrade if he didn't build the beehouses himself. He did some math as quickly as he could manage in the dirt and determined that if he built all of the beehouses personally, he could just afford to upgrade the entire apiary, while if he didn't, he could only afford to upgrade two more.

There was no choice to Belissar; his bees deserved as many homes as he could build. A decision reinforced further when he heard another chime.

New mission received: Upgrade all Apiary Beehives to Belissar's Beehouses.

Belissar nodded.
"Absolutely."

Belissar spent the rest of the week working on the beehouses. With each one he made, he was able to adjust a bit more, both improving the quality of the construction and decreasing the build time.

He noticed a curious phenomenon: every time he upgraded an apiary beehive with a new and improved beehouse, the other upgraded beehouses would adjust themselves to match. It wasn't an identical copy of the latest one; rather, it seemed to average out between the quality of the first one and the best one available, but either way, Belissar was glad. He was happy to know the first queen wouldn't be left high and dry.

Of course, that wasn't all he did. As much as Belissar enjoyed working entirely on the beehouses, the whole purification business still weighed on the edge of his mind. So, he also spent some time making whatever preparations he happened to think of, gathering and chopping a bunch of firewood throughout the week, since it would also need time to dry.

Once some of it had dried, he could start to do some work with beeswax. Unfortunately, he didn't have a strainer or any pots, but he could do some basics.

He managed to carve some grooves into a log to melt the beeswax in, then dipped some branches he'd gathered from the outside forest into the grooves. That way, he managed to make some torches that were a bit better crafted than wrapping a strip of tunic around a stick.

. . . A tunic that now left a bit of his stomach exposed thanks to the strips he'd cut off the bottom earlier. He sighed and shook his head. Fortunately, the climate in the tower seemed very pleasant at the moment. Or perhaps it was the mana of the tower protecting his body?

In any case, it was fine, since his only company at present were the bees, but he should probably keep an eye out for any plants he could use to make repairs.

Fortunately, he knew a bit of textile work. Some of the village boys called it women's work, but in a village of their size, most people knew how to do most jobs that needed doing. That went doubly so for Belissar, growing up first with just the old beekeeper, and later living completely on his own.

Unfortunately, those skills wouldn't matter unless he could acquire some suitable materials, so Belissar just resolved to keep an eye out for now.

In any case, he now had a stockpile of firewood and kindling to make fires of various sizes as necessary, as well as some torches to light. He assembled another gathering of kindling, firewood, wax, and honey in the pit traps on either side of the door between the flower meadow and the apiary, as well as in the pit trap closest to the gate to the outside.

He then built a campfire pit on the apiary side and stored the torches and his fire bow around it. He found out at that time that he could designate a section of the apiary where flowers wouldn't grow, and so was able to clear a suitable area without too much trouble.

He was thus ready to make a fire he could use to light the torches in case he needed to use the pit traps like he did before. The work slowed down his beehouse making, but he felt it was necessary.

If and when the Hunger returned to his tower, he would be ready.

CHAPTER TWENTY-ONE

BEE RESOLVED

Belissar was resting in his room after a long day of woodworking when Niobee flew inside. Belissar smiled and held his finger out for her to land on it.

"King okay?"

Belissar turned thoughtful for a second, then nodded with a smile. "You know what? I am."

He glanced out the window at the apiary's beehives. Eight had been converted, and only one of the basket hives remained. He could catch glimpses of the bees returning to their hives.

"Better, even. All of this—towers and gods and Hunger—was confusing and scary at first. But now . . . I can't say I hate it. Just me and you and the other bees, all working together. I hope we can keep doing this."

Niobee began dancing rapidly. "King best king; will always be king! Workers and queens will always help!"

Belissar chuckled and grinned. "Hope you're right about that."

The next morning, Belissar awoke to pleasant weather, as every morning had been in the tower. He stretched and ate a bit of mana honeycomb, smiling as the warmth of mana spread throughout his body. Once his fears of spontaneous combustion had faded, he'd realized he had been eating the honey all along with no ill effect. In fact, he had come to enjoy the mana honey; it was quite pleasant.

Exiting the house, he gathered some trays of honey from the converted hives. They tended to fill up if he didn't, and the bees seemed happy to offer their honey to him, so he did so every morning. He took a couple of the trays and offered them at the shrine, then went about starting his work for the day.

He began by carrying some wood over to the last basket hive remaining in the apiary, intending to assemble the beehouse right next to it. He had learned after having to drag the first one over, after all.

He was just bending down to pick up a piece of wood when a message appeared before his eyes.

Ongoing purification limit reached. Minor purification required.
Minor purification attempt in 3 days.

Belissar slowly rose back to his feet, his spine going completely straight. Niobee flew over to him.

"King okay?"

Belissar's face turned grim. "It's time, Niobee. The Hunger is coming again."

Niobee flew about unsteadily. "King have orders?"

Belissar slowly nodded. "Inform the queens. We need to prepare for battle."

He took a deep breath as Niobee saluted and flew off. The queens had received his intent even as he was asking Niobee to inform them, and he could already feel them stir. Now was the key moment. Now was when Belissar would find out how his decisions would play out, and if all had been correct.

Minor purification attempt in 2 days, 23 hours, and 58 minutes.

But there was no time for further pondering. The clock was ticking, and Belissar intended to do everything he could to turn the odds in his favor. Every preparation he could make would reduce the casualties among his bees, so he would spare no effort here. Walking over to the side of the farmhouse where firewood lay in large stacks, he grabbed as much as he could carry and made his way toward the flower meadow.

He'd kept the two pit traps by the apiary entrance stocked with wood and kindling, but now that he knew an assault was incoming, he planned to prepare as many firepits as he could, starting with the ones closest to the entrance. The sticky honey traps would help with that, but adding firewood and kindling would increase the blaze further.

He would also need to prepare campfire pits near the other traps so he could be ready to set them ablaze. And now that he had woodcutting tools and a forest beyond the tower, he could also try to prepare actual fences on the path from the gate to hopefully try to drive the shade into the first pit trap.

But all his thoughts ceased when he stepped through the apiary entrance and into the flower meadow. His eyes went wide at the sight before him. The air thrummed with the buzzing of countless wings. The sky turned yellow and black as a sea of chitin spread out above.

An army of monster bee soldiers hovered before him, led by a dozen large monster bee queens. The lead queen shook her body, and the others followed suit. Every bee soldier then curled back and thrust their abdomen forward, displaying their daggerlike stingers. Belissar felt a slight breeze from over a hundred simultaneous thrusts.

His jaw dropped open, and no words came to him. It seemed the flower meadow queens had been quite busy. Niobee flew in front of him.

"King! Queens say they fight! Soldiers want to fight!"

The queens and the soldiers hovered in place, remaining still as their eyes fixed upon Belissar. With such a scene before him, he could only manage a silent nod.

The Firstborn watched from the entrance of her hive as she waited for enough mana to lay another soldier egg. Her army was flying up in the air, the soldiers breaking off into squads of different sizes and taking turns diving down toward one of their own, who hovered close to the ground but otherwise did all they could to evade.

The target soldier suddenly shook themself, and all the bees in the air scattered in different directions before coalescing back together. The target soldier swapped out for another in the process and rejoined the attackers above as the diving practice resumed.

The Conduit had shared all that she could of the First Dynasty's fall, and the Firstborn had shared as much with her soldiers. They now trained and refined the tactics the Third Queen of the First Spawner's First Dynasty had pioneered in her final moments.

They did not attack all at once, but practiced a rotation of small squads that would prevent the invader from wiping them all out in one go. They practiced quick scattering and evasion to avoid the deadly breath attacks the Firstborn of the Second Dynasty had witnessed firsthand, and practiced hit-and-run attacks that would keep them out of the jaws of the enemy.

It went against their instincts somewhat, but even mundane bees adapted to their foes, and monster bees were something more. Besides, their King did not wish to see them perish any more than was necessary. The soldiers' instinct for sacrifice would not take precedence over the King's desire, something the Firstborn had spoken to her soldiers about until each one of them had understood personally.

The King had permitted them to fight. He had even permitted them to make the first attempt, after a discussion with the Conduit and the queens of the flower meadow. He would withhold his flames and his plans, focusing on the burning chasms toward the back of the flower meadow, and so would give the soldiers a chance to engage the enemy by their own strength. Only if they failed would the King step in to protect the hives.

And so, they would not fail. The Firstborn swore they would not fail. The destruction of the First Dynasty and the weakness of the Second would be repaid in full. She and the other queens of the flower meadow had worked solely to achieve this task.

They had cut their workers to the bare minimum and drunk as much mana honey as they could, all seeking to grow as fast as possible. And once they had grown, they'd turned every bit of mana and honey they could to raising as many soldier bees as possible, all to assemble the army training before them. They had set aside their rivalry and pooled their efforts in order to avoid even the slightest bit of waste.

The workers pushed themselves to the brink, producing as much honey as they possibly could, restricting their own meals and rest to the barest minimum. The queens held nothing in reserve; they emptied the honey storage as soon as it was filled and turned every bit of strength they had to lay even one more soldier egg.

Even now, her instincts screamed that her hive's stockpiles were empty and that she would not survive the cold of winter, were the King's domain subject to such a thing.

And even with all that effort and sacrifice, they had barely assembled enough soldiers for a single battle. That was why the soldiers now drilled relentlessly and were told in no uncertain terms that sacrifice was the absolute last resort. Each one of them was precious, each one of them necessary if they were to achieve victory.

For the fight to come, they would not have the reserves to replenish their numbers. They would not only need to fight—they would need to survive. Even minimum casualties could be enough to tip the scales against them.

But such was the will of the bees to protect the hive and right the wrongs of the First and Second Invasions. Not a worker complained about the strict rationing. Not a soldier complained about the endless drills. Not a queen complained as their abdomens burned and their mana drained to the bottom over and over.

This was why they could not be permitted to fail, especially now that the King had given them his trust. And yet . . . the Firstborn was worried. The hives of the flower meadow were all on the brink. Despite the best efforts of the workers, honey production was beginning to dip. The existing workers were at their physical limits; there was no spare honey to help them recover, and with the queens cutting worker egg numbers, there were no reserves to relieve them.

Try as they might, the queens would have to stop laying soldier eggs, or else their hives would collapse. But that . . . might be unavoidable as well. The queens had not saved any of their own mana, and the honey stores were empty. The queens would hardly have the strength to lay new worker eggs at this point.

Just then, the Firstborn heard the buzzing.

Turning to face the entrance to the apiary, her antennas shot straight up.

Waves upon waves of worker bees flew from the apiary, carrying with them glistening drops of honey. They broke apart into separate formations, and each made their way to one of the hives, including the Firstborn's own. The Firstborn's tired workers pulled themselves from their rest and moved to block the entrance to their hive, but the Firstborn waved them down.

The worker bee leading the formation landed in front of the Firstborn, and the two touched antennas, speaking to one another.

"Conduit says all help King."

The Firstborn acknowledged this in a daze, stepping away from the entrance to her hive. Every instinct told her to retaliate as another hive's bees flew into hers, yet she did not. And her shock only grew as the worker bees deposited their honey into the storage cells before exiting the hive and flying back toward the apiary.

An endless stream of them seemed to arrive, filling her entire storage in mere minutes. She could not help but gape at the sheer abundance of honey the apiary bees had brought. They, the younger queens born after the First Spawner's entire Second Dynasty, had now given away more honey than her entire worker force could produce.

She had to wonder if their hives had stripped themselves bare to achieve such a thing . . . but it did not seem so. Even as she gaped, more and more bees arrived, buzzing around the entrance, since there were no cells left to fill.

The Firstborn shook herself and got to work, rushing over to the nearest cell and drinking deeply of the honey, refilling her mana up to full. Flying over to the nearest soldier cell, she laid more eggs as quickly as she could. Her workers sipped on enough honey to get moving, and then began to expand the hive, creating more cells for the apiary bees to fill.

She realized the truth. The bees of the dungeon were not rival hives. They were all one; a colony of many, a hive *of* hives. They were all the brood of the King. And together, they would win this fight and earn his trust.

So, all the bees devoted themselves to their work. There was much to do, and only a short time to do it.

CHAPTER TWENTY-TWO

FIRST MINOR PURIFICATION

Minor purification attempt in 4 minutes and 23 seconds.

Belissar had his arms crossed while tapping his foot. He kept reminding himself to breathe, taking deep breaths while drumming his fingers on the torch he held against his arm.

He was currently standing in the apiary just in front of the door to the flower meadow. A roaring fire crackled in the campfire next to him, but his attention was on the gate at the far end, where soldier bees hovered in the air. They were gathered into small squads and spread out across the sky, waiting for the purification to begin.

He heaved a sigh. Niobee had convinced him to let the flower meadow bees take the first stab at the monster. And he needed them to, when he thought about it. He had chosen the soldier bees for this exact reason, so what was the point in keeping them from danger? Plus, he needed to know what they could do. If even the soldier bees couldn't defeat a shade, then he'd need to rethink a lot of his decisions and defenses.

As a result, Belissar wouldn't get involved right away this time. He'd remain in the apiary while the fight raged. If the bees couldn't take down the shade themselves, then they'd lure it into one of the prepped firepits near the end of the flower meadow. Belissar could then light his torch and rush out to set the pit ablaze.

Around him buzzed the workers from the apiary hives—along with some newcomers. Monster bee soldiers hovered around him, but not from the flower meadow hives. Belissar had gone ahead and added a pair of monster bee soldier spawners to the apiary. None of the apiary hives had developed enough to spawn soldiers on their own, and none of them would be able to do so in the time before the purification.

Since the flower meadow hives had been focusing on the soldiers, Belissar had needed the apiary's help to prep the firepits with extra wax. Belissar had also noticed them loaning honey to the meadow hives, perhaps allowing them to focus even more heavily on the soldiers. All of which meant the apiary queens had not had the leeway to raise soldiers.

As such, Belissar had figured he should spawn some soldiers to cover the apiary as well. If, gods forbid, the flower meadow fell and they couldn't lure the shade into one of the pit traps, Belissar didn't want to leave the apiary with only workers for defense.

With that, all the preparations Belissar could make in the time allotted were complete. They had prepped as many firepits as possible, they had spawned more monster bee soldiers, and Belissar had even seen them training for the battle. Belissar himself held his torch and his axe.

But Belissar couldn't help but worry. He didn't want to see any of his bees hurt, after all. And if the bees didn't defeat the shade immediately, it would have the opportunity to rampage across the flower meadow until they could lure it into a pit. At worst, it might destroy one or even all of the hives before then. Losing the queens there would be a heavy blow.

But the bees were resolved to do this, and Belissar needed them to if he was to be an effective tower lord. So, he did his best to calm himself and stand at the ready.

He didn't really succeed. But the timer counted down regardless, and soon, the moment was upon them.

Minor purification attempt commencing.

This time was a bit different from before. The tower's mana still heated up, but not to the burning extent of the initial purification. The gate didn't swing open this time either. Instead, Belissar felt a chill down his spine as something cold crept through the tower's mana. It inched out of the core and made its way toward the gate. Once there, it coalesced, and tendrils of the Hunger began to form and gather together. Once again, a shade of the Hunger formed and let out a roar.

Minor purification has begun.
Remaining hostiles: 1

Belissar . . . tilted his head. He knew he was looking at it from far away with his "tower sight," as he had started to call it, but . . . the shade seemed smaller than before.

However, he had no time to question it, for the bees had already begun their attack. A squad of four soldiers had started diving the moment the shade took shape, and it had barely finished its roar when they slammed into it.

Two daggerlike stingers pierced into the shade's side, which let out another roar. The other two overshot their target and missed, then all four flew up and away. The shade snapped its jaws at them, but they had already left its range and escaped unharmed.

A second squad struck from behind even as the shade bit at the first. These four had adjusted their aim, and all four stingers hit the shade's back. With another roar, it whipped its tail around, but again, the bees had flown out of the way.

The shade had apparently had enough at this point, and it took a deep breath. Most of the bees scattered as they'd practiced, but the third squad had already begun its dive and struggled to pull up as the monster unleashed a cloud of black mist from its mouth. One of the soldier bees was caught by the mist—and to Belissar's surprise, did not drop to the ground.

However, she shook about in the air and slowed to a crawl, so she couldn't evade when the shade's tail pierced through her torso. She went limp and stopped moving.

The bees renewed their assault, another squad stinging the shade's flanks even as their sister fell. The soldiers were finding their rhythm now, and stung the shade again and again. Its tail and jaws missed time after time, and the bees were careful to avoid the shade's breath now. A misty, black ooze dripped from various spots on the creature, which wasn't moving as quickly as it had at the start.

Belissar blinked. The shade hadn't even advanced from the doorway, and yet, the soldier bees had it on the ropes. Of every outcome he had thought about and planned for . . . this one came as a surprise.

"We're . . . winning?"

Niobee flew about him rapidly in response. "Yes!"

Belissar started to grin at that, but then, something changed. The bees had the shade surrounded at this point—but a cornered beast was the most dangerous.

The shade once again took a deep breath, and the bees backed away once more. But the creature didn't let out the black mist this time. Instead, it took off running as fast as it could once the bees fell back, and so broke free of the cloud of soldiers around it.

Of all the outcomes the soldier bees had trained for, they had not anticipated the shade might *run* from them. They were caught off guard and rushed to chase after it.

And that was what it was waiting for.

The shade spun around and unleashed its black breath. Several squads of bees flew straight into it before they could evade, and then the beast was upon them, pouncing into their midst and assaulting the stunned squads. Its claws took the wing off a bee, sending her falling to the ground. Its tail pierced through another two while its jaws clamped down on yet another. An entire squad fell in an instant.

The other bees in the air retaliated, rushing in to sting the shade's sides, but it mostly ignored them, whipping its tail around while focusing on the stunned bees ahead. The soldier bees' careful rotation had broken with the sudden change in situation and the plight of their sisters, and so a group of them all rushed in at once. The tail caught them and knocked them away, leaving them spinning about in the air from the force of the strike.

But the shade was not at its best, either. It had not crushed the bee in its jaws yet, though she lacked the strength to break free. Her chitin armor had saved her life, but it had begun to crack under the monster's grip, and its fangs had pierced through in places. She was bleeding heavily and could barely wiggle about at this point. She had no hope of escape.

However, escape was not her plan. Her abdomen was still free, as the monster had bit her torso, and it stretched up, her stinger extended out—and then the soldier's abdomen began to glow. Even as her chitin cracked and shattered, she swung her stinger forward, shredding her torso on the shade's fangs as she curled her body around.

The stinger thrust up into the creature's head from the bottom, a flash of light shining from the monstrosity's mouth as the soldier poured all of her remaining strength into a death blow.

The shade wobbled and staggered about before it fell to the ground. The soldier bees set upon it, stinging it repeatedly, but it responded to them no longer. A few moments after it fell, its body collapsed into a dissipating cloud of black mist.

Back in the apiary, Belissar kept staring at the vanishing mist with his eyes as wide as they could go.

"We . . . won?"

All hostiles defeated.
Minor purification successful.

CHAPTER TWENTY-THREE

BEE GRATEFUL

Belissar slowly closed his mouth. The shade may have seemed a bit smaller than the first, and never used the all-direction mist attack, but it also hadn't been particularly weak as far as Belissar could tell. It wasn't like he could have taken it by himself without the pit traps, after all.

And yet . . . the soldier bees had handled it. They'd taken it down with only a handful of losses. The shade had barely made it beyond the gate, even.

It took Belissar a moment to accept the situation.

Minor purification completed!
Please select a reward:
- +50 DP
- +10 Max Mana
- Monster Bee Soldier Strength Boost (Minimal)

But he was not dreaming. A shade of the Hunger had been defeated without needing the traps or fire at all. Belissar hadn't even lifted a finger. It was a tremendous victory.

"Bees win! King's hive best hive! King best king!"

Belissar couldn't help but smile as Niobee flew around him as fast as she could. The apiary bees all around began to buzz and zip through the air, performing quick and elaborate aerial dances as they celebrated the victory. He took a deep breath, relaxing his body as he exhaled it.

His choices hadn't been wrong. His bees could defend a Tower of the Gods, after all. He hadn't expected them to lose here, but to see the victory with his own eyes was still a relief. He really could call himself a tower lord now, without qualifiers. Well, he'd still appreciate a manual or guide of some sort, but as long as his bees were safe, he was content with how things were going.

That thought did bring a slight frown to Belissar's face. He glanced at the fallen bee soldiers on the ground, the wounded one who could no longer fly, and the remains of the one who had given her life to strike the critical blow. The victory had been great indeed, and with far less losses than Belissar had feared . . . but it had not come without sacrifice.

He nodded to himself and pushed aside the messages regarding rewards as he began to walk toward the flower meadow.

He had something to do, and all else could wait.

Belissar waited as the bees celebrated before he began his task. Once they had calmed down, he walked to the site of the battlefield. Picking up the wounded bee, he placed her on his shoulder, then gathered the remains of the fallen bee soldiers. Niobee flew over to him.

"King, what doing? That workers' job!"

Belissar shook his head. "They gave their lives for me. The least I can do is honor them."

Niobee shook about in the air. "Honor? What that?"

The rest of the bees watched Belissar as he gently held the remains in his arms, carrying them to the end of the flower meadow and laying them down by the shrine of bees. He then retrieved his axe, saw, and some wood, and got to work, digging a hole in the ground as best he could with what he had and placing the bees inside of it.

He knew that normal bees didn't seem overly concerned with their dead. The bees who died in the hive would be removed and dumped at a safe distance. The bees who died outside were simply left where they fell. He didn't know if monster bees did it differently, but Niobee's confusion seemed to confirm that they acted much the same. So, since they had no ceremonies of their own, Belissar simply did as he thought best.

He put the bees in the same hole, figuring they would have preferred to be together, before burying them back up and getting to work on the wood. He made a hexagonal honeycomb sculpture, carving some bees into it as best he could, before propping it up over the grave.

At this point, he was surrounded by bees. All of the queens had grown curious as to his actions and gathered from both the flower meadow and the apiary to watch. When he was finished, he turned to Niobee.

"Do you know who their queens were?"

"Will ask."

Niobee gathered with the queens, and then three of the flower meadow leaders flew over to Belissar, including the largest and oldest of the bunch.

"Do they have names? Or a way to call each other?"

Niobee flew unsteadily. "No name. We call by birth. This is First Queen of the First Spawner's Second Dynasty, Third Queen of Third Spawner's First Dynasty, and First Queen of Fourth Spawner's First Dynasty."

Belissar rubbed his chin and then nodded. Taking several planks of wood, he placed them by the sculpture, carving a set of numbers separated by dashes on each, corresponding to the numbers Niobee had stated. He then asked how many of the fallen belonged to each of the queens and carved a line for each into their respective planks.

Taking a deep breath, he rose to his feet and frowned for a moment, his heart beginning to pound. Belissar did not often think of the dead. What point was there in that? No matter what tears were shed or what words were spoken, the dead were gone, and that was that. It was unfortunate, but there was no sense dwelling on what could not be changed. The bees didn't bother with such things; they simply removed the corpses and kept at their work.

Belissar had tried to do the same.

But when he thought of his bees, who'd given their lives without hesitation or regret . . . he felt they did not deserve to simply be cast away and forgotten. He felt he had to do *something* for them.

So, he changed his mind. In the aftermath of the first purification, he had realized he hadn't moved on at all. That the thoughts of those he had lost still lingered inside him, as much as he tried to deny it. Even the very thought of them brought tears to his eyes, which was why he had done all he could not to think of them. Those thoughts now stabbed through his chest like a cold knife. Every muscle in his body tensed and told him to flee as the moisture built in his eyes.

But Belissar fixed his sight on the bees hovering before him and put aside his own discomfort. He would do this for them, at the very least.

He took the wounded bee soldier on his shoulder and gently placed her before the grave, then took a step back and faced her. He bowed his head.

"Thank you for your sacrifice. We won because of you. I won't forget that."

He didn't know what else to say or do. His parents hadn't even had a funeral, and he'd buried the old beekeeper himself. So, he simply stood in silence for a moment.

The wounded soldier squirmed a bit under Belissar's gaze while the rest of the bees hovered in the air, unsure of what to do.

Then, one of them began to move.

Niobee began to fly in a slow pattern, starting a new dance she had never done before. This was not something instinctive to her or taught to her by her colony. So, she slowly, unsteadily, mapped out the movements herself. She tried to match the dance to the feelings she could perceive from the King, making slow, graceful movements and beating her wings as softly as possible, yet keeping her course as straight and steady as she could.

Once Niobee completed her dance, she repeated it, now without the hesitation or doubt of her first attempt.

A slow, steady buzz rose in the air. The other bees began to follow her; first the queens of the flower meadow, then the soldiers, and then all the rest. The wounded soldier couldn't follow without her wings, but she beat her remaining pair along the rhythm of the others. The King turned and watched as the bees conducted their dance. He nodded at them as they concluded.

"Thank you all."

The bees buzzed in response.

The Firstborn trembled as the King's words vibrated through her chitin. Her mana stirred, filling her body with heat. A grand and mighty victory had been won this day. She had achieved all she had set out to do. The enemy had been defeated by the strength of their armies, felled by the sacrifice of one of her own soldiers.

The destruction of the First Dynasty had been repaid in full, and the bees had proven themselves worthy defenders to the King. If it had ended there, the Firstborn would have flown high for quite some time.

But the King had not been content with that. No, he had taken the fallen and carried them by his own hand. He'd begun a new construction; one that did not seem suited as either shelter or defense. The Firstborn had watched in confusion, uncertain as to the King's purposes here.

Until he'd called her. She stood before him as the Conduit reported her titles.

What happened next shook her from her antenna down to her stinger. The King carved *her own title* into a monument of his own design; one that stood next to the shrine of the Goddess herself, the Queen of All Bees who reigned in the skies above.

She did not know the symbols the King had carved, but the King's intent was coming through their bond, and she knew this one was supposed to represent her. He carved a symbol for each of her soldiers who had fallen in battle. He left an enduring mark that would remind all who saw it what her hive had sacrificed in the defense of her King.

The rest of the day passed in a blur for the Firstborn, even as she followed the Conduit's dance. It was not until night fell that she came to herself, even as her soldiers and workers began to tug her back to her hive. Feelings and emotions she couldn't describe surged through her, causing her wings to buzz.

Her hive all turned to her in alarm, and she began to dance rapidly as thoughts raced through her mind.

This would only be the beginning. They had defeated one invader, but more would come, and the Firstborn intended to be ready.

Nay, they would be more than ready. Her hive would build the finest army beekind had ever seen.

All for the King.

CHAPTER TWENTY-FOUR

BEE REWARDED

Belissar walked back toward the farmhouse once the ceremony was done. Niobee came and flew alongside him in silence. Once back inside, he exhaled his breath and sat down, and Niobee came and landed on his finger.

"King okay?"

Belissar gave her a soft smile. "Yes, it's just . . ." He took another deep breath and let it out slowly, glancing out the window. Thoughts of the lost passed through his mind, and he felt pain in his chest once again. "I'm remembering a lot of things. A lot of things I try not to think about."

Niobee looked up at him. "Niobee help?"

Belissar smiled and brushed her back with one of his fingers. "You already do. You already have."

He thought back to the past, to the days where he would talk and talk to the little bee drinking honey off his finger, saying all the things he couldn't tell anyone else. His heart grew warm as he remembered that said bee had been Niobee all along, and she really was his friend, just like he had imagined.

Niobee buzzed, and Belissar found himself chuckling. The painful memories were still there . . . but didn't feel as sharp anymore. Belissar shook his head and cleared his mind.

In any case, there was something more he could do now to protect his friend and his bees.

Minor purification completed!
Please select a reward:
- +50 DP
- +10 Max Mana
- Monster Bee Soldier Strength Boost (Minimal)

Another choice, another reward for a battle won. This one . . . didn't seem as dramatic as the last, all things considered, but Belissar didn't mind. He'd prefer an easy battle with minimal sacrifice to massive gains, so to him, it was good that the fight had been smaller this time around.

But the size of the rewards didn't mean he shouldn't put some thought into it.

"DP, mana, or a boost to the soldiers, huh? What do you think, Niobee?"

Niobee answered immediately. "Whatever King chooses!"

Belissar chuckled as she gave him the exact answer he'd been expecting, and then began to consider his choices. Fifty DP wasn't enough to really afford anything on its own, so felt a bit underwhelming. On the other hand, at one DP a day, that was fifty days' worth; when viewed that way, it would dramatically cut the time he needed to wait until he could afford something.

Ten max mana was small compared to his current two hundred; on the other hand, it alone was enough for another monster bee queen spawner, which would mean another four hives.

Finally, he could improve his soldier bees, giving them a bit of strength. It wasn't much, but every little bit would help.

Belissar rubbed his chin. He should also consider how all this had happened. The message that had first announced this battle had specifically stated that a minor purification was required because the ongoing purification limit had been reached.

The exact wording still confused Belissar, but it did shed some light on other questions he had. *Ongoing purification limit reached* meant that the ongoing purification had been . . . well, ongoing. So, perhaps that was something the tower did on its own, rather than being an attack by the Hunger like Belissar feared?

If he focused, he could still feel the Hunger at the edges of the tower's influence, reaching in toward the purified land beyond. So, maybe ongoing purification meant the tower holding it back?

If so . . . there was apparently a limit to which the tower could resist the Hunger, at which point Belissar was required to purify it more directly. That limit had apparently been a week—or ten days, if he included the countdown time, though Belissar didn't know yet if that was just for this time or a consistent thing.

But the important part was that the wording of all this implied that it would happen again. In fact, *ongoing purification* implied it would continue happening for as long as the tower needed to resist the Hunger. Battles were going to come consistently . . . and if he continued to win them, so would the rewards.

That made this choice all the more important. What would best defend his bees in perpetuity? The soldier boost would obviously improve their ability to fight. The max mana would allow for more bees or more traps. But, if he were going to be facing one of these minor purifications every ten days, then he could also take the DP and try to save up for a bigger purchase.

Maybe he could get a deadlier trap, or a new bee type which would let his bees fight and win with no losses at all . . . if he were willing to let them handle things for the time it took to get to that stage.

Belissar thought for a bit then made his choice. At this stage, he knew that overthinking it would get him nowhere. So, if nothing he knew would inform his choice one way or another, he'd follow his gut.

Monster Bee Soldier Strength Boost (Minimal) selected.
Monster Bee Soldiers receive a slight boost to strength!

What settled things for him this time was the memory of the soldier bees themselves. Several of them had given their lives to earn this victory, and Belissar wanted to reward them for their efforts. Maybe he couldn't make that choice every time; maybe he'd need to save up DP later or expand his mana. But today, for this first choice, he felt it was appropriate to grant the boon to the ones who had earned it.

Belissar nodded, satisfied, then headed off to bed.

The next day, Belissar took a bit of time to think as he munched on a bit of honeycomb. He would have to keep track of the days to confirm, but he figured he should assume another minor purification was coming in a week or so. So, he figured he should consider how to use that time.

All in all, the defense had gone very well, and no major weaknesses had been revealed. The death of soldier bees was regrettable to Belissar, but he was aware he was being a bit silly. Regular bees died all the time; sacrificing themselves was their main form of defense, he reminded himself. So, he should not let the death of a handful detract from their victory. The hives of the flower meadow had proven capable of handling shades with their soldiers, and their numbers would only grow.

In the end, Belissar couldn't think of anything he specifically needed to do to prepare for the next minor purification besides ensuring the flower meadow hives were taken care of. He *had* noticed the apiary queens donating honey to them during the preparations, so he may need to check on them. The soldier bees didn't seem to do much nectar gathering, after all.

Belissar himself returned to his task from before the minor purification was announced. The God of Bees had given him a mission, after all, and he was one beehouse away from completing it. And now that he had confirmed his defenses were solid, he had no reason not to finish it up.

Belissar watched as the final apiary beehive converted to one of his own.

Mission "Upgrade all Apiary Beehives to Belissar's Beehouses" completed!
Reward: One room feature selection.

Please select a room feature:
- Basic Resource Plants (Rarity: Common. Type: Nature, Resource.)
- Beehive (Rarity: Uncommon. Type: Bee, Resource, Monster Nest.)
- Hidden Wax Cell (Rarity: Common. Type: Bee, Trap.)

He smiled as the queen of that hive began a dance of gratitude and joy. "Enjoy."

She repeated her happy dance before climbing inside to resume her work. Belissar then walked back through the apiary, gathering some mana honeycomb trays from the other beehouses. The lids would pop up slightly whenever one was ready. When Belissar lifted the lid, the tray would slide itself up, and a rectangular piece of honeycomb would pop right out.

Belissar didn't know exactly how all that worked; he knew for sure that his roughly constructed trays didn't slide that easily. And he also knew that normal bees would not be producing this much honey. The Tower of the Gods was powerful indeed.

Which is why he thought carefully about the choice before him as he gathered the honeycomb. He reviewed each option in turn, hoping for more information.

<u>Basic Resource Plants</u>

> **Type:**   *Nature, Resource*
> **Mana Upkeep:**   *Depends on resource selected.*
> *A spot where resource-producing plants can be easily grown and harvested. Compatible plants will depend on the room. Existing compatible plants may be converted to nodes.*

Belissar hummed as he read it over. He was a bit worried that the description didn't specify what kind of plants or resources he would get. In fact, that would apparently change based on what room he placed it in . . . though he wasn't certain that the flower meadow and the apiary would be much different, given they had very similar plants to begin with.

But depending on what he got, plant-based resources could be very useful. If he got something appropriate for textiles, he could fix his tunic or make a new one. If he got more wood, then he could expand his construction efforts and prepare more firepits. Medicinal herbs would be a priority as well . . . though he wasn't sure if tower lords or monster bees could actually get sick.

Fruit and vegetables wouldn't change much beyond adding variety to his diet, given that he didn't seem to actually need food after becoming a tower lord. However, they would, at minimum, add more flowering plants for his bees to gather from. No matter what plants he received, he knew it wouldn't be a loss.

Still, there were two more options to consider.

Beehive

Type: *Bee, Resource, Monster Nest*
Mana Upkeep: *5 per hive. (2 with Blessing of Bees)*
A hive where bees and bee monsters may build their colonies.
Produces honeycomb at a steady rate, and boosts productivity and growth of any bees dwelling inside.

Belissar furrowed his brow. It seemed by all accounts to be the same basket hives as he'd found in the apiary, so Belissar knew what to expect and how useful they would be. The apiary had nine beehouses at present, while he had eight monster bee queen spawners that would spawn four monster bee queens each, so the other queens would certainly be happy if he had some more hives.

The question was, how would it work with the apiary? At present, Belissar couldn't actually change the number of beehives, so would this choice allow for that? He guessed that it would; it didn't seem a useful choice if not.

Well, assuming it did, there were clear reasons to take this choice. But . . . it wasn't as clear-cut as the choice might seem. Belissar could build beehouses himself, after all, and was planning to do so for the other queens as time permitted, so he tried to focus on what the tower option would provide on top of that—which was the magical daily production of honeycomb, and the boost to productivity and growth.

The growth seemed a bit subtle at the moment, while the productivity just meant more honey. That could help with more sticky honey traps, but Belissar hadn't even seen one of those in action yet.

He shook his head and moved on to the final choice.

Hidden Wax Cell

Type: *Bee, Trap*
Mana Upkeep: *1 per cell. (0.5 with Blessing of Bees)*
A camouflaged cell a monster bee may ambush foes from.
Can resize to fit larger monster bee species.

This was a more direct combat option. Belissar tried to imagine what it might look like. Perhaps soldier bees stinging a shade's feet while their sisters buzzed above it? That could be useful, though it seemed a bit straight forward. Besides, couldn't the monster bee soldiers wait inside one of the pit traps? Or couldn't he dig them some holes to do the same thing? Well, it *was* a cheaper option in terms of mana upkeep, so perhaps that was by design.

Belissar continued to look over the options as he carried the honeycomb inside the farmhouse.

CHAPTER TWENTY-FIVE

BEE RESOURCEFUL!

Basic Resource Plants selected.

Belissar didn't have much trouble with this decision, for once. Hidden wax traps just weren't impactful enough, especially since the monster bee soldiers were able to handle shades on their own.

Beehives were tempting, but weren't a priority at the moment. He already had plenty of honey production, and honeycomb was beginning to accumulate in the farmhouse's storage jars, even. The slight boost in brood growth would have been useful, but the flower meadow hives had already developed to the point of producing soldiers, while the apiary already had a bunch of beehouses. More of them just meant more of what he already had.

All in all, Belissar figured that the extra and possibly new resources would be the most beneficial to both him and the bees. More resources would increase the things Belissar could make, and thus expand his contributions to the tower.

More plants meant more flowers and more nectar for the bees to gather, which might end up being necessary before expanding the hives, in any case. The donation of honey from the apiary hives to the meadow ones implied there had been a shortfall, after all. He had been worried about that, but fortunately, the meadow queens were birthing more workers now, so hopefully, that wouldn't be an issue going forward.

With his choice made, Belissar focused on the flower meadow. As he did, he noticed several spots shining across the field. Focusing on those, he found they were the mana flowers.

Compatible plant: Mana Flower.
Upgrade to resource plant node?
Mana Upkeep: 5 per Mana Flower node.

Belissar nearly confirmed immediately. The bees loved those, and Niobee had informed him they had been crucial for the development of the meadow hives. But he figured he should hold on, at least until he checked out what else he could do. After all, each node cost more than enabling them for the entire field, and the same amount as the meadow itself, so it wasn't the cheapest thing for sure.

He double-checked his available mana.

Mana: 58/200

Enabling mana flowers for the meadow and adding the two soldier bee spawners in the apiary had cut it a bit. He certainly had enough to add some mana flower nodes, but he could find himself out of free mana if he spent it haphazardly. So, he took a look to see what other resource nodes he could add.

Available resource plants for Flower Meadow:
- Basic Healing Herbs (Mana Upkeep: 3 per node.)
- Basic Poisonous Flowers (Mana Upkeep: 3 per node.)
- Basic Textile Flowers (Mana Upkeep: 3 per node.)
- Mana Flower (Mana Upkeep: 5 per node.)

Belissar smiled. It turned out resource plants not only had one but nearly all of the different resources he had guessed, plus a few more. He could gain access to both medicine and textiles with the right nodes. Poisonous flowers also made sense, since quite a few common flowers could be toxic.

Belissar wasn't as versed in the ways of poison, nor did he have any of the tools necessary to handle and process it, but if he *did* manage to figure something out, the flowers could represent another weapon to use against the Hunger. Presuming poison actually worked on shades. The bee stings seemed to hurt them, so Belissar figured it may be worth a shot.

Worse came to worst, poisonous flowers were still flowers, and Belissar had observed bees gathering nectar from them the same as any other in the past.

And that was only for the flower meadow.

Available resource plants for Apiary:
- Basic Healing Herbs (Mana Upkeep: 3 per node.)
- Basic Poisonous Flowers (Mana Upkeep: 3 per node.)
- Mana Flower (Mana Upkeep: 5 per node.)

Belissar tilted his head at that. Seemed there wasn't anything new for the apiary. Less options, even, as textile flowers weren't available there. But he just shrugged. It made sense that a flower meadow would have more plant options than an apiary, he supposed. Bees seemed to like most flowering plants, after all, so perhaps there wasn't anything particularly unique to the apiary itself?

But it was no matter, for the meadow options were more than enough. All in all, this had been an excellent purchase. Now, he just needed to figure out how many of each he wanted.

Belissar finally decided he would test one of each node in both of the rooms. He also enabled mana flowers for the apiary, leaving him with thirty mana available when it was all said and done.

He figured the bees of both rooms would appreciate the extra blooms, and doubling up on healing herbs and poisonous flowers could prove useful if he needed medicine or poison stockpiles in the future. He was fine with one textile node for now, since he was the only person in the tower who could actually make use of it.

He placed the nodes in both rooms near the hives and spawners so the bees would have quick trips to each, then watched with interest as circles of light began to glow on the ground, followed by new plants going from brand-new shoots to fully bloomed flowers in seconds. His eyes went wide as he watched the display of the tower's power once again; it was still an incredible thing to see.

Walking out of the farmhouse over to the apiary nodes, he stood and stared as he saw the small patches of flowers that had just grown out of nothing. It was even more impressive when viewed from the ground with his own eyes.

The mana flower node was particularly impressive. A lone mana flower was a subtle thing that blended in with the flowers around it, but it was different when a bunch of them gathered together. Their subtle glow combined into a greater whole, creating little shimmers of light like the twinkling stars in the sky, or like the sun reflecting off a flowing river.

Belissar walked over to the node, feeling the warmth of mana suffusing the area around it. The apiary bees swarmed around the node yet remained at a distance from it. Belissar smiled at the sight.

"Go ahead. I made it for you all."

The bees buzzed and danced in gratitude before swarming over the flowers. Belissar chuckled and left them to it as he looked over the other two nodes.

The healing herb node was leafy green with slight blue undertones; Belissar felt it could be easily overlooked with all the flowers around it. Meanwhile, the poisonous flower node was mostly bright purple and very much stood out. Both contained a few different species, including some Belissar didn't immediately recognize. He nodded in approval and walked over to the healing herbs.

Noticing some of them seemed to be glowing slightly, he reached out to touch them. He'd only touched them lightly, but they pulled out of the soil with hardly any effort, almost removing themselves. Belissar glanced at the herb now in his hand and rubbed his chin. The apiary beehives also pushed honeycomb out to where it would be easily harvested, even before they had bees or the beehouse trays, so Belissar guessed this was similar.

"Well, that's convenient. Should help with the textiles, I hope."

He wasn't looking forward to trying to process and weave fabric completely by hand, after all. In any case, he left the nonglowing herbs for the bees, nodding at them so they wouldn't hesitate to visit the new flowers, then made his way to the flower meadow. He smirked slightly to himself as he thought that the bees were probably waiting for him there too.

His smirk only grew as he stepped into the meadow and found the bees hovering around the new nodes exactly as he'd thought. Shaking his head and chuckling as he walked over to them, he gave them permission to gather. He chuckled some more as he watched them swarm over the new flowers. It turned out *monster bees* were the politest people he had ever known.

In any case, he made his way to the textile plant node. He found a bunch of flax flowers there, several of which were glowing. He went ahead and harvested them . . . and sighed. The plants pulled off all as one piece, which meant it was up to Belissar and his bare handful of tools to process them into useful fibers.

He shook his head. He supposed it was technically better this way, as the seeds and other parts of the plants could be useful as well, but this was a job he'd never particularly enjoyed.

Still, he *would* enjoy having an undamaged tunic, so he set about harvesting what he could before taking them back to the apiary. The sooner he got started, the sooner he'd get it over with.

Still, he couldn't help but grin as he walked past the other nodes and saw clouds of bees flying to and from the new flowers. He supposed he should take on the new work as enthusiastically as they were.

THE FAVOR OF THE KING

The Firstborn of the Fifth Spawner's First Dynasty, the first of her line, paced about after laying another egg. She was . . . troubled by recent events.

She was the favored of the King, that was the truth. He had granted her ruler-ship of a magical palace just beyond the gates of his own abode. She was the first of the queens to offer him tribute, each and every day. It was the honey of her children that graced his table. And she was the queen he greeted personally on a daily basis.

She had also been the first to receive his blessing. He'd crafted for her a hive with his very own hands, turning towering trees into a dwelling without equal. When he'd finished, he'd inspected her brood personally to ensure their safety and comfort. Ultimately, he had not been satisfied and spawned guards of his own, tasked with the defense of his favored queens.

She was truly the most favored of all beekind. The first queen, above all others. Well, the Conduit had the honor of serving the King directly and speaking with his voice, but in the end, she was not a queen. The Conduit was the King's worker, and the First of the Fifth was his queen, and the queen knew which was preferable.

And yet . . . she had recently learned of troubling developments.

The queens of the First through Fourth Spawners were not like her, or any of her siblings and peers. They were simple; barbaric, even. They lived on the out-skirts far beyond the King's abode, at the very edges of his domain, right at the very edge of the beyond. They lived in humble hives of their own make, blessed not by the constructions of the King. They dwelled not within his sight. They rarely offered tribute; he never dined upon their labor.

And it was only natural. They produced the barest fraction of even the least of the apiary queens. They barely produced enough honey to feed themselves! And moreover, four of them bore the title of the Second Dynasty. A declaration of shame; a reminder that it was the bees of their spawner who had failed to defend the King and perished in vain.

And to make it worse, those of the First through Fourth Spawners had been present for the Second Invasion. It was said that the King had fought personally in that dreadful time and slain the invader with his own hand. A testament to the might of the King . . . and to the weakness of all the queens that lived then.

Where were their hives when the King was threatened? Where were their armies when the invader assaulted his realm? It was little wonder they had been cast from the King's sight, exiled to the outskirts of his domain.

Or so the First of the Fifth had thought.

That the queens of the flower meadow had produced soldier bees was known to the First of the Fifth. She had assumed this was a desperate act of necessity. Those who were not blessed with the protection of the King had to fend for themselves. It was yet another sign of their impoverishment.

The First of the Fifth would admit the soldiers were an impressive sight . . . but a wasteful one. They could not gather nectar. They could not process honey. They could not take care of the brood. They were nothing but a drain upon their colony; they consumed that which should be offered to the King. The First of the Fifth would not make that mistake.

And she was proven right. Word of the Third Invasion came . . . and the bees of the flower meadow were utterly unprepared. In their panic to boost their defenses, their meager stores had run dry long before the invader was due to arrive. They would have starved had the Conduit not convinced the First of the Fifth to offer charity.

It was only by her grace that they'd survived, for it would not do for any claimed by the King to perish without his command. And as she'd opened the endless stores of her hive and let the honey flow, she'd demonstrated once and for all the diligence and strength of her offspring, the reason why she was the favored queen.

But it was when her workers returned that she first began to doubt. She had not bothered to scout the outer realm, for why would she? Surely there was little there that would matter to her, the one who dwelled in the abundance of the King's own home. Surely the impoverished queens there required every meager scrap they could find; it was beneath her to take what little they could scrounge up.

But the reports of her workers told a different story. They spoke of a land of plenty; flowers as far as the eye could see. And worse . . . they spoke of a treasure beyond imagining. Mana flowers whose nectar overflowed with power, that did not require the mana of the workers to produce honey suitable for the brood.

The First of the Fifth had been confused by this. A treasure such as that should have enabled any competent queen to match—or maybe even *surpass*—her own brood. They should have been capable of fielding an endless tide of workers, and with the abundant fields her workers reported, they should have been able to construct truly grand hives.

She did not believe that even those disgraced queens would be so incompetent as to starve when they had access to such a treasure. She assumed they had warred among themselves for control of it . . . but the reports indicated their broods were working together. Cooperating in a way no rival queens ever should.

Even the First of the Fifth had to wonder . . . had the King truly exiled them into a place of such abundance?

And then came the battle. The First of the Fifth had had her scouts observe. They'd returned and gushed with fantastic tales of giant bee warriors flying circles around a monster more terrible than even the spider or the hornet. The creature had been felled before it even reached any of the King's defenses. The armies of the flower meadow queens had stopped it all on their own.

And then came the ceremony, where the King had gathered the fallen with his own hands and given what he called "honor" to them. He'd carved the titles of the flower meadow queens into towering monuments. He'd carried a wounded soldier on his own shoulder.

The First of the Fifth was despondent at this. The exiled ones had received those so-called honors that even she, the favored queen, had not. The strength of their arms and the gratitude they had earned called into question all she had ever known. At best, the queens of the flower meadows had redeemed themselves and more in the eyes of the King. Perhaps they would even be welcomed back into his abode.

At worst . . . she was wrong about their exile in the first place. Perhaps they did not dwell in the outskirts because the King was disappointed in them . . . but because he trusted them the most. Because he believed that they could defend themselves; a trust they had fulfilled. Why else would he grant them such grand treasures such as the mana flowers? Why else would he show them such favor when it was all said and done?

Had she been wrong all along? Did the King care more about stingers than honey? Was she kept near to him not because she was favored . . . but because she was weak? Untrustworthy?

The First of the Fifth could not remain still. She paced about every moment she was awake, even as her workers tried to calm her. But how could she be calm? All that she had worked for, all that she had built, may have been for naught if she had misunderstood so greatly!

That is, until she felt it. The rumblings in the ground and sky, the mana of the King stirring to create wonders. She flew out of her hive, wishing to see what had occurred with her own eyes. And what she saw did not disappoint.

A glowing field of flowers stretched out before her. Countless mana flowers grew before her, nothing like the lone blossom here or there the meadow queens scrounged from. No, there were so many of them, their mana began to coalesce and shimmer in the air.

This . . . This was an abundance an entire dynasty could be built upon. She glanced at the King. Before, she would have had no question as to his intent to favor her. But now, she could not help the creeping doubt. Was this a boon for them? Or did the King have other intentions with all this she could not see?

But he smiled at her, a sight that brightened the world like the dawn.

"Go ahead. I made it for you all."

The First of the Fifth nearly fell from the sky as she ordered her hive to swarm upon the flowers below.

Shortly thereafter, the First of the Fifth watched as her workers filled row after row of wax cells with glistening honey. She danced about happily as she drank from the honey packed to the brim with mana and felt her own reserves grow.

She had not been wrong. She was truly the favored of the King. She saw now his wisdom, the intent of his designs. She was the favored . . . and that meant that she was precious. She had to be protected. So, the King had grown the flower meadow queens such that they might sacrifice in her defense. And he'd tested the mana flowers upon them to ensure the gift was suitable for her.

Once he had, he had granted her an abundance of the treasures beyond the meadow queens' wildest dreams.

And that wasn't all. He had also created fields of new flowers; types the queen had never seen. And as her workers processed the nectar from these new plants, she found the honey they produced possessed new and mysterious qualities; types entirely unlike the honey they had produced before now.

As she had expected, it was honey that ruled all. The King wanted her to expand her production in ways never before conceived. And he had granted them an overabundance of the mana flowers so that she would have as many workers as she needed to do it.

Her wings buzzed as she looked over the different trays, each possessing honey made from a different source.

She truly was favored above all. She would go forth and work without doubts from now on, confident that she, more than any other, understood the King.

. . . At least until the scouts returned with reports that the King had done the same thing in the flower meadow.

CHAPTER TWENTY-SIX

YOU'LL BEE GOING MAD!

The next few days were a bit of a grind for Belissar.

First, he had to separate all the different parts of the flax from each other. He stored the seeds, since they could be processed into linseed oil, which could have uses in his woodworking and his fire traps, or even in his diet if he had surplus.

Then he had to separate the useful fibers from the straw and inner pitch. Both were steps that were noticeably difficult for a lone person who lacked the normal tools one might use for the job. The little scrapes and scratches he got processing the flax with his hands also did not improve his opinion of the task. And when that was done, it would have to be retted and dried and scutched . . .

Belissar was starting to feel that the cuts in his tunic weren't that big a deal, after all. He may not have had many fond memories of his neighbors . . . but he *did* miss being able to trade wax and mead for already processed cloth.

He broke up the monotony with some construction planning. He may have skipped out on beehives as a room feature, but he still wanted to build some for the queens who didn't have them yet. The apiary itself had more queens than bee-houses now that its spawners had filled up to their max, and none of the flower meadow queens had a beehouse at all. The only reason he hadn't gotten started was that he was still thinking about modifications to the design.

The meadow queens, after all, were no normal bees at this point. The queens and the soldiers were far larger than any mundane bee could ever grow to be. At the very minimum, Belissar would need to build the houses far larger to accommodate both the existing soldiers and any future growth.

And beyond that, there was the question of purpose. Belissar's current beehouses were a tool for a beekeeper. The trays made it easy for him to gather honeycomb from the hive or to check on the status of the bees. That was helpful for the apiary beehives, which were designed with that same purpose in mind.

But the flower meadow colonies were different. Their focus was on defense, not honey production. So the question was, how could Belissar adjust his beehouses to support them? Should he try to make them less accessible and more defensible? Did they even need trays and removable lids? Did they even need a beehouse at all?

All Belissar knew at this stage was that he didn't want to make the standard hives for them, but working out the details was slow going. He was no castle builder, and defensible beehouses went against the very idea of beehouses in the first place, so he was charting out new territory here in more ways than one.

But one thing he could distract himself with—or rather, work on right away—was a fence for the entrance. The bees had proven they could handle a shade alone, but there was no reason not to make use of all those traps he'd bought. If he could make a tall fence leading directly to the first pit trap, they could handle shades without putting anyone at risk at all.

Belissar tried to process some larger branches and smaller tree trunks into tall stakes, and plant them in the ground. He figured he needed something a bit more substantial, as a shade would probably just jump over a smaller fence.

It was . . . not working particularly well, if he was entirely honest. Digging a deep enough hole with a small enough diameter was proving difficult for a solo worker who lacked any sort of digging tools. And then there was the matter of getting those holes close enough to form a useful barrier. He even tried using the pit traps, but even their smallest size was still too large for this case. He couldn't put them close to the entrance either.

So, Belissar was left back at his flax processing for the most part. That is, until one morning when he went to gather the honeycomb. He found the queen of the closest hive waiting for him at the entrance of her beehouse. She did a little dance of greeting once he approached, and he tilted his head.

"You want to show me something?"

She signaled yes and flew up to the lid of the beehouse. Belissar opened it and pulled out the trays that were ready for harvest. He normally just took one a day from each hive. Even with his daily offerings to the God of Bees, he scarcely needed nine trays of honeycomb every day, much less more, but figured he should clear the way so they could keep making more, at the very least.

But this time, the queen seemed to want him to take all of them, so he did.

The first tray was a tray of mana honeycomb as usual . . . but something seemed different. The mana concentration in the honey was unlike any Belissar had seen before, to the point that the tray felt warm to the touch. Belissar thought for a moment before realizing this honey must have been made with nectar from the mana flowers.

And that gave him a clue as to what the other two might be. He reached out for one of them that had a slightly green-and-blue tint to it. He was surprised, however, when he picked it up and words appeared before him.

Healing Herb Mana Honeycomb Tray

*A tray of honeycomb containing Healing Herb Mana Honey. Made by monster
bees with the nectar of healing herbs, this honey has a slight medicinal
and healing effect.*

He knew honey had some medicinal qualities to it, but this was something
else. Mana honey with a slight healing effect? If Belissar didn't know any better,
he'd say that sounded like one of those healing potions from the stories. The healing potions supposed to be poisonous if drank by anyone not blessed by the gods,
and that could only be the product of foul magics otherwise.

But, well, Belissar *had* been blessed by one of the gods. He could feel the mana
inside the honey, so he knew it was magical in every definition of the word. So
perhaps the stories weren't so far-fetched, after all. If so, he could be holding an
actual treasure in his hand. Something that could heal wounds in an instant before
his very eyes, or even restore lost limbs and mortal blows.

Well, the word "slight" seemed to imply the effects might be a bit more muted
than in the stories, but Belissar would be glad to have something like this available regardless.

He had one final tray left to check; one with a slight purple tint to it. At this
point, he had a pretty good idea of what it was.

Mad Mana Honey Honeycomb Tray

*A tray of honeycomb containing Mad Mana Honey. Made by monster bees with
the nectar of toxic flowers, this honey has accumulated a significant concentration
of neurotoxins.*

*Causes intoxication and hallucinogenic effects when consumed. In excessive
quantities may cause paralysis as well.*

Belissar nodded. As he thought, this was the honey produced from the poisonous flowers. The old beekeeper had told him stories of mad honey, though he
never thought he might encounter it himself. He decided to be very careful with
where he left this tray.

He looked at the queen, who was hovering in the air and staring at him, and
smiled at her.

"Great work; this is amazing."

She froze, dipping as her wings stopped beating for a second, then she began
to fly around rapidly before rushing back into the beehouse. Belissar chuckled
and took the trays. He kept the mana honeycomb inside the house, then took the
healing herb and mad honey trays with him.

He had some ideas he wanted to try.

Sticky Mad Honey Trap

Type: *Bee, Trap*
Honey Equipped: *Mad Mana Honey*
Mana Upkeep: *3 (1 if honey is provided)*

Spreads sticky honey onto a target or area, hindering target's mobility.
Upkeep reduced if dungeon has a source of honey. Effects may vary with type of honey.

Currently equipped with Mad Mana Honey; may cause intoxication, hallucination, or even paralysis if ingested or contacted for too long.

Belissar smiled as he confirmed his idea would work. When he'd brought the mad mana honey to one of the pit traps, he'd gotten an option to add it to the sticky honey trap installed at the bottom. It would add an extra layer of defense to the trap, though it'd consumed an entire tray of the honey. Belissar would have to get to work installing it on the rest.

After that, he took the healing herb honeycomb to the flower meadow, where he found the wounded monster bee soldier standing by the entrance to her hive, unable to participate in the drills of her flying sisters. She began a dance of salute as Belissar approached, who smiled and let her finish before holding out the honeycomb.

"Here, try some of this."

The soldier bee froze and stood still for a moment, just staring up at Belissar. Then . . . she slowly began to crawl forward. She gently extended her mouth and took a small sip as Belissar chuckled.

"Go ahead and drink up."

She continued drinking slowly but did as Belissar said until a bunch of the cells were empty.

"How's that? Feel anything?"

The bee paused for a second before dancing a hesitant no. Belissar watched her for a minute, but nothing changed, and her lost wings did not regrow. He let out a soft sigh.

"Well, it was worth a shot. Let me know if you feel anything or want some more."

The bee danced a slow salute to him before he began walking back to the apiary. It seemed the healing herb honey wasn't exactly the limb-restoring potion of the stories, but it was better to have it than not.

With that, he had nothing pressing left to do, and so slowly returned to the flax processing.

CHAPTER TWENTY-SEVEN

BEE HONEY TRAPPED

Belissar sighed as he checked the first set of flax he had prepped. Retting was slow going given the lack of water in his tower. There *was* some dew in the morning, and the flowers were clearly getting watered *somehow*, but there were no bodies of water he could leave the flax in. Drying them afterward would likewise take a while since the only thing he could do was leave it out in the sun.

So, the first set he had prepped wasn't ready for further processing yet. Which meant his task today would be . . . prepping more batches. Yet another day of picking apart the stems and leaves and seeds by hand. Belissar heaved another sigh.

But there was nothing for it. The textile plant node produced more flax each day, and since Belissar would prefer not to wait for this entire process every time he needed fabric, he needed to at least build up a decent stockpile, which meant he had no choice but to keep at it.

He couldn't help but wonder if other tower lords went through all this.

Fortunately for Belissar, however, something was about to change.

Ongoing purification limit reached. Minor purification required.
Minor purification attempt in 3 days.

It hadn't exactly been a week since the last time, but close enough, apparently. Belissar smiled and leapt up . . . before frowning and shaking his head.

Right, a purification attempt meant a battle, which meant more of his bees would likely perish. It was not a happy thing. That he would have to put aside his flax work to prepare for the fight was a small silver lining, but he'd rather do flax work the rest of his life than see his bees come to harm.

But he didn't have that choice, so he'd just have to put aside his other tasks and focus on keeping the tower safe.

*

Belissar went around checking the various defenses, prepping the pit trap closest to the gate with wood and kindling. He had not done so last time to give the soldier bees their chance to fight, but now that they had proven they could do so, there was no reason not to use every tool at his disposal. He also prepared a campfire site by the front and stuck some extra torches into the ground around it.

He was going to upgrade the sticky honey traps with more mad mana honey, but found his bees had already started doing that. It turned out they could ferry the honey directly to the traps and had started doing so after they'd seen him upgrade the first one. And here Belissar had wondered why they hadn't produced many mad honey trays since then.

So, after that, his task was largely complete. Belissar crossed his arms and hummed.

The soldier bee army continued to train, and their numbers had even grown since last time. Not as dramatically—it turned out the flower meadow queens had cut workers and run into problems as a result, so they'd dialed it back a bit—but still, the army was even stronger than it had been during the last purification. In all honesty, Belissar was pretty sure they'd be able to handle it without issue.

The pit traps by the flower meadow hives and the apiary entrance were already stocked and ready. Belissar could prep more of them, but the others were scattered about the flower meadow at random. Belissar could certainly stock them with kindling and wood, but building a campfire next to each was of questionable benefit. After all, Belissar couldn't light and manage more than one or two fires at a time and didn't want to risk burning the field down by leaving one unattended.

He *could* work on the entrance fence, but that still wasn't going well, and Belissar didn't think he could make meaningful progress on it in the next three days.

He nodded to himself. Yep. Nothing he could think of would make a significant difference in the next three days. If the bees could handle a shade right in the entrance, then nothing further in felt that important.

Belissar shook his head and then got to work gathering kindling and firewood. Even if prepping the other pit traps wasn't all that helpful, it was something, and it was better to have them ready than not. Besides, it beat another day of picking apart flax.

Minor purification attempt in 2 days, 1 hour, and 12 minutes.

Filling up the rest of the pit traps took Belissar all of . . . one day.

He crossed his arms, tapped his foot, and hummed before sighing. Yep, there wasn't much left for him to do at this stage, so he guessed he would just have to work on flax again for the next two days.

It felt wrong to do something else with an attack incoming. He wondered if there was anything he could do about that . . .

Begin minor purification immediately?

Belissar shook his head to deny the question, then smiled. Looked like the countdown was a maximum time, not a minimum.

And so, Belissar did nothing. He returned to the farmhouse and resumed work on the flax.

His preparations might be done, but his bees still had more they could do. Each day meant another day of training for the soldier bees, and so reduced the chance they would be caught by the shade. Each day meant more soldier bees born, and so a greater advantage for the army.

Belissar may have wanted to get it over with for himself, but he would not deny his bees any advantage he could grant them. He was not the one who had to fight the shade, after all.

Therefore, he put aside his restlessness and tried his best to focus on his task as he waited for the countdown to finish.

Two days later, Belissar once again stood by a roaring flame next to the apiary entrance, holding a torch in his hand. The soldier bees were assembled in the sky above the gateway, waiting as the last few minutes passed.

Minor purification attempt commencing.

Another shade formed again, this one the same size as the one from the minor purification before it. And once again, a squad of soldier bees dove down and stung it, all of them hitting their mark. The creature roared and snapped at them as predicted, but again, the soldier bees flew just out of its reach.

But this time, no second wave came.

Instead, the first squad paced their retreat, flying close to the ground and just outside the range of the shade's tail and jaws. The monster snarled and ran after them, pouncing and whipping its tail around to try and catch the bees buzzing around it, but the four soldiers dodged and weaved together, passing each other by in different directions and confusing the shade's aim.

Still, the storm of fang and claw and sharp tail meant the single squad couldn't launch any attacks of their own, giving up ground as they were forced to retreat back.

And that was exactly the plan. Suddenly, the creature yelped as the ground vanished beneath it. It fell into the pit trap with a crash, and then sticky honey with a slightly purple tint sprayed all over it from a nozzle in the wall. Belissar smirked.

He wanted to test the effectiveness of the pit trap and sticky honey combo, so he'd asked the bees to adjust their strategy this time. The bees had been tasked with luring the beast onto the nearest trap, and they had succeeded. The rest of the soldiers now sprang into action and began hovering around the pit while Belissar himself lit the torch in his hand and began running forward.

Even as the monster was collecting itself, another squad of bees dove into the pit and stung its back. The shade roared and swiped its tail at them, but the honey had stuck it to the ground. It only took a moment for the beast to break its tail free, but that moment was more than enough for the bees to have escaped.

The tail strike was slow as well, weighed down by the honey and kindling stuck to it, so the next squad of bees had little issue evading and striking their mark as well. The shade thrashed about, but it couldn't reach the honey stuck to its sides.

So, it took a deep breath instead.

The next squad of bees prepared to scatter before noticing the walls of the pit trap all around them. They had no choice but to fly straight up at maximum speed as a cloud of black mist filled the trap.

Belissar frowned.

That was not something he or the bees had thought of. The confined space was working against them now. The bees couldn't approach as long as the black mist was present.

But that was fine.

The black mist began to dissipate as the shade began to stagger and sway. Belissar figured that was the mad mana honey getting to work. Between the height of the pit, the intoxication from the mad honey, and the extra weight of kindling stuck all over, the shade wasn't climbing out of the pit anytime soon. In fact, it wasn't even trying, perhaps realizing that the bees couldn't attack it down there.

What it did not account for was Belissar arriving and tossing his torch inside, lighting the whole trap up.

All hostiles defeated.
Minor purification successful.

Belissar smiled as the words appeared before his eyes. Another shade handled, and this time, with zero bee casualties. Exactly as planned.

He was starting to get the hang of this tower lord business.

CHAPTER TWENTY-EIGHT

TO BEE FAVORED

Minor purification completed!
Please select a reward:
- +50 DP
- +10 Max Mana
- Dirt Trail minor room feature

Belissar nodded as he looked things over. He didn't need long to make his choice this time either.

+10 Max Mana selected.
Max mana increased by 10 to 210!

At the end of the day, Belissar felt mana was pretty important. More mana meant more spawners, more traps, and more resource nodes. That meant more hives, more flowers for them to gather from, and more defenses to keep them safe. Even if he got something with DP, he'd probably need mana to actually implement it. Besides, he was gaining DP each day, if extremely slowly, while his mana was staying the same.

A new room feature was interesting, but dirt trails didn't seem that impactful. After all, his bees could fly, so he and the shades were the only things walking around the tower. Well, there was the wounded soldier, but she stood guard by her hive most of the time, and so wasn't making long trips in the first place. All in all, it wasn't something Belissar needed right now, so he took the extra mana instead.

With that settled and a celebratory dance by the bees underway, the second minor purification came to a close.

*

The First of the Fifth danced and buzzed as she climbed through her hive. Things were finally looking up again.

She would admit, if only after significant prompting by her workers, that she had not been at her best recently. The truth had unfortunately been undeniable. The King considered the flower meadow queens to be on par with those of the apiary and cared for them as deeply as any other. They had not been exiled, and proximity to the King's abode was not the defining metric of his favor.

So, she had been . . . *distracted* by the idea that her daily tribute to the King's meals was not proof of any special favor. Or the unspeakable idea that her tributes of honey might even be considered less vital than the defense of the King's realm. After all, when word of the next invasion had come, the King had put aside all other tasks to secure the defense. Would that not then mean that the most favored queens in his sight were those who contributed most to that defense?

The First of the Fifth may have consumed more honey than usual as that thought passed through her mind. But now, all was returning to what it should be.

The true wisdom of the King's gifts had been revealed, and it was the First of the Fifth who had uncovered their purpose. She was uncompromising in the quality of her honey. She separated the honey from different sources: different flowers, different workers, even different times. She categorized and evaluated each so that only the finest of her hive's labor would be offered to the King.

So when the King had gifted them with new flowers with exotic properties, it had only been natural for the First of the Fifth to separate, concentrate, and categorize these as well. In doing so, she was the one who had discovered that the properties of honey could be changed dramatically based on their source. By the wisdom of the King and the ceaseless efforts of her and her offspring, they'd turned honey from a meal into a weapon.

And when she'd seen the King carry that weapon to one of his chasms, she'd known he had come up with another grand plan. She'd known she now had the opportunity to be a part of it. The key part of it, even, for none of the flower meadow hives could produce the surplus of honey her hive could.

So, her hive had worked tirelessly. They'd produced as much of the mad honey as they could and carried it to each of the chasms her King had dug.

Then when the invasion came, the First of the Fifth saw the completion of the King's design. Her scouts had reported how her honey had struck the critical blow and brought the enemy to its knees. It may have been the soldiers of the flower meadow who had danced with the invader, but it had been her honey that had laid it low and left it defenseless before the King.

He had struck it down, with her help, and without a single sacrifice by the queens of the flower meadow. She could now contribute to defense as much as they—nay, more, even, for she did not need to spend a single life to do so.

The First of the Fifth had been ecstatic. The King had thanked her and her workers personally for their efforts. The whole hive had celebrated for longer than they would care to admit. But it could not be helped, for they knew they were once again the favored ones above all others.

Still, the First of the Fifth was not content to rest upon that achievement. She may have been favored, but she was a bee first and foremost. She knew that even a favored worker would not remain so if they ceased to produce results; therefore, she and her children pressed on, searching for new ways they could aid their King and bring his designs to fruition.

And this time, she had an idea as to his purposes.

As her workers produced the specialized honey from the new plants, the First of the Fifth had noticed a curious phenomenon. As she inspected the honey, she'd found that the mana her workers imbued into it resonated with certain compounds from the plants. She theorized this was why those honey types differed so dramatically from the norm.

Arriving at her destination, where cells of mad mana and healing herb honey lay open, she looked within and found the pupae resting there, some with a slight green-and-blue tint, others with a slight purple tint. She could see their heads and bodies take shape, gaining more color by the day. Her antennas twitched in satisfaction. Her newest children were growing well, and soon would hatch.

Monster bee larvae did not merely feed upon honey. They absorbed the mana from within it and used it to stimulate the growth of their own. It was why mana flowers were so valuable to them, as otherwise, the worker bees needed to imbue that mana into the honey themselves.

So, when the First of the Fifth saw the mana in the new honey types resonating with the various compounds contained within, she could not help but wonder what might result if she raised a worker fed purely with one of those honey types? Would they grow as normal? Would they fail to grow at all?

Or perhaps, they would grow differently. Perhaps as differently as the honey they fed upon?

It had taken a bit of time. These workers had not grown in a single day as normal, which had worried the First of the Fifth. But as time went on, they'd grown and developed at their own pace, so the queen had let them be, waiting to see if they would eventually hatch.

And now, her patience was being rewarded. She noticed one of them begin to twitch and thrash about, tearing through the thin cocoon covering its cell before climbing out. The bee shook about and buzzed its wings, beating them for the first time. Its antennas twitched as it glanced around. The First of the Fifth stepped forward, gently brushing her antennas against her child's. The worker froze at first, then danced before her queen.

The First of the Fifth noted with pleasure that this bee was far different from the others. Her shape and size were the same, but she had bluish-green stripes where a normal bee would have yellow. The First of the Fifth could also feel the new worker's mana, of a different quality than all the others'. She noted the worker's stinger, thinner than normal and without barbs.

And, most importantly of all, this worker was still *hers*. Its mana was different but still registered as part of her hive, the same as her other children.

The new worker stood before her, eagerly awaiting her assignment as any good worker would. The other workers nearby began to brush along her as they would any other of their siblings, and the new worker soon joined them in their work. She began to tend to the others of her generation that had yet to be born.

And then, the First of the Fifth noticed something different. The new worker flared her mana as she walked over each of the cells in a way the queen had not seen her workers do before. Eventually, she stopped on one—one which seemed to be growing more slowly than the rest.

The First of the Fifth froze as the new worker lifted her abdomen and extended her stinger. The queen moved to intervene, but she was too late. The new worker stabbed down into the cell—but gently and precisely, without piercing the larva within. She released a cloud of bluish-green liquid from her stinger, and contrary to the queen's fears, the larva did not thrash about in response.

No, rather, the First of the Fifth felt the new larva's mana begin to settle down—and grow stronger.

She watched in silence as the new worker then moved on to the next cell, using her mana to check the larva within. Slowly, the queen's wings began to buzz.

She had succeeded beyond her expectations. She had borne a brand-new type of bee, all on her own, that was unlike any other in her hive.

The flower meadow queens may have birthed the first soldiers, but those had been a gift from the King. They could not lay claim to an achievement such as this.

The First of the Fifth would not only receive from the King—she would participate in his work and give something *to* him. She would participate in his grand designs more than anyone else.

For that is what it meant to be the most favored queen.

THE HIVE OF HIVES

Belissar awoke the next day and went to check on the hives, and found the queen of the closest one waiting for him at the entrance of her beehouse, flanked by two workers.

"Hi there, want to show me something again?"

The queen danced a salute then brushed antennas with the two bees, who flew up toward Belissar.

His eyes widened as he looked more closely at them . . . and found they were the wrong colors. One had bluish-green-and-black stripes, while the other alternated between purple and black. He took a closer look.

<u>*Medicinal Monster Bee Worker*</u>

Vitality:	*Minimal*	***Defense:***	*Minimal*
Strength:	*Minimal*	***Resistance:***	*Minimal*
Speed:	*Average*	***Special:***	*Minor*
Magic:	*Minimal+*		*Herbal Shot*
			Poison Sting
		Notable Skills:	*Brood Offspring*
			Brood Tender

A monster bee worker raised on the nectar of healing herbs.

It produces healing compounds, and its stinger
is optimized to deploy them. Additionally, will improve the overall health
of its hive. These changes make it poor, though not entirely
incapable, at combat.

Maddening Monster Bee Worker

Vitality:	*Minimal*	***Defense:***	*Minimal*
Strength:	*Minimal*	***Resistance:***	*Minimal*
Speed:	*Average*	***Special:***	*Minor*
Magic:	*Minimal*		*Mad Poison Sting*
		Notable Skills:	*Sacrificial Strike*
			Brood Offspring

A monster bee worker raised on mad honey.

It now produces the neurotoxins present in the honey in its own venom glands.
Its stings, in addition to the normal bee venom effects, may cause intoxication,
hallucination, and in very high dosages, paralysis.

Belissar's eyes widened. This . . . was an unexpected development—and a massive one. Monster bees could apparently change the properties of their venom, or even their color and shape, based on the type of honey they were fed. He was starting to understand why they were considered monsters.

Bees with venom that had the same intoxicating effects as mad honey. Belissar could immediately imagine how that might be useful, for it meant even the workers would now stand a chance against larger and more powerful foes. Even if it took them a long time to take a shade down, they could now disorient and slow it down.

If he thought about it more . . . that meant these workers could now help the soldiers with their work. It meant even the smallest of his bees was now a threat the shades would have to deal with.

Medicinal monster bee workers were harder to wrap his head around. Bees that could make healing herbs in their bodies? He supposed that made sense; no reason they couldn't make medicine if they could make poison, right?

The confusing thing for him was the idea that they could deploy said medicine via their stingers. That . . . seemed a bit contradictory. Apply medicine by stabbing the patient? Or maybe they would spray it instead? Belissar didn't know, but figured the bees would know what they were doing.

In any case, extra medicine was always a good thing. He especially liked the part of their description about improving the health of their hive. Healthy hives and stronger broods always made him happy.

But the most important part of this development was not either of the two bees themselves. It was the knowledge that monster bees could change and grow into new forms *without* a reward from the tower or the gods.

Belissar's mind raced as to what might be possible. If a couple of healing herbs and poisonous flowers had led to this . . . what might his bees be able to do? How far could they take this?

He smiled and nodded his head toward the queen.

"Well done. This is amazing."

The queen in question froze solid. Belissar chuckled as he went about to check on the other hives. And as he did so, he began to dream of all sorts of fantastical and impossible bees. Fantastical and impossible bees that might be very real one day, thanks to the power of the tower and the magic of the monster bees.

"I'll have to get some more plants next time . . ."

The Firstborn froze completely as her mind processed the report. The First of the Fifth had sent her new workers across the King's lands, declaring her achievement with the approval of the Conduit. And this news . . . changed everything.

The Firstborn could admit she had underestimated the First of the Fifth. She was the eldest of the apiary queens, and yet, she did not seem to understand their purpose as the Firstborn did. They were defenders first, and all else second. Should the invaders break past the gate to the beyond, all that they had built would be torn down and destroyed. So there were no tasks more important than preparing for the fight to come.

And yet, the First of the Fifth spent her days and her efforts on the production of honey. The Firstborn could understand the need to maximize production, but the First of the Fifth took it further. From what the Firstborn had heard, she obsessed over quality and split her honey based on her assessment of each batch.

The Firstborn understood, to some extent. She, too, had the desire to offer her tribute to the King, and she agreed that he deserved nothing but the very best. Yet, she could not help but be a bit disappointed. The First of the Fifth was her counterpart in the apiary, the eldest of the queens to whom the others looked and followed.

Now, she would not go so far as to want the First of the Fifth to change her focus. The apiary hives' honey production had proved to be a critical asset in the Third Invasion. Moreover, the Firstborn was glad that the armies of the flower meadow were powerful enough that the apiary hives could devote themselves to such efforts.

Yet . . . she did wish that the First of the Fifth remembered the broader picture. She worried that her counterpart was neglecting their primary duty with her obsession and causing the younger queens to follow suit. It did not befit her role as a fellow firstborn.

But that assessment had proven entirely wrong.

The First of the Fifth's efforts had paid off in completely unanticipated ways. Her honey from the new plants had transformed into a weapon which had had great effect upon the enemy of the Fourth Invasion. And now, her offspring had taken on the qualities of the honeys she curated so obsessively.

Her workers could now deploy a venom unlike anything the Firstborn's army possessed, and her hive now had dedicated tenders to ensure every larva of her brood grew healthy and strong.

And she had done all of this with the plants that the Firstborn had neglected.

The Firstborn was ashamed to admit she had ignored the wisdom of the King. After he had gifted them with new patches of flowers, she had focused her workers' efforts entirely on the mana flowers, the blossoms that would provide the most nutrition for their efforts, to allow her army to grow as large and powerful as possible with as little work as possible.

So, when the other new plants had proven to have no more mana than the normal flowers, she had not paid attention to them. Their nectar and honey had been mixed in with the rest of the normal fare, treated no different than any other.

Which meant she had not noticed the potential lurking inside that humble nectar. She imagined what might have been if she had done as the First of the Fifth. She imagined a soldier bee with a debilitating sting, causing the enemy to stumble and fall after but a few attacks. She imagined how strong her soldiers would have grown had they been tended to by dedicated healers.

She had been truly foolish.

The Firstborn set out to rectify this, wishing to separate and organize her honey based on its source. She would not go to the extent the First of the Fifth did, but at least she would separate the nectar from the new patches so that they could feed some of the new brood upon it.

She quickly realized, however, that this was not possible in the short term. Her hive was still operating on a smaller workforce; one that could not sustain her current army if they shifted focus away from the mana flowers. They did not have the time to spend on organization nor on gathering sufficient nectar from the other low-mana patches.

As they were, they would struggle to gather enough honey from the other plants to produce even a single worker of the types the First of the Fifth had displayed, much less a honey-guzzling soldier.

The Firstborn stood still again as she realized the truth. It had not been that she had not noticed the potential of the plants . . . it was that she *couldn't* have. Her focus on the soldiers prevented her from taking the steps necessary to ever discover such a thing. It was *only* the First of the Fifth and her obsession with honey quality that could have produced this outcome. It was only her who could have revealed this new path for the army's growth.

Once again, the Firstborn realized the wisdom of the King. She had wondered why he permitted the First of the Fifth to do as she did, but now, she understood. For not all bees in the hive had the same job. The queen did not go out to scout and gather. The soldier did not give birth to the next generation. The worker was not the first to fight.

And the King had built a hive of hives. He was the king of queens. And so, each of his queens had a different role to play. Each of them had their own mission to fulfill. Each of them was vital for the success of the whole.

The Firstborn thanked the First of the Fifth in her mind as she began to lay a new generation. And for once, she lay not a single soldier egg, instead intending to dramatically expand her worker force. She would need a great many of them to gather the honey necessary, for to feed a soldier larva on mundane nectar would be a herculean task. A task that would require her to cut down the growth of her army substantially, and for a long time.

But the Firstborn wanted to produce the finest army beekind had ever seen, and to do that she could not leave a single flower unvisited. She would follow the path set out before her by the King and the First of the Fifth, and they would all work together to fulfill the King's grand designs.

For though the queens could not be more different, they were all, in the end, one hive. The hive of the King.

THE ARMY OF THE APIARY

The First of the Fifth watched her scouts' report dances as she drank some more mana honey.

So, the Firstborn was increasing her worker count and gathering from the healing and toxic flowers now. No doubt a desperate attempt to match her own hive now that her achievements had been revealed.

But that was to be expected.

The First of the Fifth dismissed the scouts and made her way to a new section of her hive. The queens of the flower meadow would have to do better than that if they wished to earn the favor of the King. The First of the Fifth had obviously known everyone would follow after her once she announced her achievement; if they did not realize she was well on her way to the next, then they were truly foolish.

But that was why she was the favored queen. She would never be content to rest on her laurels again, instead working ceaselessly for the sake of the King. And that was why no one would come to match her in the end.

So, she arrived at the site of her next project. A new bee was just breaking free of its cocoon and climbing out of its cell, surrounded by medicinal workers brushing every inch of its chitin with their antenna. One of them turned to the queen and danced a confirmation. The First of the Fifth acknowledged her and then stepped forward to address her newest child.

A child nearly the same size as her. Her first soldier.

Even after growing to the next stage, the First of the Fifth had not born any soldiers bees. She'd seen no need to do so, after all. Soldier bees could not gather nectar nor process honey, yet their large size demanded excessive quantities of it to grow. They were naught but a drain when it came to the production of the hive.

Of course, they had obvious uses regarding the defense, but such was unnecessary for the First of the Fifth. The King himself had assigned soldiers of his own to guard his treasured apiary hives, yet another sign of his favor. She would not squander such a gift by expending her honey and mana on guards of her own.

Likewise, however, it was clear that soldiers were necessary for the King's designs and the defense of his lands. The queens of the flower meadow had earned great favor, including that new one known as honor, by the deeds of their warriors. And there was a part of the First of the Fifth that wished to supplant them in that field as well; to send warriors of her own to strike down the King's enemies.

But she was not so foolish as to ignore that she was at a disadvantage in that mission. The queens of the flower meadow may not have been as productive or favored as she, but they were bee queens still. They did not shirk their duty and worked tirelessly to fulfill their role.

The First of the Fifth would admit that their armies were impressive, and their soldiers spent every waking moment preparing for battle. It would be difficult for even her to catch up to them. And most egregiously of all, it would require her to cut the quality and quantity of her daily tribute to the King. That was simply unacceptable.

So, the First of the Fifth had forgone soldiers, having no use for them, no way they could help their hive earn the favor of the King. Until now.

The First of the Fifth brushed the new soldier with her antennas. The soldier instantly stood up to her full height and began a salute dance, then the First of the Fifth gave her orders. The soldier seemed confused, but the First of the Fifth was firm in her command. The soldier gave another salute before setting out to obey, even as she beat her wings for the first time.

The First of the Fifth watched with satisfaction before laying another soldier egg in the now vacant cell.

Mighty the hives of the flower meadow may be, but the First of the Fifth was confident in her position and in her plans. For she, above all others, knew the designs of the King . . .

Back in the farmhouse, Belissar sighed as his hand slipped and the weave he was working on untangled. Again. Some of the flax had finally dried enough to work with, and so, Belissar was now trying to weave a strip he could use to fix his tunic.

It . . . wasn't going particularly well. Not only was Belissar not the best at this sort of thing, but the flax itself had not been processed well.

Normally, there were a number of tools—such as rakes and stands—which a farmer would use to process the flax and remove the unwanted pieces of the plant. Belissar, having completed those steps largely by hand, had not ended up with as clean a product as normal. Pieces of debris still stuck to the fibers, thus getting in the way here and there, forcing him to pick them off before continuing.

Belissar then froze.

He had done all this work by hand because he didn't have any of the tools and had known that this job that he didn't enjoy was going to take a long time because of that, so he had gotten to work immediately with the intention of getting it over with as quickly as possible.

So, he hadn't considered that with the axe, saw, and the trees in the forest beyond he could have made some basic wooden tools. They wouldn't match up to what he had at home, but even rough and simple implements would have made this *far* easier than doing this entire process by hand.

Belissar stared into the air with a faraway look for quite some time.

It was then that he heard buzzing. Turning to face the window he'd left open for Niobee to come and go, he tilted his head. One of the soldier bees was hovering there.

"Um, come on in?"

She danced a salute then flew inside. Landing on the table in front of Belissar, she looked at the weave in front of him before slowly beginning a dance.

"Hm? Oh, you're from the close hive, not the spawners or the flower meadow? Was wondering how you got here. And you . . . want to help?"

The soldier bee's dance was a bit unsteady, but she confirmed. Belissar smiled.

"Thanks, the gods know I need a hand with this. Let's see, um, how about you grab hold of this?"

Belissar held up the latest fiber of the weave. The soldier bee slowly stepped forward and gently grabbed it with her mandibles.

"Good, can you move it here?"

The soldier nodded and moved as he motioned. With her holding it in place, Belissar was able to easily thread the fiber into its place in the weave.

"Okay, you can let go now."

Once she did, he pulled it tight. He smiled.

"Thank you, that's much easier. Can I count on your help?"

The soldier bee did a rapid dance before moving to grab the fiber once again. Belissar chuckled, and then his smile grew. Working together directly with the bees was something he'd once dreamed of. With that dream coming true each day . . . well, even this job didn't seem so bad.

The First of the Fifth danced about happily as her scouts reported back. Her plan had been a success. Long had the King been working at his current task, and long had her scouts observed.

The First of the Fifth had wished to help him directly, as she had with the honey traps, but there had been a bit of a problem. The tasks he was performing were on a scale beyond normal bees. He uprooted entire plants and worked with bunches of them all at once. Her workers could have helped, but it would have taken dozens or even hundreds of them to move a single plant.

And so, the First of the Fifth had seen a use for soldiers. With their much larger size, they could better aid the King in his large-scale tasks. They could carry plants and fibers all on their own. They could work with the King without cutting into the production of his tribute.

The King had been well pleased by this. Even now, he worked with the soldier she had provided, showering the lucky child with praise. The First of the Fifth had no doubt she had surged ahead in his favor with this.

And so, with the confirmation that her soldiers could assist the King with the grand and complex designs he built, she was ready to move on to the next stage of her plan.

This one would not be as pleasant or as satisfying. This one would require her to humble herself and sacrifice the efforts of her hive. But she was the favored queen, the most productive and blessed of them all. For the sake of the King, she would do anything.

Which was why it was time for her to speak with the Firstborn directly.

THE NEGOTIATIONS

The First of the Fifth sent word to the Conduit, asking if she would arrange a meeting with the Firstborn. The Conduit agreed, and off she flew.

While the First of the Fifth was confident she was favored above all, even though the Conduit was not a queen, there was no doubt among any bee of the hive that the Conduit had a special place among them all. Even the First of the Fifth could not and would not contest that. She was connected to the core the same as the King; she shared in his power and in that of the realm. If the King were the ruler of all the land, then the Conduit was the land itself.

It was even whispered that the Conduit had existed since before the King's realm had been forged, as unthinkable as that thought was. That she'd known the King in some sort of past life, from before the birth of the First Dynasty of the First Spawner.

The First of the Fifth didn't know how much stock she placed in such things, for a world where her King was not king was not one she cared to imagine. And yet, she could not help but notice the Conduit's familiarity with the King, as if they had known each other for far longer than the First of the Fifth had seen.

But now was not the time to think of such things, for the First of the Fifth already had an unpleasant task before her. The point was that the Conduit danced with special authority, nearly equal to that of the King himself. No bee, whether worker or soldier or queen, would deny her save by the King's own order.

And that made her the perfect mediator for this discussion. The only mediator the First of the Fifth would accept, in fact. She and the Firstborn had each been established as the most powerful queens of the flower meadow and the apiary respectively, and none of the others could be trusted to remain impartial. And it would not do to trouble the King with such matters, seeing as this was all for his sake to begin with.

So, the First of the Fifth took her guards and flew through the apiary, passing into the flower meadow. She then waited at the shrine of the Goddess at the end of the meadow, the Queen of All Bees. She disliked coming all the way to the Firstborn's lands, but the Goddess belonged to all, so her shrine was the most appropriate as neutral ground.

And, well, the shrine in the apiary stood next to the core itself, and the First of the Fifth would not have this discussion in that sacred place. So, she would concede the journey to the Firstborn.

Soon, the Conduit came flying over, the Firstborn with her, coming without guard or escort. The First of the Fifth wasn't sure how to take that. Was the Firstborn's hive stretched so thin that none could be spared? Or was it a sign that the Firstborn was not taking her seriously?

"Hi! First Queen of First Spawner's Second Dynasty here, like First Queen of Fifth Spawner's First Dynasty asked! Queens talk!"

The Conduit danced about rapidly in the manner an excited worker would. The Firstborn began a dance of greeting.

"Hello, First of the Fifth. You want to talk?"

The First of the Fifth resisted the urge to buzz her wings. So the Firstborn wanted to get this over with when she'd been the one who'd made the First of the Fifth wait? Did she not know they were both wasting valuable time coming here?

But the First of the Fifth wouldn't waste her own time on such complaints, and so launched right into it.

"Yes. Need access to your gathering fields."

The Firstborn's antennas swayed about as she processed that.

"Apiary running out?"

The First of the Fifth's wings began to beat before she took control of them. The Firstborn would dare to imply that her apiary lacked? When it was the Firstborn who'd required her aid to avoid starvation?

"Just one. New plants that King gathers."

Yes, the First of the Fifth knew the flower meadow had access to a kind of flower the apiary lacked; the same one the King worked on even now. She knew not why the King had granted them access to it and not her, only that in his wisdom, he had. Perhaps he was testing it before gifting it to her, as he had with the mana flowers.

In any case, the First of the Fifth could not wait for him to gift her with her own; not if she were to help him with his designs. So, here she was, speaking with the Firstborn instead of growing her hive.

The Firstborn danced in comprehension, finally understanding the request. *Took her long enough.*

And now, the First of the Fifth pressed her attack, hopefully before the Firstborn could take control of the battlefield.

"Will give honey in exchange. New kinds. Know you need."

The Firstborn paused for a moment, no doubt in shock at the First of the Fifth's proposal. Even the First of the Fifth was shocked at herself. To share her honey—the fruits of her children's labor, the tribute meant for their king—with a major rival?

An emergency donation to prepare for an invasion was one thing, but in all other situations, it was unthinkable. But so was granting a rival hive access to one's own gathering grounds, and the First of the Fifth needed those flowers. So, she had no choice but to make an unthinkable offer for an unthinkable request.

Such was the will of the First of the Fifth, who would stop at nothing for the sake of the King. Besides, Firstborn needed such assistance merely to catch up to what the First of the Fifth had already achieved, all while she would be pulling ahead even further.

She watched as the Firstborn paused, no doubt working to understand her purposes. But the First of the Fifth knew she had the advantage here. The Firstborn was trying to replicate her healing herb honey and mad honey production, and then to apply that honey to her own brood.

If the First of the Fifth guessed correctly, the battle-focused Firstborn would probably try to raise soldiers on the honey. But it would take even the First of the Fifth a huge chunk of her production to raise a soldier on such fare; the Firstborn could not possibly pull it off with her hive's current worker base.

The First of the Fifth's offer would be too tempting for her. And the Firstborn did not know of the King's current designs, living as far away from his abode as she did. She would not know the opportunity she was giving up in the process. So, there could only be one answer.

The Firstborn appeared surprised, but gave her reply.

"Thanks. Helps a lot."

The First of the Fifth resisted the urge to dance happily, instead turning to the Conduit and signaling that was it. The Firstborn followed suit, and the Conduit began to dance.

"Great! Second First of First lets First of Fifth gather! First of Fifth gives honey to Second First of First! Bees help each other and help King!"

The Firstborn gave a salute dance at that.

"For the King."

That was the one thing the First of the Fifth could agree with both of them on . . . though she was a bit upset the Firstborn had beaten her to the punch as she danced her own agreement.

"For the King."

With that, the three bees parted ways, returning to their work. The First of the Fifth passed through the door to the apiary. There, she found two large gatherings of her own workers, one holding wax cells full of honey, the other preparing for a harvest. She commanded them to begin their tasks, and into the flower meadow they flew.

She could not help a happy dance as she headed back to her hive. All had gone according to plan. And the Firstborn had clearly had no idea what she had agreed to.

She would now receive the First of the Fifth's honey and use it in her attempts to raise new soldier bees, a task she could not possibly complete with her own assets at present. That meant that even should she succeed, it would not be her achievement alone. All would know that the First of the Fifth's aid had been crucial to the effort. All would see the First of the Fifth's workers bringing honey to the Firstborn's hive.

By accepting her aid, the Firstborn had granted the First of the Fifth claim to her efforts.

And on the other hand, the only thing the Firstborn had granted her was permission. Her workers would now gather the honey from the new plants on their own. The nectar would be processed in her own hive, and anything new that resulted would be hidden there.

As far as anyone would be able to see, the Firstborn would have given the First of the Fifth nothing in that process. In fact, if anything, by allowing foreign workers into her own territory, the Firstborn would appear subservient to the First of the Fifth.

In one fell swoop, she had positioned herself as the top of the queens, and there was nothing the Firstborn could now do to usurp her. If the First of the Fifth achieved anything with the new flowers, she would pull ahead. And if the Firstborn managed to raise new soldiers, they would both rise together with a joint accomplishment. There was now no way she could possibly lose.

Such was to be expected from the most favored of the King.

There was only one variable she couldn't fully address. She didn't know how much the Conduit understood of her intent, but it wouldn't matter. The Conduit was not a part of the competition between the queens, for her role was unique. And the Conduit's goal, first and foremost, was the growth of the King's realm. If something benefited the King, the Conduit wouldn't question it. So, the First of the Fifth was confident she would not interfere.

Yes, it had all gone according to plan.

CHAPTER TWENTY-NINE

A SHOCKING BEE-VENT!

It was a peaceful day in the forest around Belissar's tower. The sun was shining, the bees were buzzing, and there was even a bird singing; a newcomer who had recently flown in.

But then, the ground began to rumble, and groups of bushes began to rustle. A moment later, the ground burst open, overturning the bushes above. A dark hole opened up in the forest, leading to parts unknown . . .

With the soldier bee's help, Belissar was able to finish his work sooner than expected. He now had a simple strip of rough linen cloth; not exactly anything anyone would want, but enough to patch up his tunic.

Belissar had subsequently done what would have been the smart thing to do to start with and made some tools for flax processing. Coarse rakes and combs to help separate the seeds and other material, a board and a wooden implement he could use to scutch, and anything else he could think of which might make the process easier.

Doing so had used up a bit of his available wood, so the next day, he headed out into the forest to gather some more. He was just chopping a small tree when Niobee began buzzing around him.

"King! Scouts say something coming!"

Belissar's eyes narrowed.

"Is it the Hunger again?"

"No, different!"

Belissar blinked and tilted his head. Something other than the Hunger? But what could it be?

"Do they mean like a bird?"

Niobee repeated her same dance. "Different!"

That had Belissar puzzled. The bird that had recently arrived to the forest nearby was about the only thing he could think of besides the Hunger. After all, whatever it was, it had to have flown, for nothing could simply walk through the Hunger on the ground.

Right?

In any case, Belissar decided it would be best to act cautiously.

"Let's head back to the tower and prepare our defenses, just in case. Have the scouts keep an eye on it, but let everyone outside know to run if it's hostile."

"Okay!"

With that, Belissar returned to the tower. He didn't know what was going on, but he knew that whatever it was, he wouldn't let it take his bees.

Belissar finished stocking the campfire by the apiary entrance once again, then grabbed hold of one of the torches. Meanwhile, the flower meadow queens were assembling their army in the sky above the gate to the outside world.

Niobee finished dancing with some worker bees before flying over to him.

"Scouts say approaching."

Belissar furrowed his brow.

"Is it hostile?"

"No."

He rubbed his chin. The bees had reported an animal of some kind, with lots of brown and black color, but he still didn't have any idea what it could be. But well, whatever it was, his tower was ready.

Or so Belissar thought. As the gates of the tower opened, Belissar narrowed his eyes.

"Get ready . . ."

He gasped.

Challenger detected. Enabling Remnants.
Challengers Present: 1

In walked . . . a person? A man, judging by the body shape and facial features.

He was tall, taller than anyone Belissar had ever seen, with broad shoulders and thick arms and legs to match. His clothing was a combination of black leather and brown fur, with some light armor over his torso, waist, and upper limbs, while the fur covered his extremities. He carried a short spear and a shield, both of which were made out of bone of some sort.

Belissar's eyes then widened as he focused and realized the brown fur wasn't clothing at all. The man's legs and arms were covered in thick, brown fur. His hands were a bit wider than normal, and his fingers were tipped with large claws.

And while his face was human, his hair was more like a mane of fur combining with his beard.

But most surprising of all were the two bear ears popping out of the top of his head.

"It's a . . . demihuman?"

Belissar froze, uncertain of what to do. Demihumans were the descendants of the wicked kings of old. Those who'd survived the Hunger had been cursed and twisted into a half-man, half-beast monstrosity. Belissar had long thought they were just a tale, for he had never heard or seen of one in real life.

And now, one was standing in his tower.

Belissar blinked. The demihuman . . . was standing in his tower and *not* being smote by the gods? This situation was strange.

But maybe, as the tower lord, *he* was expected to do something? He wasn't sure; he wasn't receiving any missions from the God of Bees. He looked toward her shrine, but it wasn't glowing or anything this time. The tower itself had said something about challengers and remnants, but Belissar didn't know what that meant in this context.

Well, if he had to make his own choice, he guessed he'd try to drive it away? Demihumans were said to be extremely dangerous, but Belissar wasn't going to let it attack the hives. They were supposed to be more beast than man, so hopefully, it would be scared of fire. If not . . . maybe the soldier bees could handle it. It couldn't be tougher than a shade of the Hunger, right?

Of course, the demihuman wasn't just still while Belissar pondered. The bear man looked up and narrowed his eyes at the soldier bee army arranged in the sky, then slowly lowered his weapons and relaxed his stance, though he still held them in his hands.

And then, what happened next shocked Belissar to his very core.

"Peace, Sacred Den Master. We mean you no harm if you mean us none."

The soldier bees swayed a bit in the air, unsure of what to do, but Belissar was in no state to command them. His jaw dropped, and he stumbled back. The demihuman had *talked*.

The bear man turned to face the shrine of bees while keeping an eye on the army overhead. Bowing his head for a moment, he rested his spear against his shoulder and reached for his belt, taking a small pouch tied there. Then, opening the wax chest, he placed the pouch inside.

"A gift, for you and your patron. I pray for peaceful and fruitful cooperation, Sacred Den Master."

He inclined his head once more toward the shrine, which glowed softly in response, and then slowly backed out of the tower. Some words passed before Belissar's eyes, and Niobee asked him something in a slow and shaky dance, but Belissar wasn't paying attention.

The demihuman had talked. And that . . . went against everything Belissar had ever been taught.

He thought back to the story Mrs. Imkomos had read to him in one of her books.

Long ago, the wicked kings of old had defied the gods and brought upon themselves great wrath. The Hunger had consumed the land, destroying every vestige of their civilization and tearing down all they had built.

But such was not the extent of the gods' justice, for the wicked kings had been as cunning and cowardly as they'd been cruel. They'd abandoned their people to doom and fled alone, racing ahead of the death they rightfully deserved.

So, the gods had cursed them. They had grown bestial features and lost their humanity in more ways than one. They'd lost their tongues, the means by which to communicate. They'd lost their ability to participate in society and become like beasts. But the gods had not been so kind as to let them fall completely. They'd retained their spark, their intelligence, so that they might know what they had become and what they had lost.

They had been doomed to exist between worlds, never to be content with the life of a beast but lacking the means to live the life of a man.

Such was the tale of the demihuman, the cursed descendants of those wicked kings. A living warning against all who might defy the gods. Or so Belissar had been taught all his life.

And yet . . . here was a demihuman, the first he had ever seen. And said demihuman apparently could speak with no problems whatsoever. Even had clothes and weapons like a regular person would. Moreover, said demihuman had respected one of the gods, who had not smitten him for daring to set foot in one of the sacred towers, nor given Belissar a mission to that effect.

None of this recent turn of events made any sense to Belissar whatsoever.

He began to pace about, staring at the ground and groaning. He dropped his axe and his torch and rubbed his chin, then crossed his arms. Furrowing his brow, he concentrated.

But think as he might, he could come up with no resolution for this quandary. It'd been confusing enough when he wasn't smitten for setting foot in the tower back when he was a mere peasant, but a demihuman? Every story he had ever heard implied they wouldn't be permitted anywhere *near* a tower, much less to set foot inside of one. And yet one had, and the gods had not responded in any way.

No . . . that was wrong. The God of Bees *had* responded, just not in the way Belissar had expected.

Tribute received.
Your patron grants you this portion:

> *- Cave Mushroom x3*
> *- Cave Carrot x3*
> *- Cave Potato x3*

She had . . . accepted the demihuman's gift? Just like that? She accepted the demihuman?

Belissar sat on the ground, practically collapsing on his backside. He held his head as his heart pounded in his chest.

A peasant like him becoming a tower lord was already unthinkable, but he could handle that. He'd figured that Niobee, as the Conduit or whatever, had interceded on his behalf to prevent the gods from smiting him outright. Then, he had proven himself capable enough in the second purification, and the gods had subsequently approved of him, making an exception for him, since he was already in charge of the tower. Those discrepancies could be explained away.

But this? This was not so simple. In the doctrine, the demihumans had been intimately connected with the fall of the wicked kings of old and the Hunger itself. And that particular tale was no mere footnote. It was *the* central doctrine to all others; the very reason the world was the way it was.

So, what would it mean if it proved false?

If the demihumans could speak and were not doomed to live as beasts . . . if the gods had no quarrel with them and no issues with their presence . . . then wouldn't that mean Belissar was wrong about the origin of the Hunger and the intentions of the gods?

And if he was wrong about that . . . then wouldn't he be wrong about . . . well, *everything*?

Belissar groaned. Whatever the case, things had just gotten a *lot* more complicated.

CHAPTER THIRTY

THE EPIPHA-BEE

Belissar thought, and he thought, and he thought some more, even as Niobee buzzed around him. Eventually, she got his attention by landing on his hand.

"King okay?"

Belissar sighed and shook his head. "Not really. Just . . . give me a moment, please?"

Niobee buzzed her wings but said no more, taking off again and hovering a short distance away from Belissar. He sighed and began walking, heading over toward the farmhouse. He went inside, got a bit of honeycomb to snack on, and sat down at the table.

This was all *way* above his station . . . or would have been, were he not a tower lord now. Or maybe it wasn't? Because if the tale of the demihumans was wrong, then what else might be? He, a peasant, had clearly stepped into and been placed in control of a tower, and hadn't ended up getting smitten in the process. Maybe he had been wrong all along, and the gods didn't mind peasants in towers either. But if that was true, then what made the tower lords and the tower guard special?

Or . . . *were* they special at all? If *Belissar*, of all people, could do the job of a tower lord well enough to earn the patronage of a god, then did the job truly require someone greater than other men to pull off? Or was the case that it wasn't those chosen by the gods who became tower lords, but those who became tower lords who were chosen by the gods?

And if that was the case . . . then what of everything else he had been taught? Magic and potions being harmful to peasants? The tower lords requiring tribute to offer to the gods? Peasants naturally being beneath those the gods had chosen? The will of the gods being to obey any and all tower lords without question, lest the unworthy repeat the mistakes of old?

Belissar remembered going hungry in the cold of winter when the tribute cut into the rations on a particularly bad year. He remembered the villagers raiding his mead on orders of the village elder, for the local tower lord had requested it.

His eyes narrowed as more memories flooded into his mind.

"I'm . . . sorry, Belissar. Please . . . live . . ."

He remembered begging for help as his parents came down with the plague. A plague he later heard had been cured in the tower cities by the fantastic powers of the tower lords.

"Now, don't you worry about me, Belissar. I'm going to the gods, to the Hall of Judgement, where the God of Death shall evaluate my life. I can't say I've been perfect, but I can say now I'm happy with the life I've lived . . ."

What about Mrs. Imkomos, who'd spent her whole life trying to honor the gods and their supposedly chosen tower lords? He remembered the old beekeeper coughing in the night, believing there was nothing he could do. Even if he'd had magic or potions, he'd believed they would kill her as quickly as the pneumonia.

But if everything he had been taught was wrong . . . then all that pain, all that suffering . . .

Had it all been for nothing? Had it all been for a lie?

Belissar groaned and clutched his head.

Ultimately, Belissar could not come to that conclusion on his own. He felt he needed more information, more confirmation, before he could accept such a thing.

He rose to his feet with his eyes narrowed, heat swirling in his chest.

"Niobee . . . ask the queens to send out the scouts. I want to know more about our visitor."

She flew a bit unsteadily. "Okay . . . King okay?"

Belissar shook his head. "I don't know. But I need to know more before I can do anything."

Niobee hovered for a moment before dancing a salute and flying off to relay his command. Meanwhile, Belissar crossed his arms and frowned.

Honestly, he wanted to see things with his own eyes . . . but that wasn't an option right now. If the tales of the demihumans *were* true, then they carried a deep hatred toward all of humanity and would attack on sight.

Belissar had a feeling that would not be the case, but he wasn't about to bet his life on it. Besides, the last few times he had dealt with people, they had either confiscated his mead or else tried to kill him, so he wasn't exactly excited to meet more.

Likewise, Belissar was not particularly good at sneaking, nor was he a hunter. So, he had little confidence he could spy on the demihumans without being noticed. And this was doubly true for demihumans, since the tales stated they also tended to have better senses than the average human.

Well, again, Belissar didn't know how much of any of his knowledge he should believe at this point, but after seeing what the monster bees could do compared to their mundane cousins, Belissar decided it was best to assume the demihumans were more capable if anything.

So, he would have to rely on the scout bees. The demihuman hadn't attacked them on the way to the tower, nor had he fought with the soldier bees inside, so Belissar believed they could observe him peacefully.

The only problem was that the monster bees, while more intelligent than normal, were still ultimately bees, and focused on the things that bees cared about, such as when they'd found the mana flowers and completely ignored the nearby ruins. Even their initial reports of the demihuman had been limited to "an animal is approaching," with detail being limited to colors and shapes.

Belissar wanted to know a bit more than that. He wanted to know how the demihuman acted and talked. He wanted to know if he acted more like a beast or a man, if he used tools and tents and fire, or if he simply lived in the wild. If his spear and shield were something he'd intentionally made himself or something he'd simply picked off a human he had slain.

Getting a good sense of all that off the bees' reports would be a challenge, but what other choice did Belissar have? If only he had a way to use his tower sight outside of the tower . . .

The moment he thought that, his sight rushed from his body and through the tower, heading to the outside world until it joined with the sight of one of the scouts.

It turned out he could do just that; he just hadn't had any particular desire to do so until now. Even when the bees had reported the mana flowers, they had asked him to come personally, so he hadn't thought of checking from afar. With the ruins, on the other hand, that had been a personal curiosity, and he had not intended to distract the bees from their work with it.

He quickly tested the limits of what he could do. He was limited to what his bees could perceive with their senses, though he could move his attention from bee to bee, or even get a vaguer sense from several of them at a time for a bigger but less detailed picture.

All of which was perfect for his current purposes. Belissar looked through the sight of different bees until he found one following the bear man. The man trekked through the forest until he was close to the edge of the tower's influence. There, he arrived at a large hole in the ground and walked down inside of it while the bee watching him hovered at the edge. From what Belissar could tell, her night vision wasn't great, so she was uncertain of entering the dark hole.

Trying to send some intentions to her like he could with the bees inside the tower and finding it worked, he let her know to remain outside and keep watch. She danced a little salute before flying toward a nearby flower, gathering some nectar while she waited. He then checked which bees were closest to the hole and directed them to reinforce the lone scout.

Now, he just had to wait until the demihuman returned.

Fortunately, Belissar did not have to wait for long. The bear man soon returned—and he was not alone. Several more armed bear folk exited the hole and set up a perimeter around it. Their spears were tipped with iron and all of a similar design.

And then, after that, came a whole tribe. There were unarmed men and women carrying bundles and backpacks and even pulling carts. There were children and mothers carrying infants in slings. There were old men and women being supported by the young.

Maybe a hundred or so demihumans in total exited from the hole, all with brown fur on any part of their body not otherwise clothed save their faces and round ears on the top of their heads, all standing tall above a normal human. Even the women would tower over Belissar, and some of the children could match his height. The armed ones wore armor of leather and bone over their torsos and extremities, while the others were more lightly clothed, revealing more of their brown fur.

They began to make camp. The man from before led them to a spot nearby where the bushes weren't as thick, and the tribe got to work. They began to chop away at the trees and bushes with axes and set up tents in the cleared area. A group of them got a fire going, and even hung a large iron pot over it.

And most of all, the entire tribe was exchanging conversations throughout the whole process.

One of them, a wrinkled, hunched woman holding a large staff with all sorts of trinkets and decorations hanging on it, turned toward one of his bees. She smiled and inclined her head.

"Thank you for allowing us here. Please excuse us; we will visit shortly."

Belissar ordered the bees to fall back and then withdrew his tower sight. He staggered back and held his head, his heart pounding in his chest.

There was no mistake. There was no denying it. The demihumans were acting no different than humans would. Everything Belissar had seen pointed to them being, well, normal people, all things considered.

Which meant . . . the tales were wrong.

All of them.

CHAPTER THIRTY-ONE

BEE-HOLD THE TRUTH

Belissar paced about while clutching his head. His entire body was trembling, and his heart felt like it was about to burst from his chest.

Everything bad that had happened to the village . . . everything bad that had happened to him and the people he cared about . . . had been all for nothing?

Belissar gritted his teeth. No, it was worse. It was because the tower lords had *lied*. The lords, the priests, the guard—all of them. Mana couldn't be such a toxic poison when a humble bee could absorb it no problem. Potions couldn't be that dangerous, or even hard to make, when a monster bee could make one out of honey and a couple of common medicinal herbs. And towers needed no tribute when they grew plants and made honey seemingly out of thin air.

And if Belissar had achieved all of this as a humble beekeeper in under a month, what could a fully prepared tower lord have achieved over decades, or even centuries if the rumors were true? Why did even a small village like his own struggle when a tower could achieve such miraculous deeds?

Suddenly, Belissar froze, going completely still. He thought of the day his village had burned, remembered Niobee's words to him, that he had been hurt and she'd tried to help him. And in the process made him a tower lord . . .

A dark thought crept into his mind. What if it wasn't that only tower lords could rule a tower, but that only tower lords were *permitted* to rule a tower? Not because they were chosen by the gods but because they *killed* anyone else who tried?

What if the point of the tower lord's son's visit that day had been specifically to become the lord of the tower Belissar now ruled? And he had burned down the village to prevent any of them from interfering?

Such were Belissar's thoughts as Niobee landed on his hand and began dancing frantically.

"King! King not okay?! Need help?!"

Belissar blinked as he was shaken out of his thoughts, looking down at Niobee frantically dancing on his hand.

He took a deep breath.

Then gave as much of a smile as he could manage and brushed her back with his finger. He pushed the dark thoughts out of his mind for a moment.

"I'm . . . fine. Well, maybe not, but I will be. Because I have you now."

As he felt Niobee's legs upon his palm and her fuzz under his finger, he realized that those dark thoughts were all speculation. He now knew that most of his prior knowledge was wrong, but he didn't know how much of it was lies, how much was misunderstandings, and how much was simple ignorance.

He didn't know if all the falsehoods were intentional or not, and, indeed, not *everything* had proven false. He had also seen the Hunger and the devastation it could bring, which was unfortunately *exactly* like the tales had described. And he'd been forced to face it down himself, as tower lords were said to do. Maybe tower lords *needed* to keep the magic and the potions to themselves just to hold the line?

Belissar couldn't say right now. He couldn't change the past, either. And he couldn't do anything about the tower lords one way or another, seeing as he was surrounded by the Hunger at the moment. Most of all, whatever the tower lords had intended, *he* had command of this tower now, the one his friend Niobee was connected to. She had not been taken under their control, and he had not been killed before interfering. They were together now, and out of the tower lords' reach.

So, he tried to put it out of his mind. Stewing on what they had done and what they may or may not have intended achieved nothing for him now. But Niobee and the other bees were counting on him, so he would focus on them.

And so, Belissar decided what to do. He would not dwell on the tower lords— and he would not take their words as law. Whether they had lied or simply been mistaken, the truth was that most of what Belissar had been taught had been proven wrong. He could no longer count on the tales and the laws and doctrines he had grown up with.

His heart panged at the memory of Mrs. Imkomos, who had told him most of the stories. But he remembered that she would be the first to admit her collection of texts was not complete. She had not been sure if all her tales matched even what the tower lords claimed, much less what the gods actually intended . . .

A young Belissar's face scrunched up. He was sitting at a table with a book in front of him. Mrs. Imkomos was sitting next to him, helping him read the letters.

"We don't have all the books? Um, how do we know if we're doing the right things, then? Won't the gods be mad if we do it wrong?"

The old woman shrugged.

"I don't know what I don't know, and the tower lords have better things to do than answer an old woman's questions. But what I know is this: the gods gave us their towers and the lords to steward them. They protect us and push back the Hunger. I believe they have grace for us and wish to help.

"So I believe that even if we don't know all the doctrines, if we intend in our hearts to honor them and do the best we can with the knowledge we have, the gods will acknowledge that."

But he didn't need to count on the teachings anymore. Niobee and the others would follow and support him in whatever he did. Together, they had conquered the shades of the Hunger. The God of Bees had acknowledged and blessed him, and now sent him guidance. And Mrs. Imkomos . . . would whack him over the head for prioritizing her old books over direct experience with a tower and the God of Bees herself.

Belissar's heart slowed back down. He took another deep breath and exhaled slowly, relaxing his whole body as he did.

He felt that, even if he had to forget all he had learned before, that it would work out somehow this time. Between him, the bees, the tower, and their patron god, they could figure things out. For he was no longer Belissar, the orphaned peasant. He was a . . . He was about to say *tower lord*, but the thought of them was unpleasant at the moment.

But Belissar thought of something else, written upon the tower's status. He narrowed his eyes and nodded his head.

Yes . . . he was Belissar, a dungeon master blessed by the God of Bees. And from now on, he would face life with his eyes wide open, judging for himself what the world was really like. And as for the tower lords . . . Well, if Belissar ever encountered them again, he had already decided on his resolution before.

No one, be they man, beast, tower lord, or Hunger, would take his bees.

He looked down at Niobee and smiled, a true smile this time.

"I'm sorry for worrying you, but I'm okay now. Thank you for choosing and staying with me, Niobee."

Niobee looked up at him for a second then began dancing rapidly.

"King is best king! Niobee always choose king!"

Belissar couldn't help but chuckle at that, and the knot in his heart loosened just a bit.

Well, while Belissar had been distracted by the emotional shattering of his entire worldview, once he had calmed down, he realized that nothing much had changed. At this point, he had no idea where the tower lords or his former village even were, much less had any interactions with them, and he had already determined the gods weren't going to smite him for his control of this dungeon.

So, while the news severely changed the context of his past, it had little relevance to his current, tower lord–free life. The only serious change was that he wasn't going to call himself a tower lord from now on.

And while Belissar *did* want to think through and come to terms with all the various implications of this shocking revelation, he had something he needed to address in the immediate short term. Which was, now that he had determined that demihumans weren't actually monsters cursed by the gods, how should he deal with a group of them setting up near his dungeon?

On the one hand, they were normal people, from what Belissar could tell, and so didn't need to be treated any differently from humans or anything. On the other . . . Belissar didn't have plans for how to treat humans in the first place.

He was a dungeon master now, so his former behavior around others didn't exactly match his current circumstances. And after his latest revelations, he *definitely* wasn't going to act like the tower lords had, demanding tribute and obedience and whatnot. Maybe there were reasons for their actions, but Belissar was simply too upset to even think about them.

But that meant Belissar now had to chart his own path. And, well, he hadn't made any plans for these circumstances. He hadn't even thought about meeting people again, perfectly content with living with just himself and his bees.

His past interactions with most other people had not exactly been positive, especially after Mrs. Imkomos had died, so when Belissar thought of these bear people stomping into his dungeon, stealing his honey—or worse, setting fire to his home or his hives, his eyes narrowed, and he clenched his fist.

But he took a deep breath and shook his head. The bear man who had visited had done nothing of the sort, even leaving tribute at the shrine of bees. That much of what the tower lords said actually had some truth to it, apparently. The God of Bees had shared it with him, even.

And, if Belissar remembered correctly, he may have seen some sort of message about challengers or something, though he had been distracted very soon after that and so wasn't sure if he was remembering correctly.

Which meant that, while a part of him wanted to have nothing to do with other people—bears or otherwise—there were apparently benefits to interacting with them. Not to mention that he might be able to trade for things like cloth and tools, and so avoid having to make everything himself.

Belissar heaved a sigh. It seemed there was no choice but to give it a shot. The possibility of figuring out what challengers were, the possibility of trade, and the apparent approval of the God of Bees outweighed any fears he had regarding people. After all . . .

Cave Mushroom absorbed. Sufficient samples gathered.
Cave Mushroom now available.
No applications available.

Cave Carrot absorbed. Sufficient samples gathered.
Cave Carrot now available.
No applications available.

Cave Potato absorbed. Sufficient samples gathered.
Cave Potato now available.
No applications available.

. . . even his first interaction with these people had borne fruit. None of these particular plants and fungi were usable at the moment, but Belissar guessed from the names and the holes in the ground that these ones needed an underground environment. So, if he had gone for dirt tunnels and digger bees, he may have now had at least two new plants for them to gather from.

And if these people could potentially aid his dungeon and his bees . . . then Belissar just might be willing to put up with them.

CHAPTER THIRTY-TWO

ATTEMPTING DIPLOMA-BEE

Belissar had his bees fly around the outskirts of the tribe's camp, keeping an eye on them and learning whatever he could, but he did not have to wait long. The group spent the rest of the day making camp, but when Belissar's scouts arrived the next morning, they found a group of bear people preparing to move. A young man and a woman with a child were arguing with the old woman who had spoken to one of his bees.

"I'm against this. What will we do if something happens? If they decide to attack us?"

The old woman shook her head. "You need to come so that the sacred den master does *not* attack. We cannot show up with nothing but warriors if we wish for peace."

The young woman nodded. "It's alright, Isäppak; we'll be fine."

Another armed man, the one who had visited Belissar's dungeon previously, placed his hand on the young man's shoulder. "And we'll look after them. I swear no harm will come to your family."

The young man hung his head and took a deep breath, then nodded his head. The old woman smiled.

"You're a good father, Isäppak. And that is what we must convey to the sacred den if we wish for this to be our home."

Belissar watched as the group gathered their things and began moving toward his dungeon. He took a deep breath. "Niobee."

Niobee flew around in front of him. "Yes, King?"

"Let the flower meadow queens know I'll be heading to the gate. I'd like to bring their soldiers with me."

"Yes!"

Niobee flew off immediately as Belissar rose to his feet. Grabbing his axe, he looked down at himself and grimaced. A worn tunic patched up by his less-than-stellar linen weave did not exactly present an imposing figure. But he didn't have anything else, so there was no helping it.

Besides, the bees were the most important part of the dungeon, anyway, and Belissar figured they would be impressive enough on their own.

Belissar stood just in front of the entrance to his dungeon, watching as the group made their way toward him through the eyes of his scouts. He did not have to wait long before they reached the edge of the clearing, and Belissar nodded as they stepped out of the tree line.

"Okay, now."

A heavy buzzing resounded through the clearing as hundreds of wings began to beat. An army of soldier bees rose from the ground and from among the flowers, filling the sky with buzzing and chitin. They flew just above Belissar, forming up into their squads as they hovered overhead.

The bear people stopped and tensed. About half of their number were armed and took up positions around the rest with their weapons raised. The other half, consisting of the elderly and families with children, huddled together in the center.

The old woman stepped forward and said something to the man leading them, who motioned then lowered his weapons. The others eyed him and the bees for a bit longer before they slowly lowered theirs. The old woman and the lead man then began walking slowly across the clearing. The others glanced at each other before slowly beginning to follow.

Belissar crossed his arms as they approached. "Okay, that's close enough. Why are you here?"

He resisted the urge to wince. That had come out a bit harsher than he'd wanted, but he was trying to project confidence here. Even if every instinct in his body wanted to apologize and keep his head down.

Fortunately, the old woman took it in stride.

"Greetings, master of this sacred den. I am Chief Rohsuak, and these are my people. We have come to request your blessing to settle here."

Belissar raised an eyebrow. "You want to live here?"

She nodded her head. "We have been wandering for a long time; yours is the first unoccupied land with a sacred den we have found. Should you find it in your heart to accept, we would like to make our home here."

Chief Rohsuak motioned, and some people from the center stepped forward, spreading out a mat on the ground before Belissar. On it, they laid all sorts of goods, from seeds and preserved foods to textiles and crafts, to tools made of bone . . . and even metal.

"Of course, we shall offer you and your patron a portion of our labor, and our warriors will challenge themselves before your god if you wish."

Belissar looked down at the stuff on the ground, then up at Chief Rohsuak, then to her people watching him.

Yep.

He had no idea what to say.

Tribute? Challenging themselves before his god? Belissar's experience with negotiations was limited to acting grateful when the other villagers handed him trinkets and almost rotten food in exchange for a barrel of fine mead.

He had to catch himself from thanking the old woman by reflex, having no experience with people asking *him* for permission to do something, much less offering stuff to him.

But . . . this was good, right? They weren't trying to kill him, weren't trying to break in and steal his stuff, and they were even offering him their own stuff just to live in the area. Seemed like a good deal to him.

And, well, the only other example he had of dungeon-people relations were those tower lords he was trying not to think about, so if he thought it was good, that was fine, right?

"Um, okay. That's fine, I guess."

Chief Rohsuak smiled. "Thank you for your generosity."

Then Belissar narrowed his eyes. "Just one thing. Don't hurt my bees."

Chief Rohsuak nodded. "Of course. We will treat all of your den's residents with the utmost respect."

Belissar nodded before turning to leave.

"Sacred Den Master, will you accept our gift?"

Belissar stopped and turned around, pointing at the stuff on the mat. "Oh, that's for me?"

Chief Rohsuak smiled and nodded. "Yes, we brought it for you, after all."

Belissar felt his cheeks grow warm. "Oh. Um, right." Stepping forward, he tried to scoop up the mat as quickly as he could, stepping back while trying to hold it all in his arms. "Well, if that's everything?"

Chief Rohsuak nodded. "Thank you for your time and generosity, Sacred Den Master."

"Right . . . let's go."

With that, Belissar beat a hasty retreat into the dungeon, the soldier bee army following after him.

Belissar groaned once he got inside.

"Well, that was awkward . . ."

How was he supposed to know they were offering this stuff to him and not just showing off their wares? No one had ever just . . . given things to him before!

No one in the past had even acknowledged his presence if he didn't show up with a jar of mead!

He groaned again as he adjusted the weight of the stuff in his arms. Well, at least he'd gotten a bunch of free stuff out of all of this. He turned to the soldier bees flying around him.

"Thanks for the good work, everyone. You can go back to training now. And, um, if those people arrive, I guess don't attack them unless they attack you or try to steal your honey or something like that?"

The air roared with the beating of wings as the soldiers all performed an aerial salute dance before flying back toward their hives. Belissar cracked a smile at the sight. It was still quite impressive to see the army of giant bees flying as one.

He then made his way back to the farmhouse and spread the mat across the table to check what he had received more closely. The food was mostly the same cave mushrooms, carrots, and potatoes the first man had brought, along with some sort of hardened cake that also appeared to have some meat in it. The seeds were mostly the same, but also included some aboveground species. Unfortunately, as with the pinecones, it took more than just a few seeds to unlock any new plants.

But there was one plant that made Belissar's eyes go wide. A flower that had been dried for preservation. One that may not have registered as a flower at first, given its brown petals and stem, but that had a very familiar shape.

Absorb Ground Mana Flower?

A mana flower that was brown instead of blue, and apparently had something to do with the ground? Maybe the bear people had found it while underground? And if Belissar remembered correctly, the digger bee description had said something about Ground mana. So, if he unlocked this flower, and the bees made honey from it . . . perhaps they would come up with a new type of bee.

Ground Mana Flower absorbed.
Current samples: 1/5

Well, he only had the one, but he would have to ask the bear people if they had any more. If he was willing to talk to them again, that was . . .

Beyond that, the bear folk had given him some other useful things. The cloths meant he wouldn't have to process as much flax to get the stockpile he wanted, and the clay bowl would be useful if he made anything other than straight honeycomb. And then there were the tools, which included a set of butchery knives, mostly made of bone but including one made of metal. His own knife was getting dull at this point, so that was honestly a big help.

All in all, it was a big boon. And they had just . . . given it to him, freely?

Belissar couldn't help but be confused for a while after. His mind might know that he was now a dungeon master with a powerful monster bee army, but his heart was still surprised by the completely different interactions he'd had with these people . . .

CHAPTER THIRTY-THREE

BEE CHALLENGED!

While Belissar attempted to comprehend the meaning of people giving him stuff, the bear folk headed on back to the others. The bee scouts kept an eye on them as they reorganized, with the children and young parents returning to the camp, and a few other folk cycling in. As such, Belissar caught wind of them heading back toward the tower when he turned his attention back their way.

Belissar kept watch in silence. He wanted to know more about these people and what more they might want from him. If he could at least figure that out, he would be able to understand their actions to a degree. He had dealt with plenty of ulterior motives; it was those he was unaware of that concerned him.

He, perhaps, had not yet accepted how other people would now view him.

So, he watched through the eyes of his scouts as Chief Rohsuak and the man who'd first scouted his dungeon led another group up to the gates and stepped inside. Belissar signaled to his flower meadow queens to keep an eye out but not to interfere for now.

Challenger detected. Enabling Remnants.
Challengers Present: 12

Again, he saw a message from his tower, again confirming that the tower considered the bear people as intelligent beings who could acknowledge the God of Bees.

The bear folk then split into two groups. Chief Rohsuak gathered a group in front of the shrine, while the man led four armed individuals, who stood off to the side and watched. Chief Rohsuak gave a small smile as she walked up to the statue.

"Bees, huh? In all my years and travels, I have never seen a shrine dedicated to bees. A most curious sacred den indeed."

Turning around, she faced her group. "Remember: the gods are welcoming, but they are not blind. They will acknowledge sincerity and commitment, but they will respond to deceit in kind, and your actions today will reflect upon all of us. Step forward only if you are ready to acknowledge this god as yours and have brought the best you are capable of."

The group nodded, then one of the bear people stepped forward, walking up to the shrine of bees. Taking a pouch from her belt, she knelt before the statue and spoke in a soft voice that for some reason Belissar couldn't hear, even with his tower senses. She then placed the pouch inside the wax chest and waited, closing her eyes.

Both the chest and the statue lit up, bathing the area with soft, yellow light. The light seemed to wrap around the woman, and Belissar could feel as mana flowed through the tower into the shrine and then into her. Her eyes shot open and began to moisten as she stared up at the shrine. She said something again before rising to her feet, staring at her hands as she stepped back.

Challenger blessed.
Gained 10 DP.

Belissar stared at the message before him. He'd just gained ten days' worth of DP . . . for letting someone pray at the shrine of bees?

Five more bear people prayed at the shrine while Belissar's mind wrapped around the implications of what he was seeing. Two more of them did the same as the first woman, and Belissar gained another twenty DP. Two more acted the same, but he gained only five DP from each of them.

The final one, a young man, placed his offering inside the chest and prayed . . . but nothing happened. The shrine did not light up, Belissar did not feel any mana move, and no messages about DP appeared.

Chief Rohsuak began to frown as she watched. After a few minutes had passed, she stepped forward, inclining her head toward the shrine. "Please excuse me."

And then she went over to the chest and opened it up.

The young man glanced up and began to sweat. "Wait!"

He reached out, but the chief sidestepped him and looked into the chest. Reaching in, she pulled out a metal dagger. She narrowed her eyes—then knocked the young man over the head with her staff.

"What's the meaning of this, Toivenaq? I told you, only come if you're ready to be judged on your *own* efforts! You think a *god* wouldn't know that your grandfather made this?!"

Toivenaq averted his gaze while Chief Rohsuak sighed. She waved her staff at him, and he quickly fell back as she turned to the shrine and bowed her head.

"Please forgive us for the insult. That boy has greater ambitions than his patience would warrant. And thank you for accepting those of our people who came in good faith."

Chief Rohsuak took a small, dried flower and placed it inside the box.

"I hope this pleases you, God of Bees, as well as your sacred den's master."

Tribute received.
Your patron grants you this portion:
- Ground Mana Flower x1

Finally stepping away from the shrine, she nodded at the man leading the armed group.

"All yours, Metsaitti. May your hunt be fruitful."

The lead armed man, Metsaitti, nodded and turned to the group of four armed individuals, two men and two women.

"Remember, this is the domain of the sacred den master and his patron god, and we are guests. Do not harm his bees, and do not do anything to provoke them. Am I understood?"

The four nodded at him before Metsaitti turned around. "Good. Then, let's move."

The group began to walk through the flower meadow with their weapons raised. Two of them, a man and a woman, carried spears, while the other two held bows but had spears tied to their backs. They sniffed the air and glanced every which way as they made their way forward.

Not even a short way in, Metsaitti paused, glancing at the ground. He quietly stepped to the side. The spearwoman in front noticed and followed in his footsteps, but the spearman kept walking straight ahead—right onto the first pit trap.

He let out a cry, but Metsaitti moved quickly, jumping to the edge of the pit and catching the young man's arm, leaving him dangling over the edge. The spearwoman and the two archers rushed over as well, grabbing the spearman's arms to pull him back up.

"Watch your step."

The spearman gasped for breath before frowning. "How did you even notice? It looked exactly like regular ground!"

Metsaitti shrugged. "Experience. You need to watch with more than just your eyes. I'll show you on the next one."

The spearman balked. "*Next* one?"

Metsaitti nodded. "There's never just one."

With that, the group made their way deeper in, with the four younger folk staring at the ground ahead of them. Belissar had only been half paying attention to them up until now, as stunned as he was by the sudden DP gain, but now, something had occurred that drew his attention.

No, something that *demanded* his attention. He felt something cold move through the tower's mana . . . which he knew to be the Hunger.

Belissar leapt up as his eyes went wide. He was not prepared for a purification, for he had received no notice of it up to this point.

Sure, the amount of Hunger he was feeling was even less than that of the minor purification, but the bees weren't in position. Even worse, the first group of bear people were still gathered around the entrance to the tower. Belissar might have been wary of their intentions, but that didn't mean he wanted to see them get torn apart by a shade.

The queens of the flower meadow responded to his panicked commands, and the soldier bee army stopped training, forming up into their squads and flying across the meadow at maximum speed. Belissar turned his attention to the gate, hoping they would make it in time.

It was then that he froze, and then blinked. He was watching the gate, but the Hunger didn't seem to be gathering there. Narrowing his eyes, he tried to feel where the cold of the Hunger had gone . . .

He found it just in front of the armed group. Belissar watched as a tiny portion of the Hunger came into being and condensed in the middle of the field. But . . . this time was different. This time, the mana of the tower grew hot and wrapped around the Hunger, holding it within.

A moment later, a small shade appeared. It was like the shades Belissar had faced before, except *tiny*. Belissar's head had barely come up to the shoulder of the first shade, while the minor shades stood just below his neck.

This shade, on the other hand?

This one would barely come up to his knees.

And that wasn't the only difference. The black mist didn't ooze off, and it didn't wilt the floor beneath its feet. It also ignored the flowers around it, and even the bee workers nearby. Instead, Belissar felt the mana of the tower move, and the shade growled, walking toward the armed group.

Belissar was struck dumb as he watched.

Just what exactly was going on?!

CHAPTER THIRTY-FOUR

BEE ASSISTED!

Metsaitti stopped the group as he noticed the shade. "Get ready, everyone. Pitkäsik will take the first shot, but we all need to be prepared if it doesn't go down."

The four following him nodded. The two spear wielders took up positions by their leader, while the other two nocked arrows on their bows. One of them pulled back the bowstring as they took aim at the shade.

The arrow flew and struck the small creature in the side, who snarled before rushing toward the group, barking as loud as it could. The archer fumbled her next arrow and dropped it to the ground, missing her chance for a follow-up shot. Metsaitti called out to the nearest spearman.

"Tyhgak!"

The spearman gulped but hefted his weapon and stabbed forward as the shade leapt at them. His spear caught the beast right in the jaw, and a moment later, Metsaitti and the spearwoman stabbed into the shade's side as well.

It vanished in a cloud of dispersing black mist.

Meanwhile, Belissar exhaled his breath as he watched through his tower sight. He let the flower meadow queens know the situation had been handled for now just as words appeared before his eyes.

Remnant defeated.
1 DP gained.

Belissar blinked at the message.

So . . . that tiny shade was a remnant? And he got DP when the bear people defeated one?

Belissar rubbed his chin and fell silent as he considered that.

*

Belissar watched as Metsaitti led the group around the flower meadow for a bit. Additional remnants formed here and there, but the bear folk handled them without issue. In particular, Metsaitti had each of the four deal the opening attack to a remnant in turn, allowing them to handle it solo if they were able to do so.

After some time had passed, he returned to the entrance, where Chief Rohsuak smiled at the group.

"It appears you were successful?"

Metsaitti nodded. "We had a few close calls, but we managed. It seems the den master is fond of pit traps."

Chief Rohsuak chuckled while Metsaitti led the group up to the shrine of bees, where each of them prayed in turn. Belissar felt the tower's mana flow once again, receiving another ten DP each for the four. Metsaitti rounded it off, only granting one DP himself.

The group then prepared to leave, but just before they headed out, Chief Rohsuak had them turn toward the flower meadow and incline their heads.

"Thanks to you both, Sacred Den Master and Goddess of Bees."

With that, they departed, leaving Belissar alone with his bees . . . and his thoughts. He sat back in his chair and let out a low hum, his mind racing with the events of the day and all the various things he had learned in the process.

Soon, his ears buzzed with the sound of wings, and he held up his hand in reflex as Niobee flew around him before landing on his finger.

"King okay?"

He looked down at her, giving her a small smile, then rose from his chair and stepped over to the jars full of honeycomb. Scraping off a bit of honey with a finger, he held it up for Niobee, who flew over and began to drink. Belissar's smile grew as she did.

It had been a while since he had done this; ever since Niobee had become intelligent—or more accurately, ever since he had *discovered* that she was intelligent.

So perhaps he didn't actually need to coax her onto his finger with honey, but that didn't mean he would just stop. If anything, he should be treating her better now, knowing she could and did return his friendship.

"I . . . have a lot on my mind after all this. Would you mind if we talked like we used to?"

Niobee buzzed about rapidly. "Niobee always listen!"

Belissar smiled at that and began to talk. He poured out all that was on his mind about tower lords and lies, as well as his confusion over the latest revelations and what they would mean for his tower and the bees that lived inside of it. Niobee sat on his finger, watching him intently throughout it all.

"So, what?! I did all of that, watched everyone I care about die, took crap from the village day after day, and now I find out the tower lords lied all along? It—" Belissar blinked as he finally realized what he was feeling. His eyes narrowed. "It makes me really angry, if I'm honest."

Niobee's wings buzzed loudly, and she extended her stinger as she began a dance at a furious pace. "Others, bad! Niobee saw! Invade King's hive, steal honey! But King have workers now! We stop!"

Belissar watched . . . and couldn't help but relax a bit. "Yes, thank you for everything, Niobee. I know you and the other girls have my back now. I guess . . . things will be very different from now on."

"Yes!"

He took a deep breath and slowly exhaled it. "Okay, that brings us to the new people; what do you think of them?"

"These okay! Help King, give stuff!"

Belissar chuckled at that. That pretty much matched his own impression of the situation. To be fair, the bear people could have any sort of intentions long-term, but as far as both he and Niobee could tell, they seemed beneficial.

And that seemed to have been confirmed by the tower itself. Apparently, "challengers" like them were a significant source of DP. Or rather, maybe they were the *main* source of it?

Belissar had received over a week's worth of DP just from a single bear person praying and offering tribute at the shrine of bees. And there had been more than one of them. In total, he had earned *eighty-one* DP from their prayers and tribute. Even a minor purification didn't reward that much.

And then there was the situation with the remnants.

Belissar had thought about that and reread the descriptions of challengers and remnants, and thought he had an idea of what was going on. The description specifically said remnants allowed challengers to assist with ongoing purification, so Belissar guessed that remnants were something like a mini purification. A tiny bit of the Hunger which seemed to gather when people entered his dungeon that they could defeat so his bees wouldn't have to.

He even received DP when they did. Perhaps that was the "assist with ongoing purification" part? All in all, they had purified five more of the shades, bringing his DP total for the day up to eight-six. That was almost three months' worth, or nearly two minor purification rewards. It seemed having people around was very helpful indeed.

But . . . what was their reason for helping him to such an extent? Surely, they had to have gotten *something* out of this?

Belissar figured it had to do with the mana in the shrine of bees; if he recalled, the messages during the prayers had mentioned the challengers got blessed? If it was something like the Blessing of Bees . . . But the blessing's effects only seemed useful for a dungeon master, so Belissar wasn't sure.

His eyes widened as his mind turned back to the tower lords, and specifically, the tower guards—the servants of the lords said to have been blessed by the gods and capable of great, heroic feats. He had previously been under the impression that their capabilities were something innate to the tower guard themselves, but if that wasn't true for the tower lords, maybe it wasn't true for the tower guard either? What if it was, again, something they gained from the tower itself . . . or from its patron god?

In other words, had he just created tower guards? Only, guards who weren't working for him? Or were they working for him, and he just didn't notice?

Belissar shook his head to clear his mind, since he didn't have answers for any of those questions.

Well, he'd have to watch those bear people who had received the blessing and determine if they could perform great deeds like the tower guard were rumored to. And if so . . . Well, Belissar didn't exactly know what he'd do. Should he offer them a job? Demand they help protect the tower? Just ignore them and be happy with the DP?

He decided he'd figure that part out later, if the blessing from the shrine indeed worked the way he was guessing.

All in all, the point was that these people were acting polite toward him and actively benefiting him with their visits, and the God of Bees seemed to approve of their presence as well, which meant there was no need for Belissar to do anything about them or keep them out of the tower or anything like that, although he would keep an eye on their visits if only because of the remnants that appeared around them. Maybe he could even offer to trade some honey for more goods if he needed them.

Suddenly, Belissar realized there *was* something that had changed as a result of all of this. A very simple yet easily overlooked implication of this whole chain of events.

And that was that the bear people had traveled *through* the Hunger. Or underneath it, as the case was. Belissar had been under the impression that the Hunger seeped into the ground and reached into the skies as well, but maybe there was a limit to that? Or maybe there were towers underground as well?

The exact reasons aside, the point was that he was not alone anymore. And if the bear folk could reach him, then others could as well. Others who might not be as polite as they were.

Others like the tower lords.

And that was something Belissar would now need to consider.

CHAPTER THIRTY-FIVE

TO BEE READY

Belissar considered what would happen if a tower lord made contact with him. His gut instinct was that it would go very badly. The *gods* may not have cared that a peasant had taken command of a tower, but the tower lords still would. They were the ones who'd likely started the idea that peasants would defile a tower in the first place. So, Belissar couldn't imagine they would be happy to see him as the master of one.

And, of course, Belissar didn't really need to imagine. His entire village had been burned to the ground with presumably no survivors just for being in the area when a tower was created. He assumed the tower lords would continue such treatment should they discover him.

All of that meant that Belissar needed to be prepared to fight.

And at the moment, he had no confidence in opposing a tower lord. Even knowing some of their secrets and exposing some of their lies, Belissar couldn't shake the image of tower lords as near-mythical figures commanding godlike powers and invincible armies.

If anything, now that he knew about the powers a tower and the blessing of a god could offer, he figured the tower lords' strength might be even closer to the legends than he'd originally thought, especially those who had been around for many normal lifetimes. Who knew what sort of defenders or perks or blessings they might have in their own towers?

And then there was the tower guard. They alone were a mighty army who had never lost a fight that Belissar had ever heard about. Whenever word of rebellions or bandits or shades from the Hunger came, they all ended the same way. No matter how badly things went for the local forces, once the tower guard was deployed to the scene, the situation was handled.

So how would Belissar's tower stack up against even a conservative estimate of the tower lords and their guards?

Belissar didn't need firsthand observations or military experience to say not well at all. As impressive as his bee army was to him and maybe the bear folk, it was by no means large. The soldier bee numbers were, what, in the hundreds? Maybe? The low hundreds at best.

Belissar hadn't seen the tower guard himself, but from what he had heard, they certainly had more than a few hundred soldiers to spare. That meant even against the tower guard his current forces would be outnumbered . . . and he was under no illusion that a soldier bee would be anything close to a match. Even a token force would likely cut through everything his tower had to offer like a hot knife through butter.

He didn't imagine a pit trap or a bit of mad honey would bother them very much, either. And this was all before he began to imagine what an actual tower lord might be capable of.

So, the answer was clear. Belissar and his bees needed to grow stronger. *Much* stronger. He would need thousands, even tens of thousands or more soldier bees before he believed he had even a small chance at surviving. He would need bees who could face the shade from the initial purification one-on-one. He would need traps and weapons that could handle people capable of great and heroic feats.

And worst of all . . . he had no idea how much time he had to reach that level.

He had no idea where in the world his tower was. To be honest, he didn't even know much geography beyond his own village, much less the world beyond the influence of the towers. If the very few and incomplete maps and tales they had access to were any indication, the tower lords ruled the whole known world.

Belissar now had his doubts on whether that was true, but he had no idea what else could be out there if so, or how far he was from the nearest tower lord. They could be further apart than Belissar could ever imagine . . . or they could be right next door.

Which meant he may not meet a tower lord for an entire lifetime, or he could meet one in the next week, and he had no idea which was more likely.

Belissar realized that if he wanted to protect his bees and his tower, if he wanted to avoid a second death at the hands of the tower lords, he would need to make an active effort to grow his tower as quickly as possible, as well as learn as much about his surroundings as he could, especially the tunnel from which the bear folk had arrived.

With potentially no time to lose, Belissar got to work right away.

He took stock of all the different options he had to strengthen his dungeon . . . and frowned. He could add a couple more monster bee queen or monster bee soldier spawners, or a bunch more pit traps—and that was about it. He'd probably have to add more resource nodes in that case, too, just to ensure all the queens had enough flowers to go around. But a few more hives or soldiers would not change the overall situation. He needed much more than that.

He needed more rooms and more options, along with more mana with which to implement them. More of everything, really.

His frown deepened, and he rubbed his chin. The bear folk significantly boosted the DP income—if they kept visiting regularly, that was—but the prices in the DP shop were still exorbitant in comparison. It would take him a long time to do everything that way. He could get a bit more DP or mana from the minor purifications, but that was coming at a relative trickle as well.

What he really needed was something like the initial purification. That had given him a new room, a new defender, a new room feature, double the mana, *and* increased his room limit all at once. Of course, he couldn't rule out that was a one-time thing for getting the tower set up in the first place, but he couldn't help but wonder if there was anything similar that he might be missing.

Mana too low to initiate expansion purification.
Minimum required total mana: 300

Belissar smirked. And there it was, once again.

But then, his smile dropped. So he *could* in fact do something more than just a minor purification here and there, but not until he had improved the tower's mana pool. And the only way he could that he was aware of was through minor purifications or the incredibly expensive DP shop.

Going outside to scratch some math in the dirt, he determined he would need to conduct nine more minor purifications to get the mana required. That would mean nine more weeks at minimum if he had to wait.

However, he wondered if he could start the purifications before the countdown began, since he could start them early within the countdown?

Please purify core before initiating early purifications.
Core corruption currently at 15%
Attempt core purification?

Belissar nodded. It seemed there were things he could do to speed up the process. The flip side, though, was that this all would require his bees to fight more often . . . and die more often.

He frowned.

Was he willing to ask that of them? Would they be willing to sacrifice for that cause?

Well, he knew the answer to the latter was a resounding yes. He didn't even need to ask. The bees of the flower meadow were training and preparing to fight each and every day. The apiary bees were working hard discovering new honey types and the new bee types that might result. Each and every one of them was already working hard to grow stronger.

Belissar took a deep breath. He didn't want to see them hurt, but if he didn't take this risk now, he would risk a lot more later. He knew they could handle shades all the way up to the shade from the initial purification. Whatever sacrifices may result from that would pale in comparison to what would happen if they encountered a tower lord before he was ready.

He *had* to do this. It was not his job to keep his tower's own defenders out of harm's way. It was, rather, his job to ensure they had the best chance of defending their home. He had to take responsibility for their lives, and apparently, that would sometimes mean risking them intentionally.

He let out his breath slowly. This dungeon master business could be difficult, after all.

But he made his choice and sent word to his bees. He didn't tell Niobee to inform them on his behalf this time but sent his intentions directly to them instead. If he was going to risk their lives, he wanted them to hear it directly from him. He asked them to gather.

Before long, Niobee, all of the queens, and a soldier bee from each soldier spawner hovered in the air before him. They all watched him in silence save for the buzzing of their wings as they waited for him. He took a deep breath before opening his mouth.

"I . . . am considering conducting another purification. You will need to fight, and you might get hurt in the process. This one is not being forced on us, but it is necessary for our tower to grow, and I think we need to grow as quickly as we can. So, I'll ask you now. Are you ready and willing to fight again, not just to defend our home but to expand it?"

The bees hovered still for a moment, and then, they all burst into rapid flight, filling the air with loud buzzing. The flower meadow queens danced salutes and told him to leave it to them. The apiary queens indicated their stockpiles were full and they were more than prepared.

Meanwhile, Niobee flew up to him, and he held out his finger for her. Landing on it, she began a slow but unwavering dance.

"Bees ready. Whatever King wants, we do!"

Belissar nodded at them. "Thank you all. In that case, get ready. We'll start as soon as you are."

CHAPTER THIRTY-SIX

BEE PURIFIED!

Belissar and the bees got to work immediately. The flower meadow queens gathered up their soldiers and arranged their formations outside the tower's gate. The apiary workers flew to each of the pits, ensuring the sticky honey traps inside were stocked with mad honey. Belissar himself checked the kindling down in each before starting a campfire at the apiary entrance.

Satisfied that everything was prepared, he called out to all his bees.

"Everyone ready?"

Niobee flew next to him. "Ready!"

He could see through the tower sight the different bees all dancing their salute, indicating they were ready. He blinked a bit as he realized he was "seeing" things in multiple places at once. His tower sight was apparently not limited to a single place?

His head started to hurt a bit once he became aware of what he was doing, so he shook it and cleared his thoughts. The tower being capable of more than he'd ever imagined was nothing new at this point, so he put it aside. He would experiment more with the tower sight later; for now, he had something more important to focus on.

"Okay, I'm starting things up, then."

He thought about speeding up the purification once again . . .

Please purify core before initiating early purifications.
Core corruption currently at 15%
Attempt core purification?

Belissar nodded as he indicated he would.

Please select percentage of corruption to purify:
1–15% - Minor purification required.

Contrary to his expectations, the purification did not start immediately, and he was instead confronted with another choice. Belissar found he could adjust the first number from anything between one and the total corruption percentage. The purification required part changed when he passed twelve percent, going from *minor* purification to *minor+*.

Belissar rubbed his chin, thinking for a moment, before moving the number all the way to fifteen percent. On the one hand, he was a bit wary of taking on a purification he hadn't encountered before. On the other, his bees and traps could handle a minor purification with ease, and Belissar believed they could even deal with another initial purification level threat if it came down to it.

Minor+ didn't seem that much worse than *minor*, and so hopefully would still be weaker than the initial shade. Belissar thus felt it was worth the risk to deal with all the corruption in one go.

Minor+ purification attempt commencing.

Belissar once again felt the cold of the Hunger pass through the tower's mana, sending a shiver down his spine.

He wasn't sure he'd ever get used to that feeling, but he noted with satisfaction that the tendrils of Hunger creeping along the walls of the core room had fully receded, coalescing at the tower's gate once more, and this time, the Hunger split into two separate spheres that eventually formed into minor shades. They let out a roar in sync.

Minor+ purification has begun.
Remaining hostiles: 2

Belissar narrowed his eyes. He had not expected multiple shades. There were only two, and they were still the smaller ones from the minor purification, but it was still a situation his bees hadn't faced before, so he didn't know if they were fully prepared for this.

Still, the purification had already begun, so all Belissar could do was trust them.

The soldier bees dove from the sky, stinging one of the shades on the back and then breaking off. Only one squad had prepared to dive, so only one of the shades was attacked in the initial assault, but that was fine for their current plan. The attacked shade snarled and ran after the soldier bee squad, with the other following closely behind.

And, as planned, the first shade ran right over a pit trap and fell with a yelp, getting coated with sticky mad honey down at the bottom.

But the plan had only accounted for a single shade, and the other was far enough behind to skid to a stop just before the pit. It snarled and backed away, watching the soldier bees flying in the air all around it.

Belissar frowned. Under normal circumstances, he would light his torch and rush over to set the pit trap on fire, but now, he couldn't. Even if one of the shades was trapped, the other was still a threat.

The soldier bees dove down to attack the beast, but it was prepared and leapt to the side to evade the attack. And, worst of all, it didn't chase them as they flew off toward the next nearest trap. It remained by the first, pacing back and forth along the edge as it kept watch on the bees above.

With that plan having failed, the bees adjusted their formation and moved to fight the remaining shade directly. Bee squads began diving in quick intervals as the shade managed to dodge the first; it was about to swing its tail when the second squad arrived, and the monster was forced to redirect its attack to ward them off, only for a third to land some stings on its back.

It snarled and let out a breath of black mist, but the soldier bees were prepared this time, and all managed to evade. And this time, only the closest bees scattered, while the squads furthest back moved down toward the ground. They would not allow the shade to break the encirclement.

But once again, the beast did something unexpected.

It glanced down into the pit and found the other shade trying and failing to climb out. And then . . . it jumped down *into* the pit, using its tail to scrape honey and kindling off its staggering comrade.

The bees gathered around the edges of the trap but did not attempt to enter. With two shades in such an enclosed area, there was little chance they could evade counterattacks. Still, this was the moment Belissar had been waiting for, so he stuck a torch into the campfire and took off running once it was lit.

In the meantime, the shades began stabbing the wall of the pit repeatedly with their tails, as high as they could reach. One of them jumped up and stuck their front paws into the two indents, just managing to hold on. Belissar's eyes widened, seeing how it was about to pull itself up further.

The bees reacted, however, and a squad of soldiers swooped down to sting the shade's face. The creature snarled and lost its grip, tumbling back to the bottom while Belissar gulped and picked up his pace, trying to reach the pit before the shades escaped.

The one that had fallen barked at the other swaying around from the mad honey. The other shade shook its head and jumped up itself; however, its aim was off, and it missed the footholds entirely. It made another attempt, but its hold was too shaky, and it fell. It was not until the third attempt that the beast managed to get a grip.

The bees began to dive once again, but the shade at the bottom unleashed a breath of black mist over the other, and the bees were forced to break off their attack while the beast itself remained unaffected by the mist.

Belissar skidded to a halt as the shade pulled itself up and leapt to the top of the pit, just barely managing to grab onto the ledge.

The bees looked at one another. One among their number buzzed and danced, and then they sprang into action. A squad dove toward the creature.

Black mist erupted from the pit as the one at the bottom again covered for the other, but this time, the bees did not turn around. They flew through the mist with their stingers forward, relying on momentum and gravity to carry them forward even as the attack sapped their strength. And so, they managed to plunge their stingers into the shade.

The creature roared and whipped its tail around—which was a mistake. The move unbalanced the partially intoxicated beast as the soldier bees slammed into it, and the shade teetered over the edge before falling back. There were two yelps as it landed on top of the one still inside.

Belissar took his opportunity and sprinted the rest of the way, barely skidding to a halt before the pit. He was about to toss the torch in when he froze.

The soldier bees were still stuck on the shade. Having been weakened by the black mist, they now struggled to free themselves.

One of them glanced up at him. She danced a salute as well as she could with her abdomen locked in place, but her intentions came through to Belissar just fine, and his heart constricted within his chest.

But even as he hesitated, the two shades untangled themselves and began to tear at the bees.

Belissar closed his eyes and tossed the torch into the pit.

"I'm sorry. And thank you. I won't forget you."

He could still see through the tower sight, however, and so he caught one last, satisfied dance from the soldier before she disappeared into the flames.

All hostiles defeated.
Minor+ purification successful.

CHAPTER THIRTY-SEVEN

REME-BEE-RANCE

Belissar took a deep breath and forced down his feelings. Forcing himself to smile, he turned around to look up at the soldier bee army hovering in the air.

"Great work. Thanks, everyone."

The air buzzed as the soldier bees all danced a salute while Belissar shook his head.

Truth be told, this had been an excellent outcome. The purification had been completed, the shades had been defeated, and they had only lost a single squad of soldier bees. He had feared the worst when the shades managed to escape the pit trap, so to take them down with fewer losses than even the initial minor purification was a great victory.

Belissar, however, couldn't help the pain in his chest as he thought of the soldier bee looking up at him. After all, it was he who'd decided to conduct this purification now instead of waiting for the corruption to recede over time, and he who'd decided a stronger purification would be manageable. He was tempted to blame himself for the losses.

But he did not. He *forced* himself not to. And the reason for that was the same memory of that soldier bee looking up at him. The loss, the sacrifice—that was a choice she had made, that they all had made. They had chosen to sacrifice themselves to keep the shades down and achieve this victory. Belissar felt he should celebrate what they had achieved more than he should mourn their loss. And therefore, he could not permit himself to wallow in guilt.

Instead, he would honor their sacrifice and make use of the rewards of their victory.

And just like that, the words of said reward appeared before his eyes. Unprompted, for he did not plan to consider it until after the funeral.

Minor+ purification completed!
Please select a reward:
- +75 DP
- +15 Max Mana
- Bee Memorial room feature

Belissar froze as he stared at the golden, glowing words at the bottom of the list. All his plans and the expansion of his mana went out the window, for he knew what he needed to do.

Bee Memorial room feature selected!
Bee Memorial room feature is now available!
Compatible Bee Memorial detected. Upgrade?

Belissar confirmed as he walked toward the shrine of bees at the end of the flower meadow. Feeling the mana of the tower flow, he saw bright light surrounding the little planks he had stuck in the ground.

When it faded, the little planks were gone. In their place was a large beehouse shaped like one of his but carved from the same material as the shrine's statue. Surrounding it were tall pillars of solid wax adorned with bees.

Belissar stepped up to one and placed his hand on it. Though it was made of wax, it felt as solid as stone. The numbers and symbols he had carved into the planks had transferred onto the pillars, but he also saw markings he had not made.

Walking closer, he looked over them.

Queen 1 – Spawner One's First Dynasty, and her hive of 1018 workers.
Queen 2 – Spawner One's First Dynasty, and her hive of 564 workers.
Queen 3 – Spawner One's First Dynasty, and her hive of 186 workers.
Queen 4 – Spawner One's First Dynasty

Belissar's eyes widened, and then he bowed his head as the tears formed.

"Thank you all, for trying to defend me. I'm sorry you had to die because of me. I promise I'll do better, and I won't let your deaths go to waste."

A short while later, the bees finished their victory dances and gathered by the memorial once more. Belissar had them help him gather the ashes at the bottom of the pit trap and place them within the beehouse at the center of the memorial. His eyes widened as the bee carvings in the wax began to move and dance. Perhaps it was a written word, but for the bees themselves?

Belissar nodded toward the bee army. "Thank you for your courage and for defending our home."

They danced their salute, and then Belissar turned to the monument, bowing his head. "And thank you for your sacrifice."

Numbers and symbols began to carve themselves into the monument as he spoke, signifying each of the bees who had died that day. The beehouse began to glow with soft, golden light—and the shrine of bees next to it began to light up as well. Niobee led them in the slow song from the first funeral, the bees all dancing and buzzing slowly in the light.

A tear dropped from Belissar's eye, but his chest felt lighter. The bees were going to die. If he embarked upon this plan to grow as quickly as possible, they would even die specifically at his command. But now, he knew they would not be forgotten.

And so, he would do all in his power to ensure their sacrifices did not go to waste.

Now that the core was no longer corrupted, Belissar checked if he could initiate a purification.

Please wait 24 hours between purifications.
Remaining cooldown: 21 hours and 49 minutes.

He nodded. So, it wasn't as if he could face continuous purifications. Maybe one a day at most. But that suited Belissar just fine; he wasn't in the mood for another purification just yet, in any case.

Sitting back in a chair in the farmhouse as the sun set, with Niobee drinking from a honeycomb he'd placed on the table, he reviewed the results of the day.

Multiple shades had caught him off guard. To be fair, while every purification before now had only had one beast, it wasn't like there was a rule they had to come alone. But the fact was, Belissar simply hadn't thought about the possibility. And equally as concerning, if not more: the shades had proven they could escape from the pit traps.

All in all, it had been a miracle and a testament to the soldier bees that this purification had ended with only the loss of a single squad.

So, Belissar thought about what he could do.

Multiple shades and the ability to escape from pit traps could be dealt with by the bees. Belissar imagined they would begin training for multiple opponents from now on. If the bees could deal with one of the shades, or even just separate them from each other, then it wouldn't be a problem. The question was, what would they do about three? Or four? Or ten? Or a hundred?

The other—and perhaps larger—problem was that Belissar couldn't pull off his firepit idea under these circumstances. If there were multiple shades, the ones who didn't fall into a pit trap could hang around its edges and prevent him from approaching. Likewise, if the shades could escape, then it was dangerous for Belissar to approach, even if all the monsters had fallen into one. He would need to think of alternative methods to light up the pits if he wanted to keep relying on this method.

He also felt that he should consider the case where he *couldn't* rely on that method. If, for one reason or another, he just couldn't kill a shade with the firepit, then they would have to be defeated directly by the bees, which, as of now, would likely require sacrifice on the bees' part. This would probably be inevitable if the shades got stronger or more numerous, but Belissar still wanted to put as many of the odds in their favor as he could.

So, how could he make the pit traps more reliable? And what could he do to ensure the bees would have the best chance?

In the end, it came back to growing stronger and getting more options to work with. Which he had.

Bee Memorial

Type:	*Bee, Special*
Mana Upkeep:	*3*
Limit:	*1*

A memorial commemorating those who gave their lives in defense of the hives.

Grants all bee-type monsters a small chance to remain active for a short while after a mortal blow. Medium boost to the effect of all sacrificial-type skills.

May have additional effects under the right conditions.

Belissar frowned. He hadn't been considering benefits when he chose the memorial, so it was a pleasant surprise to find it had such effects. At least, until Belissar thought about what exact effects it had. It made his bees notably more powerful, but only when they were going to die. It would reward sacrifice in particular.

Perhaps . . . that was the point. If he was interpreting the golden glowing letters correctly, the God of Bees herself had sent this choice to him. Maybe she was reminding him that to be a bee was to embrace sacrifice?

Even so, Belissar wanted to keep sacrifice as the last resort, not the first. The memorial's effects made his tower and his bees stronger, but they would not enable the bees to handle issues without casualties, so it was not something Belissar wanted to rely on. He would have to do his best to work without the memorial's effects and leave it as a fallback for if—and likely *when*—he made mistakes.

So, he would continue with the purifications as soon as the cooldown was ready. And in the meantime, he'd brainstorm what he could do with what he had to reduce that sacrifice by even a little bit more.

CHAPTER THIRTY-EIGHT

BEE RESPECTFUL

What about this?"

Belissar had spent the night brainstorming what he could do to improve the tower's defenses. It was now morning, and he was in the farmhouse along with the soldier bee who had helped him weave linen. The soldier crawled along the table toward a stick Belissar had placed on it and tried to pick it up with her mandibles. Her wings buzzed softly as she started a slow dance. Belissar let out a sigh.

"No good, huh?"

Belissar's first idea was a simple one. If it was too dangerous and took too long for him to approach the pit traps with a torch, then why not let the soldier bees carry it instead? They could fly with it overhead and drop it into the pit from above, even if there was another shade around to interfere. It was low risk and, well, even if Belissar didn't want to accept it, the bees were willing to fly into danger if they had to.

He was running into some issues, however. Soldier bees may have been gigantic for bees, but they were still fairly small in the grand scheme of things, so a full-size torch was out of the question.

But what was worse was the lack of grasping appendages. Their legs were designed mainly for walking, save for the pollen baskets on their hind legs, so they were limited to their mandibles or hind legs. That meant the torch had to be thin enough to be held within the soldier bee's jaws or hooked within their hind leg joints, as well as light enough to be carried without excessive imbalance during flight.

But on the flip side, the torch couldn't be too small, either. The smaller the torch, the longer it would take to start a fire in the pit traps. A flame too small might even be extinguished as it fell from the sky. Likewise, a small torch wouldn't last very long, and so would have to be used quickly after being lit, which could lead to a situation like before, when Belissar couldn't get the torch to the pit before the shades escaped.

And finally, if the torch was too small, the bee itself could get burned by it, which would prevent its use entirely.

So, Belissar and the soldier bee were experimenting with different stick sizes to find the right balance, but they hadn't found a suitable one just yet.

Just then, Belissar was interrupted by another challenger message. Turning his tower sight to the entrance, he found the bear people had returned. This time, the old woman and her group had stayed home, so it was just the big guy and his warriors. His name was Metsaitti or something, if Belissar recalled correctly.

Niobee flew in front of him. "King! Problem?"

Belissar shook his head. "It's just the bear people again, but I'm going to keep an eye on them for a bit. You girls can take a break for now, too."

"Okay!"

Niobee zoomed out the window as the soldier bee gave a salute and followed after her. Belissar figured he probably didn't need to watch them, but, well, he still wasn't used to them, so wanted to observe a bit more closely.

The group acted the same as before and began sweeping through the meadow. As earlier, remnants appeared every now and again and were handled by the group, all while they kept a sharp lookout for the pit traps. Something changed, however, when they came across a certain flower. The bear folk all froze in place, and the spearman nudged the spearwoman with his elbow.

"Hey, are my eyes tricking me, or is that a mana flower?"

She slowly nodded. "For once, they're not."

The spearman began to grin and step forward, but Metsaitti held out his hand and blocked the spearman from going any further. The young man frowned.

"What gives, Metsaitti? I was going to share credit, you know!"

Metsaitti shook his head before pointing at the flower. "Look more closely and tell me what you see."

The spearman raised an eyebrow and crossed his arms. "I'm guessing you mean besides the glowing, priceless flower?"

The spearwoman rolled her eyes. "Obviously. He means the bees, you idiot."

The mana flower in question had a small swarm of bees around it, each waiting their turn to gather from it. The spearman shrugged.

"So? They're just bees."

Metsaitti stepped in front and looked the young man in the eyes. "The sacred den master has been incredibly generous to us. He has allowed us to settle in his land and visit his den all without cost or submission. In return, he has given us one condition. Just one. Don't hurt his bees. Do you plan to be the one to earn his fury and lose us our new home?"

The young man glanced away. "W-Well, how about we just . . . wave them off? As long as we don't hurt them, right?"

Metsaitti narrowed his eyes. "And how would you feel if someone stole your food? It's all fine because they didn't hurt you, right?"

The spearman threw up his hands. "Fine! We'll leave the priceless treasure alone for a couple of bees!"

Metsaitti nodded and patted him on the shoulder. "Patience. This den is still young, so it's not strange its resources are all claimed by its denizens for now. Hopefully, we'll have many more chances to visit in the future; perhaps we'll find a bit more then."

And so, the group carried on. Belissar nodded with his arms crossed and told the soldier bees he had on standby they could return to training. Belissar may have been confused regarding the bear people overall, but the one thing he was absolutely clear on was that *no one* was allowed to harm his bees. So, it was a good thing their leader had a good head on his shoulders.

Belissar took a deep breath to calm himself down. He then rubbed his chin as he thought over the bear man's words.

So, they expected to find stuff in his tower? On the one hand, Belissar wondered why that would be the case. Why would he let them just take stuff from his dungeon, even if he had the resources?

On the other, they technically *were* helping out already. They were helping to purify the Hunger and earning Belissar DP in the process. And then there was the question of why the tower had options for resources and rest zones in the first place. Perhaps . . . he was *supposed* to offer them stuff in exchange?

He wasn't sure at all. He knew that tower lords didn't exactly offer up their resources, but he'd already decided he wasn't going to follow their example. The bees would just tell him "whatever he decided," and he already knew the bear people's opinions, so there wasn't anyone else he could ask.

So instead, he left the farmhouse and walked toward the shrine of bees at the end of the apiary, taking with him some extra honeycomb. He had already made his daily offering to the God of Bees, but figured he shouldn't come empty-handed when he had a request.

Placing the honeycomb inside the chest, he looked up at the statue of the goddess.

"Um, sorry to ask this of you, but I could use some guidance. Am I . . . supposed to make stuff for those people to find? Do you have a preference on what I should do?"

The shrine of bees glowed with soft, warm light, but otherwise did not respond. Belissar sighed.

"So you want me to decide?"

The shrine continued to glow. Belissar took a deep breath and then rose to his feet.

Well, if the God of Bees said as much, he would just have to figure something out himself. But at the very least, her approval to do as he thought best gave him a little more confidence in his own opinion.

He figured he would test things out, so he added another node of healing herbs close to the entrance and let the bees know to clear the way if the bear people approached that one.

Belissar figured the bear folk would appreciate some extra medicine, and a single healing herb node wasn't *too* expensive. On the other hand, mana flowers were quite precious to his bees, so he wasn't going to hand those out for free. Maybe if they wanted to trade or something. But for now, he'd stick to healing herbs and see how it went.

Fortunately, the group hadn't made it to the end of the meadow where the mana flower nodes were, so they weren't aware that the single flowers here and there were only a drop in the bucket. So hopefully, they'd be content with the herbs.

Belissar then looked them over, for something caught his eye. He noticed the packs the bears wore and smacked his own forehead. He had found a solution to his earlier conundrum.

If the bees were having trouble carrying something, then why not use ropes and straps? Wasn't that how people carried things?

With confirmation that the bear folk weren't going to hurt his bees, Belissar didn't feel the need to watch them as closely anymore, so he got to work, getting some of the processed flax from his store and starting to weave a cord.

Well, at the very least, the bear people were reminding him of what he could do with a little civilization.

CHAPTER THIRTY-NINE

PROSPERI-BEE

The bear team had finished up their fights for the day and were making their way back to the entrance when one of the archers suddenly stopped, staring off to the side. Metsaitti brought the rest to a stop and turned to face him.

"What's the matter?"

The archer pointed toward one of the trees. "Might be my imagination, but . . . was the grass glowing by that tree before?"

Metsaitti turned and looked in the direction indicated. "Hm?" A moment later, he smiled. "I think we're in luck. Come on, let's check it out."

The group made their way over and found a small patch of herbs, several of which were shimmering. Stepping forward, Metsaitti reached for one of them, and it practically pulled itself out of the ground and into his hand.

"Hm, looks like healing herbs. The chief will be pleased."

The spearwoman narrowed her eyes. "This definitely wasn't here when we arrived."

Metsaitti smirked. "No. No, it was not."

He stood up and turned to face the group. "Something to keep in mind about sacred dens. The master can see and hear everything that goes on in one. He probably heard our earlier conversation and adjusted things accordingly."

He made eye contact with the spearman who'd wanted to take the mana flower. "He's been very cooperative thus far, but do remember that this is his home, and his domain. We are guests, and he *will* know if we act otherwise."

The spearman gulped and glanced around while Metsaitti turned and looked toward the sky.

"Thank you, Den Master."

Belissar was still working on the cord and regretting sending his helper off when the message came in.

Challenger blessed.
Gained 12 DP.

Belissar turned his attention and found the bear group back at the entrance, praying at the shrine of bees one by one. He received the DP messages, finding all of them granting one or two more than before. Even Metsaitti gave two instead of one! In total, Belissar received fifty DP from the blessing, plus the five from the shades they had hunted.

He checked the healing herb node he had placed and found they had gathered the glowing herbs of the day from it. He rubbed his chin.

So, he hadn't received any messages or anything when they had gathered from it, but they had given him more DP at the shrine than last time. Belissar thought a bit about why that was. If it were directly related to the healing herbs, then he probably would have gotten the DP when they gathered it. At the same time, though, that was the only thing that Belissar could tell had changed between yesterday and today.

His sight settled on the shrine of bees, and his eyes widened a bit. He'd gotten the DP specifically when they'd prayed at the shrine and the God of Bees had blessed them in return. So maybe it had something to do with that. Something like they had done more in the tower, or maybe they'd just been more grateful when praying this time?

Belissar nodded to himself. It appeared this was worthwhile, after all. More DP was always helpful, and the bees could still gather nectar from the plants before they were harvested.

And above all, this seemed to be related to the God of Bees. She was his patron, who had given him a powerful blessing and both guidance and rewards via her missions. Belissar was ever grateful to her, so if this brought some benefit to her shrine, then Belissar was all for it.

And then, he heard the chime.

New mission received: Help ten challengers receive full blessings.

Belissar smiled. At this point, he was wondering if the God of Bees was reading his thoughts.

Well, she *was* a god, so that was probably true. He nodded his head.

"I'll do my best."

Belissar thought a bit about what that would mean. First of all, the mission said, "full blessings." That implied that whatever mana or blessing the challengers had received thus far wasn't a full blessing. Which made sense to Belissar, as he certainly hadn't seen any of the superhuman deeds the tower guard were reported to be capable of.

The unarmed challengers had offered tribute and been blessed in turn, save the one who'd apparently tried to offer something someone else had made. Meanwhile, the armed challengers went and fought remnant shades, then got blessed. They had repeated this process the next day, and then the blessing had increased when they'd gathered herbs too.

Belissar figured they needed multiple blessings to get the full one, and that they had to do something for the God of Bees to receive that blessing. That *something* appeared to include offering tribute or helping Belissar with the purification.

Belissar frowned a bit at this. The one thing that worried him was the guy who'd offered something he hadn't made himself, and mostly because Belissar had also offered honeycomb that he hadn't made himself. Unless it counted because it was from his dungeon?

In any case, the God of Bees had accepted it without complaint or smiting. Belissar figured he would at least try to include something he had done by hand whenever he could, though.

But otherwise, to help the bear people get their blessings, Belissar should help them do things. He should help the unarmed folk make more tribute, and he should give the armed ones more to do? More to gather?

He shrugged . . . and then started to grin. For he had an idea. A wonderful, not at all selfish idea.

He made another textile node next to the healing herb node by the entrance.

Well, if the bear folk happened to gather some flax, they could process it into linen to offer as tribute, right? And if they happened to thus have some cloth Belissar could then trade for without having to make it himself by hand . . . Well, Belissar wouldn't turn them down!

Beyond that, Belissar wasn't fully sure what else to do. He wasn't certain about adding a poison flower node. What if they thought it was medicine and ended up poisoning themselves?

Well, he could always just tell them, but then, he'd have to talk to them. And when he remembered his awkward gathering of their tribute and farewell . . . He didn't particularly look forward to speaking with them again. He could send the bees, but he wasn't sure anyone but he could actually understand them. Even he hadn't known what Niobee was saying prior to him becoming a dungeon master.

Besides that, there wasn't a whole lot to do in the tower aside from walking around looking for remnants and flowers to gather. There was the apiary, but Belissar wasn't comfortable letting them snoop around in there. That was where many of his bees made their home, after all. And while they could probably gather honeycomb from the hives like they could harvest the resource plants, Belissar didn't like the idea of them reaching into his bees' homes.

Ultimately, he decided honeycomb would be something they would have to trade for.

So, in the end, the only answer was the same thing Belissar had already set out to do. He needed to expand and grow and gain more options, which meant he needed to keep performing purifications, growing his mana, and gathering DP.

He still had some time before the purification cooldown was ready, so he could continue working on his cord for the torches. He could also review his defenses some more.

Watching the bear folk walk around had given Belissar another thought, which was that putting sticky honey traps only at the bottom of the pits may not be ideal.

His rationale had been to use them to help with the firepit strategy, but he'd realized a problem with that as he watched the bear folk avoid the pit traps. If an invader managed not to fall into any of them, then the sticky honey traps didn't do anything either. This had been confirmed during the minor+ purification as well, when only the shade that fell into the pit got hit with the mad honey.

So, it might make sense for Belissar to place some honey traps beyond those at the bottom of the pits. The only downside would be that it might take more honey from the apiary to support those traps, especially if he wanted to use mad honey. Now that he was aware the bees were carrying honey to them, he'd noticed that a few of the apiary hives were producing less than normal.

Well, they were still producing *far* more than he could consume, but it did mean he should pay attention to how many traps he made.

In the end, he decided that rather than making new traps, he would move some of them out from the pits further off the beaten path; the ones less likely to catch a shade in the first place. His bees also needed the honey to grow their hives and to make new bee types, so he didn't want to overburden them with this. The honey traps, while helpful, still were only a minor hindrance to the shades. The bees were what would finish the job.

And if there was a choice between more bees and more anything else, Belissar's decision was obvious.

THE BEE-ST LAID PLANS

Speaking of honey and flowers . . .

The First of the Fifth stomped through her hive, pacing about in a dance of anger. She had been deceived. Fooled. *Swindled.*

She knew now why the King had not granted her the flower type that existed only in the flower meadow. And that was because this flower was *useless.*

First of all, it had no mana beyond that of a regular flower. What's more, unlike the other two flower types the King had spread, this one possessed no particular compounds in its nectar that resonated with mana.

The First of the Fifth had made a batch of honey from these flowers and found it little different from that of others. If anything, it felt a bit lower in quality. But the differences were minimal enough that she would not be able to produce a new honey type with it, much less a new bee type.

And that was before she even considered the reports from her workers circulating through the hive.

The flowers in question were some of the worst they had ever visited. The petals fell off when the bees landed on the flowers, the pollen was especially heavy and difficult to work with, and the entire flower would fall off the plant by evening. The nectar collection was difficult, and each flower could only be gathered from a few times, maybe even just once each.

Her honey production had dipped this latest cycle as a result, her workers' best efforts insufficient to make up for the deficiencies in the flowers themselves. All for a honey that did not improve upon any other she had made.

She did not believe any plant the King had spread would be entirely useless, but it was clear that whatever special qualities this plant possessed were found elsewhere in the plant; in its stem or perhaps its seeds. Its flowers and its nectar were largely unsuited to the production of honey. The First of the Fifth could do little with it beyond donating a soldier or two to help the King with his own work on it.

And she was paying for access to this plant's nectar with a portion of her own harvest.

Sure, she could also lay claim to any achievements the Firstborn made with it, but such was not enough by itself to justify donating honey to a rival queen. Truly, the Firstborn had played her with this deal.

The First of the Fifth's wings buzzed. She should have followed the wisdom of the King when he did not feel she would appreciate this plant.

But she had not, and now she was trapped. To simply renege on the deal was to admit defeat. And if she stopped gathering from the flowers in question, it would appear as if she was just handing over tribute to the Firstborn unprompted. Their positions in this deal would be reversed.

Yet, to continue expending her workers' efforts on a suboptimal yield was simply unacceptable. So she paced and she paced, considering what she could do. She checked the honey for the hundredth time today, searching for any quality which might justify the effort. And like the ninety-nine other times, she found nothing of the sort. She buzzed her wings once again.

She paced and she paced until eventually, she started to slow down. It was clear she would not produce an achievement from this that would earn her the favor of her King, but that did not necessarily mean she could not gain at all. There were other queens besides the Firstborn, after all, and all of them would be searching for ways to increase their favor.

She made her decision and gave her command.

"Send word to the Fourth of the Seventh. I would have words with her."

The Fourth Queen of the Seventh Spawner's First Dynasty, the first of her line, slowly flew toward the First of the Fifth's hive. As slowly as she could without angering the First of the Fifth. She almost came to a halt as she saw the flowers on the ground below. Vibrant colors filled her vision, brighter and fuller than she had ever imagined, drawing her in.

She would admit she didn't mind this break from her work. She did what she needed to, but laying eggs got old after the thousandth time or so. And that was about all she did.

Sure, her hive produced honey of quantity and quality that would not bring shame to a queen of the apiary, but she had little to do with that. Her workers were the ones who gathered the nectar and processed it into honey, so she felt they knew better than her and left them to their work. How could she, a bee who rarely even saw the flowers they were gathering from, improve upon that work with uninformed commands?

So, she spent every day like the last. Sipping on honey and laying eggs. Sometimes, she went to check on those eggs, but even caring for the brood was the job of workers, not the queen, so she just tried to stay out of their way.

She could not help but watch the dances of her workers. The tales they told of bright, colorful flowers, and of the sweet abundance of nectar they drank directly from the source. Sometimes, the Fourth of the Seventh liked to imagine what it would be like to be a worker and see such beauty directly.

But it was not to be. She was the queen, and it was her role to remain in the hive. Every moment she spent doing anything other than laying eggs or restoring her mana would reduce the size of the next generation. She could maybe peek out of the entrance of her hive, but to fly out, or King forbid, even touch one of the flowers directly would be too much.

So, she tried to content herself with the stories she heard.

She wouldn't use the word *bored*, for no bee even knew the term, but she found she didn't mind having something new to do. Though she was curious, and perhaps a bit worried, about being summoned by the First of the Fifth, the queen of the most powerful and productive hive of the apiary, above all, now she had a chance to fly out into the world and see the sights she had heard so much about with her own eyes.

It was more beautiful than she had ever imagined.

But in the end, the Fourth of the Seventh was a bee still. She slowed down to take in the sights, but she did not stop. She had her jobs to complete, after all, and she would not delay them . . . more than was reasonable, that was.

The Fourth of the Seventh stood at the entrance of the hive. The First of the Fifth came out to meet her, accompanied by two soldiers and a couple of workers.

"Finally here. I let you gather from new plants in flower meadow. In exchange, you help feed soldiers. Understand?"

The Fourth of the Seventh didn't. Or, well, she got what the First of the Fifth was saying, but had no idea why the First of the Fifth would do all this. But she didn't see any reason to refuse either.

"Okay, thanks."

The First of the Fifth buzzed her wings.

"These workers show yours where."

"Okay."

The First of the Fifth stared at her for a moment longer before returning to her hive. The soldiers and workers saluted at her as the Fourth of the Seventh looked up at the big soldiers. They were even bigger than her!

"Let's go?"

They saluted, and off they went.

The First of the Fifth rubbed her front legs together. All had gone according to plan.

The Fourth of the Seventh, being one of the last generation of queens, had very little favor and little chance to gain any. She didn't even have one of the King's magic palaces, and so could barely produce a fraction of the honey the First of the Fifth could. She was weak, unassuming, and most of all, no threat whatsoever. She wasn't even a competitor.

So, granting her access to new flowers, even suboptimal ones, was a great boon for her and no loss whatsoever to the First of the Fifth. And in exchange, the First of the Fifth got her help with the soldier bees, cutting a big drain on her honey supplies while also ensuring the Fourth of the Seventh wouldn't grow too quickly from the additional resources.

She had granted a favor and secured her influence over her subordinate queens, all in exchange for a boon that was not really a boon. An effective outcome, considering the situation overall.

With that, the First of the Fifth returned to her work, seeing what she could do with the honey types she had available.

Meanwhile, the Fourth of the Seventh stared at the soldiers and workers from the First of the Fifth as they danced a tale for her. A blessed land of plenty, with flowers as far as the eye could see. Of the grand constructions formed by the King, not from wax but from the very stems of flowers.

Her mind raced as she attempted to imagine all these wondrous things.

She made up her mind.

She had to see these things for herself.

BEE INSPIRED!

The Fourth of the Seventh hovered as still as she could. She was flying in front of the window to the King's own hive, the giant one made of entire trees. She had never dared to come so close . . . but apparently, the First of the Fifth's soldiers had been invited inside, and so had led her there.

She remained outside, but could not resist the temptation to come and see the King at work.

She also wanted to visit the flower meadow, but that trip was a bit too far for merely indulging her curiosity, so she left that to her workers. But, well, no bee could begrudge her a chance to see the King!

He was as majestic as always; a towering giant taller than an entire hive, with a body she couldn't have even imagined. He had but two legs—mighty pillars so strong he needed only a third the number to support his entire weight. He had two more that he didn't even use to walk. Instead, each of these split into five more for an unparalleled ability to grip, allowing him to reshape the world as he pleased. His eyes were smooth and colorful, like the petals of a flower, and his hair was like an entire forest.

And what he was doing was no less fascinating. The King was building something out of the plants themselves, twisting them together into a long vine of some sort. And even more curiously, the First of the Fifth's soldiers were helping with the task!

Then the Fourth of the Seventh began to buzz, for she noticed something. The color and shape of the vine they were weaving matched a part of the King's torso. She noticed now that he was not covered in some sort of hair or fur but rather that he wore some construction of plant stems over his body. It looked nothing like normal stems, so she would not have noticed had the soldiers not explained to her their current task, and if she had not then seen it in progress.

She wondered why the King put such a thing on his body.

But the surprises weren't over.

"There, how about that? Maybe if you both try at once?"

The King and the soldiers finished constructing their vine, and the King wrapped it around a large branch with a tip coated in wax. One of the King's legendary fire sticks, with which he reportedly lay waste to any invaders who intruded upon his realm.

The two soldiers crawled to the ends of the vines on either side of the fire stick, where the vines made loops. Crossing their hind legs together inside the loops, they then began to fly. The vines went taut, and then, the fire stick began to rise into the air.

The King smiled.

"What do you think? Can you fly with this?"

The soldier bees tried to fly around the room. They were a bit unsteady, and the fire stick wobbled this way and that, pulling one bee down and then the other. But ultimately, they managed to remain in the air.

The Fourth of the Seventh couldn't tear her eyes away until her workers began to pull her back to the hive.

A bit later, a wave of workers returned, carrying an abundance of nectar. The Fourth of the Seventh drank deeply from her honey reserve, which was overflowing like it never had before. Her hive had been one of the smaller ones on the outskirts of the apiary, so access to an entire patch of fast-growing flowers had vastly increased her resources, even despite the far trip and the suboptimal flowers.

One of the workers came and danced before her, and she raced over to the front of her hive. The First of the Fifth's soldiers were returning for the day, coming for their meal before they returned to the King's abode.

The Fourth of the Seventh danced rapidly before them, asking her questions without even pausing to hear the answers. The soldiers buzzed and danced as the workers brought them honey, telling their story from the beginning.

They told the Fourth of the Seventh the entire process the King had shown them; how he had gathered the flowers themselves, removing the flower and the seeds; how he had broken apart the stems and left them to partially rot; how he had processed them into the fibers she had seen him work with, and then how they and the King worked together to weave those strands into the constructs of his design.

The Fourth of the Seventh hung on their every motion, trying to imagine what it would look like. She thanked them for the tales as they thanked her for the honey, and then raced back to her reserves once the soldiers flew back to the King. She drank as deeply from the honey as she could without cutting into the growth of her hive.

She was deeply curious about this process—and had access to the very flow-ers the King used for it. But she and her workers were still tiny; too small to par-ticipate. She would need to grow if she wanted to get involved.

And so, for perhaps the first time in her life, the Fourth of the Seventh was determined to grow.

Previously, she had been content with her lot in life. Born too late, relegated to a corner of the apiary where she would ever play a subservient role to the queens that came before her. And that had been fine with her. She had her role, and she would carry it out. Any more than that could be decided by those above her.

But now . . .

Now she found herself too small to achieve what she wanted, her honey reserves too small to allow her to grow, and her worker force too small to expand those reserves. But, fortunately, the First of the Fifth had granted her access to a wealth of flowers like she'd never had in her little patch of the apiary.

And so, the Fourth of the Seventh grew. Her workers flew far and brought back the riches she had been given, and she used those riches to lay more eggs than she ever had before. A new generation would arise, until one day, they gath-ered enough honey for her to grow.

In fact, she made other plans as well. She had some of her workers begin pre-paring a second hive, much closer to the flower meadow. Once the construction had finished, she would move her entire hive closer and so cut down the length of her workers' trips. Such a location was further away from the King's hive and the flowers he had planted; no other queen wanted to live there, and so no other queen objected to her efforts. The First of the Fifth even approved of the move.

For now, she had something she wanted to do. And she would spare no effort to achieve it.

The First of the Fifth tilted her head as she watched one of her scouts' report dances.

The Fourth of the Seventh had taken to her duties with an enthusiasm that surprised even the First of the Fifth. She knew that her offer had been a big deal for the Fourth of the Seventh; an offer of resources and opportunity no queen in her generation had ever received, but tempered by the need to support soldiers that weren't her own. So, the First of the Fifth had expected a good but measured response.

Yet, from all reports, the Fourth of the Seventh was expanding more rapidly than she had ever done before. Not only that, but she apparently personally wel-comed the soldiers any time they came by her hive.

That felt strange to the First of the Fifth. If anything, she might wonder if she had made a mistake and given the Fourth of the Seventh too great an opportu-nity. Maybe the Fourth of the Seventh was making a play to rise among the apiary queens, and perhaps attract the favor of the King upon herself? Perhaps treating the soldiers well to throw off the First of the Fifth as to her intentions?

Which was what the First of the Fifth would have assumed . . . were it not for the news that the Fourth of the Seventh was planning to move *further away* from the King.

The First of the Fifth could understand it from an efficiency standpoint, given the Fourth of the Seventh's main resources were now located in the flower meadow, but the move was still unthinkable to her. Every apiary queen wished to dwell as close to the King as possible. In the early days, they had nearly fought over the locations of their hives, even. So no apiary queen would willingly move away.

The First of the Fifth thought and thought . . . and then gave up. She came to the conclusion that the Fourth of the Seventh was just happy to have a role now as more than a minor queen on the outskirts, and so was enthusiastically carrying out the task the First of the Fifth had given her.

And, well, the Fourth of the Seventh still had one of the smallest hives in the apiary. If she understood her role and wasn't making a play for the King's favor, then what she did was of no particular concern to the First of the Fifth.

Or so she thought.

CHAPTER FORTY

DON'T BEE AWKWARD!

Minor purification attempt commencing.

The cooldown had come to an end, and Belissar began another minor purification.

A shade formed once more at the gate . . . and was immediately assaulted by soldier bee squads. They flew in continuous waves this time, not attempting to lead the monster toward a pit trap.

That was intentional. They already knew the pit trap would work against a single beast like this, but the bees needed to be prepared for the case when it wouldn't work. So, Belissar had instructed them to fight this monster on their own. He already knew they could take one down, but the prior victory had also resulted in casualties. He was hoping they could manage a minor shade without sacrifice.

The bees flew in waves as they had trained to do. Belissar held his breath each time they approached, but they'd proved excellent at diverting the shade's attention. Each squad flew off immediately after dealing one sting, and so escaped counterattack.

The monster eventually stopped trying to chase the squads that had already attacked and looked for the next one on approach, but they broke off before coming within range. They then began attacking with multiple squads at a time, such that whichever one was targeted could simply break off while the others struck.

The shade brought out its lethal breath, and the bees immediately scattered. Not a bee was caught in the black cloud. The monster took another deep breath and then took off running as in the first minor purification, taking advantage of the bees backing away. But the bees further away lowered to the ground, forming another layer of encirclement while the others regrouped, and soon, their attacks began anew.

It took the bees longer without dealing a death blow to the shade's head, but eventually, the monster collapsed under their assault. The pit trap hadn't been needed, and not a single bee fell.

All hostiles defeated.
Minor purification successful.

Minor purification completed!
Please select a reward:
- +50 DP
- +10 Max Mana
- Monster Bee Queen Resistance Boost (Minimal)

Belissar nodded in approval. It seemed his bees had learned the tricks a minor shade could pull and could now take it down as a matter of course.

+10 Max Mana selected.

Belissar was slightly tempted by the perk but held to his original plans. He wouldn't turn down a particularly helpful boost, but otherwise, the sooner he could attempt an expansion, the better.

In this case, the boost had been for the queens, who did not participate in fighting outside of the gravest of circumstances, so Belissar figured they could live without it if all went well.

And if the queens *were* participating in the fight, then he probably had bigger problems than a minimal stat boost would solve.

Fortunately, Belissar didn't need to hold a funeral at the memorial this time, so he was about to go about his business when he paused, rubbing his chin and humming. He nodded to himself and walked over to the storage jars in the room. Gathering as much honeycomb as he could carry, he then walked out toward the flower meadow.

Laying out the honeycomb trays in front of the memorial, he placed one at the entrance of the memorial beehouse and one in the shrine of bees's wax chest. He was about to ask Niobee to gather the bees, but they had all come to watch him at this point. He turned to them and smiled.

"You girls won a great victory today, and nobody died this time. I think that's worth celebrating, so why don't we have a party? Here, come and eat as much as you want."

Belissar figured it wouldn't be good if he only conducted funerals, so he decided he would assist in the celebrations this time.

The bees froze . . . and then began to fly around rapidly. The flower meadow queens flew before him and began to salute repeatedly. Belissar just waved his hand.

"Go on, this is the result of your hard work. You've earned it."

The queens and their soldiers saluted again before slowly making their way to the honeycomb. One by one, they began to drink until, soon, all the bees were drinking and dancing. Belissar smiled and nodded.

The celebrations went on for longer than normal.

The next day, Belissar sighed as he walked toward the gate. He, unfortunately, had determined something he could do to increase his options while he waited to expand his mana. Something he had known he could do for a while now. Something he, perhaps, hadn't thought of because he'd really prefer not to.

And that was talking to the bear people.

Belissar was bringing with him a couple of trays of honeycomb, a single mana flower, and a couple of poison flowers. He realized if he asked them to trade, he might be able to get some new plants or something. If nothing else, he could also use new tools to expand his own crafts.

The only problem was, Belissar didn't really want to talk to them, to be honest. The last time he had had been *really* awkward, and he'd never been the one *proposing* barters before. It used to be that the other villagers would stop by and dictate the terms to him, after which he would inevitably comply.

His heart began to race as he thought of approaching the bear folk himself. But, they *had* been unbelievably nice so far. And, more importantly, expanding his options through trade could improve the odds in favor of his bees. That was worth overcoming any amount of fear or discomfort he may have felt.

Besides, it *was* a bit easier to work up the courage for a conversation when he had an army of soldier bees hovering around him. He hadn't asked them to do that this time, but they'd naturally gathered around him when he'd walked toward the front.

And now . . . he waited. And waited. And waited, his heart beating faster with each minute. He tried to distract himself, but his beating heart distracted him from his distracting, so it didn't work.

Finally, the gates of the tower opened, and Metsaitti led his group in. They paused as they took in the sight before them, then Metsaitti inclined his head.

"Hello, Sacred Den Master. Thank you for allowing us in your abode. How may we help you today?"

He motioned at the others, and they inclined their heads as well. Belissar wanted to run, but instead, he cleared his throat.

"Um . . . I have some stuff. Do you want any? Er . . . as a trade, you see."

Belissar tried not to wince. Metsaitti's eyes widened, and then he nodded.

"We would be honored, Sacred Den Master. We are not carrying any goods with us at this moment, but I will relay your offer to the chief, and we will put together something. Is there anything in particular you wanted?"

Belissar started to shake his head before remembering what he was supposed to be doing. "Yes, actually. Um, plants, especially flowers. Tools if you have them." He glanced at Metsaitti's spear. "Weapons would be nice, too . . ."

Metsaitti nodded. "Understood. I will relay your desires to the chief. Was there anything else you wanted?"

Belissar shook his head. "No . . . that should be it . . ."

Metsaitti nodded and motioned to the others, who turned around.

"Understood. Thank you for the generous offer, Sacred Den Master."

"Um, you're welcome."

With that, the bear people left. Belissar resisted the urge to fall and lie on the ground, taking a deep breath instead.

Yeah, that was still very awkward, but at least it seemed to have gone well. The bear people were still polite and had agreed to trade with him, once they had gathered some stuff.

Belissar's eyes went wide as he realized something terrible: if they were leaving and coming back . . . then wouldn't he have to talk to them *again* today?

Belissar groaned.

To distract himself—er, to continue the development of his tower, Belissar returned to his work from the day before. Now that they had figured out a way for soldier bees to lift a torch, he and his assistants were working to refine it. They tried wrapping the cord around in different ways, or tying it to different parts of the torch, or making loops to wrap around different parts of the soldiers' bodies.

In the end, they settled on tying four ropes, two at the front of the torch and two at the end, which would be carried by four soldier bees. They stuck with just having the bees pass their legs through loops at the end of the ropes, as any other method made it more difficult for them to drop the torch.

At this point, they moved to test the process in its entirety. Belissar worked on starting a fire as four soldier bees from the apiary stood on the ground next to a torch. Once the fire got going, he gave them a nod. The soldiers stuck their legs through the loops and rose into the air. They then flew over the fire and lowered the torch until the tip caught on flames.

Flying with the burning torch toward a nearby pit, flames flickering occasionally as they sped through the air, they dropped their ropes—and so the torch—toward the pit.

The torch missed and bounced on the ground next to the hole before teetering over the edge and falling in. The kindling at the bottom slowly caught on fire until a blaze was going at the bottom of the pit.

Belissar nodded at the bees. "Well, looks like it basically worked. How was it? Anyone get burned?"

The bees gave a dance indicating all was well. Belissar nodded to himself.

They had succeeded, then. A torch could be lit and carried by the bees. It would remain ablaze while they traveled, and so could still light the pit traps once they arrived. The delivery could use some work, but Belissar had no doubt the bees would practice that part to perfection.

The point was, now that the torches could be carried safely through the air, it wouldn't matter if there were multiple shades or not. They could light up any pit a monster fell into, regardless of who or what was still around the edge.

Belissar grinned . . . only to remember what he was distracting himself from. Because a group of the bear folk had just arrived back at the tower.

UN-BEAR-ABLE PROFITS

Chief Rohsuak had made her way to the sacred den once more and was currently kneeling by the shrine of bees, her eyes fixed on the sight before her. Spread out on some basic cloths were trays of golden honeycomb and several shimmering flowers.

She frowned, furrowing her brow as she looked up. There stood a young man with hardly any fur save for on his head, and tiny ears of pure flesh attached to the side of his head rather than the top. He was trying—and failing—not to fidget as he waited for her response.

She slowly shook her head. "I am sorry, Sacred Den Master, but we cannot trade for these."

The young man scowled at that. "Why not? Are you saying it's not good enough?"

Chief Rohsuak quickly shook her head and held up her hands. "Quite the opposite. We have nothing at present that would be equal in value. We would starve ourselves if we tried."

The sacred den master froze, blinking repeatedly. "Huh?"

Chief Rohsuak raised an eyebrow. "Sacred Den Master, do you not know what it is you have brought today?"

The sacred den master crossed his arms. "Um, mana flowers and mana honeycomb, right? I mean, I figured the mana part was special, right? But . . . it's still just honey, right?"

Chief Rohsuak exchanged a glance with Metsaitti. Metsaitti's fellow hunters were not so subtle, simply balking at the sacred den master's statement. Chief Rohsuak's mind raced.

Leaving aside the young man's assertion that honey itself was not an exceptional luxury, *any* object containing this much mana was a priceless treasure. Much less if it was an edible foodstuff. Such a thing could be used as is to stimulate the growth of a person's mana, which, if successful, would make them capable of deeds beyond the mundane.

Beyond that, even the most minimal of processing could turn a mana-infused food into either a powerful medicine or a deadly poison.

A mana flower, on the other hand, wasn't as readily useful, but was just as, if not more, valuable. It contained a more basic form of mana which would require further processing to achieve any particular effect, and thus greater knowledge and skill to put to use. But the flip side of that was that it was far more versatile and had countless potential uses in the right hands.

It could be cooked into magical foods, brewed into magical potions and poisons, burned to power mighty spells, or crafted into magical artifacts . . . and those were just some examples that Chief Rohsuak was aware of.

And this mana flower in particular had no discernible attribute besides the faint Nature one all plant life contained, which meant it could be used to achieve practically anything, though it would be less efficient than a flower with a more specialized attribute. But given how rare such flowers were to begin with, having a flower on hand that *could* work for *any* intended use case was beyond valuable.

Which meant the den master's statements were either made from complete ignorance or unbelievable abundance. And Chief Rohsuak needed to determine which.

The den master presented himself as the former. He seemed deeply uncomfortable, even fearful of them, despite the fact that he held their very destiny in his hands. Not to mention the army of bee monsters flying overhead. He wore tattered clothing that was clearly patched by hand and without much skill. At first glance, he appeared more impoverished than they did, despite their long and desperate travels.

But still, a part of Chief Rohsuak could not help but remain wary. While every sacred den was different, all of the masters she was aware of tended toward imperiousness. They were powerful figures who had been blessed by the gods and possessed mighty armies loyal only to them. Most such individuals did not hesitate to assert their authority.

Those who acted humbly were the most dangerous; crafty schemers who preferred to hide their hand and disarm with a smile. She could not completely rule out that this was all some sort of elaborate game, and that the sacred den master was taking their measure to adjust his schemes.

On the other hand, however, this was the smallest sacred den Chief Rohsuak had ever heard of, much less personally encountered. And this sacred den master *had* shown his hand. Even now, his larger monster bees flew overhead while their smaller members kept a constant watch on the camp.

Thus far, his overall actions were indicative of a lack of experience as opposed to an elaborate deception.

But that situation was no more comforting than the first; perhaps even less so. For if this sacred den master was truly as inexperienced as he appeared, then he would be quite unpredictable, maybe even volatile.

If he was this nervous just conversing with her, how much or how *little* would it take to make him lash out? What would he consider an insult? What would he consider a deception or betrayal? Did he truly wish for nothing from them, or was he stockpiling his grievances until the day he would break and avenge them all?

For example, Chief Rohsuak could remain quiet and trade the basic seeds and tools the sacred den master requested in exchange for the incredible treasures he offered. She could simply state that his ignorance of their value was not her responsibility, and that she'd simply accepted the price he offered. She could even take advantage of his ignorance and drive a harder bargain, using the situation to gain immeasurable profit.

But if she did so, and sometime later he came to understand exactly what their value was, and then came to realize that she had known from the start . . . how would he respond? Would he shut the doors of his tower, barring them from the blessings of his patron? Would he react in violence and rage and drive them from his lands altogether?

Long had their people wandered, driven out of land after land until they were but a shadow of their former selves. They knew firsthand what the displeasure of a sacred den master could look like . . . as well as what the friendship of such a person could provide. This one was acting like frightened prey, expecting to be hunted at any moment. But even the most docile prey was dangerous when cornered, and a herbivore provoked to violence was even more aggressive than the most vicious predator.

So, when a young man with the demeanor of frightened and cornered prey held the power of a sacred den . . . only the most foolish of hunters would dare to provoke him. How much less when the lives and futures of her people depended on his good graces?

"Sacred Den Master, what do you know of magic?"

His eyes glanced about rapidly before he looked away. "Um . . . not much?"

Chief Rohsuak nodded and made her decision.

Initially, she had intended to deal with the sacred den master cordially but distantly. In truth, her people were at the end of their rope, their numbers cut to the edge of collapse, and their resources all but drained. They could not afford to continue sojourning. They needed time and a place to rest.

So, they would have no choice but to give in to any demands the next sacred den master made of them. She had been prepared to fight such a person in the field of negotiations, to try and satisfy their desires while preserving her people's autonomy as much as she could. Such was the only way to deal with an imperious sacred den master who ruled over their lands.

But this sacred den master . . . was not imperious enough. Of everything she had prepared to deal with, no demands save not to harm his defenders was not a situation she had ever anticipated. And while it seemed incredibly fortunate for her people, she felt it was dangerous to leave the sacred den master in his present state.

If her people were to make this place their home, then they at least needed predictable reactions from the one who ruled it. They needed him to understand and protect his own interests lest they accidentally provoke him.

"Then, would you like to learn?"

The hunters gasped at that. Even Metsaitti was taken aback. One of the more . . . excitable of their numbers spoke up. "Chief, you can't be serious!"

She silenced him with a look before turning back to the den master as his face scrunched up.

"The items you have offered are incredibly useful for any number of the mystic arts. The only thing we possess of similar value right now are our own techniques in those arts. So, how about it?"

In truth, she intended not only to teach the sacred den master magic but the art of leadership as well. Of course, success in that could mean consequences for her people. It was her intention, therefore, to establish a closer relationship with the sacred den master.

However, her people had embarked on their long sojourn due to such a relationship gone wrong, and would not be eager to bow to any authority. Likewise, she predicted the sacred den master would recoil if such a thing were offered.

So, she decided to start slow and create the opportunity for further interactions. Both sides could grow more used to one another, and if she were to help the sacred den master grow, she would hopefully give him a positive opinion of her people such that he would use what she taught him on their behalf.

It would be risky, but the alternatives were to leave and give up the best opportunity for a homeland they would ever find, or else to walk on eggshells for the rest of their lives, hoping they would not provoke an unpredictable sacred den master. Chief Rohsuak would not have led her people this far if she didn't know when to take a calculated risk or two.

Besides, a close relationship with a sacred den master could bring a people unimaginable boons. And she felt like this sacred den master would not demand unacceptable terms in response.

The sacred den master frowned even more, narrowing his eyes at her. She met his gaze with a smile. "I . . . want to see what your magic looks like first."

She nodded. "Of course."

And so, Chief Rohsuak decided the future of her people. She could only hope that she had chosen wisely.

CHAPTER FORTY-ONE

DO YOU BEE-LIEVE IN MAGIC?

Get out of here, and don't let me catch you around again!"

A young boy fell back as the baker swung his fist toward his face, falling back into the dirt. He didn't know why the baker was so protective of his trash, but he wasn't going to stay around and ask. He scrambled to his feet and ran as the baker kicked at his bottom.

He limped down the road, his stomach growling. His eyes stared blankly forward as he considered where else he could search for food. The other villagers scowled at him as he walked down the street, but he hardly noticed.

He had come to the outskirts of town before realizing that his mind had gone blank, failing to come up with even a single idea. Tripping on a rock, he fell into the dirt and lay there, not bothering to get up. It wouldn't matter. If he couldn't come up with an idea to find food, walking around was just a waste of energy . . .

And then, he felt something poke his back.

"Boy, what're you doing there, blocking my road?"

He barely turned his head to glance back. An old woman was poking him with a stick, holding a sack over her hunched shoulder. He didn't respond, but his stomach rumbled. The woman's face scrunched up, and she heaved a sigh.

The boy heard a thud as the sack fell to the ground right in front of his face.

"Come on, get up, will you? Help me carry that home, and I'll give you something to eat."

The boy lay there for a moment more as his mind processed the statement. Once he did, he immediately rose to his feet, grunting as he tried to lift the sack with his scrawny arms. But the thought of food pushed all others out of his mind, focusing entirely on the task that would grant it.

And that was the start of the boy and the old woman's life together . . .

*

Belissar frowned at Chief Rohsuak's proposal. On the one hand, he had been tricked into free labor by offers of instruction before and was in no hurry to repeat those experiences. But on the other, he very much needed to learn about the mystic arts. He was a dungeon master now, with mana flowing through his body, his bees, and his tower. Learning how to put any of that into use would be *immensely* helpful.

The chief was right in that he didn't know the value of the resources at his disposal, and he *couldn't* truly know until he learned the arts they were actually used for.

His mind was also bringing up unhelpful memories at the moment. He didn't really want to think about them with an older woman offering to instruct him in front of him, so he tried to push them aside. Chief Rohsuak wasn't anybody he knew, and it would likely lead to pain if he tried to equate them. So, he focused on the situation as logically as he could.

First and foremost, he needed to confirm that the bear folk actually *could* use magic or mana or whatever; he was not just going to take their word for it. Back when he was poor and helpless, he pretty much had no choice but to trust people and hope they might one day make good on their promise.

But now? Now he had plenty of food and shelter that his body didn't even require anymore, so there was no need to deal with anyone if there wasn't a confirmed benefit. Likewise, he had a monster bee army behind him if they tried to force the issue. He could afford a bit more suspicion now.

But if the bear people actually could use magic, and if they would actually teach him in good faith . . . such a thing could dramatically improve his tower's defenses.

Chief Rohsuak smiled and motioned to the bees above. "Could you ask them to back off a bit? I wouldn't want any of them to get hurt."

Belissar nodded and let the soldier bees in the air know to move back a bit. About half of them flew up higher into the air, while the other half dropped down near the ground to hover next to him.

Chief Rohsuak then took a deep breath; Belissar could feel mana surge from within her. Holding her hand up in the air, a geometric pattern formed out of red light; with a flash, a ball of pure fire formed in its place and shot straight into the sky.

It then burst into a large explosion, causing Belissar to stumble back and fall to the ground. The bees began to buzz and form a wall between him and the bear people as Chief Rohsuak gave him a smile.

"How was that?"

Belissar squeaked out a response. That *certainly* fell under the magic category. The buzzing of the soldier bees shook him out of his stupefaction, however, as he watched them form into attack squadrons. With a wave, he let them know he was fine.

Standing up, he dusted himself off and looked Chief Rohsuak in the eyes while narrowing his own. She just kept smiling and holding his gaze until he felt awkward and glanced away. He couldn't really judge how honest she was being or not.

But she clearly knew magic, and magic of a sort that would obviously assist in his tower's defense. So, if she actually did teach him something like that . . . perhaps Belissar wouldn't need a torch to light the pit traps. No, he might not even need the pit traps to set the shades on fire in the first place.

If he could learn to do something like that, maybe the bees wouldn't need to risk themselves at all. At the very least, he would be able to fight by their side.

He knew that he was no warrior. As much as he hated to let the bees die on his behalf, he knew it would not help them to put himself in front of a shade. The best he could do was trust them and honor those who fell.

But that could change if he had access to magic.

Belissar decided that the risk was worth taking. He looked back at Chief Rohsuak again.

"That's . . . acceptable. But . . . you come here to teach me. And, um, I pay you after the lessons, not before."

Chief Rohsuak's smile grew, and she nodded. "Of course. Thank you, Den Master. It will be an honor. When would you like to begin?"

Belissar frowned. Part of him wanted to put it off, but when he thought about it, there was no specific reason to do so. Any excuse of needing to work on his dungeon's defenses could be countered by the benefits of learning magic for those same defenses. It was just that he was feeling uncomfortable around these people . . . but that wouldn't change later. So, Belissar took a deep breath.

"Right away, if that works for you?"

Chief Rohsuak nodded then glanced over at Metsaitti. "Why don't you take the others and proceed with the hunt?"

He raised an eyebrow and glanced over at the soldier bees. "Are you sure about that?"

She smiled and nodded. "Oh, I'll be fine, don't you worry about me."

Metsaitti nodded and motioned to the others. "Come on, let's go."

The others hesitated but slowly followed as Chief Rohsuak waved them off. Belissar watched them as they went. A couple of the soldier bees followed his gaze and broke off to follow them at a safe distance, then he turned to Chief Rohsuak.

"Do you mind if we sit?"

Belissar shook his head at her question, so Chief Rohsuak sat down, crossing her legs on the ground. Belissar followed suit.

"Alright, let's begin. First of all, are you aware of your own mana?"

Belissar nodded. He had felt the warmth of the tower's mana flowing through him, as well as the mana within the honeycomb whenever he ate some. At this point, he could also feel that same warmth resting in his body. Chief Rohsuak gave him a smile.

"Then you have already completed the hardest part. Are you able to move it?"

Belissar frowned at that. He hadn't done anything of the sort. Perhaps the tower lords had lied about the dangers of peasants using magic, but at the same time, Belissar had still been concerned about experimenting without any knowledge, so he hadn't attempted to interact with it. He thought about trying now, but in the end, he just shook his head. After that fire spell Chief Rohsuak had displayed, he couldn't deny that magic *was* dangerous, and he had a possible teacher now.

"Got it, then that's where we'll start."

Chief Rohsuak rose to her feet. Belissar tilted his head but did so as well.

"My master taught me a bunch of breathing exercises for this step, but I found that slow and frustrating. I find it's better to keep your body in motion. Let me teach you a couple of tricks . . ."

What Belissar did not know was that Chief Rohsuak had a *unique* perspective on the mystic arts. And a unique training method. One that the other bear people found . . . *difficult*, such that even Metsaitti's hunters feared to learn from her.

CHAPTER FORTY-TWO

TRAINING BEE-GINS!

Belissar gasped for breath as he ran across the field. Collapsing to the ground before the shrine of bees, every inch of his body on fire, he slowly strained his neck to glance at Chief Rohsuak.

"W-What . . . does . . ."

She smiled at him. "What does physical training have to do with magic?"

Belissar barely managed to nod as he lay upon the ground. Chief Rohsuak snapped her fingers, creating a small wisp of fire above her hand.

"I believe mana to be a part of the body like any other. So, the more you know your body, the easier it is to move the mana." Her grin grew wide, and she bared her teeth. "And in the worst case, if you don't learn any magic, at least you'll learn how to fight."

Belissar frowned. He was very much wondering what he had actually agreed to, for this didn't seem like magic training at all. But he didn't know the first thing about magic, so couldn't say if Chief Rohsuak's words were right or not. And, well . . . if she was teaching him how to fight, that could also help him defend his tower if he ever needed to step in personally.

So, he figured he'd stick with it a bit longer.

A few hours later, Belissar collapsed into his chair in the farmhouse, every muscle in his body trembling. He was barely capable of grabbing some honeycomb to eat, but he needed to restore his strength before it was time for a purification, so he forced himself to lift up the tray and take a bite.

He felt warmth flood through his body, soothing his aching muscles.

Tilting his head as he focused on the sensation, he tried reaching out for the mana, but he didn't really know *how* to interact with it. It was clearly present within his body, but didn't respond to any muscle he could move. He shook his head and sighed.

"King okay?"

Niobee flew in and danced around him. He gave her a small smile. "I'm fine, just tired."

She landed on the table before him and buzzed her wings. "Enemy?"

He shook his head. "No, she's trying to help . . . I think. Helping me get stronger."

Niobee buzzed her wings a bit before starting a rapid dance. "Ah! Like workers when queen needs to move!"

Belissar tilted his head. "Um, I think so?" He hadn't been aware that worker bees would train their own queens, so he'd have to take Niobee's word for it. His eyes then widened a bit.

"Hey, Niobee. You used mana when you fought the shade, right?"

"Yes?"

Belissar grinned. "Do you think you could explain how?"

Niobee began dancing rapidly again. "Okay!"

From there, a long conversation unfolded. Belissar's smile soon began to droop.

"Okay, um, twist the flow into where, again?"

"Poison sac! Then sting like normal!"

Belissar frowned. "Um, right. So, uh, what do you do if you don't have a poison sac? Or a stinger?"

Niobee flew about unsteadily. "No poison sac?"

He shook his head. "Yeah, humans don't have those."

She hovered in place for a moment before resuming her quick dance. "Can make honey, then! Concentrate into nectar!"

Belissar furrowed his brow. "Right, um, humans don't make honey, either . . ."

She came to a halt. Her next dance was quite a bit slower. "No poison sac? No honey?"

Belissar shook his head, and Niobee halted again before beginning a very slow dance. "King is . . . drone?"

He smirked at that. "Well, something like that."

Niobee barely moved with her next dance. ". . . Sorry. Don't know how to help drone . . ."

Belissar gave her a small smile and lifted his finger for her to land on, brushing her back.

"It's okay. Thanks for trying. I knew this wasn't going to be easy."

It seemed like there was nothing for it but to lean into the training.

Fortunately, Belissar recovered sufficiently by the end of the purification cooldown. He was once again amazed at what a tower could do for his body.

Or perhaps the mana from the honeycomb had helped him heal? Either way, he found he could move again with a bit of effort, so he moved to start a campfire.

He was still a bit sore, enough that he wouldn't feel confident running a torch to a pit trap. But fortunately, he wouldn't have to. The apiary soldiers stood near the campfire, their legs already holding the loops of their torch's ropes. This would be the first test of the new plan in a real setting.

Belissar was a bit worried about not being able to personally intervene should something happen, but logically speaking, there wasn't much he could do if something did. The bees could handle a minor purification without any traps at all, so it should be fine even if there was an issue with the torches. So, he buried the fear in his heart and selected the option.

Minor purification attempt commencing.

Minor purification has begun.
Remaining hostiles: 1

A minor shade appeared, alone as usual. Again, a squad of bees dove toward it as soon as it appeared and led it toward the pit trap. Nodding at the soldier bees standing behind him, they rose into the air as Belissar grabbed the torch and stuck it into the fire. Once it had caught, he pulled it out and let it go, allowing the bees to carry it on their own.

They flew off through the apiary door and across the flower meadow. The torch's flame whipped about as they sped through the air, but it remained alight, and the bees flew steadily forward.

In the meantime, the soldiers of the flower meadow had lured the shade into the first pit trap once again, taking up positions around its edges even as the beast was coated in mad honey at the bottom. Several squads set up to dive at any moment from any side of the pit such that they could attack if the shade began to climb out, while several more began a rotation of careful dives into the pit itself.

The first group made it all the way down, as the shade was still recovering from the fall, and plunged their stingers into its back. The second pulled away when the beast began swinging its tail around the pit, and the third and beyond ceased their attacks as the shade eyed them warily.

The monster eventually turned away from them and began crouching down to leap for the edge of the pit, but another squad dove toward it. It spun about instead and whipped its tail at them, but the bees had broken off the attack once the shade had abandoned its initial plans.

And so the bees danced with the beast. They attacked anytime it focused on the pit, and pulled away when it focused on them, using the threat of dives to interrupt any attempts to escape. The shade, alone as it was and beginning to sway from the mad honey, had no chance to climb out of the hole.

Then, the torch bees arrived. Flying toward the pit in a straight, steady line, just above the height that the shade's breath attack could reach, they released the ropes at the same time.

They had, as Belissar predicted, practiced the motion tirelessly before this, and so released with perfect timing. The torch fell directly into the center of the pit, smacking the shade on the head.

Soon, the pit went up in flames.

All hostiles defeated.
Minor purification successful.

Minor purification completed!
Please select a reward:
- +50 DP
- +10 Max Mana
- Monster Bee Soldier Speed Boost (Minimal)

Belissar allowed himself to smile. All had gone according to plan. The bees now weren't dependent on him to set the pit traps on fire, and multiple shades could not prevent them from doing so again. The flower meadow bees were also adapting their tactics and getting better and better at handling the monsters. And yet again, not a single bee had fallen.

Belissar then stared at the rewards for a while. With a groan, he made his choice.

Monster Bee Soldier Speed Boost (Minimal) selected!

He really wanted to get the max mana requirement fulfilled as soon as possible, but this boost was a bit too good to pass up. Stronger soldier bees were a priority in general, and speed in particular was possibly the most useful.

Faster soldiers meant faster attacks that left less room for counterattack. It meant an easier time dodging attacks and reacting to surprises. And it meant the torch-carrying bees could arrive more quickly, and so reduce the time the soldiers needed to keep the shades in the pit. Speed was perhaps the bees' main strength and defense besides numbers, and so Belissar felt a speed boost was worth delaying the expansion by an extra day.

Belissar nodded and then began stretching his body. His bees were clearly doing their best to grow, and their training efforts had shown. He figured he could show no less effort in his own training, now that he had a way to get stronger himself.

And there was one other thing he could do.

Once he had stretched, he jogged back to the farmhouse and gathered up some of the extra honey trays.

A solid victory deserved a celebration, and he would provide it.

BEE-NORMOUS EXPANSION

The Firstborn paced about as she waited for her mana to regenerate. She knew she should conserve every bit of energy she had, but she couldn't help it. She had a lot on her mind lately.

First were the newcomers. They were giants who appeared much like the King, yet they also had features her instincts warned her about, indicative of vicious threats. But the King had asked the soldiers to hold their assault, and apparently, the Queen of All Bees approved of their presence here, so the Firstborn's soldiers were holding back their stingers.

Still, she could not be comfortable with the presence of outsiders in their midst; ones who could not even dance to convey their intentions! The King could understand them, as powerful and wise as he was, but even he was wary of them. Fortunately, they had not approached the hives. The Firstborn wasn't sure how to respond if they did.

And now, one was pushing the King to run, and driving him to the point of exhaustion. The Firstborn had been ready to strike them low, but the King apparently did not consider this a hostile act. The Conduit had conferred with him and revealed that he was training.

It was that news which had the Firstborn pacing about. The King was training. Which meant . . . he was planning to join the fray once again.

The Firstborn's hopes had been dashed. Now that the army of the flower meadow was powerful enough to face the invader head-on, and now that the apiary soldiers could carry the flames on their own, she had hoped the King would withdraw from the fighting and remain in safety. But apparently, he was not satisfied yet.

It was no mystery why, for the Firstborn had been there when the Queen of All Bees blessed the King's memorial. She'd seen the way he looked upon each of the symbols displayed there, especially those for the fallen queens of the First

Dynasty, and honored her own fallen warriors, lavishing praise upon the wounded one; the one she had only continued to feed because of the King's attention.

The Firstborn detected the stirring of mana and turned her body. A new soldier was pushing against its cocoon and starting to emerge. Medicinal workers helped pull away the cocoon and brushed their antennas across the soldier as it stepped out of its cell. A soldier with purple hairs.

Thanks to the aid of the First of the Fifth, the Firstborn had raised a new type of soldier: one that would have the same toxins used by the King's honey traps.

Crawling over, the Firstborn brushed the soldier's antennas. Her new child responded with a salute dance before marching off to join the army in their training.

This was a good first step. Medicinal workers had taken over the task of tending the brood, improving the health of her hive as well as freeing up her other workers for increased foraging, and the new soldier would hopefully increase the impact of the army's attacks.

But the Firstborn felt it was not enough. She had made a stronger bee army, but she had not yet created the strongest bee army. She had not yet raised an army so powerful that the King could send them into battle without worry.

So, she began to ponder. What more could she do? How else could she increase the strength of her armies?

But think as she might, it would not be her who would come up with the next step.

The First of the Fifth had finally calmed down. The deception of the Firstborn had caught her off guard, but it was to be expected. The Firstborn was the one the King trusted with the defense of his realm; she had to be capable of at least this much.

The First of the Fifth had made the most of it; passing the soldier feeding onto the Fourth of the Seventh had freed up a lot of honey for her. She would simply need to be careful in her future dealings to ensure she was not sent scrambling again.

And, once the First of the Fifth had calmed down and taken stock of the situation, she'd realized this incident had borne unexpected fruit. It had given the First of the Fifth a new perspective; one that helped her divine the purposes of the King.

She'd realized there was a huge abundance of resources in the realm that were not being put to good use. The Fourth of the Seventh's move to an unoccupied section of the apiary and her subsequent growth had made the First of the Fifth realize just how many flowers were left untouched by the foragers.

It was, perhaps, only natural. The bees of the apiary had only two concerns: honey production and proximity to the King. As a result, they focused entirely on the mana flowers that could produce the greatest amount of the highest quality honey and competed for the areas closest to the King's personal hive.

And because of that, the First of the Fifth had missed an obvious opportunity. But no more. She had conferred with the queens of the apiary, for she needed their help with this. She had set forth her plans, and now, they were about to pay off.

Standing before a small wax cell, she watched as a new bee, fully grown, emerged from her cocoon. She was far, *far* smaller than the First of the Fifth or a soldier bee, yet she was larger than any of the workers now tending to her.

For she was a princess, soon to be queen. Yes, the First of the Fifth was starting a new hive.

None of the apiary queens had thought to do so thus far, for none of them wanted more competition for mana flowers and the space around the King. But the Fourth of the Seventh had revealed that there was far more room to grow for those who were willing to accept less.

Likewise, recent events had revealed a need for expanded honey production. The King now shared the honey of the apiary with the bees who did battle on behalf of the hive. The First of the Fifth wanted to ensure there was sufficient honey of . . . less than top quality available so that her own labor would remain at the King's table.

It had been a significant expense. A single queen took even more mana than a soldier bee did, and the First of the Fifth had had to imbue honey with her own mana to create the necessary royal jelly. It would have been a costly endeavor had the Fourth of the Seventh not accepted the burden of the soldiers.

And beyond that, a queen would require drones, and that meant cooperation from other queens. None of them were ready to bear queens of their own, so the First of the Fifth had been required to offer concessions in exchange for drones. Some of the other queens would now be permitted to gather from the new flower patches the King had made. The First of the Fifth did not enjoy sharing the King's gifts, but it was necessary.

For now, she would have *her* offspring utilize the space and resources that the rest of the apiary overlooked. It would be her line who fulfilled the designs of the King when he filled the entire realm with flowers.

And now that the new queen had been born, the First of the Fifth realized something else. As a monster bee queen, she had an innate ability to command her own brood. And contrary to her expectations, she still felt a connection with the young princess. The new queen was not exactly a member of her hive, and the connection was not as strong as with her workers . . . but there *was* a connection.

The First of the Fifth danced happily. The new queen would not be an additional rival but instead a part of the First of the Fifth's strength.

The First of the Fifth began to buzz and tremble. The King himself had made a hive of hives. And now, the First of the Fifth had begun to follow in his path.

The young queen stood before her. The First of the Fifth brushed their antennas together, commanded her to go and grow, and then assigned some workers to attend her. The young queen saluted before making her way out of the hive.

And so, the First of the Fifth began to build her own hive of hives.

Meanwhile, workers from the Fourth of the Seventh caught sight of the new princess on her maiden voyage. They brought news of this to their queen, who loved to hear about all that went on outside her hive. And when those workers then went to gather from the flowers of the flower meadow, they exchanged scouting reports with the workers who lived there, intending to gather more news for their queen.

The Firstborn stood completely still after she heard the report. Of course. It was so obvious now.

A new queen would double the number of bees born. More workers, more honey, and therefore, more soldiers. The Firstborn and the other spawner queens had largely focused on the mana flowers, so there was an abundance of normal blooms available. The flower meadow could support many more hives than it currently did. The King was building a hive of hives, so it was only natural they should raise more hives of their own.

It was so obvious that the Firstborn had to spend quite a while pondering why exactly none of them had thought of it until now. In any case, she would have to thank the First of the Fifth. Thanks to her ceaseless efforts, yet another path had opened up for the King's army.

And so, the Firstborn got to work.

CHAPTER FORTY-THREE

BEE FOCUSED AND COMMITTED

Belissar met Chief Rohsuak the next morning while Metsaitti's group passed them by. He didn't say anything to them, but he did glare at the spearman who wanted to mess with his bees. Chief Rohsuak let out a sigh.

"Tyhgak's got more courage than sense, but Metsaitti will keep him in line."

Belissar's expression didn't change. "He'd better."

Chief Rohsuak shook her head before taking a look at Belissar and raising her eyebrow. "You seem to be doing well. I expected you to be in much more pain after yesterday." Belissar glared at her, but she just smiled. "You grow the most when pushed past your limit."

He sighed and shrugged. "I recover fast."

Looking at him for a bit, she nodded. "Well, you do have a lot of mana. Ah! You ate mana honey as well?"

Belissar eyed her for a bit before nodding slowly. Chief Rohsuak grinned with a glint in her eye that made Belissar take a step back.

"That's good to know. That's *very* good to know."

She began to chuckle, and Belissar felt a chill go down his spine. The training that day dramatically increased in intensity.

When it was over, he barely made it back to the farmhouse, collapsing upon the bed with a groan. Niobee flew around him rapidly, but he didn't respond, so she flew out the window as fast as she could.

"Ow!"

A short while later, Belissar felt a sharp pain. Looking at his arm, his eyes widened.

"What . . . Why?!"

A bee was stinging him. Belissar's heart pounded in his chest. He was no stranger to being stung; the nonmonster bees he'd raised before didn't exactly like it when he gathered honey from their hives. But he thought that had changed after becoming a dungeon master, now that he could talk directly to them. So what had gone wrong? What had he done that they'd resorted to stinging without even talking to him?

And worse, why had this little bee given her life for that purpose?

Belissar's eyes moistened as he reached a trembling hand toward the bee. He would try to pull her stinger out without hurting her, but he knew that was a difficult task. Which made it all the worse that she had stung him. If she had just told him what was wrong, he would have stopped whatever he was doing. There was no need for her to sacrifice herself—

The little bee pulled out her stinger without issue, with no harm done to herself. Belissar stared at her, then felt a soothing warmth spreading by the stung area. He now noticed the bee who had stung him was colored blue and had a thin, smooth stinger. One of the medicinal bees.

"Oh . . . Is this how you apply the medicine? You're trying to help me?"

The little bee danced a salute, and Belissar exhaled his breath, also remembering that monster bees didn't necessarily die when they stung, now that he had calmed down. With a smile, he reached over and gently brushed the bee's back.

"Thank you."

More medicinal bees were hovering around him, and Belissar nodded at them. He felt little pricks as they stung him, but now that he was paying attention, he noticed they weren't as bad as a normal sting. Looking around, he found Niobee watching, along with the queen from the nearest hive.

"King okay?"

Belissar smiled. "Yes, and better thanks to you two, I'm guessing?"

Niobee wavered a bit in the air. "King hurt. Needed help."

The queen danced her agreement. Belissar held out his hand, and the two landed on it.

"Thanks. I'll be fine thanks to you both."

They paused for a second before they both began a happy dance. Belissar grinned, and then lay back down on the bed, letting the medicinal workers do their thing.

The next day, Chief Rohsuak brought a pair of staves, and after an excruciating amount of physical training, she began to teach him how to wield a spear.

Belissar raised an eyebrow at the older, hunched woman as she picked up the staff, but she twirled it around her with ease, then thrust it forward in a powerful stab that sent forth a small gust of wind. She turned to Belissar and grinned.

"Oh, I'm not as frail as I look. Age is a formidable foe, but I never yield without a fight."

Belissar began to sweat. He had a feeling that the training was going to get a lot worse.

He was correct.

Metsaitti's crew couldn't help but stop and stare at the sacred den master the next day. The young man had been through *three* days of the chief's training, and not only did he keep coming back but he looked no worse for wear than on the first. Even Metsaitti raised an eyebrow at that.

"Have you been taking it easy on him?"

Chief Rohsuak smiled. "No."

Metsaitti looked to the sacred den master and straightened his back somewhat. He knew now he was facing a man of focus, commitment, and sheer grizzly will, whatever his appearance or demeanor might suggest otherwise.

He was unaware the sacred den master was used to doing what he was told without complaint, regardless of how unpleasant it was, and that it hadn't occurred to him that he could quit.

Tyhgak the spearman, on the other hand, stared openly with his jaw wide open.

"You're surviving the demon?! Is that the power of a sacred den master?!"

Of course, everyone turned to look at Tyhgak when he shouted, and the sacred den master's eyes narrowed. Tyhgak took a step back and started to sweat. "Um, hello?"

The sacred den master continued to glare. "Don't touch my bees."

Tyhgak gulped. Metsaitti sighed. "Told you he could hear you."

Chief Rohsuak smiled as she walked up behind Tyhgak and placed her hand on his shoulder.

"Worry not, Den Master. I'll make sure to give Tyhgak here some instruction. The demon will certainly whip him into shape."

Tyhgak's face paled.

Belissar winced as he sat on the ground. His muscles ached, and he had bruises all over. Niobee and the soldier bees nearby started to hover around him before he assured them he was fine. Chief Rohsuak, despite all the sparring, seemed no worse for wear. She smiled as she sat down in front of him.

"Now should be a good time. Let's work on mana control."

Belissar sat up as well as he could, fixing his eyes on Chief Rohsuak. This was what he was ultimately working for.

"As I said, I believe mana to be a part of the body, or at least heavily intertwined with it. Your body is already subconsciously moving it around, sending it toward the parts in need of healing. Try to focus on it and feel it moving." She grinned. "From what I've seen of you, it should be easy."

Belissar nodded and focused on himself. He could indeed feel streams of mana flowing through his body, concentrating on the sorest muscles and the worst bruises. Chief Rohsuak nodded.

"Looks like you found it. Now, pay attention to *how* the mana is moving. Try to remember that feeling and see if you can replicate it. It may help to move around your limbs to get a feel for how the flow changes." She grinned again. "The sorer the limb, the easier the changes will be to notice."

Belissar flinched at that but did as she suggested, moving his arm around. He winced as he felt the bruises on it once again . . . and then felt the mana surge slightly toward that exact area.

Chief Rohsuak nodded. "It looks like you got it. We'll end our time together here for today, then. Focus on remembering that feeling for the rest of the day. Once you've healed, try to see if you can replicate it."

Belissar nodded, and the two parted ways. This time, he declined the help of the medicinal bees so he could focus on his own mana. It certainly made the rest of the night more painful, but the tower's powers were as impressive as ever, and he had made a full recovery by the next morning.

As he sat up in his bed, he took a deep breath and closed his eyes.

"Okay, here it goes . . ."

Belissar tried to make his mana move like it had the previous day.

His eyes shot open. The mana was now flooding into his arm where he once had a bruise. He tried to make it flow to the other arm, and it responded immediately. It was so easy, Belissar wondered why he couldn't do it before now.

Niobee was just flying in to greet him, but before she did, Belissar grinned at her.

"Niobee, I did it!"

"Did what?"

He held up his hand. "I moved the mana!"

Niobee paused for a second, then began a rapid dance. "King is best king! Niobee knew! King not useless drone!"

Belissar was so happy with his achievement that he didn't catch that last bit.

He leapt out of his bed and ran to the entrance of the tower. Up until now, everything he had achieved had been through the bees or through the powers of the tower. But now, Belissar, the former peasant, was moving mana around and about to learn some real magic.

Now, he could truly say he had become something more than he had ever been.

CHAPTER FORTY-FOUR

EVERYONE BEE GROWING

Chief Rohsuak raised an eyebrow. She and Belissar had just finished the physical training part for the day and had sat down to practice moving his mana.

"Already?"

Belissar nodded. Chief Rohsuak rubbed her chin with a nod.

"I suppose a sacred den master would have some advantages. Very well, let's move on to the next step, then." She held out her hand, and a small ball of dim light appeared. "You must learn to move your mana outside of your body but remain in control of it."

She went on to explain how to do so. Belissar nodded and then held out his hand. He tried to move his mana once more, concentrating it in the palm of his hand before trying to push it out—

A huge flash of light blinded him. Belissar cried out and fell back.

Chief Rohsuak, on the other hand, had already shielded her eyes and was grinning.

"Happens to everyone. Yours was brighter than most, but that's to be expected."

Belissar rubbed his eyes as he sat back up. He held his palm out again . . . but turned his face away.

Which turned out to be wise, as flashes of light filled his view time and time again.

Belissar sighed as he walked back to the apiary. Thanks to the large quantities of mana he could feel from the tower, the first steps of accumulating, sensing, and moving his own mana had been quite simple. This step was not. The mana did not want to leave his body, and when it did, it would do so all at once. Trying to control that burst was proving difficult.

Still, it was only the first day, so Belissar tried not to get too discouraged. He was learning *magic*, after all.

Glancing around as he stepped into the apiary, he watched the bees as they visited the nearby flowers. He had heard one of the queens had moved out here, so he wasn't surprised to see them this far from the beehouses.

However, he did see something that surprised him. A second, relatively new hive was under construction. He could feel the queen inside like the others, but something felt a bit different about her.

"Hey, Niobee."

Niobee flew into his vision. "Yes, King?"

Belissar pointed at the hive. "Did another of the queens move out here?"

"No. New queen!"

Belissar's eyes widened. "A new queen?"

The spawners had long since reached their maximums, and Belissar hadn't made any more recently. So, there was only one way a new queen could exist.

"The queens can reproduce? Have new queens as children?"

Niobee flew rapidly. "Yes!"

Belissar began to smile as a small queen bee crawled out of the hive and gave him a hesitant salute. Somehow, he had not considered that the monster bee queens could give birth to each other, but it made sense. And it would very much change his strategy.

Because he checked his mana and found that it hadn't changed.

He could tell now what felt different about this queen. The tower's mana flowed through the spawners and the monster bee queens. It did through this queen as well, but it felt a bit weaker than with the others. Which made sense, since the other queens had been born from the tower, while this one had been born from more normal parents.

Which apparently meant she didn't require a spawner or an upkeep of mana from him. And that meant that from now on, Belissar didn't need to make any more monster bee queen spawners. The current queens could expand the bee numbers on their own, and he could subsequently devote his mana to other uses; perhaps to more flower nodes to support the newcomers if the current flowers weren't enough.

He nodded at the new queen.

"Welcome, and great work. Let me know if you need anything, or if you don't have enough flowers."

She began dancing a salute as fast as she could before returning to her hive to continue setting up. Belissar grinned then continued home in a good mood, imagining how he could grow the tower to support more bees. He looked forward to the day the tower expanded that much more.

The days began to fall into a rhythm for Belissar after that. The magic practice went slowly with no discernible progress, but Chief Rohsuak told him that such was normal, so he kept at it.

Belissar and his bees performed minor purifications in the late afternoon, and at this point could consistently pull them off without issue. No new perks or room feature offers caught Belissar's eye, so he steadily expanded the dungeon's mana reserves, working toward the day he could attempt an expansion.

But for other residents, some things did change in that time . . .

Light died down within the hive. The Fourth of the Seventh shook her body, then stared down at the honeycomb, at her limbs, and at the little workers crawling around her.

She had done it. She was big now! It had taken a while, but when the Firstborn had learned of her intentions, she'd shared access to the mana flowers, which had dramatically sped up the process. And now, she could begin to lay some soldiers of her own. Once they hatched, she could put her plan into motion.

She couldn't wait!

The Firstborn and the other queens of the flower meadow gathered before the memorial. She felt it appropriate to meet there, a place that belonged to all the bees of the King. The place that reminded them of the sacrifices required to achieve what they had.

The wounded soldier stood up and danced her salute and greeting. After the King had lavished honor and attention on her, the Firstborn could not simply discard her. Yet, with her missing wings, the soldier could not participate in either the training or the battles, nor could she do much work around the hive, so both the Firstborn and the soldier were at a loss for her purpose.

But that had changed with the new memorial. Now, the soldier stood guard at the entrance of the beehouse, the hive of the fallen, where the sisters of her squad lay buried beneath. While the Firstborn knew the soldier would not be capable of handling any threats, it felt appropriate, somehow. A job that she couldn't justify devoting healthy bees to, and yet, a job that she felt needed to be done.

After greeting the soldier, she flew over to one of the monuments and paused before the symbols there.

> *Queen 1 – Spawner One's First Dynasty, and her hive of 1018 workers.*
> *Queen 2 – Spawner One's First Dynasty, and her hive of 564 workers.*
> *Queen 3 – Spawner One's First Dynasty, and her hive of 186 workers.*
> *Queen 4 – Spawner One's First Dynasty*

The Firstborn liked to remind herself that the King had built a hive of hives. And there was no better way to do that than to remind herself of those who had come before her: The queens of the First Dynasty who had sacrificed everything; their children, their hives, and even their own lives.

She danced her own salute before making her way to the meeting place. The other queens soon arrived, each greeting the soldier and pausing before the memorial as she had.

And then, they began their conversation. The Firstborn had wanted to follow the First of the Fifth in raising a new queen, but she had run into an issue. To do so required drones, which meant the cooperation of one other queen, and the drones the First of the Fifth had used had already perished.

At first, she was going to see if the First of the Fifth would be raising a second queen, and if they could collaborate, but she quickly realized that wasn't going to happen. The Firstborn had been stunned when she realized how much mana and honey it would require to bear a queen, so she knew the First of the Fifth would not be ready to bear a second one anytime soon.

So instead, she gathered the queens of the flower meadow. She greeted them, then explained her plan, which was simply to follow their instincts. If all the queens released both new queens and drones at the same time, all of them could bear a new queen at once while sharing the burden of raising drones.

The First Queen of the First Dynasty of the Third Spawner asked for more details. "A queen and drones. How much mana, honey needed?"

The Firstborn told them, and all the queens fell still. The Fourth Queen of the Fourth Spawner eventually began a slow dance.

"My hive can't. Not enough."

The Firstborn had expected as much and gave her prepared reply. "Will help. Give honey." She looked around at all the queens. "We all one hive. All help when in need."

One by one, the other queens gave their approval. Afterward, however, the Third Queen of the Second Spawner began to dance.

"But if all spending mana and honey, will need cut soldiers. If all cut soldiers, army not grow?"

The queens once again fell still at that. The Firstborn danced her acknowledgement. "Yes. But more queens mean more soldiers later."

The Third of the Second stood still before beginning an even slower dance. "But . . . King planning something. Something big. Need army now?"

The Firstborn paused at this. She . . . had not considered that. She stood in silence for a bit.

In the end, it was the First Queen of the Second Spawner who replied.

"Ask Conduit? If King need army, wait until King's plan, then try? If not, try now?"

The other queens began to agree. The Firstborn quickly agreed as well, for that was a much wiser idea than she'd had. She, perhaps, had been a bit overexcited, but now that she thought about it, coordinating with the Conduit and the King's plan was only natural. If anything, she should have done that to begin with.

But that was why the queens were gathered now, and why they were a hive of hives. Even if she should miss something, another bee might notice.

"Then, everyone agree?"

The queens all danced their affirmatives, and the meeting adjourned. The Firstborn sent messengers to find the Conduit, and the Conduit quickly sent her reply.

The King was indeed planning something big; something which would likely require a fight more dangerous than the daily assaults. It had been immensely fortunate that the Firstborn had asked before enacting her plan, for now, the queens of the flower meadow could focus on soldiers until that battle came.

The Firstborn was left deep in thought. Had the Third of the Second not spoken up, she may have made a major mistake. But because they had cooperated as a hive of hives, they had found the most efficient course of action. So, she thought, perhaps the queens should get together to speak more regularly.

CHAPTER FORTY-FIVE

TIME TO BEE BRAVE

And so, time passed. Belissar still hadn't managed to control his mana outside of his body yet, but today, his lack of progress did not cross his mind.

No, today, Belissar had other things to consider, for he had just finished the latest purification.

Selecting another ten mana, he brought his numbers to the current values.

Mana: 124/300

With this latest increase, he had reached his goal. He could now conduct an expansion purification.

Attempt expansion purification?
Estimated purification strength: Small.

Belissar hesitated at that. He did not know how strong a small purification would be, but he couldn't imagine it would be weaker than the minor purifications. It could be as strong as the initial one . . . or stronger, for he didn't know what the initial purification was classified as.

His bees were both capable and numerous at this point, and his traps were all stocked and prepared, but they had only been tested by the weaker shades thus far. He still didn't know if they could handle the beast from the initial purification as easily as they did its smaller kin.

And if the next purification was stronger than that . . . then sacrifice would be inevitable, and victory would not be guaranteed at all. Belissar would almost certainly have to watch his bees fall, and could end up losing everything he had built so far. He had been so focused on reaching this point that he hadn't truly considered the risks involved.

He got up from his chair and gathered some honeycomb. Making his way to the shrine of bees in the flower meadow, he placed the honeycomb in the chest and knelt in front of the statue of the God of Bees. Niobee followed along quietly, as she always did.

"Do you have any guidance for me? I . . . don't want to see my bees get hurt again."

Feeling a slight warmth, he opened his eyes. The shrine was glowing slightly. The glow then faded, which allowed Belissar to catch a glimpse of another light. Turning to the side, he saw the nearby bee memorial. Both the beehouse at its center and the pillars surrounding it glowed faintly.

Belissar stared at the memorial for a minute before walking over, looking over the pillars and the numbers inscribed there. He saw the carved bees dancing up and down, then looked over to the beehouse which held the remains of the fallen. The wounded soldier bee stood guard there and began a salute dance at his approach.

The frown on Belissar's face shrank, and his body relaxed even as his eyes narrowed. The bees never hesitated to sacrifice themselves. Niobee, the workers and queens of the First Dynasty of the First Spawner, the soldiers who had perished in the purifications that followed. The soldier who stood before him now, and who had not once complained about her permanent crippling. And the memorial itself, which *encouraged* such sacrifice.

Even though she had not spoken with words, Belissar knew what the God of Bees was trying to say. It made sense. She was the God of Bees, and bees were born to sacrifice for the hive. She would not fear those sacrifices.

And, if he were to be a king of bees like they called him, neither could he.

Belissar took a deep breath. "For the good of the hive, huh?"

The soldier bee immediately danced a salute, and Belissar's eyes widened as the bee carvings in the memorial followed suit. Belissar looked to Niobee, his constant companion. She did not wait for his question before beginning her dance.

"Bees ready. King is best king; bees follow."

Belissar gave a small smile and nodded. He did not wish to see any of his bees fall. He did not wish to see his tower devastated once again. He did not want to take this risk. But he knew he must.

If the tower and the hives were to grow, Belissar needed new options. New rooms, new flowers, new bee types, new perks. Now that he knew the existing queens could bear new ones, the tower's current space had started feeling small. It may not be long before all the existing flowers were claimed.

As for the worst case . . . Well, the worst case was *why* Belissar needed to take this risk in the first place. A shade could slay all of his bees, tear down all he had built, and corrupt his core, and that still wouldn't be the *worst* thing that could happen to his tower. Belissar had had a chance to rebuild and recover even from that disaster. It would be painful beyond belief if he had to do so again, but he at least knew it was possible.

The tower lords, on the other hand, were an unknown threat. Belissar had no idea what they might be capable of—or if it would be possible for him to recover from what they could do. The risk presented by a small purification now might be dwarfed in comparison to the threat of the tower lords down the line.

Belissar resolved himself. For the good of the hive—for the good of all the hives—they needed to take some risks now.

He sent a call to the bees—to *all* the bees. He requested all the queens and as many of their brood as could be spared. Soon, the sound of buzzing wings grew as loud as a roaring fire. The sky and the ground turned yellow and black as bees hovered in the air or landed on the flowers below.

Countless eyes looked at him as the queens flew ahead of them. Niobee took some distance from him to join them at their head. Belissar's heart constricted as he thought of subjecting them all to danger, but he forced himself to speak.

"We now have an opportunity for greater growth than we've seen so far. But . . . it comes with greater danger. We, um, will probably have to face a battle worse than anything we've encountered so far. I . . . cannot guarantee that we all will survive." He furrowed his brow as he thought of the initial purification. "I cannot even guarantee that we will win."

He paused as he looked at each and every queen. They hovered in the air, waiting for his next words. "So, um, I wanted to ask you all. Are you ready to face the greatest challenge you have faced so far, even if you must risk death and destruction?"

Belissar nearly took a step back as he was battered by the roar of buzzing wings. Every bee immediately danced a salute, all as one.

"Then . . . I think we need to do this. For the good of the hives, and to grow strong enough to face whatever threats come later. We'll attempt the expansion purification tomorrow at the normal time. Um, do whatever you need to do to prepare."

The air roared with another synced salute, then exploded into motion as the bee swarm began to move. The queens raced back to their hives, the soldiers immediately began to split into squads and conduct maneuvers, and the workers spread out across every flower they could find.

Belissar exhaled his breath. Niobee stayed and flew before his eyes.

"King okay?"

He slowly nodded. "Yes. I'm just . . . I think bees are going to die tomorrow."

Niobee flew straight and steady. "Bees ready. Fight for hive."

Belissar nodded. "I know. But I still don't like seeing you all get hurt."

She paused for a minute before flying slowly. "When Niobee caught, was going to die. That fine; Niobee just worker, queen had many. But then King helped, saved. Gave honey."

Belissar's eyes were fixed on Niobee as she danced. She slowly began to speed up. "Niobee not even King's worker then. So, Niobee knew King best king. But King was alone, needed workers, needed hive." Her wings began to buzz louder. "Then, others hurt King. Niobee couldn't help then." She slowed down a bit. "Now, King has hive, has workers. Now, hive protects King, helps king."

Belissar smiled and lifted his finger. Niobee landed on it, and he gently brushed her back.

". . . Thanks, Niobee. How about we try to protect each other from now on?"

Niobee flew off his finger and began dancing rapidly. "No! King is king! Workers, soldiers protect King!"

Belissar chuckled as Niobee continued to dance. His steps were just a little bit lighter as he returned to the farmhouse for the night.

Chief Rohsuak lifted an eyebrow. "A break, you say?"

The sacred den master nodded. "We have a big fight coming up, so I want to make sure everything's prepared."

She rubbed her chin and nodded. "I see. Is there danger approaching?"

The sacred den master paused for a moment before shaking his head. "Um, I don't think so. Not unless you saw something on the way here?"

The chief shook her head, and the sacred den master continued.

"It's more . . . I have to do this to expand the tower."

Chief Rohsuak nodded. She didn't know many details of a sacred den's inner workings, but that made sense, given what little she knew.

"I see. In that case, it is wise to prepare for battle. Should I return tomorrow?"

The sacred den master paused again. "Um, maybe? I, um, might be busy."

Chief Rohsuak gave him an encouraging smile. "How about I check in the day after to see how things are going, and we can decide our future schedule from there?"

The den master nodded. "Um, yeah, that sounds good."

Nodding, the chief turned to Metsaitti and his hunters. "Let's all take a break, then."

The other hunters began to complain, but Metsaitti just nodded and told them to pack it up. Soon, they were walking with Chief Rohsuak back to their camp.

"Metsaitti."

"Yes, Chief?"

"Take your hunters and scout the Underway. I'll make sure everyone is prepared."

Metsaitti nodded. "Right away."

The other hunters, bless their hearts, just looked confused. Fortunately, Metsaitti had caught on, and took them ahead. Chief Rohsuak let out a sigh.

She had heard tales of sacred dens falling. It was rare, but it *did* happen. The sacred den master was clearly anxious—or rather, more anxious than normal, as far as she could tell. If he was attempting something big, then the risks would be big as well.

She considered offering assistance for a brief moment before burying that idea. Her people were teetering on the edge of a knife as they were. The situation would already be extremely grim if they had to pack up and continue their sojourn now. If the sacred den master lost his fight, they might have to do just that, and would need every advantage possible to survive. So, if they lost *any* of their hunters to injury or death trying to help, it could mean the death of them all.

The sacred den master, for his part, did not seem to trust them yet. He had not even told them his name, nor made any attempt to engage with the hunters passing by him every day. He hardly spoke to Chief Rohsuak outside of their lessons. It did not seem to occur to him to even request their help, which was fortunate, since she could not offer that help.

As much as she wished to keep this sacred den around, their relationship was not close enough to risk everything on it.

So, she would prepare for the worst.

She turned back toward the tower and bowed her head, lifting a small prayer up to both the God of Bees and her own patron.

"Best of luck to you, Sacred Den Master. I sincerely hope to meet you again."

PREPARE THE BEE-FENSES!

The Firstborn scrambled to the next soldier cell as her mana filled back to the minimum necessary. A part of her longed to join her soldiers, to see her army's preparations firsthand. But she quashed such feelings, for such was not her role.

The King had spoken, and had appeared as solemn as the day she was born, just after the fall of the First Dynasty. Not even when he had honored the fallen from her hive had he appeared so. It was obvious that this had been a decision he made only with great deliberation . . . and perhaps resignation. Such was the nature of the danger they would soon face.

The truest test of her army. A threat on the scale of the one that had ended the First Dynasty . . . or perhaps even greater. The Firstborn would like to believe she was ready, but doubts still crept into her mind. The King was preparing for a bloodbath. There was a risk of loss with every purification, but this time, the King seemed to be *expecting* deaths.

Such was the purpose of her army. Neither the Firstborn nor a single one of her soldiers would hesitate to give their lives for the sake of the King, yet still, the Firstborn was troubled. She no longer wished for mere victory—she wished for perfection. The strongest army that could win any fight without grieving her King.

To see the King as she saw him today was perhaps her greatest failure yet. Proof that as strong as her army was, it could not yet avoid troubling the King. That falling as the First Dynasty had before was still a very real possibility.

Unfortunately, there was little the Firstborn could do about that for this battle. The time was upon them; the soldiers she laid now would not be ready in time for the fight. The queens of the flower meadow were not striving to grow their numbers, but to replenish them if the battle turned out as bloody as the King feared.

So, she allowed her heart to burn. She would trust that her warriors would carry the day tomorrow, whatever the cost. And then, she would do all in her power to cut that cost and ease the King's burden.

After laying her next egg, she rested right next to the cell, willing her mana to regenerate that much faster.

A soldier bee sat at the entrance of the memorial's beehouse. She watched as her sisters flew in the distance, practicing as many different maneuvers as they could think of, preparing for as many different scenarios as they could. She could not help but beat her single remaining pair of wings, but without the other pair, she would never fly again.

The King had preserved her life right when she was about to leave her hive in a final exile. She believed it had been for a reason, and that reason was beginning to take shape. She now had a job as the guardian of the fallen, the one who looked after the home of her sisters who had sacrificed for the hive and the King. Yet still, now that the eve of battle had arrived, her questions returned as well.

Was this truly all that was left for her? Was this truly worth the continued support of her queen and her worker sisters? Would she truly never join her sisters in battle again? Was she truly doomed to remain here even as the sisters of her squad passed on? Was this all the King had preserved her for?

There was no one to answer her questions, nor would she ever ask them. She would not dare take the time of even a single worker. After all, she contributed the least to the hive of any bee within the King's realm, despite having received many gifts from the King himself.

So, she was left alone with her thoughts as everyone else prepared.

The First of the Fifth watched as her workers scrambled. The sound of buzzing filled the air as her workers fanned their wings in sync, creating an air current across the latest batch of honey.

The First of the Fifth's mana surged and touched that of the honey. She knew then that the honey in tray three was drying faster than expected, so she could reallocate some of those workers to the mana-processing chain. She brushed antennas with the nearest workers, sending them to relay orders to that effect. Her mana surged through them, and they instinctually responded to her touch, renewing their efforts as the balance of workers shifted.

A great battle was coming; greater than any within her lifetime. That meant the Firstborn would have a great opportunity to gain the King's favor through the victory and sacrifices of her soldiers. That was a field the First of the Fifth could not compete on.

So, she wouldn't. Instead, she would utilize her strengths to remind everyone of who she was and the critical service she provided for the King. She would ensure that she could not be forgotten even in the midst of the Firstborn's moment.

And that meant honey. Lots and lots of honey.

She followed the workers as they transferred from tray three to the entrance, where her workers were assembled into large lines.

Foragers arrived at the entrance and landed in front of designated lines, passing the nectar in their honey crops to the first workers in the chain. The workers then began blowing the nectar into bubbles while cycling their mana through it, starting the process of converting it into honey while also imbuing it with mana. They then passed it to the second row, where a large strip of greenish blue interrupted the yellow lines.

The First of the Fifth was not merely producing honey. A great battle was coming, and the King was expecting blood. And unlike the Firstborn, the First of the Fifth could address the King's concern directly through the creation of healing herb honey.

She would prepare vast stockpiles in order to heal as many of the future wounded as she could, reducing the sacrifices required of the flower meadow queens. She would become a balm for the King—and would turn the flower meadow's sacrifice into her own triumph.

But the nectar she'd gathered from the healing herbs was not enough, not least of all because she had allowed the other queens access to it in return for producing drones. So, the First of the Fifth did the unspeakable.

She mixed the honeys.

She combined her rigorously categorized products into a single amalgam where quality could not be guaranteed. She turned her hive to brute mass production and focused on expanding the healing honey stockpile as much as possible.

The first step of doing so was to have the medicinal workers participate in the honey processing. The workers could produce the same healing compounds as the herbs, and so could imbue any nectar they processed with a bit of it.

Of course, diluting the healing compounds by mixing the honeys also reduced its potency, which was why the First of the Fifth was also mixing the nectar of mundane blooms with that of the mana flowers.

The additional mana from that precious nectar resonated with the scarce healing compounds from the healing herbs and boosted their effects, allowing a much lower concentration to reach the same level of effectiveness. Combined with the additional compounds from the medicinal workers, she was able to produce acceptably effective healing herb honey even though the majority of the nectar came from other flowers.

She would not dare serve such shoddy honey to the King, but it was sufficient to heal the wounds of the soldiers. And nothing, not even her own pride in her honey quality, would prevent the First of the Fifth from being of service to the King.

For that was what it meant to be the most favored queen.

Even the Fourth of the Seventh had been stirred to action by the words of the King. She had not the strength of the Firstborn, for her first soldiers hadn't even hatched yet. She could not produce even a fraction of the honey the First of the Fifth could, even if she had been blessed with a magical hive like the best of the apiary queens. But she still did all that she could.

The workers she sent to the flower meadow to forage were redirected to the flower meadow hives, dropping off their nectar to the queens that would do battle. The workers gathering from the apiary nearby offered their nectar to the First of the Fifth.

The First of the Fifth would normally reject such an offer, but today, she accepted the nectar, to the Fourth of the Seventh's surprise. And then, she sent some of her workers to the newest queen, the First of the Fifth's child.

The First of the Fifth had loaned some workers to help her out at first, but had recalled them in the current time of need. The Fourth of the Seventh was the closest queen, and didn't seem to have as urgent a task as the First of the Fifth, so she figured she could lend a hand.

Her workers said the new queen danced a gratitude dance like they'd never seen before. She wished she could have seen it, but that would have to wait. There was work to be done, and not a bee in the realm would rest for even a moment until it was finished.

Belissar himself spent the time reviewing the traps. He moved some of them about, such as placing one of the honey traps by the door to the apiary. It would spray its honey just before a shade reached the pit awaiting there, hopefully knocking them off-balance so they would stumble into the hole.

He set up a couple of traps like that, then double-checked the kindling and firewood at the bottom of each pit and refreshed them as needed. He wove a couple more rope torches for the bees to carry, and double-checked that the campfire in the apiary was ready to go on a moment's notice.

He then went ahead and added more traps; as many as his current mana could buy. He figured that would make more sense than monster spawners, given they wouldn't have time to reach their spawn limit, and he also needed to keep his mana for after the new choices came in. Traps could be removed once they were no longer needed, but spawners would keep hold of the mana for each monster they spawned.

And there was no world where Belissar even *thought* of getting rid of bees to reclaim some mana.

And so, everyone in the tower prepared themselves for the fight to come as the purification cooldown slowly ticked down.

CHAPTER FORTY-SIX

FIRST EXPANSION PURIFICATION

Yellow and black covered the sky, with the occasional purple interspersed here and there. Flowers swayed in the wind generated by rapidly beating wings as the bee army assembled into its formations and squadrons, deploying around the tower entrance. A handful of mad honey soldiers joined their ranks, ready to fight alongside their sisters.

The worker bees retreated to their hives. There, they assembled into formations of their own, ready to fly out should the worst come to pass. The queens stood at the entrances, trying to see the soldiers in the distance as best they could.

A roaring flame crackled at the front of the apiary. Several squads of soldiers stood nearby, their legs already holding the loops of their ropes. They would be ready to light their torches and fly at a moment's notice.

Belissar stood next to them with his woodcutting axe beside him. Niobee hovered nearby.

Attempt expansion purification?
Estimated purification strength: Small.

Belissar took a deep breath and then spoke, sending his intentions to all his bees. "Here we go."

Expansion purification attempt commencing.

By this point, the flow of the tower's mana had faded into the background for Belissar, but it was still there. It permeated every inch of the tower and beyond. Trace amounts of mana flowed through the surrounding area, condensing again when it came into contact with the Hunger at the edges.

But now, Belissar could clearly feel that flow once again.

His body began to heat up as the tower's mana burned, the currents growing rapid and intense. It began to pour into the surrounding area, racing across the fields and trees and past the camp of the bear folk. Then, it hit the edge, where the Hunger awaited.

Belissar shivered as the cold of the Hunger responded in kind, creeping back along the trails of mana. As it approached the center, the gates of the tower swung open once more.

"Everyone, get ready! Here it comes!"

The Hunger soon grew visible at the edges of the gate, an amorphous black mist spreading across the empty air. Soon, it covered the entrance entirely, appearing as it had when Belissar had first opened the gate.

A high-pitched screech cut through the air. Belissar winced as the noise stabbed into his mind, and soon, something began to emerge from the mist.

But it was not a paw. Not this time.

Belissar's eyes widened as the shade began to emerge from the top of the gate rather than the bottom. A long beak, longer than Belissar's arm, came first, with sharp teeth sticking out from both top and bottom.

A big head emerged next, with five glowing red eyes arranged in a tight circle right in the center. Two wings spread out across the length of the gateway, and small bolts of black lightning leapt across the shade's body. Razor sharp claws that appeared more like daggers tipped its feet.

The shade beat its wings, remaining aloft as it hovered above the ground. It opened its beak, revealing rows and rows of teeth, and then let out another high-pitched screech.

Expansion purification has begun.
Remaining hostiles: 1

Belissar felt a chill go down his spine. He couldn't help but shout, "Watch out! It can fly!"

Unfortunately, he was a bit too late. The first squad of soldiers began diving the moment the shade started taking shape, but they had been positioned for a target on the ground and had not reached full speed by the time they reached the beast. The shade swung its wings and pulled its body back, and the bees passed right before it.

With a snap of its jaws, the first bee of the day fell. Belissar gritted his teeth.

The rest of the soldiers reacted immediately. Several close squads began to fly in while the rest pulled up. The close squads couldn't gain the speed for an attack dive, so instead ran interference for the first squad, flying in but preparing to take evasive action once the beast turned its attention toward them. In the meantime, the rest of the bees tried to gain altitude and set up higher-speed dives.

The shade snapped at the bees around it, but now that the nimble bees were focused on dodging, they managed to evade its beak. Two of them even managed to get behind the creature and sting its back. The beast screeched again.

Belissar held his breath as the close-range bees danced around the shade while two of the squads above began to dive. It seemed that beyond their initial surprise, they were still faring well. The shade might be able to fly, but its large size meant it couldn't outmaneuver the agile bees in close combat.

It snapped its jaws again, but bit only air as the target soldier suddenly changed direction, and yet another bee landed a sting on its back.

But then, the shade looked up into the sky and saw the bees above, including the two squads on approach. Lifting its wings up as high as they would go, it then pushed off, the wind from its wings blowing away the closest bees, which spun in the air as they tried to right themselves.

It shot up toward the bees overhead with frightening speed. The bees in its path began to scatter, but the diving squads weren't so fortunate. The shade slammed into them as they tried to kill their momentum and turn away, snapping up two of them in its jaws. One perished immediately.

But not the second.

The second began to glow and continued moving despite being impaled by the creature's teeth, channeling her mana into her stinger and driving it into the shade's shoulder. A moment later, the glow around her body faded, and she, too, was torn apart, leaving her stinger imbedded in the shade. The beast screeched again.

The rest of the bees began to fly around the monster, trying to encircle it, but the creature beat its wings and shot into the sky faster than any of the soldiers could follow. Its eyes glowed as it looked down on the bees climbing after it, then tucked in its wings as it twisted its body, beginning a dive even faster than its climb.

Again, the bees were forced to scatter. Two more soldiers failed to do so and ended up in the shade's jaw. It bit down on them then swung its beak to toss them away before any survivors could strike again.

The other bees tried to entrap it once more, but the beast was climbing again before they could catch it. It began to prepare itself for another dive.

Belissar's heart leapt to his throat as his grip on his axe tightened.

They were losing. His tower had *nothing* to deal with a flying foe that could outrun the bees. There was nothing but clear, open skies up above. His mind raced as he tried to think of something to do, but nothing came to mind. As a human on the ground, he was helpless against a flying enemy. He had no ranged weapons to even attempt to help. No bows, no javelins, not even a sling.

He stared at his hand and gritted his teeth. Maybe, if he had learned magic successfully, he could have done something. But he had not, so he had no choice but to hope his bees could find a solution.

One of the soldiers began to dance, and the others saluted before rearranging themselves as the beast began to dive once more. And as it approached, the bees compressed together, as close as they could fly. They did not scatter, instead flying *toward* the shade and its beak.

The shade could not pull out of its dive at this point, so it dove forward instead, chomping down with its beak. Three soldiers were caught in its jaws.

But at the same time, five more right next to them were not, instead crashing into the monster. One was struck by the side of its beak and knocked away. Another was blown down by the shade's wing. But the other three landed on the monster's back and belly, and immediately stuck their stingers into it.

The shade screeched, but this time, the bees didn't bother flying away. They clung to the beast and stung it over and over again. The monster reached down and snapped up the one on its belly with its beak, but she responded by just stinging the bottom of its head. It screeched and released her, though she tumbled from the air due to her wounds.

And, of course, the rest of the bees had not been idle in the midst of all this.

The shade had come to a stop as it tried to deal with the bees clinging to it, so taking advantage, the other soldiers began flying toward it at maximum speed. The monster could not even remove the two bees on its back. If more could begin piling on, they could overwhelm it. They could bring it down.

They could win. Belissar held his breath.

Suddenly, the air began to crackle.

Black lightning began to surge and coat the beast. It struck the bees on its back, and soon, they fell off, smoke and lightning clinging to their bodies. The shade then spread its wings wide and screeched as loud as it could.

A wave of black lightning surged in all directions. The closest bees were struck, either falling from the sky or twitching in the air, while the rest were forced to fall back.

And the shade didn't miss that chance.

Even before Belissar could react to the horror before his eyes, the monster beat its wings. And this time, it did not fly up.

No, this time, it flew *forward*, shooting through the sky away from the cloud of soldier bees.

And straight toward the door to the apiary.

CHAPTER FORTY-SEVEN

BROKEN, NOT BEE-TEN

Belissar gasped as his mind caught up to the scene before him. The shade was soaring across the flower meadow, flying at about the height of the trees as it raced toward the apiary door. And the flying shade, of course, ignored every single pit and sticky honey trap Belissar had placed. Not a single one of his preparations would slow the shade down in the slightest.

The soldier bees raced after it, the air buzzing as they beat their wings as fast as they could go. But the sheer size difference between their wings and the shade's meant they couldn't match its top speed. Now that it had gotten ahead of them, they wouldn't catch it.

Belissar's mind went blank, and his expression slowly twisted as he realized there was *nothing* to stop the shade from reaching the end of the flower meadow. It could tear the meadow hives to shreds before their soldiers arrived to defend them. It could continue on straight into the apiary and attack him or the beehouses behind him. It could even keep going and fly straight into the core room.

Niobee frantically danced commands in the air while Belissar remained stunned, and the soldier bees from the apiary spawners began to assemble. But the soldier bee spawners capped out at fifteen each, and there were only two of them. The small force of thirty soldiers seemed paltry in comparison to the shade heading toward them.

But Belissar couldn't think of anything else to do. He wasn't even sure if he *should* do anything, or if he should run and tell the bees to hide. Maybe the shade would target the core, and some of them could survive.

Either way, he was too late. The shade was fast approaching the entrance and did not divert its course. It would fly into the apiary—and into Belissar—within moments. Niobee was frantically dancing in front of him, but he didn't notice. There was nothing and no one between him and its snapping beak.

Save one.

The little head of a soldier bee popped up above one of the memorial pillars, the one closest to the entrance. One single soldier bee with a missing pair of wings climbed to the top of the pillar. The wounded soldier watched carefully as the shade approached, tensing her legs. She waited for her moment . . .

And leapt off the pillar.

She beat her last remaining wings as she glided through the air, willing herself to go even a little bit faster, hoping that she had timed her single chance correctly.

And she had. She was on a direct collision course with the shade's back, so she spun about as best she could and extended her stinger forward, filling it with mana.

The beast screeched as the stinger plunged into its back. Since it had not seen any bees flying overhead, it had not anticipated being attacked from above. As a result, it dipped down, an instinctual motion to move away from the sudden assault.

And as a result of that, it came just barely within range of the sticky honey trap Belissar had placed on the ground by the apiary entrance. A plume of honey erupted into the air as the trap triggered and bathed the shade as it flew by, and the monsters found its wings coated in sticky, damp, thick honey.

It quickly lost lift and crashed into the ground.

The wounded soldier continued to sting the shade—and she wasn't alone. The Firstborn had leapt into action, leading her workers into battle. She arrived and dealt a sting of her own to the beast's back. She may not have had the strength of the soldiers, but the large queen had quite the reserve of mana she could push into her attacks. A cloud of worker bees swarmed over the shade as well, making up for their tiny size with raw numbers as they dealt a thousand stings at once.

The shade shook as it tried to escape, but the sticky honey held its wings to the ground, and the bees on its back were out of range of both its beak and claws. So, instead, it took a deep breath.

The Firstborn's antennas twitched as she felt the gathering mana. She quickly flew off the shade's back, her workers following. A surge of black lightning coated the beast and began to burn at the honey. Thanks to the Firstborn's quick actions, all the bees managed to escape the attack . . . save for one. The wounded soldier convulsed as she was covered in black lightning.

"NO!"

A shout filled the flower meadow. Before he even knew it, Belissar had rushed out of the apiary with his axe held high. He brought it down and struck the shade's head, who screeched as it slammed into the ground. The lightning stopped surging and began to fade.

"King!"

Niobee flew after him and straight toward the beast. Her abdomen glowed bright with mana, and the shade screeched again as she stung it. The apiary soldiers came after, landing on the monster, dealing stings of their own. With the lightning gone, the Firstborn and her workers resumed their attack as well, and they were soon joined by the other queens and workers of the flower meadow.

Shortly afterward, the fastest of the meadow soldiers began to catch up and join in while Belissar continued striking the shade's head over and over with his axe.

"Don't! Touch! My! Bees!"

Over and over the axe fell. The monster struggled at first, but the sheer number of bee stings had taken their toll, and it was unable to retaliate. Soon, it was unable to move at all, and its head fell against the ground as Belissar continued to strike it.

He didn't stop until the shade burst into a cloud of black mist and his axe dug into the ground.

All hostiles defeated.
Expansion purification—

Belissar ignored the message, as well as the growing heat of the tower's mana, as he rushed forward. Kneeling on the ground, he slowly picked up the fallen soldier bee. Her chitin was charred, her legs, antenna, and remaining wings twitching now and then. Bits of black lightning danced across her on occasion, causing Belissar's hands to go numb, but he ignored that as well. She was still alive, if barely.

Belissar quickly turned his head toward Niobee. "Get some healing honey, quick!"

Niobee flew off toward the apiary as the queens of the flower meadow rushed to check their honey stockpiles. Belissar gritted his teeth as he held the soldier bee, his mind racing as he tried to think of a way to help her.

"Don't die on me!"

Her antennas twitched faintly at his words. He felt her mana stir, trying to repair her body. She had more than the average soldier bee, but it was quickly fading.

He narrowed his eyes, then stirred up his own mana.

"Come on . . . Come on!"

Taking one of his hands, he moved it away from the bee, trying to condense his mana above it. He didn't want a blast of mana to hit her if he failed, but if he could just condense his mana externally, maybe he could give her some of his own. He didn't know if that would actually help, but he felt he had to do *something*.

The mana burst into light, and Belissar snarled.

"Come on, work already!"

He willed with all his heart for his mana to obey his command. And as he did, the nearby shrine of bees began to glow. Belissar didn't notice as both he and the soldier took on a similar glow.

"YES!"

The mana released from his body but did not explode beyond its control. Instead of a burst of white light, it condensed into a small ball of yellow light above his hand, which began to stretch into lines. It formed hexagonal patterns reminiscent of honeycomb, then flashed. The yellow light began to condense further into a ball, becoming more and more solid until it soon became a shimmering yellow liquid.

It became honey.

Belissar had no idea what was happening, and he didn't care, bringing the ball of floating, glowing honey to the soldier bee's face. She slowly extended her proboscis and began to drink.

The wounded soldier had been satisfied. Despite her injuries, she had been able to join the battle. She had been able to strike a blow against the invader and ensure victory for the hive. For a soldier bee, there was no greater joy than that. Though she would perish, she would gladly join the sisters of her former squad who had gone before her. She was no longer ashamed to have endured, to have spent the resources of the hive on a soldier who could no longer fight.

Until she heard the words of the King.

"Don't die on me!"

For her, that was enough. The command of the King was absolute, for her above all. She only lived to this day by the will of the King. Her life was his to end.

And so, she fought back, stirring up her mana and trying to purge the enemy's attack from her battered body. But it wouldn't be enough. She would fail the King's final command to her.

Until suddenly, she was bathed in the warmth of the King's mana. A ball of honey appeared before her, brighter, sweeter, and more beautiful than any she had ever seen. She began reaching out before stopping herself. She wanted it, more than anything, but was she truly permitted such a thing? She, a mere crippled soldier?

But the King's mana filled her with warmth. As well as another's . . .

Reaching out, she began to drink. Warm mana flowed through her body and began to burn, heat scorching her as the mana attempted to heal her wounds. She trembled as the black lightning resisted, surging through her once again.

So, she began to beat her remaining wings and move her body, rubbing her legs and hairs together as best she could. She filled them with mana as the movements began to create the tiny lightnings that workers used to help gather pollen. The tiny lightnings began to carry her mana and the mana granted to her from the honey, and it joined with the black lightning surging across her chitin.

Soon, the lightning began to change color. Black became black and yellow as she warred with it for control. But the black lightning's source was long gone, while she was filled with more and more mana every moment, and soon, she was coated in golden lightning only. Moving about it, she began searching for a place to put it so it would stop harming her body and the King.

And she found one. An empty void which both her mana and her mind wanted filled.

The yellow lightning condensed and gathered together along her back, then extended out before looping around. It formed a long curve that grew wider the further it got, with smaller bolts zigzagging across the interior.

A pair of wings formed of yellow lightning now extended from her back, replacing what she had lost.

And then, the remaining mana within her flowed to her wounds, which began to heal.

CHAPTER FORTY-EIGHT

BEE-FITTING GROWTH

Tears welled up in Belissar's eyes as he looked down at the bee in his hands. The lightning had changed color and turned into a pair of wings. He had *no* idea what had happened, but the important part was that the bee was going to be okay. Her body was no longer twitching, and she was still alive; he could feel her mana growing stronger by the second.

She slowly began to move around and climbed up his arm to rest on his shoulder. Belissar smiled and laughed as he wiped his eyes with his free hand.

It was only one out of all the bees who had died that day so far, but he had saved at least that one from death. And hopefully, she wouldn't be the only.

He placed her down as the medicinal bees began to arrive and pour over her, brushing her with their antennas and mana. Niobee returned with an *army* of worker bees from the apiary, each carrying cells filled with healing herb honey. He nodded at her then turned to the army arriving from the front.

"Gather up the wounded; we're going to take care of them all."

But as he spoke, Niobee suddenly began to glow. Belissar's eyes widened. "Niobee?!"

A moment later, she was covered in light so bright Belissar had to shield his eyes.

As Belissar was moving to help the wounded bees, Chief Rohsuak and her people were gathered by the entrance to the Underway. Soon, though, she heard the perimeter scouts begin to shout, and she turned her head in the direction of the sacred den.

She could see a bright light shining from that direction, even with all the trees between them and its entrance, then felt a wave of mana pass them by. Even those without mana of their own glanced around from the slight warmth.

She smiled, even when for her it felt more like a roaring flame.

"I guess I was worried for nothing. Well done, Sacred Den Master."

She motioned to her people to return to their home.

Belissar lowered his hand as the light faded . . . and then his jaw dropped. A soldier bee now flew where Niobee had once been. A soldier bee with a missing antenna.

"Niobee?"

The soldier began dancing. "Yes, King?"

Belissar let out his breath. If Niobee was fine, he could deal with whatever had happened later. Like he would with those messages trying to distract him, or those intense currents of burning-hot mana rushing through the tower and beyond. Right now, he had bees to heal.

The first wounded soldier crawled back on his shoulder right before he was about to set out.

"You should stay and rest."

She began a slow but firm dance, as quick as she could. "Can help; others need."

Belissar frowned, but he had no time to argue the point, so he decided to bring her. He guessed at the end of the day her resting on his shoulder wasn't all that different from resting on the ground or in her hive, and even if it wasn't, she was right that the others needed help as quickly as he could provide it. So, he set off with her riding along.

Medicinal workers were guiding hurt soldiers to cells full of healing herb honey, lightly jabbing them with their thin stingers on occasion. More soldier bees came and went, carrying their injured sisters to the medicinal workers.

Meanwhile, others led Belissar to the most heavily wounded; those who could not be moved at all. He did the magic honey thing his mana had done for the first soldier, filling them with mana in hopes of stabilizing them.

Some made it. For others, the mana honey simply seemed to ease their pain as they passed. Belissar teared up each time that happened but kept moving to the next one who needed his help.

As for the soldier on his shoulder, he quickly learned why she had wanted to come. They found other bees who had been burned by the first lightning surge, still twitching as jolts of black lightning occasionally arced across their bodies.

Whenever they came upon them, the soldier climbed down his arm, then one by one, she crawled to the wounded and brushed them with her golden wing. Soon, the black lightning arcing from their bodies turned yellow as well, after which Belissar's honey could heal their wounds.

They worked hard until every bee who could be saved was stabilized, and every bee who could not was accounted for. After that, everyone gathered by the memorial. All those who were wounded stood on the beehouse, while the rest hovered in the skies around.

One by one, Belissar placed the remains of the fallen inside the memorial, and new words appeared on the pillars as the bee carvings danced. When it was done, Belissar took a step back and lowered his head. "Thank you for your sacrifices. We won today because of you."

Niobee led the bees in their solemn dance once more. The wounded soldiers joined in as they were able, and the bee carvings followed suit. Belissar watched as the shrine of bees and the memorial itself began to glow faintly.

Today had been a victory, but at a great cost. Twelve soldier bees had perished, and another fifteen had received wounds to varying degrees, mostly due to lightning burns.

Belissar thought he had done all he could to prepare, but the shade had defied all of his expectations, and the bees had paid the price. In fact, had it not been for the wounded soldier's attack at precisely the right time and place to trigger a honey trap, they likely would not have won at all.

He himself might have died, and he didn't know if he'd come back or what would happen to the tower if he didn't. He was reminded once again that he had a *long* way to go as a dungeon master. His defenses may have been impressive compared to the wolflike minor shades, but they fell apart immediately against a new kind of foe.

But, though Belissar's heart ached at the thought of all the bees who had perished, this time, he did not regret it. This exact scenario was what he had been worried about when he'd made the decision to expand. His tower had not been prepared for a flying enemy that could channel lightning. They *couldn't* have been.

More queens, more flowers of the types he had, and more soldier bees would not have changed the outcome today. The pit traps and the fires he had prepared had been entirely useless. And most of all, he couldn't have known the threat he was facing before he started the purification. His tower and his bees needed more options to deal with future threats, including ones he couldn't predict ahead of time.

And thanks to the courage and sacrifice of the bees, they had gained just that.

Expansion successful.
Reward: Floor limit increased to 2. Receive one perk choice and two random reward choices.

But he would deal with that a bit later.

Soon, the dance came to a close, and Belissar gave a smile. "Let's celebrate. Today, we won thanks to you all."

The air exploded into motion as thousands of bees began to zip about, and Belissar brought out as many trays of honey as he had; even the mad honey trays, which apparently didn't poison the bees. Workers buzzed around and brought honey to the soldiers while countless bees of many different hives danced together and brushed each other's antennas.

Belissar looked over to the apiary queens and nodded at them with a smile.

"Thanks for making all that honey for this."

The apiary queens danced happily at his thanks. Belissar felt a bit of the ache in his chest fade as he watched the bees all around him. This was why he didn't regret his decisions. The bees themselves were full of nothing but joy tonight, the wounded no less than the healthy. They didn't mind the sacrifices, and they didn't fear death or pain.

So, Belissar would honor that courage and celebrate what they had achieved. He would still do what he could to minimize the sacrifices, but would not run from them if they were necessary.

And he would bring ruin upon those who caused them.

At that point, Niobee flew over to him, carrying a chunk of honeycomb with her new, larger body.

"King! King should eat too!"

He smiled and held his hand out. Niobee placed the honeycomb in it.

"Thanks, Niobee."

Taking a bite, he held out his other hand. Niobee landed in it, barely fitting now. He then held out the honeycomb for her, and she drank from it. He grinned as her wings fluttered.

The celebrations continued even as the sun went down.

CHAPTER FORTY-NINE

BEE-MUSING CHOICES

The next day, as Belissar woke up, he looked around for Niobee. He frowned when he didn't find her, then paused as he saw a soldier bee hanging around his bed. He rubbed his eyes as she shook herself and began to fly before him.

"King!"

His eyes widened as he caught sight of her antenna and remembered what had happened the night before. He smiled.

"Good morning, Niobee."

He now remembered that she had grown dramatically. He had wondered about that at first, but put it aside to treat the wounded, honor the fallen, and then celebrate the victory.

But now that he thought about it, he guessed it made sense. Niobee was listed as the conduit, and so was connected more deeply to the tower than any of the other bees, Belissar guessed. So perhaps she would grow as the tower did? In any case, Belissar figured it was a good thing, and moved on to the next order of business.

It was time to take stock of the tower's growth.

The tower had grown another floor, becoming a two-story structure. It now achieved the bare minimum to be called a tower in the first place, though it was still shorter than the surrounding trees.

Belissar thought for a moment if he should keep calling it a tower at all, especially since he refused to call himself a tower lord. The bear people called it a "sacred den," while the tower's own status referred to it as a dungeon. But at the same time, Belissar thought "Tower of the Gods" was still an appropriate name, given the role of the God of Bees in all of this.

He shrugged and moved on as he rose from the bed and grabbed some honeycomb to eat. He had bigger things than the name to think about.

Dungeon Status

Patron:	*God of Bees*
Floors:	*1 (Rooms: 2/2)*
	2 (Rooms: 0/2)
Available Mana:	*0/300*
DP:	*664*
Available Monster Types:	*Monster Bee Queen*
	Monster Bee Soldier
Available Room Types:	*Flower Meadow*
	Apiary
	Basic Pit Trap
Available Room Features:	*Sticky Honey Trap*
	Basic Resource Plants
	Bee Memorial (Limit Reached)
Core Corruption:	*0%*
Dungeon Master:	*Belissar*
Dungeon Conduit:	*Niobee*
	Blessing of Bees
	Bee Breeder
Perks:	*Monster Bee Soldier Strength Boost (Minimal)*
	Monster Bee Soldier Speed Boost (Minimal)
Current Missions:	*Help ten challengers receive full blessings.*

One perk choice and two random reward choices available.

And now, for the moment of truth. Belissar opened up the new rewards from the latest purification.

Please select a perk:
- Monster Bee Soldier Defense Boost (Small) (Rarity: Common.)
- Cross-Pollination (Rarity: Uncommon.)
- Boosted Beehouses (Rarity: Uncommon.)

The soldier bee defense boost was pretty straightforward, so Belissar focused on the other two perks.

Cross-Pollination

May grow hybrids of dungeon plants.
Rate of hybridization improves with pollinator-type monsters.

Belissar rubbed his chin. The description was a little vague for his tastes, but he knew of farmers who tried to grow new and better versions of their crops. Mostly because they would yell at him because his bees were "contaminating" their prize crops or some other nonsense like that. Belissar would have liked to see how their prize crops grew *without* his bees.

He shook his head to rid himself of currently irrelevant memories. The point was, this perk would probably let him get new and improved plants, which meant more flowers for his bees. And bees were the best pollinators that Belissar knew, so the perk would work nicely in an all-bee tower.

Still, the benefits of that weren't specifically defined, so there was a bit of risk with that choice, unlike with the next perk.

Boosted Beehouses

Beehive features produce honeycomb 10% faster and can store
+1 maximum products.

The beehouses were making at least one honeycomb a day, sometimes more, so a ten percent increase meant . . .

After about ten minutes of trying to make numbers with the honey that had dripped on the table, Belissar gave up on figuring out the exact amount and settled on the conclusion that this perk meant more honey.

More honey was good. Chief Rohsuak had even claimed that honey was priceless! So priceless that they couldn't trade for it, even though Belissar had no idea what to do with it besides sticky traps and meals.

So, those were his options. Tougher soldier bees, maybe new flowers, or more honey.

Belissar wasn't going to decide right this second, however, as he still had two more choices to review. He figured what he chose for one might affect his choices for the other, so it would be best to check all of them before deciding on any one. He definitely wasn't just putting off the decision.

Please select a reward:
- Uncommon Room Choice (At least one uncommon or better option.)
- Uncommon Room Feature Choice (At least one uncommon or better option.)
- +100 Max Mana

Belissar clasped his hands together, rested his elbows on the table, and held his hands in front of his mouth. So now, he had a choice of choices. Or he could pick more mana. He had two of such rewards, but apparently, he could only pick one at a time. Would they offer the same selection, or would what he could choose change each time?

He would apparently have to pick his choice before he could find out.

Belissar sat there for a moment before deciding he'd make this pick now, at least. A choice of choices was too vague to inform his choice of perks. And he could at least rule out the max mana option. He could get ten mana a day from the minor purifications, so it didn't seem worth giving up new options. New options were, after all, the point of having risked an expansion in the first place.

So that meant a new room type or a new room feature. He apparently now had a second floor, which had two room slots he could fill. The question was, did he want to put something new there? Or would he rather add more flower meadows and apiaries, and then add something new to those? What would help his tower and his bees the most?

For once, Belissar was able to decide.

Uncommon Room Choice selected.
Please select a room:
- Orchard (Rarity: Uncommon. Type: Nature, Resource.)
- Hedge Maze (Rarity: Common. Type: Nature, Labyrinth.)
- Dirt Tunnels (Rarity: Common. Type: Ground, Labyrinth.)

He'd made his decision thanks to the latest purification. Neither the flower meadow nor the apiary had anything that could help his bees deal with a flying enemy. And maybe it was because he lacked knowledge, but he couldn't imagine what sort of room feature might help them do so. A lot of the ones he had seen weren't battle-oriented at all, even.

Belissar guessed a new room would offer more options than a room feature. Not to mention that with the resource plants feature, a new room might offer new flower types for his bees. It just seemed an altogether better choice to him. And if the next reward selection was the same, he could always just pick room feature then.

His previous room choices had included a forest or dirt tunnels, either of which could have helped with the latest purification. Trees may have made it harder for the shade to use its speed, since it wouldn't have been able to fly in a straight line. Even if it had gotten above the canopy, at least it wouldn't have been able to see and target the bees underneath. And if Belissar could place sticky honey traps on the trees themselves, then maybe the bees could have driven the beast into one more easily.

Dirt tunnels, on the other hand, may have prevented the shade from flying at all, though that mobility restriction would have also applied to the bees.

In any case, it was now time for him to review the available rooms.

Orchard

Type:	*Nature, Resource*
Innate Features:	*Fruit Trees*
Mana Upkeep:	*10*

A farm dedicated to fruit-bearing trees.
Decent for Nature-type monsters and features. Excellent for resource production.

Orchards were a natural companion for apiaries, at least outside of towers. Belissar figured that wouldn't be much different here. An orchard would presumably come with fruit-bearing trees, which of course meant more flowers that his bees could gather from. Additionally, they would provide more resources that he could trade with the bear people—assuming the fruit produced wasn't also some sort of priceless magical treasure, that was.

On the other hand, however, an orchard may not assist as much with the defense. Belissar didn't know how dense the trees would be, but he guessed they wouldn't be as tightly packed as in a forest. So, would it offer anything more than the flower meadow or apiary in that aspect? Especially compared to the other choices . . .

Hedge Maze

Type:	*Nature, Labyrinth*
Innate Features:	*None*
Mana Upkeep:	*5*

A maze made of tall, dense hedges. Beware of ambush by root and branch.
Excellent for Nature-type monsters and features.

A maze made of tall bushes would be an excellent battleground for his bees. They could hide within the branches or fly over the maze to attack at will. And, depending on what sort of bushes the hedges were, maybe the maze would even produce flowers the bees could gather from.

But such an environment had downsides as well. If the roof of the maze was open to his bees, then it might be open to a flying shade as well, in which case, the hedge maze wouldn't be much better than the rooms he already had against such an opponent. And, even considering a ground-based beast, a tight, restricted maze might work against his bees, like when the wolf shades in the pit had used the close environment to defend themselves.

Although, thinking of the pit trap, would it be possible to set the entire hedge on fire? That could be a powerful defense if so, though it would mean none of his bees could set up their hives there. It was something to consider, at least.

Dirt Tunnels

Type: *Ground, Labyrinth*

Innate Features: *None*

Mana Upkeep: 5

A network of tunnels dug directly into the ground. Soft walls mean new tunnels may be dug by defenders and invaders alike, and that plants and fungus may take root with ease.

Excellent environment for Ground-type monsters and features.

Finally, there were the dirt tunnels he had seen before. These didn't have many special features, but did have two notable advantages over all the other options. One was that they were underground, with no open sky. While that would work against his bees if they faced ground-based enemies, it would help them immensely against another flying shade that could outrun them in the air.

The other advantage was that the bear people had come from underground and brought with them crops, and even flowers they had gathered there. At the present moment, Belissar couldn't use any of them, as he had no place to put them, but that might change with this room.

Likewise, if he were to acquire some monsters who could operate in the dirt tunnels, they could also scout the tunnels the bear people had come from. His current bees couldn't see well enough in the dark to venture down there at the moment.

Of course, that meant they would also have trouble fighting in the dirt tunnels should he choose that option. He would be all but forced to acquire a new monster type if he wanted to make use of that environment, which might come back to bite him if the next reward choice didn't include monsters.

And that meant it was time to pick the next reward.

CHAPTER FIFTY

BEE-FUDDLED

Please select a reward:
- Common Perk Choice
- Uncommon Room Feature Choice (At least one uncommon or better option.)
- Uncommon Monster Choice (At least one uncommon or better option.)

So, it turned out the second round of choices wouldn't be the same after all. That was fortunate in this case, since this set included monsters. Or Belissar could go with the feature choice, but he was pretty certain of his decision this time. Traps were powerful in the right circumstances but weren't particularly flexible. At the end of the day, it would be his bees facing the enemy when all else failed.

Please select a monster:
- Monster Bee Captain (Rarity: Uncommon. Type: Bee.)
- Monster Bee Sprayer (Rarity: Uncommon. Type: Bee.)
- Monster Mason Bee (Rarity: Common. Type: Bee, Ground.)

"Ugh."

Belissar couldn't help but groan. Unfortunately, monster digger bees, the option he was secretly hoping for, had not appeared this time. If they had, he could have selected them to go with dirt tunnels, as well as to scout the tunnel used by the bear people. But he was not so fortunate, and he had now learned that choices would not necessarily repeat themselves. He could not make plans based on something he had seen before.

Which meant he now needed to make plans based on a bunch of new choices.

Monster Bee Captain

Vitality:	Minimal	**Defense:**	Minor
Strength:	Minor	**Resistance:**	Minimal
Speed:	Average	**Special:**	Minor
Magic:	Minor		Poison Sting
		Notable Skills:	Death Blow
			Brood Offspring
			Brood Commander

Evolves from: Monster Bee Soldier

A monster bee soldier specialized in command. More intelligent than normal and able to command and buff squads of soldier bees. Not much stronger than a normal soldier, but a key part in improving the sophistication and coordination of the hive.

In addition to existing monster bee soldiers evolving, a few monster bee soldiers may be born as captains. If born from a monster bee queen, may relay commands from her.

Monster Bee Sprayer

Vitality:	Minimal	**Defense:**	Minimal
Strength:	Minimal	**Resistance:**	Minimal
Speed:	Average	**Special:**	Small
Magic:	Minor		Toxic Spray
		Notable Skills:	Death Burst
			Brood Offspring

Evolves from: Monster Bee Soldier

This monster bee soldier has evolved a deadlier venom that can affect a target through exterior contact. It has replaced its stinger with a pore capable of spraying its venom at range, making it dangerous at a distance. It gives up some of its strength, bulk, and its stinger in exchange.

In addition to existing monster bee soldiers evolving, a few monster bee soldiers may be born as sprayers.

Monster Mason Bee

Vitality:	Minimal+	**Defense:**	Minimal
Strength:	Minimal+	**Resistance:**	Minimal
Speed:	Average	**Special:**	Minimal

Magic: *Minimal*   ***Notable Skills:***   *Poison Sting*
Mud Pack

A mason bee who has accumulated enough Ground mana to become something more.
Capable of forming mud and other chewable materials into basic structures.

Belissar frowned and rubbed his chin. *Maybe* the mason bees would be able to see in the dark? They also mentioned Ground mana like the digger bees did. The problem was that Belissar wasn't sure of that. Additionally, the mason bees were regular sized and were not a brood offspring that the monster bee queens could lay eggs for.

The captains and the sprayers, on the other hand, would improve his existing hives and give them new options. The bees had already shown how much they could improve with training, so how much might they improve if they had dedicated leaders? Or how powerful would the army become with sprayers that could attack from a distance? A dangerous shade like the first big wolf or the lightning bird might be a lot easier to handle if they could poison it without ever putting a bee in danger.

But neither of those options would be any more capable of operating in the dirt tunnels than his current bees. If he was going to go with one of those, he would need to rethink selecting dirt tunnels, as he would have no bees specialized for that environment.

And he would have no new ways of gathering information about his surroundings.

He could feel the Hunger at the edge of the expanded territory, so it seemed he hadn't made contact with any other towers aboveground, but there was still the underground path to deal with. Just how exactly was he supposed to figure out what was down there—

Belissar froze. He had an idea. A simple, straightforward idea. An idea so simple and straightforward he had to wonder why exactly it had taken him until now to think about it.

Why didn't he just ask the bear folk? The people who had already traveled through that very tunnel he was worried about?

He took a deep breath as he felt his heart begin to pound.

No, he knew why he hadn't thought of it. Because up until now, he hadn't trusted them. How could he? The number of people he had ever trusted could be counted on one hand, and all three of them were dead. Every other person he had ever met had either deceived him, stolen from him, hurt him, or ignored him entirely. He had no desire to rely on anyone other than his bees and his patron god.

But now, he had no choice. If he wanted to know what was beyond the influence of his tower, if he wanted to know exactly how close the closest tower lord was, he had no choice but to ask the bear people, wait for the next monster choice, or hope that mason bees could operate underground.

And, if he put aside his beating heart and thought about it, it was a better idea to ask the bear folk regardless. Better to find out how worried he should be and *then* choose his next monster rather than the other way around.

He took another deep breath. He didn't want to ask these people anything more than he had to, but if he thought about it, they had been different from the villagers and the tower lords so far. They had agreed to his requests. They had not touched his bees. And Chief Rohsuak had taught him magic.

Holding out his hand, his mana coalesced in the air, forming the honeycomb pattern and then a floating sphere of honey. Chief Rohsuak had not lied to him. It was thanks to her instructions that he'd gained this ability. It was thanks to her that he'd managed to save the wounded soldiers.

Maybe—just maybe—he could trust them, if only a little.

Belissar felt his heartbeat calm after that. Taking one last deep breath, he let the tension leave his body while he exhaled. He owed Chief Rohsuak some honeycomb and mana flowers just as payment for the training. He owed her more when he considered that she had saved the life of his bees with her teachings.

He was still wary, but he felt he could trust her with a question like this. After all, the bear people were living here now, too. It would make sense for them to warn him of any impending danger, right?

Belissar got up with a grunt and started to gather some honeycomb and flowers. It was time to do what he should have done a while ago.

Unfortunately for Belissar, Chief Rohsuak had specifically agreed *not* to come to his tower for the next few days. That had made sense when Belissar had originally planned to expand his tower before resuming the magic lessons, but now, he needed to speak with her *before* expanding his tower, so he had no choice but to go to her.

Gathering up his things, he made his way out of the tower. Niobee followed, along with a good bunch of soldier bees. He had to admit he did feel a lot better when they came with him.

He traveled toward the bear folk's camp, along the small trail they had cut when visiting his tower. Soon, he arrived and found them making camp. They were setting up their tents and getting a fire started. Belissar tilted his head at that, since he thought they had done all that the first day they arrived.

Belissar's own arrival did not go unnoticed. The bear folk began to back away, eyeing the monster bees hovering overhead; a few of them even grabbed weapons. Belissar nearly backed away at that. Fortunately for both parties, Chief Rohsuak made her appearance and gave him a smile.

"Sacred Den Master, it is good to see you. Congratulations on your victory."

Belissar raised an eyebrow, but then realized she'd probably noticed the Hunger being pushed back and determined he had succeeded that way, so he nodded.

"Thank you."

Her smile grew. "Of course. Now, how may we help you? It's an honor that you've come all this way to visit us."

Belissar held up a sack. "I owe you. And, uh, I have some questions, if you don't mind."

Chief Rohsuak's eyes widened just a bit before her smile recovered. "I see. Why don't we find a comfortable spot to sit?"

Belissar nodded. Chief Rohsuak gave some instructions, and the other bear people returned to their business, putting away their weapons as well. The chief then walked out alone and pointed to the edge of the clearing. There were a couple of tree stumps over there where the bear folk had recently cleared some of the trees. Belissar followed, and the two sat down.

CHAPTER FIFTY-ONE

A BEAR-Y IMPORTANT QUESTION

Belissar handed over the sack to Chief Rohsuak. "Here."

The chief took the sack. "Thank you." Opening it up, she double-checked the contents, then gave him a smile. "Does this mean you were successful?"

Belissar nodded, holding out his hand. His mana condensed and formed into honey once again. Chief Rohsuak's eyes widened, then she smiled again.

"Well done. This is the fastest I've ever seen someone pick up magic."

Belissar felt his face warm and scratched at his cheek. "Oh. Um, thanks? I, uh, think it's because of the tower. And, uh, thanks to your help."

Chief Rohsuak nodded. "I and the sacred den may have helped, but you put in the work to make it happen. Don't discount your own efforts."

Belissar looked away before taking a deep breath. He didn't really know how to respond to that, so he simply didn't. "I, uh, had some other questions for you."

She nodded. "Of course, how may I help you?"

Belissar glanced over to the hole in the ground. "You, uh, came from beyond my tower, right? I wanted to know what's out there."

Chief Rohsuak hummed and rubbed her chin. "I don't mind speaking of our journey, but was there something specific you wanted to know?"

He slowly nodded. "I need to know if there are more tower lords—or, uh, you call them sacred den masters, right? Yeah, if there are more of those, except, um, like me, and calling themselves tower lords, um . . ."

Chief Rohsuak gave him a smile. "So, more sacred den masters who call themselves tower lords and appear more similar to yourself, as opposed to us?"

Belissar nodded as he felt his cheeks grow warm again. "Yes, that."

Chief Rohsuak rubbed her chin again. She sat in silence for a moment before beginning to speak.

"My people were driven from their homes when I was still a young lady. Most of our records and history were lost or destroyed. What we managed to pass on has faded as well, as our journeys took their toll on the people that knew them. But I can say from what stories remain and what I have personally seen that I have not seen anyone like you before. I know every people has their own name for the sacred dens and their masters, but I've not heard the name tower lord before."

She gave him a smile. "It does make sense, though, given their appearance."

Belissar gave a hesitant smile at that, then Chief Rohsuak continued. "There are legends of lands far to the east and to the west where peoples with less fur live. But to us, they were little more than myths and legends. Until I met you, I had found little evidence of such things."

Belissar rubbed his chin. "So . . . they're really far away?"

Chief Rohsuak shrugged. "As for actual distance, I cannot say, only that my people have never recorded meeting them that I can recall."

Belissar fell from his seat and groaned. Chief Rohsuak tilted her head. "Are you alright, Sacred Den Master?"

He groaned one more time. "Fine, just . . . I've been worried about something that's not going to happen anytime soon."

Chief Rohsuak rubbed her chin. "Not a fan of your own sacred den masters, huh? Well, I don't think you were wrong to prepare."

Belissar sat back up. "Huh? What do you mean?"

Her face turned serious, and she made eye contact with him. Belissar wanted to look away but managed to hold her gaze, if barely.

"My people passed through many dangers to arrive here. Savage peoples, deadly monsters, and sacred den masters who were not as kind as yourself, on top of the ever-present threat of the Hunger. It is wise to gather your strength."

Belissar frowned. "Anything close by? How long do we have to prepare?"

Chief Rohsuak shook her head and waved her hands. "Ah, nothing in the immediate future. The last sacred den master was far away, thus why we had to travel the Underway for quite some time. We aren't under any imminent threat so long as you can hold back the Hunger." She made eye contact again and smiled. "Just keep in mind that you should not neglect the growth of your defenses and you should be fine."

Belissar exhaled his breath before nodding his head.

Chief Rohsuak waved to the sacred den master as he left their camp. Once he was gone, she immediately frowned and began rubbing her chin.

The sacred den master had advanced more quickly than she had ever imagined he would. She had thought it would take him weeks at minimum to learn how to move his mana around his own body, then weeks more to do so out in the open. That should have given her a month or two at the bare minimum to warm him up to herself and her people, and impart a lesson or two on leadership.

She held up her finger and created a small flame, then waved her fingers about, causing the flame to dance between them. The problem was that the mana manipulation steps were the *only* steps she could really teach him. She had not learned magic as some sort of formal trade. No one among her people had; not since they had lost their home.

What she had was the blessing of the God of Fire, which, once she'd had the requisite control over her mana, granted her an innate ability to manipulate her patron's domain. She had assumed, rightly, that the sacred den master would have a similar blessing from his sacred den's patron and would automatically learn that patron's magic once he managed to manipulate his own mana.

Which meant that at this point, she no longer had anything specific to teach him. She could share her experiences exploring her blessing, but the blessing of each god was mysterious and unique. She couldn't truly say she knew how her own magic worked, and so could not teach him to use fire as she did. Nor did she have any idea on how the God of Bees's magic might work, or how he should develop it.

She heaved a sigh. She knew sacred den masters possessed great magical powers, so she supposed she should have expected this. Would a person who had the power of a sacred den flowing through their body struggle to move their own mana? Perhaps she had underestimated the boy due to his apparent age and demeanor.

So, the question was, what would she do now?

She also needed to consider the sacred den master's concerns. He had seemed worried, fearful even, of the ones he called tower lords. She had to assume such individuals to be on the worse end of sacred den masters from the way this one spoke of them and how relieved he seemed that she hadn't encountered any. If a sacred den master was worried about them, then they were certainly a threat to her people.

And finally, she needed to consider what the sacred den master himself was capable of. He had his bee army, had picked up magic in about a week, and had emerged victorious from his recent fight.

Opening the sack, she gazed once more upon the golden honeycomb shimmering inside, as well as the lightly glowing mana flower.

He also had some incredible resources available that could dramatically improve the capabilities of her people. Even now, ten of their number were working on receiving blessings from his patron; if they could be fed a diet of mana-infused food as well, then they would put Metsaitti to shame. There might even be a hunter who could surpass her in her prime.

And . . . what if the entire next generation was raised on food such as this? If her entire people were one day capable of using mana like herself? Such a people would not fear any challenge whatsoever.

But all of that was contingent on establishing a good, cooperative relationship with the den master, who was still quite wary of them, when she had just lost her main reason for consistent interactions with him. But Chief Rohsuak hadn't led her people this far for nothing, so she started to come up with some ideas. Including one that had nothing to do with her people at all.

She glanced around. There was no one around her, all of her people focused on their work at present. No one seemed to need her right this second, and no one was watching her.

She glanced down at the sack in her hand and frowned at the golden sight within.

She knew she shouldn't. She was old, and she already had solid mana reserves. She didn't need it. This was a priceless treasure, and it was her duty as chief to utilize it in a manner that would best benefit her people.

She glanced around once more. "Well, just a taste wouldn't hurt . . ."

After all, it had been her effort that earned this. She deserved this much, at the very least. Reaching down, she scraped a bit of the honey onto her finger and quickly brought it to her lips.

She soon discovered that just a taste could hurt, after all. Because now . . . Now, she would do *anything* to get another. She was just fortunate that no one happened to be nearby, lest she lose her dignity as the chief.

CHAPTER FIFTY-TWO

COUNSEL AND DELI-BEE-RATION

Belissar stood in silence in front of the bee memorial, gazing up at the names on the pillar. He took a deep breath and closed his eyes.

He had panicked at the thought of meeting the tower lords. He could still remember the smell of smoke and blood from that day. He could still hear the screams of people he had known his entire life as the soldiers cut them down. He could still feel the pain from when the arrow had pierced his back.

He reached to scratch at the spot, though he couldn't reach the exact place.

He had rushed in his panic, and bees had died as a result. If he had spoken with the bear people from the very start, he would have learned that he had plenty of time. The bear folk hadn't even heard of *humans*, much less tower lords. Who knew how long it would be before he met one again, or if he ever would?

So, was there a reason for those bees to have died? Did he truly need to grow as quickly as he had? Couldn't he have waited? Couldn't he have learned magic first, then participated in the fight directly? Or maybe traded with the bear people for one of their bows, now that he remembered they had archers. Couldn't he have done more?

He opened his eyes and reached up to touch the names. But as he did, the bee carvings moved, and one of them flew as if to land on his finger. His eyes widened, his heart bursting in his chest as his vision began to blur.

He rubbed his eyes before glancing over to the beehouse as he heard a crackling noise. He saw the wounded soldier there, stirring up her mana. A pair of wings made of yellow lightning appeared on her back. She tried to swing them around like she did her original wings, though she did not manage to take flight. Belissar took another deep breath and closed his eyes once again.

"Right . . ."

He reminded himself once again that the bees did not regret their sacrifice. In the case of the soldiers, fighting and—if necessary—dying for the hive was what they were born to do. And though the cost was high, the tower and the bees *had* grown through this.

If Belissar looked up into the skies of the flower meadow, he could see the soldier bees practicing new movements and formations in response to the latest battle. He could look down to the flowers where countless workers continued their tireless gathering. If he used his tower sight to look to the apiary, he could watch the newest queen building her hive, with workers from a nearby one offering to assist her.

He couldn't change the past. He couldn't fix mistakes he had already made. All he could do was do better in the future. The battle had been fought. The bees had fallen. The rewards had been gained. All Belissar could do now was ensure that it was worth the cost. That was his duty as their king.

He stepped back from the memorial and glanced around until he found Niobee.

"Hey, Niobee, can you ask the queens when would be a good time to meet? I'd like to speak with them, though I don't want to interrupt their work."

"Okay!"

Belissar watched as Niobee flew off. He decided first things first: he wouldn't act alone. He had missed critical information by ignoring the bear people when he'd rushed to prepare for the tower lords. At the very least, he wanted to see what his bees thought of their home.

The First of the Fifth didn't even wait for the Conduit to finish her dance. She rushed out of her hive and soared through the air. The King was calling for her. He desired her counsel.

She immediately dropped everything to rush to his side . . . and then froze in the air. The Firstborn and her council of brutish queens were already there, surrounding the King, likely filling his head with all sorts of nonsense. She nearly charged at them.

And worse, she saw the Fourth of the Seventh and *her own kin*. The queen she had born, along with all the other queens of the apiary. She had been the *last* to arrive.

A betrayal most foul.

But she calmed herself. No, this was better, wasn't it? If she thought about it, the queens that arrived first had to wait for those who would come later. They had to waste their time while she would lose none at all. If she thought about it that way, it absolutely made sense the Conduit had told her last. It was proof that her time was the most valuable of all.

Surely.

But as she pondered, the King laid eyes upon her. He smiled with the warmth of the sun, a face as inviting like the petals of a flower.

"There you are; we've been waiting for you."

The words rocked the First of the Fifth to the core, and she forgot all else that was occurring around her.

Belissar stood surrounded by queens and scratched the back of his head. The queens were the most important members of their hives, for the hives would not exist without them. Yet, every single one had dropped everything they were doing and immediately rushed over to him.

He had *hoped* to schedule this for a time he wouldn't interrupt, but at this point, he couldn't say he was surprised by this turn of events. Any time he had spoken, the bees had responded to his requests immediately and without complaint. It was clear they regarded him extremely highly and took his words as absolute.

All the more reason for him to get better at this job.

Opening his mouth, he paused. He closed it and rubbed his chin. He was going to start by laying out the choices and asking the queens what they thought, but Niobee had answered that question often enough that he could predict exactly what they were going to say.

"Whatever King chooses!" was endearing, but it was not what he wanted to hear today. So, he took a moment to think about how exactly he should approach this.

"Um, the tower is about to grow. I, uh, want to hear from you all. What do you think the tower needs? Or, um, what would you want to do your job better if you could have anything?"

Belissar smirked as a lot of "Whatever King chooses!" dances started.

Well, he wasn't exactly good at leading just yet, so he figured he wouldn't get his point across right away. But to his surprise, there was one bee who hadn't joined in the dances. One bee who stood still . . . and then slowly started to move.

The Firstborn was about to join the others in affirming the King's authority. The King had built this entire land before they'd even been born. He could create entire fields. He could grow mana flowers in an instant. He could build grand constructions the likes of which they couldn't imagine. He bent destructive infernos to his will and set them upon their enemies. All the other bees acknowledged the wisdom of the King and indicated as much with their dances.

After all, what was the opinion of a mere queen in the face of such power? Could anything she imagined add even the tiniest bit to the wisdom of the King? How could she contribute to plans on a scale she couldn't comprehend? Especially her, for she had failed. Her army's latest performance had put all the hives and even the King himself at risk. She had failed in the one task the King had entrusted her with. The one task she had expended all of her efforts for.

She had proven less than all of the other queens. She did not even deserve to be a part of the hive of hives. So what worth was there in her opinion?

But something caused the Firstborn to hesitate, for after everything, she could not get this wrong as well. Such thoughts were obvious . . . and so, surely, the King had thought of them as well. Surely, he knew how far the depths of his wisdom outstripped their own.

And yet, he had asked them anyway. He had requested their opinions, their desires.

She thought of her own meeting with the queens of the flower meadow; how a queen younger than herself had brought up a concern she hadn't thought of. She thought of the First of the Fifth, whose efforts had revealed paths the Firstborn had never dreamed of. She thought of the hive of hives the King was building.

The King wanted to know their thoughts. Not because they were worth anything, and not because he needed their help to design his grand plans but because they might be different. Their very limitations may force them to face concerns the King never would, not in spite of but *because* of his overwhelming power and wisdom.

And perhaps she, who seemed to have even more limits than most, might be best positioned to understand them. So, the Firstborn thought about his question. What did she think the hive of hives needed? What was she lacking? What did she *need* to fulfill her own role within it? What could resolve her failures?

And then, slowly, she began to dance. The King fixed his eyes upon her, as well as all the other bees. She nearly stopped. How terrible would it be if she were wrong? If, after everything, she dared to question the plans and wisdom of the King?

But she was the Firstborn. She had resolved to defend the lands of the King. She aimed to build the greatest army beekind had ever seen. She had failed at that, but not in her desire to see it done with or without her. So, she pressed onward and spoke her mind.

Belissar watched as the largest of the queens gave an answer.

"Army not strong enough."

He smiled. It was a simple answer, but it *was* an answer. Indeed, the soldier bee army had weaknesses that needed to be addressed.

"Um, can you think of anything which might help fix that?"

The queen stood still for a while before slowly beginning another dance.

"More soldiers; bigger soldiers. Need queen that can raise. Need better queen."

Belissar rubbed his chin and nodded. A moment later, another queen, the largest from the apiary, flew in front of him and began a dance of her own.

"More flowers! More nectar means more bees! New bees!"

Belissar nodded at that. "That's a good point; those medicinal bees really helped."

All the bees had frozen at this point, but soon, they slowly began to dance.

"More flowers is good."

"Soldiers should be tougher."

"Should be faster."

"Mana flowers best!"

"More palaces!"

Soon, each of the queens was dancing their own dance. Some of them even began conversing with each other. Belissar nodded as he tried to take in all of their suggestions. Slowly, ideas began to form in his mind, and he couldn't help but grin.

He knew asking the bees was the right choice!

Belissar listened for a while until he had a good idea of the queens' general opinions. After that, he cleared his throat, and the dancing soon died down. Every bee fixed their eyes on him, and he smiled.

"Thank you, everyone. I think I have a good idea on what to do now. Feel free to head back to whatever you were doing . . . or you can stay if you want. Whatever you feel like."

A thunderous buzzing accompanied the joint salute of all the queens before they began to return to their hives. Well, almost all; one of them tried to stay, but was dragged away by her workers. Belissar chuckled then rubbed his chin one more time as he started to walk back to the apiary, and then to the core room.

At first, he had been largely committed to the idea of dirt tunnels. Neither the hedge maze nor the orchard seemed like it would help against the flying shade, while the dirt tunnels undoubtedly would. But now, his conversations with Chief Rohsuak and the queens had changed his perspective.

The queens had had much to say. Some had asked for more flowers, others for stronger soldiers, and others still for beehouses. But none of them had asked for more traps or terrain that would restrict the shades. Belissar had realized at that point that he had been focusing mostly on the latest monster and how to defeat it.

But was that the right way to go about things? Which was more important: defeating shades or supporting his bees? Again, Belissar remembered that he had defeated the first beast as a beekeeper, not as a tower lord or dungeon master or sacred den master or whatever else.

Perhaps defeating shades would have been the correct priority if the tower lords were coming for him. However, he had confirmed with Chief Rohsuak that they were nowhere nearby. He would have plenty of time to prepare for them . . . assuming he ever met one again at all.

And in that regard, promoting the growth of his bees was the top priority. It was the soldier bee army who ultimately dealt with the shades. It was the honey traps who had caught the flying monster in the end. It was the God of Bees who blessed his tower.

Besides, thinking about the latest beast might prove to be a trap. In fact, it already had. The reason this shade had dealt as much damage as it had was that Belissar's tower was overprepared for the monsters that had come before it. There was no guarantee that the next creature would be anything like either the wolf shades or the bird, so making choices solely to defeat the flying beast might not help at all against the next foe.

So, Belissar changed his line of thinking. He decided that rather than trying to restrict the shades, he would choose whatever would help his bees the most. His bees growing stronger and more versatile would give them more options the next time a shade surprised them.

Not to mention it would make him, the bees, and maybe even the God of Bees happy.

With that in mind, Belissar made his first choice.

Orchard is now available!

The orchard did the most for his bees out of the available rooms. It gave them more flowers to gather from and more trees to make hives on. What's more, Belissar guessed that resource plant nodes would do something different in the orchard than they did in the flower meadow or the apiary. An orchard would *probably* have trees rather than flowers, right?

Still, while the nectar from fruit trees would allow for different types of honey, he didn't imagine it would be different enough to result in new kinds of bees like the healing herbs or poison flowers had. Which was why he made his next choice.

Cross-Pollination selected.

This perk was a bit of a risk, but Belissar felt it was worth it. More flower types meant more options for his bees, and this perk would grant that. And if the orchard unlocked new plant types entirely, then it would combine nicely with this perk.

Plus, the bear folk had given him underground crops he couldn't utilize at the moment. He'd thought of taking dirt tunnels for that purpose, but even if he had, would his bees have been able to gather nectar from them if he didn't have an underground-specialized bee?

So, he'd gone with the orchard, which his bees would definitely be able to use, and would try to figure something else out for the new plants. Maybe they could grow at the bottom of a pit trap, or he could try to dig a hole? If so, then maybe cross-pollination might work between the underground plants and the regular flowers and give him something his bees could gather from aboveground.

Of course, none of those options helped the bees fight directly, which informed Belissar's last choice.

Monster Bee Sprayer now available.
Monster Bee Soldiers may now evolve into Monster Bee Sprayers.
Some Monster Bee Soldiers will now spawn as Monster Bee Sprayers.

Mason bees would give him a new type of bee separate from the queens who would not be directly useful in combat, so he'd ruled them out. Of the remaining two, he figured sprayers were the better option. Sprayers gave the army entirely new options for attack, while captains just seemed to make them better at what they already did.

Besides, in Belissar's admittedly inexperienced opinion, his bees were already pretty smart. They seemed to adjust their strategies and formations after each battle already, so as far as Belissar knew, it seemed like they were already doing what captains were supposed to do. In any case, the sprayers definitely did something his current soldiers could not and would help with foes his soldiers couldn't get close to.

With his choices selected, Belissar could now get to work rearranging his tower.

The first thing he did was remove most of the traps he'd placed before the expansion purification. He even cut down on the number of traps from before then. He originally had nineteen pit traps and sticky honey combos placed around the meadow and the apiary, but that had proven to be excessive. He decided to cut it down to an even ten, with an additional five sticky traps placed aboveground.

All that brought his current mana total to one hundred thirty-eight out of three hundred available for his new rooms. Now that he had a second floor, he could place another two rooms.

Belissar had arrived back in the core room at this stage, so he placed his hand upon the orb and got right to it.

First things first, he would place an orchard. He wanted to see exactly how the new room functioned and what options it unlocked for him, especially with the new perk. He would determine what to do with the fourth available room after that.

Once again, a map of his whole tower appeared within the core, and a transparent image of an orchard floated above the apiary. A door formed on the edge of the apiary leading to a large staircase that connected to the new room. Belissar found he could also move the orchard down, which automatically made the apiary move above it.

He rubbed his chin as he considered how he should rearrange the space. With a nod, he moved the orchard in between the flower meadow and the apiary, moving the apiary up to the second floor. He figured it should be the furthest back because he wanted to keep the beehouses and beehives there safe. The queens there focused on honey production and had few soldiers, so it was best to keep them away from the fight.

He also hoped that the orchard, by its very definition, would have more trees than the other two rooms. That could be useful for setting up defenses, since the trees would provide obstacles for both air and ground-based shades. Maybe he could use them to make a walled path to a pit trap like he originally wanted to do in the flower meadow?

Belissar thought about putting the orchard first for that reason, but its ultimate purpose was to give his bees fruit trees to gather from, so he didn't want to move it *too* far away from the apiary.

Although, the memorial, which was becoming the gathering place for his tower, was in the flower meadow, so maybe it would make sense to keep that in the middle? Besides, there were already hives in the flower meadow, so if they had to retreat to the orchard, those hives would be left vulnerable if the flower meadow came first . . .

Belissar began to rub his chin and groan a bit. And here he thought he had finished making difficult choices already.

Belissar thought, and he thought, and he thought some more until he grew tired of thinking and just put the orchard in the middle. He could always move the rooms later if he wanted to, so he would deal with it later if it didn't work.

He made no adjustments to the location of the entrance and exit, leaving them in the center of the front and back walls, then confirmed the changes.

CHAPTER FIFTY-THREE

A BEE-AUTIFUL DAY

Belissar felt the mana of the tower surge once more as his changes went into action, feeling a new room growing in the corner of his mind. He could have checked it immediately with the tower sight, but decided to be patient. Instead, he stepped out of the core room and turned to Niobee with a smile.

"Shall we check it out?"

"Okay!"

Belissar walked through the apiary with Niobee following along. He could see his bees stirring, the workers pausing on their flowers as the tower's mana passed through them. He smiled as he thought of them discovering the newest room.

Reaching the end of the apiary, he stepped through the entrance, entering a room made of yellow wax arranged in hexagonal patterns. The space was empty save for a doorway leading to a stairway; Belissar could only see a couple of steps before it curved around a corner. He glanced around, shrugging when he found nothing of interest, then made his way to the stairs.

When he stepped onto the first step, his vision blurred. He had the distinct feeling of falling, and a moment later, found himself exiting into another empty wax room. He frowned.

"Weird . . ."

Glancing around the room, he again found nothing of note. He wondered if he had somehow gotten turned around until he glimpsed the room's exit. He could see a slightly blurry image of a field filled with trees.

"Is that it?"

"Think so!"

He'd asked mostly to reassure himself, since he knew the answer already, but Niobee answered anyway. His tower sight—or maybe tower sense, since he was not actively using the vision at the time—let his intuition know he had moved "down" a floor.

Shaking his head, he walked toward the exit.

His eyes widened and a smile broke out on his face as he entered the next room.

Before him were rows upon rows of trees standing in a grassy field, their green canopies filled with red apples and pink-and-white flowers. Belissar was pretty sure apple trees weren't supposed to have fruit *and* flowers at the same time, but figured that was an effect of the tower, and so put it out of his mind. Instead, he walked up to the nearest tree and placed his hand upon it.

Manage tree types?
Available types:
*-**Apple** (Mana Upkeep: 0) (Selected)*

He gave a satisfied smile. It was about as he'd expected. The orchard grew fruit trees like the flower meadow did flowers, and just like the flower meadow, he got one type for free.

He guessed he would have to start gathering pinecones, after all. Maybe if they searched the surrounding forests, they could find some juniper trees? If that happened, Belissar could even resume work on his mead with juniper berries!

Belissar paused for a second as he thought of mead for the first time in a while. Between almost being killed by the tower lords, almost being killed by the Hunger, becoming a dungeon master, learning of the tower lords' lies, and most of all, gaining the companionship of intelligent monster bees, Belissar hadn't had the chance to think about his old hobby.

His bees were giving him more honey than he could ever eat, and he no longer had to supply tribute to either the village chief or the local tower lord . . . so didn't that mean he could use as much honey as he wanted on recipe experiments?!

Not to mention, his bees were making magical honey. Honey filled with mana, medicinal honey that healed wounds, and mad honey with intoxicating effects; Belissar couldn't help but imagine what sorts of mead he could make from those.

Okay, maybe not the last one until he *really* knew what he was doing, seeing as it was poisonous and all, but the point still stood.

Belissar shook his head. He had a lot to do before he could think about hobbies. Not to mention, he would need some more equipment first; watertight containers at the very least. And water.

Now that he thought about it, his tower didn't really have any water in it, did it? He wondered how all the plants were growing without a raincloud or river in sight.

But he still couldn't help but have a smile on his face as thoughts of mead danced through his mind. He reached up and grabbed a low-hanging apple, taking a bite as well.

His eyes widened. It was crisp and sweet and juicy, much unlike most of the apples the villagers traded him.

He turned to Niobee and motioned to the fruit.

"Want a taste?"

"Okay!"

Belissar held out his free hand for Niobee to land on, then brought the apple up to her face. She couldn't actually take a bite, but there was some juice dripping out of the side he had bitten. Turning that side toward her, Niobee extended her mouth and sipped a bit of the juice. She began dancing around happily, causing Belissar to smile even more.

All in all, Belissar thought this was a good day indeed. Regardless of whether it helped fight shades or not, the orchard was a wonderful place.

The Fourth of the Seventh paused as she felt the King's mana flow through her. Something had happened; she knew that the King had just performed great and wondrous deeds. She knew because the mana had imprinted new knowledge onto her instincts. New foraging instincts that encouraged workers to visit different types of flowers within a single trip. A new type of soldier, one that could fight in a completely different manner than any other type of bee.

And . . . something else. Something had changed about the world around her, though she knew not what.

She could not help but take a short walk to the entrance of her hive, moving her antennas about in the air, trying to see if she could see, feel, or smell anything different.

Well, she didn't notice anything, but she did get to see the King and the Conduit walk by her home. Unfortunately, she couldn't figure out anything else, and her workers wanted her back inside the hive. Since she didn't know what had changed, she had no specific reason to refuse, and so went back as her foragers began their next trip to the flower meadow.

Not even a minute later, her foragers rushed back into the entrance of the hive and began a frantic dance. The Fourth of the Seventh noticed the disturbance and rushed over to find out what had happened.

She froze as the workers spread their news.

The flower meadow . . . had disappeared? When the workers had passed through the normal entrance, they'd found an entirely different environment.

The Fourth of the Seventh began to tremble. She now knew what she had sensed: The King had *reshaped the world*! He had built an entirely new land in between the flower meadow and the apiary! That was where he and the Conduit were going earlier!

The Fourth of the Seventh nearly flew out of the hive immediately, but her instincts held her in check. Instead, she began to dance and brush her antennas against the surrounding workers, giving them her commands.

A third of the foragers who normally visited the flower meadow would stay in the apiary today and focus on keeping up honey production by gathering from the flowers around her hive. The rest would head into the new lands and scout them out.

Surely the King had not removed the flower meadow entirely, so the Fourth of the Seventh figured there must be a new route to get there; her foragers just needed to find it. Finally, she told them to speak with the Conduit if they had the chance, to discover the King's purposes with this new land.

Her workers stopped their frantic dances as their queen gave her speculations and orders. Now that they knew how to respond, they immediately began organizing themselves as she had said. Before long, workers began flying out to the new lands, and the Fourth of the Seventh couldn't help but dance about as she watched them leave.

What wonders would they find? What new lands had the King created? What sort of grand design was he building this time? The Fourth of the Seventh couldn't wait to find out!

While Belissar and Niobee were sharing the apple, he heard buzzing. He turned back and noticed worker bees flying from the entrance to the second floor and the apiary. He hummed for a moment.

He considered whether he should add some spawners to the orchard or not. They would spawn new queens to fill up the new room very quickly, but since he had much more time than he originally thought, was that necessary? One of the queens had moved her hive already, so maybe some of them might want to check the orchard out? Or they could raise some new queens to populate the room.

Nodding to himself, Belissar decided he would wait and see before adding new spawners. Instead, he checked what he could do with traps and basic resource nodes.

Available resource plants for Orchard:
-Apple Tree (Mana Upkeep: 3 per tree.) (1 due to room discount.)
-Basic Wood Tree (Mana Upkeep: 3 per tree.)
-Mana Flower (Mana Upkeep: 5 per node.)

Belissar tilted his head at that. Apple trees were a resource plant? He tried to place one to see if it would make a bunch of trees like with the flower nodes, but only a single transparent tree appeared before his eyes.

Did that mean all the trees in the orchard were resource plant nodes? Or would a tree made with a resource node be different? Belissar figured it was probably the latter. Maybe it would produce fruit faster, like the difference between the bee-houses that came with the apiary versus a normal beehouse he just made himself?

Other than that, there wasn't much new. Wood trees might be pretty useful if making them a node made it easy to harvest useable wood. On the other hand, while he could easily gather flax plants from the textile flower node, he still had to process them himself, so he might end up having to saw and dry the wood himself anyway. He would have to try it out.

Beyond that, he was limited to the apple trees that came with the room—and the mana flowers, for some reason. Not as many new options as Belissar had hoped for, but he supposed that was what cross-pollination would help with. In any case, it might be good to scout the forest more thoroughly and pay attention to what sort of trees were out there.

Belissar finished his apple while Niobee took to the air once more. It was a good break, but he should finish up the room as much as he could. Stretching, he started to consider where to put the traps.

FAILURE AND VICTOR-BEE

The Firstborn lay still on the floor of her hive. The last few days had been . . . confusing. The hive of hives had won a great victory, yes. But once the celebrations had come to an end and she'd had time to reflect, she realized that her hive had *not*. No, her hive had *failed*. Her army had been beaten.

Yes, the soldier bees had overwhelmed the shade and driven it to flee from them. Had they been facing a normal enemy, perhaps that would have been enough. But these invaders were different. They did not fear death. When they ran, they ran *toward* the hive, not away from it. Such a foe running away from her army was not a victory but a failure.

During this latest battle, the enemy had slipped out of her soldiers' grasp, and there was *nothing* they could have done to catch it. It could have killed her, destroyed her hive, and slaughtered her brood before her defenders returned. And worse . . . it could have moved deeper into the hive, where the King and the honey-producing queens took shelter. It could have even reached the core itself, the very heart of the King's domain.

So, in truth, her army had been defeated. They'd failed to stop the enemy's advance. They'd failed to protect the hive. Had it not been for the extremely fortunate attack by the wounded soldier and the intervention by the King himself, that day would have been a disaster.

It was the greatest failure any of the King's queens had ever suffered. Even the doomed First Dynasty had not allowed the enemy to reach the King before every last bee in their hive had perished. Forget building the greatest army beekind had ever seen; the Firstborn had not even built an army sufficient to defend her home. A crippled soldier had done more to save the hive than she.

She had assumed when the King called for her that it would be her end. Workers would fly until they died enroute. Soldiers who could not fight would leave the hive, never to return. So, it would only be right that a queen who had failed as egregiously as she had would do the same.

But once again, the King had defied all of her wildest expectations. Not only had he not punished her for this failure—he hadn't even *mentioned* it. He had instead gathered all of his queens together and asked for their counsel. As if a failed queen such as she had anything to offer him.

But she would not defy the King's intentions. So, she had spoken up in the moment. She'd told the King the truth. He needed a stronger army. He needed better soldiers.

She told him he needed a better queen to lead the defense. And then she returned to await her fate.

But it never came.

She felt the tower's mana stir and then flow into her, granting her new knowledge. Her antennas twitched, and she began to crawl about, her wings fluttering.

In the new knowledge came information of a new kind of bee. A new type of soldier; one who could do things no normal bee was capable of. It had an entirely different method of fighting and would revolutionize the army.

She trembled. The King had granted them better soldiers. He had seen her dance . . . and interpreted it differently. He did not replace her with a bigger, better queen who would raise bigger and better soldiers. No, he saw beyond normal soldiers and came up with something *entirely* different.

And then, he granted it to her, the queen who had failed. To all of them.

Regarding things that were entirely different from the norm, her mind drifted to the wounded soldier. It turned out the King had been incredibly wise to keep her around. Though she could not fly and fight like the others anymore, her contributions had proven critical to defending the hive.

And now, she was becoming something else entirely. She had been fed mana by the King's own hand and gained powers unlike any other bee in the hive of hives. Even now, that power moved in place of her lost wing. Her injury was slowly becoming her strength.

None of that would have occurred had the crippled soldier been discarded as the bees' instincts indicated she should have been. The battle would have been a loss if they had done so.

The Firstborn stood up on her legs and shook herself. She realized again the vast wisdom and distant sight of the King. The average hive tossed aside all whom it felt were lacking, but not the King. In the hive of hives, the wounded and the broken and the failures remained. They had a place by the King's side until, one day, he found a new use for them. Not a single moment of his bees' lives would be wasted.

And so, neither would hers. If the King came to punish her for her failures, she would accept it as was right. But if he did not, then she would continue on.

She would find a way to be useful in her failure. She would not stop until the King commanded her to.

Crawling through her hive once more, she took stock of her honey reserves and the growth of her brood. At the soldier cells, she found a curious sight. One of the soldiers had returned, her purple hair identifying her as one of the mad honey bees. She stood by one of the empty cells and turned to the Firstborn, her antennas twitching. The queen walked up to her, and the two exchanged brushes then began a dance.

The Firstborn fluttered her wings at what the bee told her before dancing her assent.

Crawling into the cell, the soldier curled up inside of it as the Firstborn ordered her workers, who brought as much of the mad honey as they had left, pouring it into the cell. The queen then filled the honey with her own mana, charging it up until her instincts told her it was enough, before the workers covered the cell with a layer of wax, and it began to glow softly.

The Firstborn moved to her next task. There was no time to rest if she was to rebuild the army. There was no time to rest if she was to overcome her own failures.

And so long as she remained within the hive of hives, she would give it her all.

The First of the Fifth was over the moon. First, she had been thanked personally by the King for the contributions of her honey. Her medicinal honey had saved many lives, and then she had provided for the grand celebration of the King's victory. She would not even dance of the abject failures who had put the King himself in harm's way, so it went without saying that her position had been utterly secured after the latest battle.

Next, the King had called for her, personally, and asked for her counsel. Her! Nothing could take from her elation at the King's trust in her. Nothing! Not even the small, irrelevant, infuriating detail that an abject failure of a queen had been the first to speak, as if *she* understood the King's will in that gathering. As if!

The First of the Fifth always knew the King's heart the best and understood his desires better than any mere bee could. It was only that *she* was not utterly shameless enough to dare lecture the King on his domain!

Even if he requested it, only after she had made her complete trust in his wisdom unmistakably clear would she let the King know what was on her mind! Only a shameless, disloyal fool would do otherwise! Especially one whose failures had put the *King himself* at risk!

So great was that fool's failure that the First of the Fifth would no longer refer to her as the Firstborn. She would be the First Queen of the First Spawner's Second Dynasty, if she was worth even *that* title!

The First of the Fifth stopped the frantic dance she didn't remember starting. The point was, the King's favor for her had reached new heights never before seen. Truly, she was the most favored of all bees. Even the Conduit, with her sudden and concerning growth, could not compare to her! And the Conduit was just about the only bee left the First of the Fifth needed to pay attention to!

But of course, she would not stop here. The King's favor was boundless, and so her efforts must be. For now, though, she simply waited, for she, above all others, understood the designs of the King. The King was planning something big, and had even taken her counsel to do it. She had no doubt something incredible was coming, and that anything she could plan now would pale in comparison.

So, she would wait to see what the King had wrought, then do her utmost to support him.

She did not need to wait long. As mana passed into her, she knew she had been right. New instincts filled her regarding the gathering of nectar. The King . . . wanted them to gather from multiple different *types* of flowers on each trip?

The First of the Fifth paused at that, then began pacing in a circle. She had spent a while instructing her workers not to gather in that very manner. Each worker gathered only from a single type during a single trip. The nectar was then categorized and organized in different sections for each type of flower. This system was critical to maintaining the First of the Fifth's exceptional honey quality.

Mixing nectars during processing was already bad enough. If they mixed the nectars during the gathering, her workers would be completely unable to categorize and sort them out. The outcomes of each batch would become entirely random, completely out of her control. Such a thing was unthinkable to the First of the Fifth.

But again, she, above all, understood the King. She understood the depths of his wisdom, and *she* would never presume to know better than he. As she had before, she would not even offer her opinion until she had completely reassured him that was the case! So, she knew the King saw something she did not when this knowledge was passed to her.

She assembled the workers currently within the hive and gave out her instructions. Half the foragers would continue in the normal gathering method, while half would act as per the new instincts. New sections were to be set aside and dedicated to the mixed nectar they would bring in. And while they were abandoning rigorous sorting of the nectar by source for that batch, she still expected exceptional quality in every other aspect of the honey processing.

The workers set off immediately to fulfill her commands and pass them along to the foragers as they returned. The First of the Fifth could not help but continue dancing. The King had taken her counsel and returned to her detailed instructions on the nectar-gathering process. She had no idea what would result from this at the moment, but she knew it would be incredible. It was a collaboration between her and the King, so it could only be so.

She couldn't wait to see what exactly the results would be.

A WHOLE NEW WORLD

The Fourth of the Seventh stood with her eyes fixed upon the scouts before her. There were two groups giving their reports. One was the first wave back from the new room, here to report the initial findings while more of their number combed the area in detail. The other was the group assigned to finding the flower meadow, who had flown far and fast while trying to relocate the path.

The tale the two groups danced together was truly astonishing.

The King had created an entirely new room in between the apiary and the flower meadow. This room was filled to the brim not with small flowers but with massive trees, their canopies filled with gorgeous blooms and ripe fruits. The flower meadow and the apiary had the occasional tree, but the scouts reported the sight was unlike anything they had seen in the King's domain before. A field of flowers not on the ground below but in the skies above.

The Fourth of the Seventh wanted to see it for herself but put her own desires aside. Her first soldiers had just hatched, and she now could put her plans into motion.

She desired to participate in the weaving of plant strands she had seen the King perform, and now, she had bees large enough to gather and transport them. She needed, therefore, to focus on the management of her hive and ensure said project could proceed nicely and without disrupting normal work.

She would need to work extra hard at this now, in fact. With a new room between her hive and the meadow flowers she had been granted access to, her foragers had a much longer trip. She would need many more foragers to keep up the same honey surplus as she had before—

Suddenly, the Fourth of the Seventh's thoughts stopped entirely.

She had an idea. A simple, *incredible* idea.

Rather than adding a bunch of foragers to maintain a long gathering route, which would in turn require more honey themselves and thus require even more foragers to achieve the same honey surplus, why didn't she just move the hive closer? She had already done so once before, and making the route shorter was far more efficient than trying to fix the extended supply line.

For example, why didn't she move her hive *into* the brand-new, apparently amazing room the King had built? Wouldn't that be the most efficient option of all? Not only would that shorten her foragers' trip to the flower meadow, it would also give her hive access to an abundance of brand-new flowers from the new room.

The fact that she would then be able to personally explore said place was just a happy coincidence.

Her workers had grown worried at her lack of movement and were buzzing around her, trying to get her back to work, when she suddenly exploded into a dance, calling for a general assembly of the hive. Her workers reluctantly began to gather. Once they had, she began a passionate explanation of her plan to move the hive.

Her workers just stood still. One slowly began to dance.

"But, moved already? Moving again?"

"Inefficient."

"Unnecessary."

One of the workers who often followed her around danced rapidly. "Queen just want to escape, see new things."

The Fourth of the Seventh glanced away for a moment before beginning a slow response. ". . . Yes. Want to see. Only see, not escape! But not only reason. Flowers we gather are far away. New room has new flowers, and closer to current area. Lots of work now but gathering more efficient once done. Need more honey to feed soldiers; efficient gathering will help."

The worker stared at her for a while, but this time, the Fourth of the Seventh held her gaze. The worker reluctantly began to dance.

"Seems . . . right? Suspicious."

But one of the scouts began to dance as well. "Have seen new room. Flowers incredible. Queen has good idea."

The other scouts began to dance their assent, and the workers of the hive began to ponder. One by one, they agreed, until the suspicious worker was the only hold-out. She, too, began to dance slowly.

"Okay. But ask Conduit first."

The Fourth of the Seventh danced happily. "Yes! Of course!"

The workers dispersed to begin preparing the hive for a move while the scouts headed out to begin evaluating possible locations in the new room. The Fourth of the Seventh moved about, sending a messenger to the Conduit.

This was, of course, premised on the King's own plans for the room, but he hadn't had a problem with her moving before, so the Fourth of the Seventh was hopeful. Her dreams would come true; she would be able to see new sights for herself while still fulfilling her duties to the hive!

Suddenly, she paused as another thought passed her mind. Wasn't she supposed to be the queen? So why did she need her workers' permission again?

She pondered this as the worker who followed her gave commands to the rest of the bees and arranged the move . . .

The First of the Fifth listened to the reports from her own scouts, who had also discovered the new room the King had created. An abundant land with brand-new flowers that grew on trees and that formed into fruits so large only the King could consume them.

This gave her pause. She very much desired nectar from these new flowers, for who knew what sort of honeys she could produce from them? After all, shouldn't she, the producer of both the most and best honey of all the hives, be the first after the King to drink of his latest flowers? She very much wished to order a foraging mission immediately.

But there was a problem this time around. Even her worker force was not endless; in fact, her hive was nearly overextended at the moment. Her bees needed to clear the hive of the mixed healing herb honey she had created, which while suitable for the soldier bee army, was not nearly of a quality she would dare serve to the King.

They then needed to rebuild her stockpiles of top-quality honey and resume providing for the King's table. They also needed to create new stocks of nonblended healing herb honey; mad honey as well.

She, too, was aware that a new type of soldier bee was now available, and presumed that the Second First of the First would be moving immediately to raise some, so she could not suddenly cut the agreed-upon donations . . . assuming the King allowed that failure to remain in his domain, that was. Even if the Second First of the First had deceived her and then failed in her own mission, the First of the Fifth would not deign to be seen reneging on her own word. She was above such a blunt refusal.

On top of all that, her workers were now experimenting with the new gathering method provided by the King and trialing the production of blended honey. A new group had to be set aside for that if she were also to maintain the production of her normal honey at the same time, further reducing her available worker force.

So, to gather, produce, trial, sort, and refine a new type of honey from flowers in another room was one job too many. She would have to make compromises elsewhere if she wished to do so, and the First of the Fifth never compromised when it came to her honey.

But what then? If she waited until she could expand her worker force, another queen might move upon the new fields and lay claim to them. The First of the Fifth had no wish to conduct another negotiation, not after she had been swindled by the first. She also needed to consider the possibility of the King creating new spawners, and new queens being born—

Her thoughts came to a halt. She had it. She had the solution. Her hive was not sufficiently large enough for the task. But her hive was not a mere hive anymore. Hers was a hive of hives, like the King's. A new queen had *already* been born.

Her own daughter.

The First of the Fifth commanded that word be sent to her daughter. If her daughter were to move to this new room, she could lay claim to it in the name of the First of the Fifth. The First of the Fifth could even requisition her daughter's workers to deliver the new nectar directly to her own hive.

She would, of course, pay her daughter for the effort, for she was not so crude as to steal from her own kin, but the terms would be far more favorable than if she had to negotiate with a separate queen.

And if the King planned to create a new spawner to populate the new room, then the First of the Fifth could assist him! Her daughter would represent an established, experienced queen who could help lead and guide the new queens as they began setting up. It would give her a chance to assist the King directly . . . while ensuring that the new queens found their proper place in the hive of hives under the watch of the most favored queen and not any of those who had failed.

The First of the Fifth returned to her work, satisfied that she had found a solution.

Later, she heard the Fourth of the Seventh was moving to the new room as well, but that was fine. The Fourth of the Seventh had an agreement with her and had even helped her daughter out of her own initiative, so the First of the Fifth was confident the move wouldn't interfere with her own plans.

No, since the Fourth of the Seventh was already working under her, this was even better! All was going in the most favored queen's way.

THE CHILD

The First Daughter of the First Queen of the Fifth Spawner's First Dynasty, the Second of Her Line, lay flat against the floor, her antennas drooping, even as her mother's worker repeated the dance.

She had received a new command: she was to move her hive at once to an entirely new, unknown land and lay claim to it in the name of her mother.

This . . . did not excite her. Her mother was the greatest and most productive of all the queens of the apiary, and as such, demanded excellence from all of her children. Her first daughter was no exception to that. Her mother had great expectations as to the growth of her hive, the quantity and quality of her honey, and the numbers of her workers.

But a queen was not a worker, and working as hard as she could was not a simple matter. A queen needed to carefully balance the growth of her hive against her currently available workforce.

Her workers had many jobs to do: gathering nectar, processing honey, making wax, and tending the brood, all of which were necessary for the growth of the hive. If she tried to lay as many eggs as she possibly could, her worker force could end up overwhelmed by the extra tasks the new children created.

Too many workers needing to build honeycomb could end up cutting their nectar gathering. Too many workers needing to gather nectar might leave the eggs and larva untended. And, of course, all of those workers required honey to sustain themselves, on top of the honey and mana required for the new brood to grow, as well as what the queen needed to replace her own reserves and keep up egg production.

The First of the Fifth's expectations had driven her first daughter to the brink. Her hive had *barely* managed to balance honey production, hive expansion, and brood tending. She did not have the magical palace built by the King's own hand her mother did, and so her workers just couldn't produce honey as quickly as her mother's could.

Likewise, without access to the mana flowers her mother had, her workers had to work even harder to ensure the honey was fit for the larva. Her hive was operating at the very edge of sustainability and consuming every last drop of honey produced. She had no reserves whatsoever, and any disruption to her production would put her hive in trouble.

Her mother was not unreasonable, however, and had sent her own workers and donations of her own reserves to help her daughter achieve the stated goals . . . at least at first. However, events elsewhere had recently interfered. A great battle had occurred, and her mother had moved to support the King directly. She had, as a result, withdrawn her support for her daughter.

Whether or not she had withdrawn her expectations as well had never crossed her daughter's mind. She had a job to do, and she did her utmost to fulfill it, no matter the efforts or sacrifices required to do it.

Her hive had come close to collapse in that time, but timely assistance by the Fourth of the Seventh's hive had managed to carry her through. With that help, she'd managed to reach her mother's expected goals for her growth. She was just stabilizing to the point she wouldn't require assistance when her mother's latest order came in.

This would be her greatest challenge yet. Moving her hive would require her to send scouts to find locations, rebuild her entire hive, move all the honey and brood, and then locate and arrange for new foraging routes.

All of that would take time and effort from all of her workers, time during which they couldn't be making honey, which for her hive, meant that production would drop below daily consumption. And since they had no reserves to tide them over, that meant, in the short term, either her workers or her new brood would have to go hungry until the new hive was established and honey production restored.

She slowly crawled over to her brood, watching her workers tend the eggs and the larva lying within. Her antennas drooped once more. She would have no choice. She could not starve her workers when they would be needed for the work of setting up the new hive and gathering the next wave of honey. Her entire hive would starve if she did. So that meant . . . she would have to cut rations to her children who were not contributing.

She would have to let her latest generation starve to fulfill this command. The generation that would be the quickest to perish should their rations cease.

But to fail the command of her mother was unthinkable. To beg another queen for assistance was equally inconceivable, especially for her, who had already received much. She was a queen bee. To be a bee was to complete her job or die trying. To be a queen was to guide the hive—and to accept its failures as her own.

She rose upon her legs as she resolved herself. She would not fail in her task, no matter the cost. And if she flew into disaster, she had no one but herself to blame.

Just then, one of her workers brushed antennas with her. She turned her attention, and the worker began to dance while she stood still, for she wasn't sure how to respond to the report she was receiving.

The Fourth of the Seventh . . . had come to visit?

The First of the Fifth's First Daughter slowly crawled to the entrance, her antennas twitching about. The Fourth of the Seventh was the queen who had saved her earlier. It was thanks to her that she had been able to meet her mother's expectations and avoid collapse. The Fourth of the Seventh had offered said assistance unprompted and asked for nothing in return, so the First of the Fifth's First Daughter could not help but hesitate.

What would the Fourth of the Seventh say to her? What was she like? What should she say back? How should she act before such a queen? Such thoughts nearly paralyzed her, but she was a bee queen with a great deal of work ahead of her, so she had no time to meander. As such, she made good time and crawled out of her hive.

She froze as she gazed upon the visiting queen. The Fourth of the Seventh was a mighty thing, nearly as large as her mother. Her wings were strong, carrying her extended abdomen in the air without strain. Her mana shone bright like the fires of the King.

"Hey! Nice to meet you!"

The First Daughter was stunned as the giant queen began to dance, and so was a bit slow in her response. "Hello. Nice to meet you?"

The Fourth of the Seventh danced happily in response before continuing.

"Just want to tell. Moving to new room. Will keep trying to help but might slow down."

The First Daughter froze. "Fourth of the Seventh moving . . . to new room?"

"Yes!"

The First Daughter was having trouble thinking, and so just danced out something related.

"Me too."

She nearly took a step back as the Fourth of the Seventh flew right up to her. "Really? You too?!"

"Y-Yes?"

The Fourth of the Seventh began a dance more rapid than the First Daughter would have thought possible for her size. "Let's move together! Help each other. Build hives together!"

The First Daughter froze. An unrelated queen . . . wanted to build hives together? It took her a while to respond.

"... Can't."

The Fourth of the Seventh drooped midair. "Why not?"

The First Daughter's antennas twitched about rapidly at the sight of the Fourth of the Seventh drooping. The First Daughter did not wish to speak of her own failures, but the Fourth of the Seventh was her savior and deserved to know.

"My hive, no reserves. Can't help."

The Fourth of the Seventh rose back in the air. "No reserves? Hive okay for move?"

The First Daughter couldn't bring herself to admit it, but she also couldn't bring herself to lie, and so just stood in silence. Unfortunately, that in itself was enough of an answer for the Fourth of the Seventh. "It's okay! My hive has! I help! New room has lots of flowers and can ask Firstborn if not enough!"

The First Daughter took a few steps back at that. The Fourth of the Seventh was offering to help her? She quickly began a dance.

"No. Won't bother. Is my problem."

But the Fourth of the Seventh flew up to her, overwhelming the smaller queen. "Not bother! Firstborn and Conduit says we hive of hives! One's problem is all's problem, so all King's bees help! We help now, you help later! First of Fifth helped me too, gave new flowers! Now I help First of the Fifth's daughter!"

The First Daughter couldn't respond to that. Her mother . . . had helped the Fourth of the Seventh? Gave her flowers? If all this were true, then maybe it was alright?

And even if it wasn't, the alternative was to watch her brood starve. No bee queen would ever allow that to happen if she had any means to avoid it.

The First Daughter very slowly danced her response, more of a crawl than a dance.

"... Okay. Please help."

"Yes! Let's go! Need get hive ready!"

The Fourth of the Seventh danced happily midair, leaving the First Daughter to collapse on the floor of her hive once more as she stared up at the mighty and glorious queen flying around, the sun shining off her chitin.

Once again, the Fourth of the Seventh was helping her unprompted. Once again, the mighty queen didn't even think to ask her for anything in return. And once again, the help was truly necessary. If the Fourth of the Seventh helped her, if she shared her reserves during the move, then the First Daughter's hive would not need to cut rations. Her youngest children would not starve.

She could fulfill her mother's command without sacrificing her hive in the process.

"Hey, you okay?"

The Fourth of the Seventh noticed her on the ground and flew over to check. The First Daughter looked up at her for a moment.

She didn't remember what happened after that, only that she began to dance. She didn't know what sort of dance it was, only that she needed to convey her gratitude, and that the normal dance was insufficient to express what she felt. She danced until both the Fourth of the Seventh's workers and her own retrieved their queens and began to prepare for the impending move.

The First Daughter then walked over to the brood and brushed an antenna against one of the larvae, ignoring the honey sticking to her as a result. She swore to herself in that moment.

One day, she would repay the Fourth of the Seventh for all she had done.

CHAPTER FIFTY-FOUR

BEE-NEFACTORS

Chief Rohsuak sat in her tent. A certain bag sat on the mat spread across the ground. She didn't take her eyes off of it for even a second. She barely even blinked.

Chief Rohsuak may have seemed calm and steady now, but she had not been known for her self-control in her youth. A berserker directed her emotions; she did not suppress them. But she took a deep breath and did her best. Now was not the time to indulge. Not yet.

After a seemingly endless moment, her guest finally arrived.

"You wanted to see me, Chief?"

"Yes, please come in."

A young bear woman stepped inside the tent. Chief Rohsuak didn't bother to look at her. The woman stood there for about a minute before she began fidgeting.

"Um, Chief? How can I help you?"

Chief Rohsuak slowly tore her eyes away from the bag and to her guest. "I have something to show you."

With that, she opened the bag. The woman's eyes opened wide. "Chief . . . what is all this?"

Chief Rohsuak removed the contents one by one. "Mana flowers and . . . mana honeycomb."

The woman glanced up and looked at the chief, her eyes opening even wider. "Mana . . . honeycomb?"

Chief Rohsuak just silently nodded. The young woman stood still for a moment before a wide smile broke out on her face.

"That's amazing! To infuse mana into the honey, it must have been condensed into the nectar while the bees were still processing it. Or is this what happens

when bees gather nectar from a mana flower? Honey already has medicinal properties, so I'm certain the mana will enhance it; it might serve as a basic potion as
it is. There are so many tests I'll need to—"

Chief Rohsuak slapped away the hand that was reaching for the honey with
only *slightly* excessive force.

"Ow! C-Chief?"

Chief Rohsuak looked the woman in the eyes. "Calm down, Juosiutik. You're
getting ahead of yourself."

Juosiutik flushed and bowed her head. "Sorry."

The chief shook her head with a smile. "It's fine. This truly is an exciting find, so
I understand why you're excited. We'll need to arrange for you to gain some soon."

Juosiutik froze. "Gain some? Um, chief . . ."

Chief Rohsuak leaned forward and looked her in the eyes.

"As you may have gathered, this is from the sacred den. Specifically, it was
given to me by the sacred den master himself in exchange for teaching him how
to unlock his blessing. And yes, I know that normally, such a treasure would go
into the communal stock. But this was a reward from a sacred den in exchange
for the completion of a challenge. That means, by the will of the gods, it belongs
to me, and me alone. Just like your blessing will belong to you, should you complete it."

Juosiutik frowned. "I . . . guess that makes sense?"

Chief Rohsuak nodded. "Which is why you must also earn these materials
for yourself if you wish to experiment with them. But don't worry. The sacred den
master has already agreed to one such exchange; I'm sure we can arrange another."

Juosiutik furrowed her brow. "But . . . what can I offer him, Chief?"

Chief Rohsuak smiled. "For now, teaching. Share your craft with him, both
knowledge and results, and he will share his bounty with you. And who knows?
Perhaps his patron will look favorably upon your collaboration, and you will progress toward a full blessing as well."

Juosiutik rubbed her chin for a moment. Eventually, she slowly nodded her
head. "Mana honey . . . It's too incredible to pass up. I'll do as you say, Chief."

Chief Rohsuak grinned and nodded. "Excellent. We'll be waiting here for a
few more days, but plan to come with us when Metsaitti's group next returns to
the sacred den."

Chief Rohsuak nodded in satisfaction as Juosiutik left her tent. She had found
a simple solution to the question of the sacred den master. If she had little else to
teach him regarding magic, then she just needed someone else to take over.

Direct manipulation of spells and elements represented only one small fraction of the mystic arts and was one of the rarer uses of mana outside of those with
the blessing of a god. One of the most common, and indeed, one she thought
would pair with this sacred den quite nicely, was herbology and potion making.

And Juosiutik was the foremost student of that craft left among them who was even seeking the blessing of the sacred den's patron to boost her skills to new heights.

It had other benefits as well. Introducing the sacred den master to more of her people should hopefully warm him up to them as a whole. And it just so happened that Juosiutik was one of the most eligible bachelorettes available. If a young man and a young woman working together happened to grow a bit closer . . . Well, Chief Rohsuak would simply take things as they came.

She wasn't sure if Juosiutik would be initially attracted to a man with so little fur, or, alternatively, if the sacred den master would be attracted to a woman with so much from his perspective. But he seemed close enough in form to her people that she couldn't help but speculate.

Chief Rohsuak wasn't going to count on either case, but at the very least, she hoped the sacred den master might be receptive to a young woman around his age. Even a simple friendship would go a long way to establishing her people in his good graces.

But even if nothing came of that, this method would establish a precedent. If each member of her people had to individually deal with the sacred den master to trade for his incredible treasures, then he would slowly get to know more and more of them and establish more and more friendly connections. It would lay the groundwork for a close relationship in the future, or so Chief Rohsuak hoped.

Of course, the fact that she got to lay claim to the honeycomb she already had was just a side benefit and had *definitely* not factored into her decisions. Especially not as she reached for the honeycomb again.

Belissar was getting to work when a couple of worker bees flew over to Niobee and began to dance in the air. After that, she turned to Belissar and began to dance as well.

"King! Fourth of Seventh and First of Fifth's First Daughter want to move to new room! Okay?"

Belissar nodded immediately. "Yep, that's fine. The queens can expand anywhere they want."

Niobee began zipping around. "Okay! Will tell them!"

Belissar chuckled as he turned his attention back to the room. Confirmation that the queens, including the newly born one, were moving to the orchard was quite helpful. Thanks to that, Belissar put off any plans to build more queen spawners. Instead, he planned to add a new mana flower node and some wood trees once the queens chose the location for their new hives.

As for traps . . . since pit traps had been rendered useless against the latest shade, Belissar chose not to place too many of those. One right outside the entrance to the room, one by the exit, and then one in the middle. He would have to build a campfire site by the entrance as well, since the apiary's was an extra room away at this point.

He then thought about where to place the sticky honey traps. They had proven key to defeating the latest shade, but their range was a bit of an issue. It was only a stroke of luck and the efforts of the wounded soldier bee that had enabled them to work in this last battle.

Belissar rubbed his chin as he looked over the room, moving a transparent honey nozzle about as he considered where to put it.

Then, he had an idea. Trying to move the nozzle toward one of the trees, he found it moved right along the trunk. He grinned.

"Well, that's convenient."

More than convenient, even. Placing the honey traps up on the trees would greatly expand their ability to hit flying targets.

Belissar tried to move the nozzle as high as it could go, but found he couldn't move it onto the branches once they got too thin. So instead, he put it as high up as it could go on the main trunk, then proceeded to place over a dozen more honey traps on top of various trees.

After a moment of thought, he placed some lower on the trunks as well so that they would be able to trigger on ground targets. Just because the latest shade had flown didn't mean the next one would.

With that done, the last thing to do for his new room was finalize the resource plant nodes. Niobee was off talking to the queens, so Belissar would have to wait a bit before he could ask her where the bees were setting up.

Or did he? Belissar rubbed his chin, then turned to his tower sight, looking through the orchard.

When focusing on his tower sight, he gained an intuitive sense of his bees' locations, so he managed to identify worker bees scouting through the room. A bunch of them were congregating around the door to the flower meadow.

Belissar frowned. He would prefer if they didn't set up right there, since that would leave them vulnerable to any shade that reached the orchard. But at the same time, if they had a reason to move there, he didn't want to interfere. He would ask them, but he knew they would take even a casual suggestion from him as law, so he hesitated.

Suddenly, he came up with an idea. Or rather, remembered one from earlier.

Trying to see if he could move the apple trees, he found that he could and began to rearrange them into a tight grove a bit to the side of the entrance, as close as they could go. He put pit traps in the ground between them, and honey traps along their trunks and branches. Then he put a mana flower node in the center.

With that, there was a hopefully well-defended location where the bees could set up their hives. It was a bit off to the side, about halfway between the entrance and the side walls, so hopefully it would be out of the way should a shade assault the orchard.

Belissar nodded with a smile as he saw the worker bees pause and then fly to the nearby area. They began to buzz and zip around before racing back toward the apiary. Belissar hoped that meant it was a job well done.

THE ROLE OF A QUEEN

The Fourth of the Seventh flew into the room and just hovered midair for a moment, taking in the sight stretching out before her. She then shot forward to the nearest tree, zipping up its length and flying right up to one of the apples, the bright red fruit as large as her torso.

Brushing her antennas against one of the pink-and-white flowers, she took it in with all her senses, memorizing its colors with her eyes, its scent with her antennas, its touch with her legs, and even the charge of the petals that changed if she brushed her legs and wings together to make tiny lightnings. She unfolded her proboscis and drank directly from the flower's nectar, dancing about at the sweet taste she had never experienced before.

One of her workers watched from a polite distance, swaying back and forth. She wanted her queen to get moving, but she did not approach, hanging back and continuing to watch. Her queen was unlike any other in that she wished to see the world outside of the safety of the hive, much to the chagrin of all of her children.

But it was the workers' duty to see their queen's will fulfilled, however strange that will may be. Besides, their queen knew her role and her importance, and so held back her desire to see the world. The workers wished she could do as she pleased, even as much as they wished she would remain safely within the hive, but the circumstances where they could allow her to were rare.

So, the workers let her fly about, and even act like a worker would, while they moved the hive. It was the least they could do, since this was one of those rare circumstances.

The bee thus ignored her instinct to pull her queen to safety and glanced back at the rest of her siblings. The move was well underway, with countless workers carrying single wax cells filled with honey or with the brood. She flew over and danced a command to a group of scouts, sending them to assist a group of bees who were falling behind.

Normally, coordinating like this would be the role of the queen, but the worker did not wish to interrupt her mother in her moment of joy. And well, at this point, she was used to it. It wasn't the first time she had taken care of details on behalf of her queen.

Their hive was a bit unique in that regard, in that the workers were left to their own devices to an even greater extent than other hives. They didn't have the efficient, uncompromising discipline the First of the Fifth's hive did, nor the urgent energy the workers supporting the Firstborn's army strove with. Instead, they had grown used to taking matters into their own hands and organizing themselves, leaving their queen free to do whatever it is she chose to do, within reason.

For example, raising soldiers.

The worker glanced over as the two soldiers who had recently hatched carried larger pieces of comb. She still didn't fully understand her queen's intention with those, since their hive did not participate in the grand war, but at present, their bulk and strength was proving invaluable. One of them was even carrying the First Daughter of the First of the Fifth on her back, since the young queen had grown exhausted by the trip.

It was moments like these that the worker was reminded why she was not queen.

For monster bees like them, the queen was more than just the mother of the brood. She was larger, stronger, and more intelligent than any of the rest of them. She could see the world in a way they couldn't. She could think thoughts that never crossed their minds. And more than that, she connected them. Each of them had a bond with her through which mana—and more—flowed. She elevated them all, and they, in turn, acted as the implements of her will.

For monster bees, the queen truly was the heart of the hive.

The queen could, therefore, see further and *more* than the normal bee could. Even this worker, who had taken on many duties beyond her instinctual tasks, generally saw the world through her instincts. She saw flowers and predicted whether or not they would produce good nectar. She saw the brood and felt the urge to check them for healthy growth and illness. She saw the hive and sought to ensure its security. She saw the rest of the world and saw only threats and danger.

Not the queen. She saw the world and saw *possibility*. That was why she was so excited to go and see more of it, even though every instinct in the worker's body told her to keep the queen secure and safe. But she only needed to look out at the sight before her eyes to understand the value of the queen's perspective.

Countless trees stretched out as far as her eyes could see, creating a field of flowers above their heads. It was an abundance that filled her with the urge to fly to them and to report the location to the rest of her sisters, even though she knew they were currently flying with her. And there was not a rival bee in sight, save for the ones travelling alongside them.

Had the queen not pushed them for this move, they wouldn't have had access to even a fraction of the resources that would soon be theirs for the taking. Their hive could grow exponentially once this move was completed.

And to think she, along with most of her sisters, had thought this move was unnecessary. *Inefficient.* She now saw with her own eyes that she had been overwhelmingly wrong.

That was why she took on some of her queen's duties without complaint. That was why she and the workers strove to let the queen indulge her desires as much as they could. And that was why she now assisted a rival queen without complaint. She had no doubt that, once again, her queen had seen something she had not.

So, she turned away from the flowers and her queen and continued to manage the flight of the hive. The queen was doing what only she could, so the worker would manage the rest.

The worker herself froze at the sight ahead of her once the group had arrived at their destination.

There was a mighty grove of trees, tightly packed together in a location that would give them ready access to the flower meadow while remaining out of the immediate path should danger come. Their canopies overlapped and interweaved in a way that would be *perfect* to support an elevated hive. Massive hidden chasms guarded the ground approach, while honey traps would surprise any aerial invaders.

And, above all, there was a patch of *mana flowers* in the center of the grove, a treasure previously reserved only for the greatest and most powerful of the hives the likes of the Firstborn—the eldest of the living queens and commander of the mightiest army—and the First of the Fifth—the largest and richest of the hives whose honey fed the King himself.

And most of all, this entire grove had *not existed*, according to the most recent report by the scouts. It, therefore, must have grown entirely within the past hour, for the worker did not believe her sisters would have managed to miss such a perfect location. She began to tremble at the implications.

This could only have been the work of *the King*. He must have taken notice of their move and prepared a perfect location for their arrival.

The King was an existence beyond her. If the queen could see things beyond a normal worker's instincts, then the King saw things beyond a queen's wildest imagination. He built the world by hand, creating trees and flowers like a worker molded wax, and laying the spawners from which the queens came. He commanded flames and fires, and struck down foes thousands of times the size of any bee. Only the wisest and mightiest of the *queens* would dare interact with him.

As for a worker like her . . . only the Conduit could approach him, and that was if they considered an existence like the Conduit to be equivalent to a worker based solely on their previously shared external form, which no worker would dare to do.

And now, his attention was on *her hive* specifically, and he was moving personally to assist them.

The worker trembled at the foresight of her queen. What she and her sisters thought was an unnecessary, inefficient move, *the King* approved of and *changed the land itself* to support. What they thought was the queen's attempt to indulge her desires proved to be part of the King's grand design.

Only truly great queens like the Firstborn and the First of the Fifth were worthy of such attention, or so the worker had accepted as fact. Until now.

This was why, for all the authority their queen conceded them, she would ultimately remain queen.

The worker once again thanked her and resolved to expand the freedoms afforded to her, even if it went against her instincts. She could not possibly have come up with the decision that her queen had, nor earned the personal support of the King himself.

As such, she did not move to fetch her queen now that they had arrived on the site. Instead, she began to instruct her stunned sisters. They looked at her warily, but then slowly agreed with her dancing. The workers, therefore, began to set up their new hive—without waiting for the presence and instruction of their queen. They would do anything and everything they could so that their queen could do that which only she could.

And then, the bee flew over to the First Daughter of the First of the Fifth and requested her instructions. The queen hesitated to respond, but the worker insisted that her queen had instructed them to assist. Slowly, the First Daughter began to dance, asking to set up her hive right next to their own. The bee agreed and started giving out commands to that regard, and workers from both hives began to mold wax in the boughs of the grove.

The worker knew not what would result from cooperating with a rival hive like this. And that was why she knew she needed to do it. All for the queen.

CHAPTER FIFTY-FIVE

THE TOWER BEEKEEPER

Belissar smiled as he watched two hives migrate to the orchard. One of the queens in particular seemed quite excited as she zipped around the new room. That, above all, convinced Belissar he had made the right decision.

At this point, the day was growing late. Belissar decided to give the bees a break from the routine purifications, so he headed for the farmhouse instead. As he settled in to rest from the day, he considered all that had occurred.

One day, he was a beekeeper on the end of his rope, wondering how he was going to survive the winter. The next, his village was burning to the ground, and he was about to embrace death. The one after that, he was suddenly put in charge of a Tower of the Gods, elevated from the lowest position to the highest overnight.

It had gone about as well as anyone might expect, but he had learned from that failure. He, a mere peasant beekeeper, had defeated a shade of the Hunger and earned the approval of the gods, including the God of Bees.

He had then met the bear people and discovered that the tower lords had lied about almost everything. That had been a shock and had made him realize just how unprepared his tower was for true challenges. He'd resolved to grow, and he had, though only by the sacrifice of his bees.

It had been a flurry of activity; crisis after crisis. Belissar had barely had time to breathe, and certainly none to consider who or what he was becoming.

But now, things were finally settling down. The orchard was now set up, and none of the new features required any more direct and immediate action from him. The migrating queens needed to set up their hives, the flower meadow queens would need time to raise or evolve some sprayers, and he had no idea how long it would take cross-pollination to start working.

In any case, all three of those were the work of his bees, not him, so he would need to find something else to work on in the meantime.

His bees barely even needed him for the normal purifications at this point. He would need to set up a campfire site in the orchard and start the fire before the purification, but after that, the bees could handle it themselves. In fact . . .

Belissar turned his tower sight to the memorial and saw the wounded bee still flapping her lightning wings as she stood outside the memorial beehouse. Since she still had access to lightning, she might even be able to start a fire on her own, in which case, Belissar would be entirely unnecessary . . . against the normal wolf shades, at the very least.

Point was, the bees could and would take care of the fighting and growing aspects of the tower work for the near future. Belissar's role there was setting up traps, leading the celebrations, and making decisions on the rewards, none of which would take up the majority of the time he had each day.

His tower was finally getting settled, and he was getting settled into the role of its master. The bees were no longer helpless, the tower was no longer undefended, and he was no longer afraid of violating some rule made up by the tower lords.

But Belissar wasn't just going to sit around and do nothing while his bees were working their hearts out. Fortunately, he had come up with a task; one that the bees had specifically requested. One of their dances at the meeting had stood out to him, when one of them had requested more beehouses.

Yes, Belissar had stopped making those. He had put that task aside after upgrading the apiary beehives, but there were far more queens than that who were currently building their own hives. Including all of the flower meadow queens; the ones who had been here the longest and who were bearing the brunt of the fighting and the sacrifice.

Belissar frowned. It was a travesty that he hadn't made anything for them as of yet. He may have been distracted by world-shattering revelations and heavy panic on account of tower lords and shades, but there was no excuse to delay any further.

Now that he'd confirmed the tower wasn't in any immediate danger, he would make that task priority number one, especially now that the queens were starting to reproduce, so their numbers would only grow. If he didn't get started on it soon, he might fall behind permanently.

Ultimately, despite everything, Belissar was still a beekeeper at his core. To battle the Hunger on behalf of humanity and the gods may now be his duty as a dungeon master, but to support and care for his bees would always be his heart's desire. And from what he had seen so far, he believed the God of Bees did not disapprove of that.

So he may have had other tasks—such as the magic training with Chief Rohsuak; he had learned how to use magic, but surely that wasn't all there was to it, right? And there was also the quest about helping the bear people acquire blessings or something—but for Belissar, the bees came first, and they deserved a roof over their heads.

Belissar nodded and rose to his feet, walking to the bed. He had his path set forth now, so now, it was time to rest and prepare for the work to come.

The next day, Belissar walked over to the flower meadow, glancing over at the wounded soldier. She was no longer trying to flap her wings to fly. Instead, she was apparently trying to make the lightning move on its own, as parts of her lightning wings distorted and curved about.

It was fascinating to watch, but Belissar had a job to do, so he pressed on.

He finished walking over to the flower meadow hives. The largest queen there—the First Queen of the First Spawner's Second Dynasty if Belissar had the name right—crawled out of her hive and greeted him. He nodded and smiled.

"Hello, are you busy?"

She danced a negative; Belissar let out a small sigh and then chuckled. As she was a bee—and a queen no less—he was pretty sure that was a lie, but she'd probably always make time for him, so he'd just have to be quick.

"I'm going to build you and the others here some beehouses. I figure that the soldiers might need a different design, however, so I wanted to check my ideas with you first. Would now be a good time to take a look?"

The queen froze solid. Belissar's smile was just starting to drop when she suddenly burst into action, her dance so rapid and chaotic that her legs got tangled and her torso fell to the ground.

Belissar started to panic, but Niobee flew to the bee first, brushing her antennas against the queen's; Belissar could feel her mana moving as well. The queen stopped writhing about, then slowly rose to her feet. Slowly, she began to dance. Niobee flew off as she did.

"Honored, gratitude."

Belissar held back a gulp. After her initial reaction and the care she was taking with her current dance, Belissar felt that the words told to him by the tower's translation power were not enough to convey the queen's current feelings. He could tell this was a big deal to her.

He had the urge to reconsider the plans he had come up with casually, as they did not seem to be worth such a reaction, but he held it in. He may have felt that way, but the bees were apparently happy with his work. However bad he might feel about it, letting the bees go without a home would be worse, so instead of second-guessing himself, he would just have to do his best to build them something nice.

"Okay, um, so . . . since you girls already have well-built hives, I was thinking of building a larger home around them all, and then building some larger trays for raising soldiers. I'm guessing you make larger cells for the soldier eggs, right?"

The queen watched him intently and responded immediately. "Amazing. Yes, larger cells."

Belissar nodded. As he did, Niobee returned with more of the flower meadow queens. He nodded at her as he turned to the Second First of the First.

"Got it. So bigger trays for the soldier cells. I was going to split it up into larger rooms for each of you . . ." Belissar took some sticks and stuck one in the ground, then walked around in a square and placed a stick at each corner. "Would about that big be enough for each room? Not just for your current hives but in case you want to expand?"

The newly arrived queens stared for a moment before exploding into rapid dances. "Amazing! Incredible!"

Belissar shook his head and chuckled before he got serious.

"Okay. Next . . . I want to talk about defenses, since you girls are in the most danger. We'll keep the entrances small and high, maybe with one large ground-level one at the back for me. But I also want to try and dig a ditch around it with as many pit traps as we can fit together, and then maybe a fence of some sort on the other side. How does that sound?"

He was treated to another flurry of "Amazings" from most of the queens. The Second First of the First was about to join them but stopped. She slowly changed course and began a new dance.

"Protect us from enemy?"

Belissar nodded. She paused for a moment, then started another slow dance.

"We protect hive of hives. King . . . should protect all."

Belissar frowned a bit and tilted his head. "What do you mean?"

Her dance slowed even more. "If King make for us . . . King should make to help all. Help soldiers fight, stop enemy."

Belissar crossed his arms and hummed. "So you're saying you would rather me make something that would help you fight rather than something just to protect your hives?"

The queen slowly danced her affirmative, and Belissar hummed and rubbed his chin.

Obviously, it didn't sit well with him for the queens not to have some protection, but it was true that the soldier bees were the first and best line of defense. If a shade were attacking these queens, it would have already bypassed the soldiers.

Helping the soldiers defeat the shade *would* be the preferable option, and yes, if he was going to devote the time and effort to building a ditch and a fence, it may make sense to make something that would benefit the defense as a whole. But how could he do that while also helping keep the queens safe? Belissar knew he should consider the tower as a whole, but he didn't want to lose any of them if he could help it.

He thought, too, about the last shade. How it had nearly beaten them, and how it had been beaten in turn. What could he build which would help the queens face it?

His eyes lit up.

"How about this? What if we move the house and the ditch right in front of the exit to the orchard? We put a big entrance through the house here where you girls don't put any of your hives. The shades will have to pass through to get to you or to the other room, and we can place some honey traps too. If a shade gets past the army again, you can plan to trap it in there while they catch up. Like, wait on the house here to ambush it like the wounded soldier did?"

The Second First of the First looked at him for a moment before responding. "Amazing. Incredible."

Belissar chuckled at that.

After confirming the details of the flower meadow beehouse, Belissar heard a pair of chimes.

New mission received: Construct new type of beehouse.
New mission received: House all queens.

He nodded as the God of Bees officially sanctioned his current efforts. He really had put that task aside for far too long. But no longer. With nothing but the small, daily purifications on the horizon, he had nothing more urgent to deal with.

Belissar had once been a beekeeper. He had now become a dungeon master; maybe even a competent one. And now, with the help of his bees, his friend Niobee, and his patron, the God of Bees, he'd set off and try to become both at once.

AUTHOR'S NOTE

Hi, everyone! Author here! Did you know this series was originally a web novel released one chapter at a time? In that version, I included a short commentary at the end of each chapter with my own reactions to its events. In order to preserve the intended experience, I have now gathered all that commentary in one place for you to enjoy.

Please visit Bee Dungeon on Royal Road to learn how the author feels about each chapter of this book!

ABOUT THE AUTHOR

Icalos is a lifelong fan of sci-fi, fantasy, and video games, and the author of the Terminate the Other World! series, which was originally released on Royal Road. To learn more, visit his website at icalosbooks.com.